WINTOUR'S LEAP

Morton Ross

Copyright © Morton Ross 2020
This book is sold subject to the condition that it shall not, by way of trade or otherwise, be lent, resold, hired out, or otherwise circulated without the publisher's prior consent in any form of binding or cover other than that in which it is published and without a similar condition including this condition being imposed on the subsequent publisher.
The moral right of Morton Ross has been asserted.
ISBN-13: 9798651080915

This is a work of fiction. Names, characters, businesses, organisations, places, events and incidents either are the product of the author's imagination or are used fictitiously. Any resemblance to actual persons, living or dead, events, or locales is entirely coincidental.

DEDICATION

For my children Sam and Beck who never tired of listening to their father's impromptu stories each night before bed. Here's another.

CONTENTS

ACKNOWLEDGEMENTS i
AUTHOR'S NOTE iii

P A R T I 1
CHAPTER 1 3
CHAPTER 2 10
CHAPTER 3 17
CHAPTER 4 20
CHAPTER 5 29
CHAPTER 6 38
CHAPTER 7 46
CHAPTER 8 52
CHAPTER 9 60
CHAPTER 10 70
CHAPTER 11 81
CHAPTER 12 88

P A R T II 93
CHAPTER 1 95
CHAPTER 2 101
CHAPTER 3 105
CHAPTER 4 118
CHAPTER 5 131
CHAPTER 6 142
CHAPTER 7 152
CHAPTER 8 159
CHAPTER 9 163
CHAPTER 10 174
CHAPTER 11 177
CHAPTER 12 186
CHAPTER 13 196
CHAPTER 14 206
CHAPTER 15 212

CHAPTER 16	217
CHAPTER 17	222
CHAPTER 18	235
CHAPTER 19	245
CHAPTER 20	250
CHAPTER 21	257
CHAPTER 22	267
CHAPTER 23	277
CHAPTER 24	288
CHAPTER 25	298
CHAPTER 26	306
CHAPTER 27	314
CHAPTER 28	320
CHAPTER 29	330
CHAPTER 30	339
CHAPTER 31	344
CHAPTER 32	347
CHAPTER 33	357
CHAPTER 34	361
CHAPTER 35	364
CHAPTER 36	372
CHAPTER 37	380
CHAPTER 38	383
CHAPTER 39	386
ABOUT THE AUTHOR	400

ACKNOWLEDGEMENTS

I am indebted, as always, to my wonderful wife Christine, without whose constant support and enduring patience, I would never have reached the last full stop.

My sincere thanks are due to Craig, my editor at Cornerstones Literary Consultancy, who saw past the shortcomings of my original manuscript to the novel that it could become.

Thanks must also go to Paul who, for many hours, stood patiently at the foot of Wintour's Leap holding my ropes as I oh-so-slowly pulled myself up to those tiny ledges on which the tale told herein was born.

AUTHOR'S NOTE

Part I, set in the English Civil War, is based loosely on the legend of Sir John Wintour and his infamous leap from the cliffs, which today bear his name, into the River Wye. Historians cannot agree on the exact events leading up to the leap; nor, indeed, can they agree on the leap's precise location. What they do agree upon is that in 1645 Wintour was ambushed at the Lancaut Loop on the River Wye by a superior parliamentarian force – Roundheads – and a large number of his men were drowned in the river attempting to escape. Their deaths are listed in parish records to be found at nearby Chepstow Castle. The tale told in Part I of this novel is therefore, for the most part, a work of fiction based on the merest scattering of facts. Sir John Wintour, his wife, Mary, and father, Edward, together with Colonel Massey, the parliamentarian commander, certainly did exist. However, their attributes and actions are the product of the author's imagination. All other characters are fictional and any resemblance to actual persons is entirely coincidental.

Part II, set in 2019, is entirely a work of fiction. Names, characters, businesses, organisations, events and incidents are again the product of the author's imagination or are used fictitiously. Any resemblance to actual persons, living or dead, or events is entirely coincidental. The author has based much of the contemporary action in the village of Tidenham which does exist. However all locations within the village are entirely fictitious.

PART I

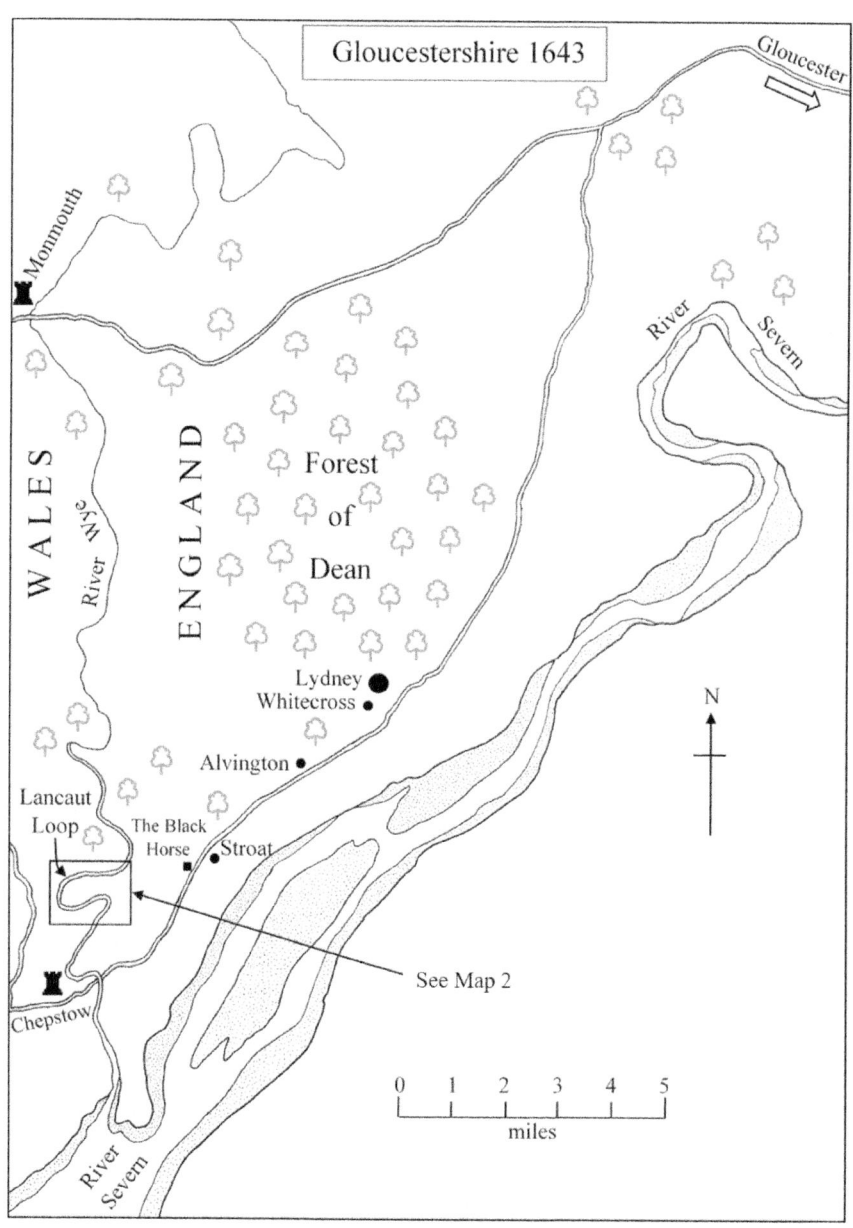

Map 1. Gloucestershire, 1643.

CHAPTER 1

15th October 1643

The instant that Grace set eyes on the stranger, she was certain he would set her free from the hell she'd endured since her ma had died; free from the witch of a woman who had marched through the door and occupied the inn with the flowers still fresh on the grave. *Please God, be merciful, I beg you. Let this be him, the saint who will write the letter.*

She guessed from his appearance that he was a gentleman – a squire perhaps or a merchant – though why he had chosen to take supper at The Black Horse she couldn't imagine. Weaving through the clutter of tables, slapping away the attentions of roving hands, her gaze remained fixed on the man on whom she had rested all hope of freedom.

'Come far, sir?' she greeted him, brushing down her ale-stained skirt.

'Four mile, maybe more, though I'm wishing now I'd continued on awhile,' he replied, nodding at the bawdy rabble behind her, 'but my horse has thrown a shoe. Where's the nearest smithy, might I inquire?' His accent, flat and refined, spoke of education and wealth.

'That would be Stroat, sir, not a mile away on the Lydney road. I'd ride there now and fetch him for you but...' She glanced nervously over her shoulder towards the kitchen. '...collecting eggs is the furthest she'll let me go.'

He looked up at the girl. The taut lines stretched across her face spoke of hunger and neglect. 'No matter. I'll walk him there since the hoof is clear of nails. Supper and cider with haste, my dear, if such a thing is possible at The Black Horse.'

Before Grace could reply, the kitchen door flew open to reveal a giant of a woman, her huge, corpulent body filling every inch of the door frame. No sooner had she thrust herself into the room than a voice cried out:

'Look sharp, boys, 'cos there's a Mundy-mountain on the prowl.' That brought a cackle of laughter from a few. The rest knew better.

Alice Mundy glared at the voice's owner. 'You mind yer filthy tongue, Sam Blackall, or I'll be serving it to you on a plate and that ain't a jest, d'you hear?'

Her eyes swept across the tables until they came to rest on her stepdaughter. Feeling the woman's glare on her back, Grace turned to go.

'Supper and cider it is, sir,' and she hurried back to the kitchen.

Alice moved to block her path. 'Hope you're treating that one real nice, girl, 'cos I'm losing patience with the insolence you show the men.'

Grace said nothing and squeezed past her stepmother into the kitchen, flinching from the slap which usually followed a reprimand, though none came for Alice was too busy staring at the stranger.

In the kitchen, Grace's mind was made up. She would speak to the gentleman before he left, sensing she might never get another chance to execute her plan. It relied entirely on the charity of an educated man and few such individuals ever stopped at the inn. The moment had to be seized. She returned with an earful of Alice's instructions and a tray of pork and cider.

'My stepmother says it's a pleasure to welcome a gentleman to the inn.' She struggled to hide the fear in her voice. The fear of failure. 'She asks your name, sir?'

'Charles Melville. She'll not know it for I'm new to the shire.' He looked down at the bone on his plate, almost entirely devoid of meat. 'Does she not think a gentleman is worth better fare than this?'

''Tis the best we have, sir,' Grace replied. 'My stepmother insists you stay the night and let my father fetch the smithy in the morning. She says your horse ain't fit for walking.'

'I think I'm best placed to make that judgement. Let her know I'm grateful for the invitation but my wife expects me home tonight and I'll not disappoint her.'

'I wouldn't press you, sir, but my stepmother, she don't take no for an answer that easy.' Grace brushed back her long, dark hair to expose an ugly, yellow bruise on her neck.

'She beats you often, does she?' he asked gently.

Grace nodded, hope welling up inside her so she could almost taste freedom. 'Every day, sir. Beats my brother Tom even worse. Says it's good for us. Teaches us what's right 'cept no matter what we do, it's never right.'

'Not easy raising children in this world. I've a daughter your age. Twelve, am I right?'

'Fifteen, sir. I don't look it, I know. Ain't been fed proper since my ma died.' She felt her stomach churning as she stared down at the pork. 'I got to go but please, I must speak with you again before you leave. 'Tis an urgent matter, sir, I swear it.'

Melville frowned at this. 'Then speak it now, dear.'

'I can't, sir, not here. I'll tell my stepmother you can't stay. She's got designs on your money so you'd best leave prompt. I'll meet you in the stable out back when you've finished.' She turned away before he could reply.

When Grace stepped through into the kitchen, Alice looked up from a tub of scummy water where she was washing plates. 'So is he staying or what?'

'Mr Melville's mind is not made up,' Grace lied, 'but let me speak to him awhile and I'll persuade him 'tis best for his horse that he stays the night.'

'*Speak* to him, girl? You don't persuade a man by speaking to him.' Alice's grin revealed gums sparsely decorated with black, rotting teeth.

'I told you, I ain't doing that. *Never.*' Her encounter with the stranger had given Grace a courage that had long lain buried. 'Beat me black and blue if you must, but I ain't stooping that low.'

Alice straightened, her pockmarked face no longer wearing a grin. 'Don't tell me what you can and can't do, girl. If you want to eat, then you got to stoop low and earn a few shillings. It's time you started earning 'cos you're old enough now and there ain't no shortage of customers, that's for certain. Our gentleman friend, Mr Melville, he be no different from the rest just 'cos he's dressed all fine and fancy.'

Grace stared at the woman who had taken the place of her mother five years before and silently prayed that her plan would succeed. She knew the fate awaiting her at the inn if it didn't. As she stepped back into the public room, one glance at the corner table caused her heart to miss a beat. He'd gone. In a flash, she crossed to the porch, swung open the heavy oak door, and ran out into the road. Melville appeared from the stable yard leading a fine-looking gelding, closely followed by Tom who was so preoccupied with the horse that he didn't notice her.

'Tom,' she called, hurrying to him. Melville threw a glance over his shoulder and promptly set off on foot as fast as his horse would allow in the direction of Stroat. She lowered her voice. 'Listen, tell Alice I'm speaking with the gentleman. She'll get suspicious if I've disappeared for long, like she always does.'

'It's a fine horse, don't you think? Lost a shoe, mind.' Tom's gaze remained fixed on the animal. 'He gave me a shilling for tendin' him, and here, payment for his supper.' He held out his hand but she pushed it away.

'Tom, listen will you? Give the money to Alice and tell her what I said. She'll come after me if you don't. Now go!'

He looked up at her questioningly. 'What's your business with a gentleman like that?'

'I'll tell you later. Get gone!' She gave him a sharp shove and then hurried off down the road in pursuit of Melville, calling after him. He stopped and turned, shaking his head.

'I want to be in Lydney before dark so I've no time for whatever business you might have in mind.'

Reaching him, Grace paused, breathing hard, all the while staring back down the road, expecting at any moment her stepmother to come barrelling out of the inn after her. 'Sir, pardon me but I needs just a moment of your time and…' Though she had rehearsed the speech a hundred times, now that she had an audience, she could remember none of it.

'I cannot wait, miss. If I'm not home tonight, my wife will send out servants looking for me.' He turned to go but Grace reached out and caught his sleeve.

'Sir, please, hear me out. We're not long in this world if we don't get away from her, me and Tom. You've seen what she does. We works the whole day, every day and she pays us nothing more than a beating. Been this way for five years, ever since our ma died. Food's a reward and some days we don't get any.'

He looked down and removed her hand. 'What exactly are you asking of me? I can't take you with me. The law won't allow it and neither would my wife.'

'No, sir, you misjudge me. The favour I'm asking is much simpler. Like I told you, my stepmother won't let us travel a hundred paces from the inn. I ain't been this far in months, but if I could persuade her that by travelling to Gloucester for the day, we would bring her good fortune, then she might agree to it.'

'Good fortune? And how, pray, might the pair of you come by good fortune?' Melville made no effort to hide his scepticism. When

Grace had finished outlining her plan, he stared at her for a moment before shaking his head.

'I should walk away right now for there's a fine line between bravery and foolery. It's not hard to guess my role in all this. And this aunt you speak of, is she part of this deception?'

Grace nodded. 'My ma, she had four brothers and ten sisters though most died young. Father don't remember any of them 'cos the drink has addled his brain. Some days he don't even remember my ma's name, so when he gets a letter from an Aunt Catherin, he won't blink an eye.'

'So, Catherin Croker, she lives only in your imagination?'

Grace nodded. 'It's easier that way 'cos she ain't going to complain if word gets out about the letter.'

'And your father, he can read, can he?'

'My ma, she taught him but he don't read anymore. My stepmother learnt to read 'cos her father, he were a prosperous man until he were hanged for murder. She'll read the letter. When she learns Aunt Catherin has invited me, Tom and father to her home in Gloucester so's she might pass on a sum of money for me and Tom's education, she'll…'

'She'll let you travel more than a hundred paces. Well, there's a gaping hole in your trickery for it's most unlikely that a girl would be gifted an education.'

'I know that, sir, particularly a girl of my position but like I says, my stepmother, she was taught to read though it ain't done her much good. Oh Lord, here she comes!'

The elephantine figure of Alice Mundy waded up the road towards them, her arms thrusting back and forth like the oars of a rowing boat.

'Sir, I beg you, write the letter. It's our only hope.'

'And when you get to Gloucester, then what? Your father will hunt you both down and you'll be back here with bruises worse than before.'

'My father ain't got the wits for hunting, sir. We'll find work.

There's always a household needing a maid and Tom's good with horses. Now sir, you must go for she has a wicked temper and cares little who's on the receiving end.'

Mr Melville stared at the hideous creature growing steadily larger by the second and then he was away, tugging on the reins.

'Grace Mundy's my name,' she shouted after him. 'And my father is Silas.' But she got no answer.

Charles Melville hadn't travelled far when Alice Mundy's venomous cursing punctuated by Grace's screams shattered the early evening peace.

CHAPTER 2

Two weeks passed and Grace gave up all hope of her plan succeeding. She'd been a fool, she thought, to imagine for one moment that Melville might agree to such a scheme. What had she been thinking? Had her foolishness now become a tale re-told in inns across the county? Would word of it reach her stepmother's ears? There'd be no mercy if it did. She'd been so stupid.

So, when a carriage drew up outside the inn and a portly coachman stepped down holding a letter, folded and sealed, addressed to Mr Silas Mundy, a flame of hope burst into life.

'And who gave you this,' Alice demanded of the coachman, 'since Mr Silas Mundy ain't in the habit of receiving letters?'

The coachman shook his head. 'Ain't my business who's they from. Read the seal, woman.' With that, he pulled himself back aboard the carriage, slapped the horses with the reins and was gone.

Alice studied the wax seal. 'C. C.,' she read aloud, slamming the oak door behind her. 'Get your lazy arse down here *now*, Silas Mundy,' she yelled up the stairs, ''cos there's a letter here with your name on it.' She broke the seal, unfolded the paper and began to read in silence. Grace watched her from the kitchen doorway, scarcely daring to breathe. C.C. – the aunt who didn't exist. Would the man who slowly descended the staircase nursing a sore head remember the names of her aunts, the ones that *did* exist? She'd been certain he wouldn't when she'd devised the scheme but now she was tortured with doubts.

'Catherin Croker. Why ain't you ever spoken her name before?' Alice stared at her husband.

Silas looked blank. 'Catherin? Don't remember.' He wiped the sleep from his face with both hands. 'What's it say?' He motioned to the letter.

'Says Tom and Grace got to go to Gloucester to meet their aunt three days from now and you with them.'

'Gloucester? With them two wastrels? She can think again 'cos I ain't riding all that way just so's the woman can lay eyes on 'em.' Silas turned back to the stairs. 'Road's not safe, neither,' he added.

'Not so fast. There's more.' Alice shot a look at Grace, her eyes full of cunning. 'There's much more but the girl don't need to hear it.' She pointed at the kitchen. 'Get in there and clean the mugs.'

Grace turned and closed the door behind her. It was all she could do to stop herself from dancing around the room. Her plan was working. She'd seen it in her stepmother's face, the lure of money working its magic.

It wasn't long before Alice burst into the kitchen clutching the letter. 'Your mother ever speak of Aunt Catherin?'

'Aunt Catherin?' Grace feared the tremor in her voice would betray her lies. 'Most of Ma's sisters died before they was a year old but Ma said Catherin was stronger than the others. She never came here. Don't think she and Father were close. But Ma travelled once to Gloucester to see her sister, I'm certain of it.'

'Your father don't remember the woman. How's that?'

'Father never took much notice of Ma's family, so it don't surprise me.' *He never took much notice of Ma, neither.*

'Thursday next, you's going to Gloucester, you and Tom with your father. Letter says you've both got to go though I don't know why. Yardes Cottage in Quay Lane. You'll stay the night and then return here on Friday. You understand me?'

Grace nodded. They were almost free. She longed for the moment when she could share the deception with her brother.

'But hear this, girl.' Alice bent lower until Grace could feel her stepmother's foul breath on her face. 'Either of you tries anything clever when you's away and God's my witness you'll wish you ain't been born, you listening?' She grabbed a handful of Grace's hair and yanked her head back so that Grace squealed in pain. 'I will whip the skin off your back. You hear me?'

Grace wanted to say *the day you moved in, I wished I ain't been born* but instead she just nodded again.

The instant her stepmother was gone, Grace hurried out through the back door into the yard to find her brother. If Alice got to him first, she thought, he might sow doubts in her mind as to Catherin's existence. She found him behind the stable block chopping wood.

'Tom! Stop for a moment and listen to me.'

Tom ignored her and swung the axe with his lanky arms, his face screwed up with the effort.

'Tom, stop for heaven's sakes! We're going to Gloucester!'

For a moment, he stood resting the axe head on the ground, breathing heavily. 'If I don't get this done, she'll horsewhip me like she always does. Anyways, you're lying. We ain't never going to Gloucester.' With that, he lifted the axe but before he could deliver a blow, she rushed onto him, grabbing the axe handle with both hands.

'I ain't lying, God's truth. Now let go of it and hear what I got to say.'

'Alright,' he said, releasing the axe, 'but you're taking the whipping.'

'Don't mind if I do, Tom, 'cos there won't be many more of them.' As soon as she said it, she wished she hadn't since the less Tom knew about the deception, the better.

'What do you mean? She'll not stop whipping us till she's dead. Maybe not even then.'

'Just listen to me.' She pulled him round to face her. 'A letter arrived for Father from one of Ma's sisters in Gloucester. She's asked him to bring us both to see her. This Thursday coming. Alice has agreed to it. Don't ask me why, but she told me we're to spend a night with Aunt Catherin and then return the next day.'

'Aunt Catherin? Ma's sisters died before she did, so how's we got an Aunt Catherin? I told you, you was lying.' He moved to pick up the axe.

'I ain't lying. We're going to Gloucester with Father. Ma never talked about Catherin but sure enough, the letter says she wants to see us. Alice will ask if you remember her and when she does, tell her Ma spoke of Catherin to you but she never came to visit. You got that, Tom? If Alice thinks she don't exist, then we ain't going.'

'You swear it's true? We're going to Gloucester?'

'Tom, I swear it. Thursday next.' She longed to tell him that they would not be coming back, that in three days they would be free from the hell they'd endured since their mother's death but it was safer that Tom knew nothing of her plan. Not yet.

*

On Thursday morning, before the cockerels had announced the dawn, Grace was awoken by the sound of her brother groaning loudly beneath the ragged pile of blankets on his straw mattress, an arm's length from her own. She sat up, suddenly possessed with a terrible sense of foreboding.

'What is it, Tom? Are you not well?'

'The pot, Grace!' he cried out, pushing back his blankets. 'I needs the pot, urgent! My belly – it wants to puke.'

In an instant, his sister flung aside her blankets and leapt to her feet, grabbing the chamber pot and, not a moment too soon, thrust it in front of the boy for at the same instant, Tom retched up the contents of his stomach. She waited until his heaving spasms had died away before laying the pot down, then she reached out with both arms and held him close to her.

'Poor boy,' she said softly. 'You're hot with the fever. 'Tis just as we both had last winter. Does your belly hurt, Tom?'

He nodded, clutching his stomach. 'I've got to go.' With that, he picked up the pot and made for the door.

'I'll come,' she offered but Tom waved her back. Grace knelt down on her blankets in the dawn twilight, listening to her brother's hurried footsteps along the landing to an empty room at the far end.

'Why today?' she whispered, wringing her hands. 'Please God, tell me why. Does the boy not deserve to be free? Has he not suffered enough?'

She sat waiting, praying that she was wrong, that Tom did not have the affliction which had laid them both low for almost two weeks the previous Christmas. Back then, Alice had been fearful that the illness might steal them both away, leaving her to run the inn single-handed since her husband's contribution grew less with each passing day. Somehow, she had nursed both children back to health before the beatings resumed once more.

Faltering footsteps sounded on the landing and Tom's hunched figure appeared in the doorway.

'My guts are burning,' he gasped, clutching his belly. He collapsed on his mattress and curled up into a ball. Grace wrapped his blankets around him for he'd begun to shiver violently.

'Are you strong enough for the journey?' she asked though she already knew the answer.

'Don't know,' he muttered. 'It's the devil's work. He'll not give me two days without a beating.'

It's not two days, Tom, it's a lifetime. If Tom was too weak to travel and she left him behind, then Alice was sure to wreak vengeance on the boy when Silas returned without his daughter. Yet delaying the visit would risk exposing her plan.

Grace lay down with him, an arm around his shoulders, the frightful dilemma playing over and over in her mind. It was now or never, and never was not an option that she could bear. She would have to go alone and return for Tom as soon as she had work and a roof over her head. A month at most, she told herself.

It wasn't long before Tom sat up and retched into the pot again, his whole body shaking worse than ever. She rose to get some wet rags from the kitchen but no sooner had she set foot on the stairs than Alice appeared on the landing.

'You ain't dressed yet? And where's the boy? You both got work to do 'fore you leave so get him out of his bed and fetch water for the kitchen.' She turned back to her room but didn't get far.

'Tom's got the fever and ain't fit for the journey. If you make him go, he'll burn up 'fore he gets to Gloucester.'

Alice turned, her face twisted with a cold fury. 'Ain't fit for the journey, you say? We'll see about that,' and she pushed past Grace and waded into the children's bedchamber. 'Still in bed, you good-for-nothing little runt!' She bent down, eyeing with disgust the contents of the chamber pot, and laid a hand on Tom's forehead. In a trice, her mood changed. 'Fetch cold towels, girl. Boy's got the fever bad and I won't have him drop dead on me, so make it quick.'

When Grace returned, she handed the towels to Alice who laid them across Tom's forehead. She turned to her stepdaughter. 'Get yourself dressed, nice and pretty like. Don't want your aunt thinking you ain't well kept. You'll tell her about the boy being with the fever. She'll understand 'cos you'll make her understand.' With that, she squeezed out through the door and thumped along the landing to waken her husband.

Grace knelt down beside her brother and turned the towels on his head. 'Tom, I must speak to you,' she began as the tears rolled down her cheeks. 'There is something I've kept from you. For your own good, you understand.'

Tom lay quite still, his eyes closed though she sensed he was listening.

'I'm not coming back.' Saying it made her feel sick.

His eyes opened and he looked up at her. In the early dawn light, she could plainly see the look of horror on his face.

'What do you mean? You'll return tomorrow.'

She shook her head. 'Tonight, Father will go drinking like always. As soon as he does, I'll slip away from the house and he'll not know I'm gone till he wakes next morning. Then it will be too late since he's not the wits to find me.'

'But you can't! You can't just go and…' His voice began to break and tears welled up in his eyes for the thought of life without his sister was unbearable.

'Tom, it was supposed to be both of us, but you heard the woman. She won't wait till you're well. If you want to be free, then you must let me go. 'Tis the only way. I'll find work and make enough to rent a room and then I will come for you, I promise.'

'She'll make me do the work of two, you know that, don't you, and she'll beat me all the more for what you've done.'

'I know it, Tom. Of course I know it and it breaks my heart to leave you here. But this is our only chance to be free, do you see? I will return in the night when it's safe. A month, six weeks at most, I swear it.'

'Six weeks? You need not bother for she'll have beaten me to death by then.'

'Tom, please,' she sobbed, 'you must not say that.' She kissed him on his cheek, her tears mingling with his. 'I have to go, precious brother. Be strong till I come for you. It won't be long.'

She quickly dressed and, with one final, tortured glance at her brother, slipped out of the door to begin her escape.

CHAPTER 3

10ᵗʰ December 1644

In the icy blackness of his bedchamber with dawn still two hours away, Tom Mundy awoke from his dream and promptly sat up.

This dream was not like the others that had tormented his sleep for months. At first, they had been no more than the briefest glimpse of Grace lying asleep, her face illuminated by candlelight until the flame was abruptly extinguished. Then, as the weeks passed, the dreams had become more vivid and more frequent. Grace would wake, stretch out her arms and call for him, her voice filled with such sorrow that even in his sleep, Tom wept silent tears. With the onset of winter, more than a year since his sister had vanished on the way to Gloucester, her cries invaded his sleep every night, her mournful voice begging him to escape the inn and find the prison cell where she was held captive. Sure enough, what the dream revealed of her surroundings looked for all the world like some ghastly dungeon, its roof no higher than a man's waist.

'You can set me free, Tom, for you have the key.'

'Key? I have no key,' he would call out in his sleep. 'Tell me where you are? I cannot find you unless you tell me.'

'Escape and you will find me,' she answered, 'for I will guide you.'

For weeks, Tom had thought of nothing but escape since he'd given up all hope of Grace ever returning to keep her promise. His stepmother, however, had become increasingly vigilant ever since her husband had returned from Gloucester without his daughter. She could not afford to lose another workhorse. Scarcely an hour went by each day without the woman checking on his whereabouts, while at night, she slept with her door wide open.

What if the dreams were true? Grace held captive in some frightful prison cell, fighting for her life. It would explain why she had not come back for him.

Tonight, however, the dream had been different. 'Tonight, precious brother. You must escape tonight. Take the Lydney road. I'll guide you.'

'Tonight?' he whispered, blinking away sleep. 'Why tonight?' But his question was met only with the sound of rats foraging in the thatch above his head.

His mind made up, he rolled out from beneath his blankets onto the floor and peered down through a gap between the floorboards, looking for the flicker of candlelight in the room below, a sure sign that his stepmother was on patrol with a fire iron. But nothing stirred in the inky dark.

He had to hurry. The instant his stepmother found him gone she would have his father saddle the horse and ride out in pursuit. If he could reach Lydney, five miles away, before his father, then he'd melt into the maze of back streets where Silas was unlikely to find him.

He dressed quickly, shivering in the frigid air, the cold burrowing its way into his scrawny frame. He pulled on his boots, picked up a small leather bag and crossed to the door. He opened it a pinch and listened. Two sets of deep, laboured snores issued like some infernal duet from rooms a short distance along the narrow corridor. The stairway lay immediately opposite his father's bedchamber but Tom had no fear that he would wake the man since six quarts of ale rendered him inert until dawn. But his stepmother, she was a different beast, often roused from her slumber by nothing more than a fox's bark.

Carefully avoiding the steps that creaked, Tom reached the door at the bottom of the stairs and gently pushed it open, moving silently into the public bar. In the kitchen, he found the remains of a loaf and some cheese which he stashed in his bag. The door from the kitchen into the yard at the back of the inn was shut fast by three huge bolts, none of which he had the strength to unlock. In any case, the noise would have woken his stepmother. Back in the public bar, the massive oak door which led directly out onto the road was likewise bolted shut.

But there was another way out.

Dying embers from the huge fireplace filled the room with a ghostly glow as Tom edged carefully along the bar until, on reaching the far end, he dropped to his knees, searching the floor for the trapdoor leading to the cellar. Almost at once, his hand found the bolt. He'd opened it a thousand times before and with practised precision, he eased it back. With all his strength, he pulled the trapdoor up and stepped down into the black void, lowering the door behind him. At the bottom of the staircase, he stopped to listen, straining for any sounds of movement above. Satisfied, he crossed the cellar floor to where a wooden ramp led up to a pair of hatch doors, not much taller than a barrel, opening onto the road. He climbed the ramp and, at the top, freed the bolts on the back of one door and pushed it open.

'Almost there, Grace,' he whispered.

He climbed out, closed the hatch door and set off as fast as he could along the road to Lydney.

'Grace,' he called out into the night, 'I've done just as you told me but I ain't a notion as to where you might be. Alice will send Father out after me so you've gotta help me now like you said you would.'

Silence.

CHAPTER 4

The road to Lydney ran north-east from the inn through a scattering of woods and fields, punctuated now and then by tiny villages and ramshackle farmsteads. A heavy mist brought an eerie silence, broken only by Tom's footfall and laboured breathing. His heart leapt as a wild boar shuffled out from the undergrowth in front of him, no more than a dark smudge uttering a gravelly roar before shambling back into the woods.

Almost an hour passed before he dared stop to rest, his skinny legs throbbing from the effort. The villages of Wibdon and Stroat lay behind him but Lydney still lay three miles away. The mist had thickened into dense fog, slowing his progress further. It would slow his father too, he realised, but with dawn approaching, Tom knew the race to Lydney was one he might not win. He reached into his bag for some bread but before it reached his mouth, a far-off cry drifted through the darkness from the direction of Lydney, muted by the fog but still recognisably human. Tom crept forward along the edge of the road, ready at any moment to dart into the woods.

Again! A man's voice barking orders. And there, a second! Four hundred paces, perhaps less. Drawing closer, invisible to the strangers ahead, Tom began to catch fragments of the exchange playing out between them.

'You hard a' hearing or some'ink 'cos we's running outta patience.' There was a pause, the silence deafening. 'You touch those bloody pistols one more time and I'll blow your head off. Now get off the horse or you's a dead man.'

'You've picked the wrong man for your foul trade, sirs. You pull that trigger and God's my word, my men will hunt you down like pigs in the forest before they drag the guts from your body and…' The pistol shot made Tom jump. A horse let out a shrill whinny as the body of a man crashed to the ground. Moments later, the horse pounded out of the darkness like some wild phantom, causing Tom to dive headfirst out of the way.

'Shoot the bloody animal!' A pistol shot whistled above Tom's head, smashing harmlessly into an overhanging branch, while the sound of hooves hammering the road faded into the night.

'Missed it, you damn fool, an' a horse that size. Now we ain't got nuffin'.'

'We got *him*, ain't we?'

'We got him but I'll wager he ain't carrying nuffin'. They never do.' There was a moment's pause. Tom guessed they were searching the dead man's pockets; at least, he assumed he was dead. 'What did I tell you? Pockets are empty. It's all on the bloody horse.'

'I can't shoot what I can't see. He says he's got men. What if he's one of parliament's men up Gloucester way? They say Massey's gathering an army there.'

'Nay, he ain't a Roundhead, not with long hair and a fancy coat. More likely a Cavalier riding back from Chepstow. Hey, leave the coat! You get caught with that, they'll hang you. We gotta go 'fore the sun's up and they comes looking for us.'

The road fell silent as the men slipped away into the woods, leaving their victim stretched out on the road. Tom scrambled to his feet. He'd lost precious time but it wasn't right to leave the man without knowing whether he was dead or alive. Few men would survive a pistol shot from point blank range and, when he found the body – a dark shape lying face down – he was certain the man was indeed dead. The shot, it seemed, had found its mark on one side of his skull. Tom tried turning him over, his hand feeling the warm ooze of fresh blood. He was a large man and it took great effort. The thieves had been right about his coat. It was made of thick leather and heavily embossed. The horse, too, betrayed the man's wealth. A beast of such monumental size could not be bought cheaply. As he ran his hands across the coat, Tom felt the man's chest rise and fall. He was still alive but not for long, he guessed, unless the bleeding from his head could be stopped.

'Damn you,' Tom muttered. 'You'll steal my freedom lying here, bleeding out. Father'll be on the road at dawn and that ain't far away. I've gotta leave you, you understand.' No sooner had he turned his back than a familiar voice spoke to him from the darkness.

'Bind his head, Tom, though he scarce deserves it. You'll be rewarded.'

'Grace!' he cried out. 'Grace, is that you?' He whirled about, unable to determine from which direction the voice had come. 'Where are you? Show yourself!' He stood quite still, straining for the sound of footsteps but heard only the soft whisper of the wind in the trees. Had he imagined it, his sister speaking to him as though she were standing scarcely an arm's-length away?

'"Tis more than a year, Grace, since you left me. You told me six weeks at most and now you won't show yourself. Why are you doing this?' He stood staring into the darkness.

'You don't deserve this, precious brother, I know. You've paid the price for my wickedness but now you must help me. No one else can do it. Bind his head and in time, you will find me.'

'In time? Why don't you tell me now? I've done as you asked and escaped but where am I going?'

'Bind his head and I'll guide you.'

'You've lied to me once so how can I trust you?' Without waiting for a reply, he knelt at the man's side, pulling furiously first at one sleeve of his coat then the other. It seemed to take forever but finally both arms were free. He set to work, stripping the man of his cotton shirt, tugging and tearing as if possessed, listening all the while for his sister's voice and for the sound of hooves on the road behind him. When at last the shirt slipped over the man's head, Tom folded it several times into a narrow strip and laid it across the bloodied head, pressing hard on the wound. Then he tied both ends together as best he could. Wrapping the man's coat around him, Tom's fingers felt the cold metal of a slender chain around his neck. Running his hand along it, his fingertips fell on a locket, no bigger than a copper penny. He felt for the catch, thinking that its contents might shed light on the man's identity but quickly gave up. In the dark he could barely see his own hand, less still a tiny locket.

He let it go, wrapped the leather coat as tightly as he could and quickly got to his feet.

'Take the locket, Tom. You can open it when dawn comes.'

'Ahh! This is madness!' he yelled, staring out into the night, craving some sign of his sister. 'For so many weeks you've tormented me in my sleep and now here, in the forest.'

Wiping away tears, and uncertain what to do, he paused a moment before bending down and removing the chain from the man's neck. He dropped it into his bag whereupon the dark shape uttered a frightful groan and promptly sat up, feeling first his head and then his right shoulder. He let out an anguished cry of pain. Only then did he notice Tom.

'You'll pay dearly for this,' was followed by another groan as he tried to stand.

'Sir, I played no part in it save to wrap your head,' Tom protested. 'The thieves are gone, both of them, off into the woods. Took a shot at your horse, they did, but I fancy they missed 'cos he just galloped past me. I came on you lying here, God's truth.'

'You wrapped my head, eh?' More concerned about his shoulder, he made no attempt to remove the shirt. 'Shoulder's out of place, boy.' He groaned again. 'Filthy maggots. Roads are crawling with them. You'll have to help me up on the horse, you understand. Can't do it on my own.'

'Sir, you ain't going to do it 'cos you ain't got no horse.'

The big man rose unsteadily to his feet. 'Forrester won't have gone far.' He put two fingers in his mouth and let out a deafening whistle. Somewhere in the distance, a horse whinnied and a short while later, the sound of pounding hooves drew closer until Forrester appeared through the fog, steam blowing from his nostrils.

'I need your back, boy, though you've not got much of one.' He peered down at Tom in the darkness. 'God's truth, you've not got much of anything. Bend down there now. It's going to hurt, you understand. I'll put a foot on your back. Hold still if you can.'

Tom cursed himself for not leaving the man when he had the chance. Dawn could not be far away yet Lydney was still an hour's walk. He knelt by the horse, stealing himself for the crushing weight but it never came.

'Can't do it, boy.' The man staggered backwards before dropping to his knees. 'Head's spinning. Can't ride...' He lay in the road now, his voice no more than a slurred whisper. 'Whitecross, boy. Ride to Whitecross and fetch...' He slipped into oblivion and lay still.

Whitecross? Tom had heard the name countless times, a name that men uttered with loathing more often than not, for the man who owned the Whitecross estate had made many enemies on both sides of the civil war. Could this man lying half dead at his feet be Sir John Wintour of Whitecross? The huge beast towering over him lent weight to his suspicion, as Wintour's horse was rumoured to be the largest in the west of England.

'And how am I climbing up there?' Tom muttered aloud. The saddle's pommel lay out of reach while the stirrups dangled by his shoulders. What he needed was a rock or tree stump to stand on. 'Forgive me, Sir John,' he whispered, as if a louder voice would wake the man, and led the horse over to his master. Standing on the man's barrel chest, Tom managed by a series of painful contortions to pull himself up onto the saddle. Panting hard from the effort, perched high on Forrester's back, a thrill ran through his body, an elation he had not felt since his mother had been alive. 'Forrester, I'm hoping your eyes are better than mine.' The horse pricked up his ears. Grasping the reins tightly in both hands, Tom shouted, 'Whitecross, do you hear? Home, boy!' and with that, he kicked his heels hard into the animal's flanks. Forrester shook his mane, uttered a disapproving snort and dropped his head to nuzzle the body lying on the road.

'You're not leaving without him, eh?' Tom thought for a moment, then slid down from the saddle. 'There's a hat somewhere here. No one travels without a hat.' It didn't take him long to find it, a wide-brimmed cavalier hat lying where its owner had tumbled from his horse. He grabbed the reins and held the hat up to the animal's muzzle as though feeding him. 'That's him, ain't it. So now you got to follow. Come on!' A sharp tug at the reins, a moment's hesitation and then Forrester swung round to follow the hat and the walking boy. 'Ha! You's as dull as the old nag we used to have. Size don't mean nothing, eh?' A hundred yards or so further on, Tom stopped by a fallen tree half-blocking the road. He glanced back nervously, straining to hear the sound of his father's horse but heard only the far-off hoot of an owl.

'Grace,' he called out, 'if you're there, you must show yourself now before I go,' but there was no answer. *You've been gone too long and now I'm losing my mind. Seems I'm fit for nothing but the madhouse.* Climbing onto the trunk, he swung up into the saddle, took firm hold of the reins, and kicked hard at Forrester's flanks. He wished he'd been less forceful as Forrester took off at a loping canter, almost unseating him. With the stirrups far out of reach and astride such a broad back, his legs had nothing to grip. 'Whoa!' he exclaimed, pulling hard on the reins. 'You'll be the end of me!' Forrester slowed to a trot, picking a line down the middle of the road. They continued this way, setting off howling dogs in Alvington and Aylburton until, with the first rays of dawn chasing away the darkness, Forrester veered left off the main highway and slowed to a halt outside a pair of massive wooden gates set in a high stone wall. Wrought iron letters nailed to the doors spelt out the word "Whitecross".

Tom quickly dismounted and hammered on the doors. 'Open up! I got news of Sir John!'

At first, he got no response but, certain the gates would be manned with sentries, he continued pounding until at last, an angry voice the other side called out, 'Piss off, boy. You go on with that hammering and your arse'll get hammered next.'

Undeterred, Tom tried again. 'Pardon me but Sir John's taken a pistol shot to his head and is lying in the road maybe four mile away. I ain't lying to you 'cos I've got his hat and horse right here. Told me to ride to Whitecross. Quick now, 'cos he's bleeding bad.'

A peephole in one of the gates suddenly opened and a voice exclaimed 'Boy's got the master's horse, all right. And his hat.' With that, bolts slid back, the gates opened and a posse of well-armed men spilled out, circling around him. An older man, Sergeant Matthewe Hoskyns, stepped forward.

'Speak up, boy. Your name first.'

'Tom, sir. Tom Mundy. Sir John, he were set upon by brigands on the Chepstow road not far from Stroat. I tied cloth on his head 'cos it were bleeding bad. He were alive when I left him. Spoke a little then slept again. But he ain't good. Told me to ride to Whitecross. That's what he said, God's truth.'

'Sir John ain't gonna send a runt like him to save his neck,' someone called out.

'There weren't no one else,' Tom insisted.

The sergeant intervened. 'Only one way to find out. Nicklas, take the boy to the kitchen and feed him. Truth or lies, he needs a meal, and find him some decent clothes. Miracle he hasn't perished with cold in those rags.' He turned to the others. 'Five with me and Forrester. Prime your pistols. Sun's almost up but there's mischief on that road, day or night.'

Nicklas led Tom through the gate. 'You'll ride up with me. Half mile to the manor it is so you can tell me your story like why's you out on the road in the middle of the night?' He looked back at the boy and grinned. 'Go on, then. Get started.'

Tom's version of the night's events indeed proved a good story, decorated here and there with an occasional fact. He'd been out on the road hunting boar since, as anyone could tell you, the best time to catch them was under cover of darkness. As for the brigands, he'd chased them off by hurling stones.

'Hunting boar with your bare hands?' Nicklas roared with laughter. 'Good story, Tom, if it were true, which it ain't.' He was still laughing when they arrived at the manor. The fog concealed the true size of the building but walking around it to a door in the south wing, Tom got a sense of its impressive proportions. The cook was already at work in the huge, high-vaulted kitchen and the aroma of baking bread brought a rush of saliva into his mouth. Nicklas pointed at a bench. 'Sit there. No tricks, now. Hey, Mistress Allen, we got a visitor. Sergeant Hoskyns thinks he needs feeding, which to be honest, ain't hard to see.' He turned to Tom. 'You'd best pray that the sergeant returns with a living Sir John 'cos you ain't long for this world if he don't.' Nicklas disappeared into the bowels of the great house.

'Bread's not made yet so barley gruel's all I got. It's cold, mind,' Agnes Allen announced, setting down a plate in front of him. 'There's more but I'll wager you ain't eaten much of late so don't make yourself puke.' Moments later, she returned with a mug of ale. 'Wash it down with this, nice and slow.' But it was too late. Tom had already launched an all-out assault on the gruel, spooning in mouthfuls of the pale brown soup as fast as he could swallow it until suddenly he remembered the bread in his bag. Reaching in, his hand fell upon the locket. He glanced over at the cook to make sure she wasn't watching him, then removed it from his bag. Holding it up, the nascent glow of dawn from the window illuminated its bright yellow lustre. Carefully, he prised open the clasp and peered inside. His strangled cry diverted Agnes' attention from the bread ovens.

'What's with ye, Tom? The gruel not to your liking?'

'No, ma'am,' he answered feebly. 'I mean it's good, like my ma used to make.' But despite his hunger, the gruel was forgotten. Instead, his whole mind was focused on the face that stared out from the open locket.

The face of Grace Mundy.

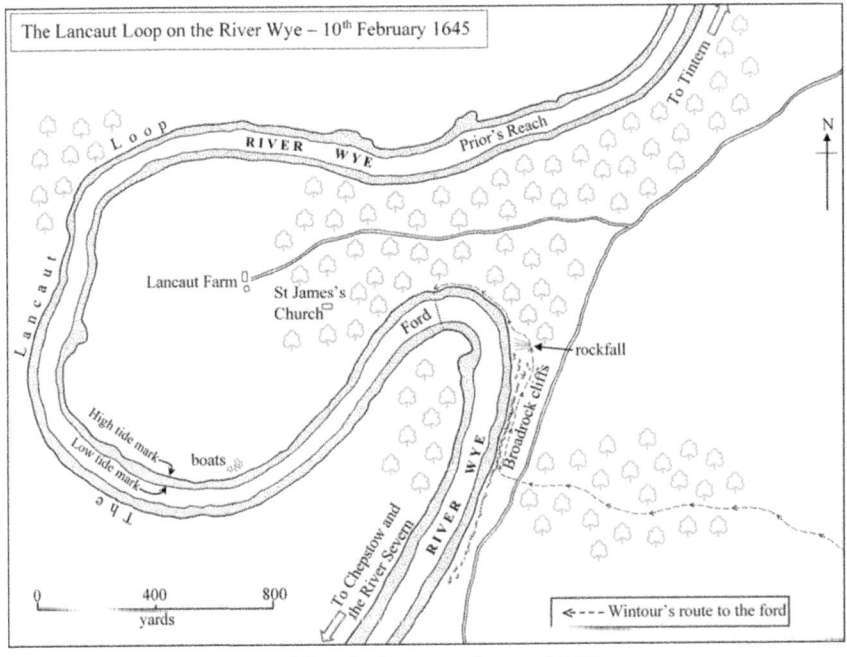

Map 2. Lancaut Loop, 1645.

CHAPTER 5

10th February 1645

'Three bloody years, Tom, and no sign of an end to it.' Will Whytton sat shivering on the edge of his bunk, rubbing what little sleep he'd had from his eyes. 'Hey, boy, Sir John wants his horse!' He rose and aimed a kick at the pile of woollen blankets on the adjacent bunk. That brought a howl of protest followed by,

'An end to what?'

'The bloody war, that's what. Sick of it. Who cares if it's King Charles or parliament what makes the laws?' He lit a candle and crossed the long attic room running above the Whitecross stables, ducking roof beams, to a bucket of water at the far end. Using his elbow, he broke the quarter inch of ice. 'Don't matter if the tax collectors are the king's or parliament's, they're thieves, the lot o' them. Money's gone, just the same, and where's it going, Tom? Making rich men richer, that's where.' With that, he plunged his head into the bucket.

Tom emerged from his blankets and pulled a shirt over his head. 'It's too early for bellyaching, Master Whytton.'

Will gasped as he shook the freezing water from his hair. ''Cos what d'you think we're doing this time of night, saddling the horses and freezing our arses? War business, Tom, that's what it is.'

'But Sir John ain't riding for either side, so what's his business with the war?'

Will shook his head, wondering how the boy had lived two months at Whitecross and not yet understood Wintour's business. 'The forest, Tom, that's his business. King's leased him every tree and every mine in the forest, or so he says. Ore from the mines and charcoal from the trees to fire the furnaces which bleed the iron from the ore. Every Royalist cannon bears the stamp of Wintour's iron furnaces and every gold crown in his coffers comes from the king's purse in payment. D'you see?'

'Sir John makes iron and iron makes the king's cannons; I know that. But the talk is he lets other men do the fighting.'

'You've been listening to gossip in your father's inn. Three times Sir John has brawled with the enemy. Not pitched battles but ugly affairs, mind.' He raised his left arm as far as it would go and grimaced. 'Now word's out that Colonel Massey commands six hundred of parliament's cavalry at Gloucester and God knows how many infantry, well-armed, well-armoured and they's coming, Tom. Today, tomorrow, who knows, but they's coming, believe it. Whitecross stands in their way, see, between where they are in Gloucester and where they wants to be, in Chepstow. Parliament takes Chepstow, then parliament takes Wales, and when the king loses Wales, the war's over, and the men who rode with Sir John will be swinging from forest oaks.'

Tom stood over the bucket of water, summoning up courage for the morning ritual. 'Well it ain't me that rides with Sir John. I just mind his horse.'

'And that's where you're wrong 'cos you've been nagging me ever since Christmas past to ride out with the company and today you gets your wish. Sir John needs every pair of hands he can muster so get yourself dressed. Maybe I'll have your company swinging on that tree.'

Tom's face lit up. 'Me? Riding out with the men? And when was you going to tell me this?'

'Truth is, I wasn't. There's no place for a boy in a company of dragoons. I were going to tell Sir John that you were sick but since you needs convincing that Whitecross ain't safe no more, then maybe a day in the saddle's good for you.'

Tom could barely contain himself. Every night since Wintour had given him a home at Whitecross, a reward for saving the knight's life, he'd dreamt of riding out with Sir John's dragoons.

'Where we headed?'

Will smiled at the boy's innocence. 'Sir John don't share that with no-one till we get there. But you gotta hope that when we do, there's not a ball of lead waiting for you from a Roundhead musket.'

They were interrupted by hammering on the attic door. 'You're late, the pair of you. Get your arses down here now and saddle up. Sir John wants to leave in a half hour.'

'They's coming, Tom. Colonel Massey and his Roundheads. You'll wish you'd never wrapped that shirt round Sir John's head.' Will lowered his voice. 'Better he were dead and we could all go back to working in the forest.'

'But I'd not be here if I hadn't wrapped his head. Father would have found me and taken me back to a beating from my stepmother.'

'Well, you won't be working here much longer if Forrester ain't saddled when Sir John comes looking.' Will stamped his feet into a pair of knee-length boots, threw a woollen cloak around his shoulders and made for the door. He turned, a grave expression written into his face. 'It's not your father you gotta fear, Tom, it's Massey, and Sir John ain't got enough men to stand against him.' With that, Will slid down the ladder to the stables below.

Tom sat for a moment on his bunk, Will's words filling him with a sense of unease. He pulled out the locket that had hung around his neck ever since he'd taken it from Wintour more than two months ago, opened the clasp and stared at the portrait of his sister. He'd not heard her voice since the encounter with Wintour on the road and part of him had begun to doubt that he'd ever heard her at all; and yet, it was Grace's portrait concealed inside the locket that the voice – her voice – had urged him to steal.

The day following his arrival at Whitecross, he'd been assigned to the stables under the watchful eye of Will Whytton. At first, Will had not taken kindly to his new charge but the boy's skill with horses together with his appetite for work soon softened his mood towards him. As for Tom, it wasn't long before he felt it safe to show his new master the locket.

'That's Emma for certain,' Will had observed without hesitation. 'Pretty girl she was. Older than you, Tom, so why's you got her picture round your neck, eh?'

'Emma? Are you sure?'

'Course I'm sure. Plenty of the men had a fancy for her though none gained her affections. Mind, there was gossip an' all, but best not to set much store by it.'

Tom's heart leapt at this news. 'Her name's not Emma. It's Grace. She's my sister, Will. Ran away from home a year and a half ago. She told me she'd come back for me but she never did.'

'Your sister?' Will studied the boy's face and laughed. 'Now I see it. So she never came back for you and now you's run away like she did. Well, you's got to run a bit more if you wants to find her, Tom Mundy, 'cos she ain't here now. Gone last summer, if I remember right.'

'Gossip you said. What kind of gossip?'

'There's always gossip in a place like this and most of it's the work of troublemakers so I won't bother you with it. You should ask Agnes in the kitchen. That's where your sister worked. Queen of gossip, is Agnes.'

Tom had sought her out the following day, determined his questions should not be brushed aside.

'Emma!' she exclaimed, peering at the tiny portrait in the locket. 'Now that's a fancy piece you got there, Master Tom. Gold if I'm not mistaken. Where d'you get some'ink like that, eh?'

'She's my sister, miss.'

'Your sister?' Agnes paused, waiting for an answer to her question but none was forthcoming. 'She were mighty friendly with the men was Emma, but she worked hard. Served at the Wintours' table up in the Great Hall. Sir John demanded it. I think he... well, you know.' She turned away, immediately regretting the remark. The girl's brother ought not to know.

'But where is she, miss? She doesn't work here now, does she?'

'No, she don't. One day, months back, she were just... well... gone. Not a word to me, not a word to anyone. Left everything behind, what little she had, and there's no one knows why. Sad 'cos I liked the girl.'

'What did you mean, miss, "Sir John demanded it"? Are you saying...?'

'You never mind what I'm saying, Master Mundy.' Agnes gave him a forceful push towards the door. 'It won't do your sister much good now 'cos, like I say, she don't work here no more.'

But Tom wasn't ready to leave. 'Sir John was wearing this when I found him that night on the Chepstow road. It don't belong to me but I deserve to know what's happened to her.' He held the cook's gaze, refusing to blink until she answered.

'Come here and sit.' Agnes glanced around the kitchen to make sure there were no listening ears. 'If he finds out you took this from him, then you'd best get ready to meet your maker.' She sat shaking her head. 'Listen, I don't know where she is, God's truth, but it don't surprise me that Sir John wore her portrait round his neck 'cos he were mighty stricken with Emma.'

'Her name's Grace,' Tom corrected. 'I think she must've changed it 'cos she were scared she might be sent back home.'

'Grace? Well, he's a wicked man is John Wintour and that ain't no secret. When he wants something, God help anyone standing in his way. Emma... Grace, she weren't here more than a week before...' She paused, a grave expression on her face.

'Before what, miss? You've got to tell me. I've not seen Grace for more than a year. She promised she'd come for me but she never did.' Then without thinking, he added "cept she came to me in dreams, begging me to find her and then...' He paused, suddenly aware of how foolish he must sound.

'And then?' Agnes asked quietly.

'And then she spoke to me on the road when I found Sir John. Spoke out of the darkness. It was her, I'm certain of it. She's trapped in some dreadful prison cell and I'm to set her free but she won't tell me its whereabouts. I've been here a month and she ain't said a word to me, night nor day.'

Agnes stared at the boy, thinking how sad it was that all that remained of his sister was a voice in his head. 'Tom, there's only one man who can answer your questions but if you value your life, you'll not ask them. They were sweet on one another, that I do know. Everyone knew it, Mary Wintour too, poor woman. But then your sister was gone and for a while Sir John's mood was blacker than night. That's it. Now, he might not know you're her brother but if you keep on asking questions like this, then he's sure to find out and believe me, it won't end well.' With that, she stood up. 'There, I've told you all I know, but don't say a word to no one, you understand?'

Tom nodded, a thousand questions still circulating inside his head.

'You understand?' Agnes repeated loudly, shaking him. 'Not a word. Promise it.'

'I promise. Not a word.'

'Good. Now be off with you.'

*

February had brought little snow, but for weeks the land had been gripped in a vice of bitter cold. Dawn was still two hours away when the column of one hundred and fifty dragoons, Sir John Wintour astride Forrester at its head, moved at a fast trot through the village of Aylburton. Wintour was, like his horse, a giant. Not a man, woman or child in Lydney would ever forget the lavish Whitecross Fayre four years past when Sir John had challenged all comers to a wrestling match with a handsome purse of twenty gold crowns as the prize. A disapproving audience of gentry, with their approving wives and daughters, watched as the big man stripped to the waist, revealing his huge, muscled torso. For a man of forty he was still in excellent shape and, much to his wife's disgust, the rough-hewn features of his face, decorated with its curled moustache and pointed beard, had not yet lost their seductive powers. One by one, he dispatched his challengers, tossing them about the great lawn like playthings. Sir John bowed low at the end of each bout, his thick locks of long, black hair cascading to the ground. The men who worked his estate roared their approval and Sir John glowed with pleasure, for he loved the stage and himself and precious little else.

Many found the big man crude and graceless, unfit to hold the title of Knight of the Realm, unfit to rub shoulders with English aristocracy and certainly unfit to run such a wealthy estate. Mary Wintour, the sole surviving child of a rich Gloucester merchant, had, twenty years ago, fallen for Wintour's cunning, blind to his motives despite the advice of many who knew the knight's deceitful character. Love clouded her judgement and she willingly tied the knot, yet six months later she wished with her very soul that she could untie it. Twenty years later, she was still searching for a way to be rid of the man who from the very beginning had treated her no better than his hunting dogs.

Wintour glanced behind him at the line of men riding two abreast, serpentine beneath a brilliant full moon. They had fallen to silence some miles back, their minds paralysed by the cold. A biting wind sprung up, blowing down from over the wooded hills to the north. At the back of the column, a hushed voice broke the silence.

'It ain't no secret where this road leads, Master Whytton.' Tom slapped his gloved hands together to restore some feeling.

Will ignored the boy and leaned forward in the saddle, pressing his chilled body against the hard, brown neck of his courser, hoping in vain to gain some warmth from the beast.

'This is the Chepstow road; leads past the inn.'

'I reckon I might hand you back when we gets there.' Will was in no mood for conversation.

'You wouldn't do that.'

'Lord knows, I'd have some peace if I did.'

Tom fell quiet as the company rode on, the road and its ruts clearly visible in the moonlight. Stroat and Wibden passed in quick succession until suddenly, Tom's heartbeat quickened as the familiar outline of the Black Horse Inn came into view, hunched low and menacing beside the road. Before the company had even reached the building, a tiny window set deep into the crooked thatch flung open and a woman's head appeared.

'A woman can't get a wink o' sleep with that bloody noise!' The shrill voice rent the night air sending shivers down Tom's spine. 'Ha! John Wintour, I sees you! Up to no good like you's always is. Been telling folk to stay away from the Black Horse, I'm hearing, is that right?'

As Wintour drew level with the inn, he raised his hand to halt the column, removed his hat and looked up at the woman. 'And I'm hearing that you're having to do a day's work now that Mundy's boy's run off.'

That silenced Alice briefly. Then, in a quieter voice laced with venom, she asked, 'What the bloody hell d'you know about the little runt, Wintour?'

Tom could hardly breathe, waiting for the answer.

'I heard he's gone south to Chepstow.'

'Chepstow?' she screamed. 'You're lying, John Wintour! Bridge is down. Ain't no way he could get there.'

'Even the rats in your bedchamber have heard of boats, woman. Now get back to bed and close that window. The stink's making me retch.' He replaced his hat and motioned the column forward.

At the rear, Tom leaned forward in his saddle, pulling his hat low over his face and prayed that his stepmother wouldn't recognise him. He needn't have worried. She was too busy hurling a torrent of foul insults at the big man. When they were finally out of earshot, Will turned to Tom.

'God in heaven, I'd have run away from that, too. War's going to get bad, for sure, but least you ain't got that in your ear no more. Your sister did the right thing, too,' he added.

'But where *is* she, Master Whytton?' Tom whispered. 'No one knows where she's gone.' There was a pause and then he added 'Except one.'

Will looked across at him. 'Except one? Cook tell you that?'

Tom nodded.

'There ain't nothing that woman don't know. Well, something happened between them, it's true, but now Grace ain't here and that's got to be the end of it.'

So, you've known about Wintour and Grace all along, Will Whytton, and you never spoke a word. Tom shook his head. 'The end of it is when I find her.'

CHAPTER 6

With the Black Horse Inn behind them, Tom's curiosity finally got the better of him. 'Master Whytton, why's we on the Chepstow road? The bridge is down like the witch said, so how's the river to be crossed?'

Will had been thinking the same thing. A man, of course, could cross by boat but he'd have to leave his horse, and a dragoon without a horse was a dead dragoon. 'We'll know soon enough but you wake the bloody Roundheads and you'll be fighting sooner than is good for you. And dying sooner,' he added.

Tom lowered his voice. The first seeds of fear, sown when the company had departed Whitecross, had begun to take root. 'You think Massey has men on the road, waiting for us?'

'Enough!' Will snapped. After that, Tom fell silent, lost in his thoughts.

*

A little more than an hour had passed since the company had set out when Wintour, navigating from memory, veered off the main road onto a vague and sinuous path heading due west across heather moorland, well clear of any habitation. Many of those living east of the River Wye had little sympathy with the king's cause and might well have sent word to Massey that a company of Royalist dragoons was on the move. Wintour knew he could not remain undetected for long after dawn, yet if all went well, by noon the task would be complete and he could beat a hasty retreat back to Whitecross.

A half mile from the river, Wintour led his men into woodland. Branches of beech and birch sagged low over the path, weighed down by a thickening rime of hoarfrost. Those at the front of the column were showered by a storm of sparkling ice crystals as they weaved their way through the trees. At the far side of the wood, the company reached a stone wall beyond which lay a narrow road.

'Sergeant Hoskyns.' Wintour turned to the man behind him.

'Sir?'

'We go on foot from here. The top of the Broadrock cliffs lie about one hundred paces beyond the road. We should find a path there to take us down to the river. Then we start work. Give the orders.'

Matthewe Hoskyns dismounted and ran back along the line, passing on Wintour's instructions.

'What's it mean, Master Whytton? Are we laying an ambush?' Tom whispered, sensing that something was about to happen.

Will grimaced as he dismounted, stamping his numbed feet on the ground. The dragoons led their horses through a gap in the wall, across the road and out into open heathland. Despite the approaching dawn, it remained too dark to see far ahead. At fifty paces, Wintour could make out the dense screen of hawthorn that hid the very lip of the cliffs. More than one poor soul had met their maker by walking straight over the cliff edge in the dark and plunging almost three hundred feet to the river below. At seventy paces, Wintour found the path and swung right, following it for a quarter of a mile until the cliffs faded into broken rocky outcrops scattered about the hillside. Here the path turned sharply left and led steeply downhill through an oak wood to the river below. Wintour turned to his sergeant.

'Post Topham and Fitzjohn to keep watch here. We'll take their horses down to the river. I want to know without delay if we're threatened.'

The rest of the company were glad to escape into the cover of the trees. The first hint of dawn had touched the eastern sky and paled the stars. Halfway down the hillside, the path reached a clearing in the wood. Wintour swung up onto the saddle of his great horse and turned to face his men.

'Gather round, men of Whitecross,' he began, gesturing them to come closer. 'You've waited long enough. Leave your nags and I'll tell you what we're about.'

The men were in better spirits now, the walking restoring their circulation. A low murmur of anticipation swelled then fell quickly to silence as the dragoons formed a tight circle around Forrester.

'I'll wager there's not a man here who still believes the king's cause can be won. England no longer has the stomach for a fight and parliament takes whatever land it pleases from His Majesty. There is little you or I can do to save the king. I fear his days are numbered for his judgement is no longer sound.'

Wintour glanced around the clearing, as though someone might be listening then, bending forward, lowered his voice.

'The man's a fool, am I not right, men of Whitecross?'

No one spoke for this was treason but some heads nodded. Sir John straightened.

'We'll not save the king but we can save ourselves. I've received word from Gloucester that Massey is gathering strength to attack Whitecross. We stand in his way and before long he will move to brush us aside. He has tried before, as you know, and failed. Next time I fear he'll bring an army – a thousand infantry or more. Cavalry too. We've not the men nor cannon to prevail against such a force.'

A black silhouette flew silently across the clearing, disappearing like a ghost into the wood. Will Whytton waited to hear something he didn't already know.

'We must prepare our means of escape. Your families are safe, I'm certain of it. Massey has no interest in your wives or children but when the time comes he will no doubt take an interest in you. Any man who has ridden with me can expect no quarter. Tongues in Lydney will wag soon enough when a Roundhead army marches down Main Street.'

This brought a low murmur of agreement.

'I've spies in Gloucester who will give us warning of Massey's march on Whitecross. He'll not find us there, for long before he reaches Lydney we'll have retreated across the Wye into Wales. The Welsh, as you well know, remain loyal to the king.'

'Sir John! The bridge at Chepstow is destroyed. Do you mean to cross at Monmouth? My uncle has seen the bridge there and it's well defended by parliament's forces.'

'I recognise that sweet voice. It belongs to Master Bellamy if I'm not mistaken. Step forward, man, so we can see your feeble frame.'

Martin Bellamy pushed his way to the front. There were few men at Whitecross who could claim to be taller than Wintour but Bellamy, who stood fully six foot and ten inches, was one of them.

'You've spoken well, Master Bellamy, and I'll not argue with you. The only thing to be gained by riding to Monmouth is an early grave. Our passage to Wales lies right here in front of you.'

'Sir, I don't mean no disrespect, but there's few here would take their chance in that water.' Every man nodded. The Wye was a treacherous river, its bed of bottomless mud a sticky grave for those who tried to walk across, its powerful currents too strong for those who dared to swim.

'True enough. Massey will think the same when he pursues us from Whitecross. He'll ride north to Monmouth, expecting us to cross there, but we will disappoint him. In centuries past, monks from Tintern Abbey walked across the river here. Now we're going to walk in their footsteps when Massey comes calling.'

'What was you saying about boats back at Mundy's inn 'cos I for one ain't walking across the Wye.'

'Boats won't serve our purpose. When we cross, we'll need horse and cart, loaded with provisions. It won't be safe to return till the war is over and who knows how long that will be.'

'Well, the good Lord might have walked on water but we're just simple woodsmen who ain't learnt miracles like that.'

'Enough. No more talk. We've work to do. I will show you how the monks crossed the river.' Without another word, Wintour dismounted and led his charger steeply downhill towards the Wye. The company emerged from the oak wood onto the riverbank at a sharp bend in the river. Here it veered away to the left around the Lancaut loop. To the south, the great sweep of the Broadrock cliffs soared skywards. Wintour turned north along the narrow strip of grass that lay between the edge of the wood and the long mud slope running down to the dark waters of the Wye, his eyes scanning the grass ahead. There! An ancient slab of limestone, no more than two feet square, slightly raised from the grass and covered with a thick layer of moss – he'd found it. He knelt by the slab, scraping the moss away to reveal a rough cross carved into the surface, its long axis pointing down the mud slope towards the river. He knew it would be there. As a boy, he had ridden out from Lydney with his father to fish the Wye for salmon at this very place. More than once, sitting beside the slab, Edward Wintour had spoken of the monks. 'They crossed here when the river was low. We could stand out there now, midstream, if the tide was out, and cast a line. You see, John, there's solid rock beneath the water.'

'Then let's try, for midstream makes a better cast.'

'That's true, but you can't just walk out there now. The mud will suck the boots from your feet. Might suck more of a boy than that. In any case, the water's too high. The current will take you.'

'Then how did the monks get safe across?'

'I'm thinking they made a ramp in the mud on either side. Beams of waterlogged oak placed on a bed of stones. They'll be gone now, washed away by the winter floods.'

Looking down the long mud slope, its thick grey-brown ooze emitting a foul stench of decay, John Wintour could not imagine why monks did not walk the extra four miles and cross the bridge at Chepstow. Now, with the bridge destroyed, he had no choice.

'Hoskyns, tell the men to tie their mounts out of sight in the woods. No time to waste. Master Mundy, where are you?'

Tom stepped forward, full of trepidation at hearing his name. Wintour handed him Forrester's reins. 'Take him out of sight beneath the trees but keep him away from the others.' He put a hand on Tom's shoulder. 'Anyone comes near him, you bring him back out on the bank quick where I can see him, you understand? That's *anyone*.'

Tom nodded though he understood nothing. Why should his own men approaching the horse concern him?

With their coursers tethered among the trees, the dragoons crowded around Wintour and the stone slab. It was light enough to see confusion written across their faces. They still possessed no clue as to how man and horse could cross the Wye here. The mud slope ran down some thirty yards to the river. There, muddy water little more than three feet deep flowed downstream to Chepstow and its confluence with the mighty River Severn. From Chepstow all the way north to the ruins of Tintern Abbey, a distance of five miles, the River Wye was tidal and when the sea swept upstream from the Severn twice a day, the mud slopes quickly disappeared beneath a powerful surge of seawater. Before long, the swollen river at the Broadrock cliffs reached twenty feet in depth and more than a hundred yards across.

'Master Bellamy, you're a head taller than most of us and well suited to the task I have in mind.' Wintour strode into his men, clapped an arm around Bellamy's shoulder and led him out to the top of the mud slope. He dropped his voice. 'You've got to trust me, Martin. I wouldn't ask you, but we need this passage across the river, you understand.'

'Not sure I do understand, sir. You ain't asking me to walk in there now, are you, 'cos I ain't doing it.'

This was no less than the knight expected. 'Water's not warm, I grant you, but aside from a chill, no harm'll come to you. The stone slab's been there hundreds of years, set in place by the monks to mark the exact position of a ford. Hidden beneath the water but it's there, I swear it.'

'A *ford*, you say?' Martin Bellamy scanned the river below him. 'I never heard of one hereabouts.'

'It's not been used in a long while so Massey will have no knowledge of it either. The men must see you do this, Bellamy, if they're to trust me today. There's fifty crowns for your trouble, man, so don't delay.'

Bellamy sighed, shook his head, removed his bandolier of musket charges, then coat, tunic and shirt. 'And why should I trust you, Sir John?' to which he got a blank stare. 'Well, if it has to be done, then best it were done quickly.' He strode down the mud slope towards the river.

Tom, standing with Forrester on the edge of the wood, watched in horror, scarcely able to believe what he was seeing. 'It's madness, boy,' he whispered to the horse. 'Agnes was right for this is an evil deed, sending a man to drown. Look, see yonder, there's boats on the riverbank but Sir John, he ain't seen them or else he don't care much for his men.' Dawn revealed a clutch of small boats lying pulled up on the bank a quarter of a mile away upstream on the Lancaut Loop. Could they not make good use of them, he wondered?

At first, Bellamy found the mud no more than ankle deep, but with each step down the slope, the mud swallowed more and more of his boots. Each time he wrestled one leg free to take another step, the mud issued a malevolent belch as if some monster lurked in the lifeless hell that lay beneath the surface, a monster with an appetite for fools. Further down, as Bellamy neared the water, he sank up to his knees, thick, glutinous mud spilling over the rim of his boots. He glanced back up the slope, hoping for a reprieve but none came. Instead, Wintour shouted,

'One more step, man. You're almost there.'

'Almost where?' cried Bellamy. 'My grave?' The big man had stood still too long and his long legs had all but disappeared. In an effort to free them from the mud, he lost his balance and fell forward into the water. Fearful of drowning he began to thrash his arms wildly, searching for something solid. Then, just when he began to think that all was lost, his hands struck rock beneath the surface. Pushing down on it with all his strength, he managed to pull each of his legs free from the vice-like grip of the mud. Slowly, he struggled forward onto the rocky platform and stood up, the river no more than shin-deep around his legs. 'By God, that was a close thing,' he gasped. '"Tis no wonder the monks have long since vanished if this is how they chose to cross the bloody Wye.'

On the bank, a cheer split the dawn silence, each man's relief as great as Bellamy's. Wintour slapped his sergeant on the back.

'Exactly as I told it, Hoskyns. Now it's time to go to work. We've found the ford.'

CHAPTER 7

The ford, no more than twenty feet wide, stretched across the river, disappearing into the mud slope on the far side. Walking across it was an act of faith since the smooth strip of limestone remained hidden from view by the muddy water. Bellamy stumbled across to the far side. Two minutes later, he returned, pulled from the sucking mud back onto dry land by a forest of hands.

Wintour turned to his men. 'To the nonbelievers among you, repentance is due, as this is where the monks of Tintern crossed and so shall we. It's not an easy passage – Master Bellamy has proved that. The mud won't let horse and cart pass so we must sink more stones into it on both sides. Once there's a good foundation, we'll lay planks of wood across the stone. I've had them brought here in readiness. You'll have seen them piled up among the trees where you tied your nags.'

At this, a voice called out. 'Sir, beg pardon, but the planks will be washed away when the next tide sweeps up from Chepstow.'

'Don't mistake me for a fool, Master Baker. They're taken from the wreck of the Margaret. She went down when the great storm hit Chepstow boatyard forty years ago and her timbers are waterlogged. The shipwrights were glad to be rid of them. They'll not last a year, I grant you, but a week or two will serve our purpose. Now, time's not on our side so we must get to work.'

'*We?*' murmured Tom. 'I don't see Sir John getting his boots wet today.'

'There's no shortage of stone.' Wintour pointed downstream towards the Broadrock cliffs. Where they faded into scattered outcrops on the wooded hillside, a huge rockfall created a ribbon of scree reaching almost to the riverbank. 'We can only work on the ford while the tide is low. Two hours from now the sea will flood the Wye and chase us back to Whitecross. We have just two hours to pack these mud slopes with stone and lay the planks. Sergeant Hoskyns, there are three carts waiting for us at St James's church. You'll need twelve horse, twelve men. Take Master Prestcote with you, he knows the way.'

Moments later, twelve dragoons galloped away along the riverbank towards the church.

'Planks and carts, Sir John?' Martin Bellamy stood shivering as he emptied the water from his boots. 'You've been a busy man these past days. How's it you know about the ford when word of it has never reached our ears?'

'I heard of it from my father, though I never saw him cross the river here. Mud's too deep, he would say.'

'Ha! He were right! A smaller man might perish before he reached solid ground.'

'You're fifty crowns better off so put your shirt back on and stop whining. We need to get those stones moved but, before you go, there's another matter.' Wintour glanced around to ensure he could not be overheard. 'I have two pistols of great value which you will deliver in person to Sir Nicholas Kemeys at Chepstow Castle and no one else. He commands the castle for the king. They will pass from your hands to his, do you understand?'

Bellamy nodded. 'So I'm crossing your precious ford, eh? Tell me you ain't doing all this on account of a pair of pistols. A boat would have been a better choice.'

'I told you, the ford must be made ready so that every man here may cross. But the pistols must go first. I sent word to Sir Nicholas some weeks back and he expects them today. There's fifty crowns more for this. I'm counting on you being a rich man by day's end, but know this, Master Bellamy: if the pistols fail to reach him, then it's not just the crowns you'll forfeit but a damn sight more. You understand me?'

'Very good, Sir John. Let's hope the ford is done before the sea tide comes 'cos I ain't riding across a waist-high river, not for a thousand crowns.'

The cold air trapped in the valley chilled every man to the bone and they were desperate to start work, if only to warm their frozen limbs. Wintour split them into two groups, sending one to the rockfall to begin picking out suitable stones, the other to the ford and the less enviable task of unloading the rocks and sinking them into the mud.

Wintour went in search of his horse. He found Tom stamping his feet, anxious to be out with the others.

'Be off with you now, Master Mundy. Join the men downstream. I sense you're in need of some gentle exercise.'

Wintour lifted a flap behind his saddle and ran his hand over two slender leather pouches. Satisfied, he mounted his horse and rode out from the trees along the bank, his eyes scrutinising the river, mindful that before long seawater from the River Severn would begin to do battle with the Wye's meagre flow. For a while it would be an even contest until the ever-rising tide would finally triumph over the river, sending a surge of seawater – the Wye bore – upstream.

Suddenly, cheers broke out from the men waiting at the ford as three carts, each pulled by a team of four horses, came tearing out of the trees from the direction of the old church, careering along the riverbank like charging war chariots. At the rockfall the real work began. Heavy stones got loaded into the carts until their axles groaned beneath the weight. The coursers were small, fast and agile, trained to carry a man into battle, not to pull a wooden cart loaded with a ton of limestone and it took a good deal of persuasion to get them moving. Load after load of stone arrived at the ford to be dragged from the back of the carts and flung into the mud. Despite these efforts, progress proved agonisingly slow. The mud seemed bottomless and Wintour began to think he'd badly miscalculated the size of the task. If the ramps were not completed, it would mean a return visit, and yet Massey's strike could come at any time. For too long, Wintour had been a thorn in parliament's side, his iron foundries amongst the most productive in all England.

A triumphal cry came from the ford. The ramp on the English side was complete, a layer of wooden planking leading down from the bank and across the stones to the causeway, still hidden by the muddy flow of the Wye. A team of horses raced down the ramp, pulling the first loaded cart across the ford to the far side where its cargo of stones was unloaded into the mud. Exhaustion began to take its toll, yet a profound sense of urgency now gripped the company, driving them on.

Wintour dismounted by the ford and stared at the men laying stones. If Master Bellamy was to reach Chepstow by horse with his precious pistols, he needed to cross the river before the flood tide swamped the ford. He reached inside his coat to check his watch. It was gone ten o'clock. Something was wrong. The depth of water at the ford had not changed and yet he had fully expected it to rise quickly after low tide had passed since it was well known that tides in the Bristol Channel were the largest in England.

'Low tide at half nine,' he muttered to no one, 'so where in God's name is the sea?' It made no sense. If the sea flooded the Severn shortly after half past nine, should it not have raced up the Wye and reached the ford by now? Instead, almost an hour had passed and still there was no sign of it.

Just when the men were almost completely spent, the sun burst over the Broadrock cliffs, bathing them in its warming rays, instantly lifting their spirits. Wintour glanced nervously up the hillside. Their luck was holding – no sign of enemy troops and the task all but finished.

Two miles downstream, an enemy of a different kind rushed headlong towards the ford, its killing power as lethal as a thousand Roundhead muskets. It roared beneath the towering ramparts of Chepstow Castle, perched high on a cliff overlooking the river, before continuing north. Sentries posted high in the castle watchtowers stared spellbound at the torrent of sparkling surf passing beneath them.

Upstream, William Whytton sat motionless on the scree. The effort of lifting stones had begun to tear at an old musket wound in his shoulder. Oblivious to Will's torture, Tom was enduring his own. Every muscle in his body screamed for rest until, lungs gasping for air, he collapsed at the foot of the slope.

Suddenly his eye caught sight of something on the Wye, moving swiftly upstream towards him. For a moment he stared at the thin white line stretching across the river no more than five hundred yards away. As he tried to make sense of it, one of the men higher up on the rockfall saw it too and cried out in alarm.

'Get the men off the ford! It's the bore! For God's sake, it'll drown 'em all!'

The thin white line, growing in size as it swept towards him, suddenly made sense. Tom leapt to his feet and sprinted as fast as he'd ever run along the bank towards the ford. As soon as he was within earshot, he screamed, 'Get off the ford! Get off the ford!' but the ford lay around a sharp bend in the river and none of the eight men presently unloading a cart could see the six-foot wall of seawater surging towards them. Catching sight of Tom, still running for all he was worth towards them, waving his arms frantically and pointing downstream, they stopped work and stared.

'Look sharp! We've been ambushed! Get to the bank!' shouted one of the dragoons. The others needed no further persuasion and instantly began splashing back across the ford as fast as the river would allow. All except one.

'The horses, for God's sake!' Martin Bellamy roared after them to no avail. Cursing the men, he grabbed the bridle of the nearest horse and pulled for all he was worth to turn the cart but the team of four proved stubborn.

The huge bore wave rounded the bend and thundered towards them. One by one, those who had been on the far side reached the ramp and scrambled up to safety. Only Bellamy and the horses and cart remained in the path of the wave.

'Leave the bloody cart, man!' Sergeant Hoskyns yelled. 'Save yourself!' But Bellamy had no intention of abandoning the horses. Instead, he leapt up on the cart, grabbed the reins and slapped the horses repeatedly. 'Move, damn you, move!' he shouted but the horses stood motionless, transfixed by the torrent bearing down on them. With a deafening roar the mountainous tidal bore surged up and over the ford, sweeping away Bellamy, the horses and the cart.

CHAPTER 8

The company stood in stunned silence, staring at the wave as it disappeared around the Lancaut Loop towards Tintern. Every eye searched the surface of the river for signs of Bellamy and the horses but there were none.

Wintour dismounted, cursing beneath his breath. He'd known a bore wave would announce the incoming tide but such a wave on the Wye was normally no more than knee high. His father had never spoken of waves that could sweep away horse and cart. Now the ford was impassable and his precious pistols would not reach the safety of Chepstow castle.

'The day here is done.' Wintour could sense the unease in his men, and it needed to be scotched quickly. 'There's five feet of water across the ford and soon the depth will measure twenty. Tomorrow we must return to complete the task since Massey's threat grows with each passing day.'

Tom stood listening, a sense of outrage beginning to boil in his belly. Did Wintour not give a damn that one of his men had been washed from the ford and was likely drowned?

'But, Sir John, there's no knowing whether Master Bellamy has...'

'Has what, Mundy, you young fool?' Wintour cut in. 'Has swum out from the wave and pulled himself ashore? I'll wager there's only one man who can swim here and you're looking at him. Truth is, Master Bellamy refused to save his own skin and now he's paid the price. A pity, for sure, but pity won't save him now. Whitecross sits poorly defended while we're standing here. Fetch your nags and...'

Wintour's orders were abruptly cut short by the sharp crack of a musket shot from the top of the hill behind him. It echoed up the river valley, scarcely fading to silence before a second shot rang out. Bellamy's plight was forgotten, a far greater danger threatening them all.

'Sergeant, did you arrange for a signal?' A sense of dread spilled out from Wintour's voice.

'The sentries – Topham and Fitzjohn – they were ordered not to fire unless challenged, sir,' Sergeant Hoskyns replied.

'Then they've been challenged. Send two of our fastest men up the hill to discover what they can. I want the rest in the trees where we cannot be seen from above. The enemy must not know our numbers or see our horse.'

Bart and Edmund Cole weaved their way up through the wood to where Topham and Fitzjohn had been posted. Before covering half the distance, through the trees they caught sight of someone running down towards them. Drawing their swords, they flung themselves flat onto a deep bed of decaying leaves. Neither had brought their heavy musket and both began to regret it.

''Tis Fitzjohn!' Bart whispered to his twin. 'Where's Topham?'

Sam Fitzjohn sprinted down the hill, ducking under branches and all but ran straight over the two men lying on the ground.

'Sam!' Bart exclaimed, 'Are you followed?'

Seeing his companions, Fitzjohn threw himself into the leaves beside them, panting hard. It was a few moments before he could speak.

'Massey,' he blurted out, 'with horse and foot. Hundreds of 'em. They's armoured back and breast, all of 'em. Professional soldiers, that's what they are.'

'Slow down, Sam.' Edmund got to his feet and sheathed his sword. 'How can you be so certain it was Massey?'

'I saw his ensign. It's Massey for sure. They was looking for us, muskets loaded, the infantry spread out like ants with cavalry lined up on the road. It's a bloody army! Topham had no chance – they almost walked into him.' He paused for breath. 'He fired first and hit one of 'em. You could hear him screaming but then they shot Topham before he could reload. Shot him real close. He's dead. He must be dead. I had to run like the Sergeant ordered. I couldn't help him. It were too late.' Fitzjohn looked at the twins in turn, searching for reassurance.

Bart pulled Fitzjohn to his feet. 'Course not, Sam. You can't fight an army. But did they see you?'

'Don't think so. But they knows we're down here, I'm certain of it.' There was anguish in his voice. 'Day's turning sour.'

'Day's sour enough already.' Bart Cole started back down the hill. 'Come on. Sir John needs this news, though it won't improve his mood.'

Wintour did not receive the news well at all: Massey with a force of foot and horse greatly outnumbering his own. Worse still was Fitzjohn's conviction that Massey had known exactly where to find the Royalists.

'How is it, Sergeant, that Massey knows of our whereabouts?' He spat it out as though Hoskyns were to blame. 'If we were sighted on the road this morning by one of Massey's spies, then word would not have reached him in Gloucester till sunrise at best and yet his infantry arrive up yonder just two hours later. Infantry cannot march thirty miles in two hours.'

Matthewe Hoskyns stood a foot lower than the knight and yet his immense barrel chest and broad shoulders spoke of great strength gained from a life felling trees in the forest. It wasn't Hoskyn's brawn, however, that had earned him promotion in the company but his brain. Now a sickening sensation was gnawing at the sergeant's gut.

'With respect, Sir John, this surely has the stink of a trap. We're exactly where Massey wants us. By now, like you say, there's five foot of water across the ford and deepening fast. We could chance it, and drive the carts across. But the horses won't get up the far bank since we ain't laid the planks on it. And men would drown for certain if they tried it on their own. Current's too strong.' He spun to face the way they'd come down. 'The wooded slope's too steep to ride a charge. Massey will have ranks of muskets waiting for us right across the neck of the Lancaut Loop. We'd have no speed by the time we reached them and they'll shoot the horses from under us. Then he'll send in his cavalry and none of us would survive that. Upstream is Prior's Reach and the valley slopes there are steep and wooded, right down to the river. We could find a passage on foot as it ain't fit for horse but, if I were Massey, I'd have musketeers hidden in those trees and it sounds like he ain't short of those.' He swung round to face downstream. 'No way south past the cliffs since the mud reaches right up to them. Fact is there ain't no easy way out.'

Wintour stood silent, seething with rage, staring up in the direction of the musket shot. 'Mary,' he whispered. 'I see it now, you traitorous bitch.' He turned to the sergeant. 'My wife travelled to Gloucester this past week, did she not?'

'She does regular, Sir John, to visit her parents.' Hoskyns knew exactly where the knight's question was leading since he'd harboured the same suspicions for some time now.

'It's well known, is it not, that her mother despises me.'

Hoskyns nodded. *And not just her mother. Your wife's family have thrown their lot in with parliament and would gladly see you hang.*

'This is her work. Mary has fed the woman details of our visit here and she's passed them to Massey.' He grabbed hold of Hoskyn's coat and pulled him close. 'Tell me I'm mistaken,' he snarled.

No, you ain't mistaken and now every man here will pay the price for what Mary Wintour has suffered these past twenty years. 'Sir John, pardon me, but we've got no time for this.'

Wintour pushed Hoskyns away. 'You're right but there's a day of reckoning coming. I should have rid myself of the blood-sucking leech years ago.' He swung round to search the riverbank upstream. 'You said there's no easy way out but I'm seeing boats sitting on the bank. Your sight failing you?'

'Sir, I seen them boats but it seems to me that they're mighty convenient, just where we needs them.'

'And why would Massey give us an escape across the river?'

'Escape? I don't think so. Men packed into boats like that would make a perfect target for musketeers. In any case, I ain't sure there's enough boats for all of us. It's hard to see from here.'

A curious look came over Wintour's face as he stared at the boats. 'Like you said, Sergeant, there's no other way out of this. Get the men in the boats.'

'But sir, what if...'

'Don't question me. Get the men in the boats! Now!'

The two men glared at each other before Hoskyns turned and walked over to where the dragoons waited anxiously to learn their fate. Needing little encouragement, they mounted their nags and sped away along the bank to where nine boats had been dragged up beyond high tide.

'Sergeant!' Wintour beckoned him over. 'A word before you go.' He lifted the leather flap on his saddle and removed one of the pouches. 'I'd charged Master Bellamy with taking both of these across the ford to the castle at Chepstow but it's too late for that now. I'll not risk them in the boats so instead, I'm giving one to you to hide in the church yonder.'

You're risking the men in the boats. Are they worth less to you than the precious contents of your pouch?

Wintour handed his sergeant the pouch. 'Heavy, eh?' Wintour could see the surprise on Hoskyn's face. 'That's because the pouch contains a pistol with a butt of solid gold. King's payment for fifty Whitecross cannon. There's another on my horse. 'Tis safer that they are kept separate for now. Take this to the church where you'll find a crypt beneath the chancel floor. Lift the stone – it's heavy but not beyond a man of your stature. There's a cavern below with steps leading down into it. Place the bag on the top step. Go no further for the air below is bad.' He waited until Hoskyns nodded. 'Lower the stone back into place, then hide among the trees.'

As Hoskyns turned to go, Wintour added 'Tell no one. If the pistol ain't there when I return to retrieve it, I'll hold you responsible and that won't end well for you. And remember, go no further than the top step. Now get going.'

Hoskyns darted into the wood, mounted his horse and kicked hard to reach the boats. Ahead of him, Tom had slowed his horse to a walking pace.

'Can you not ride faster, Mundy!' Whytton shouted over his shoulder as he steadied his horse to wait for the boy. 'We'll arrive last, for God's sake, and then we're sitting ducks.'

But Tom was listening to another voice. 'You'll die in the boats, Tom. It's a trap. There's a better way.'

'Master Whytton,' he yelled, 'you've got to stop! This ain't right!'

Whytton swore loudly and swung his horse round, galloping back to where Tom had stopped and dismounted.

'You want to die, boy!' He bellowed. 'Get back on your bloody horse or I'm leaving you.'

'You're wrong. It's a trap. There's a better way.'

'You're talking pig shit, Mundy, 'cos there ain't no better way.' Whytton glanced along the bank to where dragoons were frantically dragging the boats down the slopes to the water. Already, scuffles were breaking out as men fought to get aboard. 'It's too late. You just cost me my passage across the river, you bloody fool! I should knock you senseless for that,' and he swung down off his horse and made to swing a punch at Tom.

'I'm not lying, Will!' Tom steeled himself for the blow. 'She spoke to me – Grace – clear as day, just like she did before.'

'You've lost your mind, Mundy. Should never have brought you, a bloody child in a man's war.' He remounted his horse. 'You're on your own now 'cos I ain't wet-nursing you no more. Enemy scouts'll be down…' The sound of hooves pounding towards them from the ford cut him short. Sergeant Hoskyns slowed only long enough to bellow orders:

'Whytton, Mundy, with me. Look sharp 'cos we ain't got time,' and then he was away, racing towards the remains of the company, little more than thirty dragoons who'd lost out in the race for the boats. Here the river began its loop around the Lancaut peninsula, the trees giving way to open farmland, offering little cover to men fleeing from an army of trained infantry. Hoskyns could see the fear in their eyes as he dismounted. Out on the river, the dragoons who'd won the race were doing battle with the tidal surge as its powerful current swept the boats upstream around the Loop towards Prior's Reach. Deprived of oars, the men resorted to musket butts and hats, paddling frantically for the safety of the far bank, but with little coordination of their efforts, the overloaded boats spun wildly, all the while shipping water as they rocked violently from side to side.

'No oars,' Hoskyns observed. 'If I was Massey, I'd have done the same. The boats'll be in Prior's Reach before they get across to Wales. It's a bloody trap, just like I told him.' He turned to the men who'd gathered round him. 'Too late for them now, God rest their souls. We got to save ourselves. Leave your horses. You won't need them where we're going. Follow me and keep quiet!' He turned and ran back along the bank to the edge of the woods, desperately hoping they wouldn't be seen by enemy scouts. Tom cast Whytton a black look but the dragoon ignored him and followed the others. When they reached the cover of the woods, Hoskyns beckoned for the men to gather round.

'As I sees it, we got two choices and fighting ain't one of them. We surrender or we hide. I ain't too keen on the first 'cos Massey has a habit of hanging his prisoners from the nearest tree. So we're hiding.'

This brought protests from a few of the men but Hoskyns raised his hand.

'Let me finish. You'll be wondering what's in the bag I'm carrying.' He lifted the pouch that Wintour had given him. 'It's a pistol but no ordinary pistol. Made of gold. Sir John's been carrying two of them from Whitecross. Gave me one, he's got the other.'

'And where is Sir John and his priceless pistol 'cos I didn't see him getting in the boats and he ain't with us?' Will Whytton voiced what everyone was thinking.

'Reckons he can find a way past the enemy back up the hill to the cliffs. Taken his horse too 'cos he wants to get back to Whitecross.' Hoskyn's news was greeted with a rumble of outrage.

'We all want to get back to Whitecross, for God's sake, but we're stuck down here and the poor devils in the boats, they're…'

'There's no time for this, Master Whytton. Like I said, Sir John gave me the bag and told me to hide it in the church – St James's. He says there's a crypt beneath the chancel floor. Told me not to go down there – bad air, he said, but bad air or not, that's where we're going.' Whytton wanted to ask why Wintour had not sent the pistol across the river like he'd sent most of his men, but time was precious. Every minute, the enemy drew closer. 'So from now on, we're ghosts, you understand? Not a sound.' The men nodded. They understood perfectly.

CHAPTER 9

Running in single file, low and soundless across the thick carpet of leaf mould, thirty-four ghosts weaved their way through the trees towards the church. Hoskyns led the column out into a clearing. In the middle stood the ramshackle remains of a small church. Years had not been kind to St James's. The nave had lost its roof and willow trees, sensing the opportunity, had thrust their stems skywards between the rows of rotting pews. The narrower chancel at the eastern end of the nave had fared better, the roof remaining intact while at the western end a square tower rose some forty feet, its roof surrounded by a low, castellated wall.

The sergeant quickly instructed the men to lie down, out of sight, while he scouted ahead. He supposed it wouldn't be long before Wintour's dragoons were spotted in the boats and that would bring Roundheads sweeping down the hill onto the bank. In doing so, they'd be certain to come across the church. Fortunately for now, it remained deserted. He signalled the all clear.

'Tread careful and disturb the leaves as little as you can.' He stepped through the porch and into the nave through an arched doorway. It had long lost its oak door, thieved for its massive wrought iron hinges.

'Now, Sir John,' he whispered to no one, 'where's this crypt of yours?'

He led his men down the nave and up two steps through the remains of an ornately carved wooden screen into the chancel. Hoskyns handed Wintour's leather pouch to the nearest man, then knelt and swept away the leaves from the middle of the floor.

'Well I'll be damned,' he muttered, staring down at a large, rectangular stone slab, slightly raised above the surrounding floor. into which was set a rusty iron ring. A simple Latin message had been inscribed into the slab: *Requiescant in pace ad finem temporis.* Rest in peace until the end of time. He noted that the moss growing thickly over the whole slab had been carefully scraped away to reveal the inscription. Someone else, it seemed, had visited the crypt in recent times, perhaps descendants of the dead below. He unsheathed his sword and struck the stone gently with the hilt. It rang hollow.

'Master Fitzjohn, get up the tower and find out what you can. Don't be seen or we're done for.' He turned to the others, his voice hushed yet urgent. 'It ain't going to lift by staring at it.'

It took the brute force of two dragoons to lift up one side of the slab until it balanced precariously on edge. Two others held it steady. A mouldy stench belched out from the gaping hole in the floor. A narrow stone staircase led steeply down into the darkness.

'All of us going down there, is that right?' asked Swithin Sixtrees, at forty-five, one of the oldest of Wintour's dragoons. A volley of musket fire thundered down the valley from the north, sending crows cawing up into the air from their roosts. A second volley followed, and then a third, the sound of ordered ranks of infantry firing in succession. Sam Fitzjohn rushed into the chancel with news of the enemy advance.

'Musket fire's coming from across the Loop in Prior's Reach. The tower ain't high enough to let me see them, but there must be hundreds over there, a bloody army.'

'What of the boats? Did you see them?'

'Didn't see none. Current's taken them out of sight round the Loop.'

Into Prior's Reach the sergeant thought. *They'll be slaughtered. I should have stopped them. It's exactly what Sir John wanted, a bloody distraction.* Hoskyns turned to his men. 'Make your choice. Hide with the dead down there or join the dead up here, but make it quick.'

Another volley of musket fire exploded from somewhere to the north. Swithin Sixtrees needed no further persuasion. Clutching his musket, he disappeared down into the crypt.

'How's the air, Master Sixtrees? Sir John says it's bad.'

'And how the bloody hell would he know? He ain't here, is he. Air's like you'd expect in a hole in the ground but it ain't bad.'

'Is there room enough for all of us?'

'It ain't wide but it goes back a way.' A silence followed, then, 'It'll be a bloody squeeze.'

A bloody squeeze was better than a bloody musket shot, Hoskyns reasoned. 'In!' he barked. One by one, the others joined Swithin Sixtrees, dreading what they might find but dreading more the chilling darkness that would fold around them when the stone was lowered back into place. The crypt was a crude construction, no more than a short, narrow tunnel hacked out of the limestone bedrock, barely four feet in height. The walls on either side had been hollowed out in places to form coffin-sized niches, but at first glance, the crypt appeared empty.

'You gotta pack closer than that,' Hoskyns demanded. 'There's a few more up here.'

Will, clutching his left shoulder, waited with Tom until the rest of the dragoons had descended into the crypt. 'You still happy Wintour let you ride with us today, Tom?'

'No more than you are, Master Whytton.' Tom almost wished he was back in the kitchens of the Black Horse. 'There's blood on your coat. Is the shoulder bad?'

'Not as bad as what them poor bastards in the boats are getting right now.' Then he turned to the sergeant. 'Matthewe, I ain't going down there. Tight spaces, they make me sick in the head, I mean real bad and you don't want that when there's Roundheads looking for us. Someone's got to put the leaves back and signal when it's safe to come out.'

Hoskyns hesitated for a moment but Whytton was right. 'Tom, get down there 'cos you ain't staying up here. Master Whytton, knock three times, then three times again when you're certain Massey's men have finished looking for us, and for God's sake keep out of sight best you can. You know what they'll do if they find you.' With that, Hoskyns followed Tom down into the darkness while two men lowered the flagstone back into place. Will quickly covered it with leaves as best he could but it was a hopeless task. It would be clear even to the least observant that feet – many feet – had not long churned up the leaves in the middle of the chancel.

The musket fire from Prior's Reach sounded unrelenting now though it seemed to Will that it was growing fainter. He wondered if any of the boats had reached the far bank. He thought it unlikely.

Snatching up his musket, he ran through the nave, looking for the stairs to the roof of the church tower. At the back, a wooden balcony had all but collapsed on its rotting timber supports and beneath it, almost completely hidden from view, Will found a low wooden doorway leading to a narrow spiral staircase. At the top, a heavy wooden trapdoor lay open and he emerged onto the flat roof of the tower into brilliant sunshine. He crawled across to the south side and slowly raised his head so that he could look out through a gap in the castellations. Not far away, the sea continued its relentless flow upriver, swelling the Wye and submerging the mud slopes. He watched a group of men, the sunlight glinting off their breastplate armour, making their way along the bank to the dragoons' horses before walking slowly among them. *Counting*, thought Will. *Hundred and fifty. Massey wasn't expecting such a large force. There's only enough boats for a hundred, hundred and twenty if they're overloaded. So when he hears there's a hundred and fifty horse, he's going to come looking for the dragoons that didn't get in his boats.*

Lying beneath a warming February sun, his shoulder felt as if someone had thrust a dagger into it. He stared up at the cloudless sky, the pain amplifying his rage. Wintour, the damn fool, had walked straight into Massey's trap, one that could not have been laid with such precision unless details of the knight's intentions had been leaked to the enemy: numbers, times, locations. Sir John was right about one thing – Massey could not have marched his troops from Gloucester that morning. He must have been waiting and watching while the dragoons laboured at the ford, staying his hand until the bore wave had made escape across the river impossible. And the men at Prior's Reach? For how long had they been posted there, waiting for the boats filled with Wintour's dragoons to be swept around on the rising tide? Wintour's plans had been leaked, of that there was little doubt.

All at once, his thoughts were interrupted by a barrage of musket fire from the top of Broadrock, followed by the tortured whinny of a horse. He raised his head just in time to see the animal plunging from the cliff top towards the river far below before slamming viciously into the mud. A second later, the sound of the massive impact reached him, a boom as loud as a cannon shot. Even from that distance, the identity of the horse was never in doubt, a huge black behemoth silhouetted for a few cruel seconds against the brilliant white of the cliffs. Forrester! Had Wintour fallen with his horse? Surely he would not ride him so near to the edge. He saw movement on the cliff top at the very place where the horse had fallen. As he watched, something flew over the edge into space, tumbling, flapping and then almost floating through the air until finally it landed softly on the mud, not far from the horse. Someone had thrown it over the edge – a coat or riding cloak, perhaps. It was a trick! Will had seen it used before – a hat thrown onto water to give the impression to the hunter that the hunted had fallen in and drowned. Now he was certain that Wintour had thrown down his coat, hoping the enemy would think he, too, had fallen from the cliff. But where would he hide to escape detection? The enemy would be certain to search the dense thicket of hawthorn. Sure enough, the cliff top was suddenly crawling with enemy soldiers. *You're looking for him, eh? You can see his horse easy enough, lying in the mud at the foot of the cliff; but what's that shape lying beside it?* Shortly, the Roundheads disappeared and Broadrock lay still again while Wintour's fate remained a mystery.

The musket fire from Prior's Reach had ceased now, the dreadful silence broken only by the distant cries of wounded men, their desperate appeals for help silenced as they slipped beneath the surface of the Wye.

Will pushed back from the parapet, closed his eyes and tried to make sense of it all. Wintour, he guessed, had climbed through the trees to the top of Broadrock, hoping to make his way along the lip of the precipice undetected. The hawthorn grew thick a short way back from the edge where its roots could find soil, though without leaves it would provide a poor screen for a big man and a bigger horse. If Wintour had thought that Massey would concentrate his force on the river and leave Broadrock unguarded, he was mistaken, another blunder in a growing list.

He came to his senses and sat up. There was nothing he could do for the men in the boats, but the fate of those who hid beneath the chancel floor now lay in his hands. He tried to imagine what it was like down there; thirty men – and Tom – packed like apples in a press, cramped and contorted beneath the low roof in soot-black darkness, ears straining for the sound of footsteps on the floor above. Some of the men had toiled in Wintour's iron-ore mines in the forest and were well used to hours spent crawling through waist-high tunnels with nothing more than a flickering tallow candle. Often the candles were spent long before the shift was done and far below the forest oaks, miners wielded picks and shovels blindfold, adding crowns with every blow to Wintour's coffers.

For most, however, the crypt was hell, the utter darkness made worse by the silence.

And the waiting.

Tom could stand it no longer.

'Sergeant,' he whispered, 'why's Sir John brought golden pistols to the Wye? Seems mighty risky to me.'

'Every man here is thinking the same, Master Mundy, so I'll tell you.' Sergeant Hoskyns threw caution to the wind. The men had a right to know the truth behind Wintour's plan to resurrect the ford. 'The golden pistols are worth more than any of us will earn in a lifetime's toil in the forest. But even they are nothing compared to Sir John's fortune hidden away in the vaults of Whitecross. Nothing else matters to the man; not the Manor, his family, the forest – the little that we ain't felled – nor you or I or the men packed in the boats. The ford ain't for us. It's for Wintour's riches, starting with these pistols. Sir John tasked Bellamy, God rest his soul, with taking the two pistols across the ford today but he ain't taking them anywhere now. I'll wager he planned to have us take the rest of his treasure – plates, goblets, candlesticks, jewelry and Lord knows what else – over the ford to Chepstow castle tomorrow. Sir Nicholas Kemeys holds the castle there for the king and it's well guarded.'

'So why's he not sending his precious pistols across the river in a boat?' asked Sixtrees. 'Don't make sense hiding one of them down here and taking the other. Unless he *knew* the boats were a trap. Tell me that ain't right, Sergeant.'

Swithin Sixtrees was no fool. Hoskyns admired that in the man. 'I told him it were a trap and I could see in his face he believed me. But he needed a distraction if he were to escape from the valley along the cliffs; needed Massey's men drawn away to the north.'

'Christ, Sergeant, this is too much! The slaughter of his men – a distraction?'

A rumble of outrage filled the crypt until Hoskyns appealed for silence. 'That's bad enough,' he continued, 'but save some of your wrath for Mary Wintour.'

'Mary?' Sixtrees sensed his world was falling apart around him.

'What part has she in all this?'

'You know her part, Master Sixtrees. Every man here knows her part. Aside from Sir John and Sir Nicholas, who else knew the details of our business at the ford today? Even the men who brought the carts to the church and the planks of wood from Chepstow knew nothing of Wintour's intentions, nor the timing of them. But Mary Wintour, she still has access to his bedchamber, to his writing desk, to the letters that he's written to Sir Nicholas and Lord knows, she has reason to send her husband to hell.'

'A curse upon the woman if it's true 'cos every man but him is down here or in the boats,' Sixtrees snarled.

All at once, Howey Brown, who'd crawled into a niche in the crypt's end wall, let out a sudden howl of terror.

'Lord help us, who was that?' hissed the sergeant. 'Someone put the bloody arse out of his misery.'

''Tis the dead,' Howey whispered, his voice shaking. 'Didn't see him 'cos there's no coffin. He's just lying here in his clothes.'

'Howey Brown, that you?' another voice asked.

'He ain't long dead. Skin's still stretched over his bones.'

'You'll be joining him, Master Brown, if the Roundheads hear you.' Sergeant Hoskyns softened his tone. 'Move away if you can.'

'Can't move. There's nowhere to go.' There was a pause, then Howey added, 'There's a candle on the ledge here. Ain't much of it left, but...'

'Master Sixtrees, is your fuse still burning?' Swithin Sixtrees had refused to relinquish his old matchlock musket when Wintour had received the king's payment of two hundred flintlocks, a weapon vastly superior to the matchlock.

'Give me a moment.' The sound of blowing was soon rewarded with a faint glow from the match cord hanging from his musket. 'Pass over the candle, Howey.'

In a trice, the flicker of candlelight chased away the darkness, revealing to everyone's horror the true size of the void into which they had squeezed.

'Christ, Swithin, we were better off in the bloody dark.'

There were murmurs of agreement. In their imaginations the men had created a far larger crypt. In the same way, the darkness would have saved Howey Brown from the full horror of what lay beside him in the niche. Instead, in the faint, yellow light thrown along the tunnel, his eyes were drawn to the emaciated corpse, every inch of its skeleton covered by a shiny layer of stretched, black parchment. Scraps of rotting cloth still clung to what remained of the body while a few tufts of coarse, white hair, long since released from the scalp, tumbled across the shoulders.

'It's a woman,' he gasped.

'Ain't no telling if bones are a man's or a woman's, Howey. Look the same.'

'There's no mistaking.' He could barely speak. 'It's a woman. I gotta move. Please, I gotta get away...'

In a panic, he pushed out from the niche, falling onto the sprawl of men on the floor.

'Bloody hell, Howey, what's with you, man? It's no more than a corpse. You seen a few of them before.'

'No, he's right,' someone whispered. 'It *is* a woman. Here, pass the candle.'

'No, leave her!' wailed Howey. 'This ain't right!'

It was too late. The dying candle was held aloft to reveal the corpse lying fully stretched out on the ledge. Every eye in the crypt was drawn to the swelling in her belly, the shrunken contours of her parchment skin revealing the merest, yet unmistakeable outline of another tiny human inside her. A hand reached out from someone crouched below the niche.

'No secret how she died,' he whispered, running his finger over the neat, circular hole above her left eye socket. 'Pistol shot. Who'd do such a thing? Ain't nothing she could have done to deserve this.' He spied a tiny golden locket attached to a slender chain which had fallen to one side of her ribs. 'All she's got left now,' he whispered.

'We've got no business stealing from the dead, Master Butcher.' Sergeant Hoskins said, 'so leave it.'

'Open the locket, Tom. The truth lies in the locket.' Grace's voice filled the crypt and it seemed to Tom impossible that no one else could hear it.

'No, open it, Master Butcher! Please!' Tom pleaded, a look of utter dread on his face. 'Open the locket before the candle dies. I have one just like it – look.' He slipped the locket from around his neck and held it up. 'I need to know the truth. Please!'

A puzzled silence fell across the men until Hoskyns said, 'Alright. Open it and then we'll leave it with her.'

The candle's wick had all but consumed the wax and the flame began to flutter wildly, casting dancing shadows across the walls like ghostly wraiths. Butcher's clumsy fingers struggled with the tiny clasp but suddenly the locket sprung open. 'Can't see nothing. Hold the candle near.' The candle's final death throes gave him the briefest glimpse of a face before the crypt was plunged once more into darkness.

'Master Butcher,' Hoskyns whispered, 'tell us what you saw.'

'He's here,' came the reply.

'What d'you mean? Who's here?'

'Sir John.'

'It's her,' Tom burst out. 'I knew it. It's Grace!' With that, he pitched forward, covered his face with both hands and wept.

CHAPTER 10

Voices! They were coming out of the trees towards the church. Someone was barking orders. Instinctively, Will grabbed his musket and checked the priming pan. It was full. He had not intended staying on the roof – it was too exposed with nowhere to run – but now he was trapped. The Roundheads would reach the church before he had a chance to escape. He cursed himself for being so witless.

Massey had done his sums: the number of dragoons in the boats was fewer than the number of horses which meant only one thing. The rest of Wintour's men were hiding somewhere around the Loop. Will guessed he'd send small groups of ten, maybe fifteen infantry to flush the dragoons out – the beaters on a pheasant shoot. They'd work slowly uphill from the riverbank to the brow of the valley where snipers armed with long-barrelled muskets would lie in wait.

Warily, the Roundheads circled the church, pistols in one hand, swords in the other. Twice they hoisted one of their men up into a window frame to peer into the nave and twice he shook his head and jumped down. Two men were posted outside the porch while the others rushed through the empty doorway into the nave, expecting to be ambushed by the remnants of Wintour's force, but instead they were greeted only by the husky caw of a crow as it flapped away into the sunlight.

'This place ain't been used in a while, no mistake,' one of them observed. 'What did the colonel call it? St John? After Wintour maybe.' The others sniggered at this.

'St James, it is,' replied another. 'Anyways, Wintour ain't no saint. Saints go that way,' he motioned upwards, 'and Sir Mighty John, well, you seen him fall. Ain't so bloody mighty now, eh.'

'Enough talk.' The corporal was growing tired of the ill-disciplined rabble under his command. 'Nappe, search the tower. Rest of you out and search the clearing.'

Titus Nappe bowed mockingly. 'As you will, Corporal Grey.' The others grinned as he turned theatrically and made his way to the back of the nave. The corporal resisted the temptation to shoot the insolent man in the back.

On the tower roof, Hoskyns lay motionless, listening to the muffled sound of voices in the nave. It was only a matter of time before they searched the tower and if they climbed the staircase, they were certain to lift the trapdoor and check the roof. Crouching as low as he could, he silently lowered the trapdoor and then gingerly placed first one foot and then the other on the ancient oak timbers, fearing they might give way at any moment; but they held firm. There was just a chance whoever pushed the door from below might reason that, after long years of neglect, the swollen timbers had jammed the door shut. It was a long shot but what else could he do?

Forty feet below, Titus Nappe sat on the bottom step, a loathing for the corporal burning inside him. The man's name had won him promotion, nothing more, and Titus, with twenty years soldiering under his belt, was taking orders from a boy scarcely weaned from his mother's breast. Search the tower? Hah!

'Well?' Corporal Grey inquired when Nappe returned, a little too soon for the corporal's liking. 'What did you find?'

'Didn't find nuffin'.'

'What do you mean you *didn't find nuffin'*,' the corporal imitated.

'Did you search the roof?'

'Nuffin's what I found. It ain't hard to understand, not for a man of your breeding, *Corporal*.'

'You watch your tongue, Nappe, or you'll answer for your insolence when we return.'

'Insolence? Now there's a fine word. Learned that from your father, I'm thinking, a man of fine words when he was sober, so they says.'

This was too much. In one lightning motion, the corporal's sword swept out from its scabbard, its point coming to rest on Nappe's breast plate immediately below his neck. 'Damn you, Nappe, another word and you'll be speaking through a hole in your neck, do you hear me?' The two men stared at each other through their helmet bars with no attempt made to disguise their contempt for one another. 'Twenty years a soldier, so you say, and still a private and you dare to speak of my father.'

Titus Nappe sneered at this. ''Cos my name ain't Grey, that's why.'

'I've heard enough. The enemy escapes while you practice your insubordination. I cannot trust you so you'll remain here until I send for you, is that clear?'

'Enemy's long gone, Corporal Grey. Colonel ain't going to be too pleased 'bout that.'

Grey lowered his sword. 'They're long gone when we can't find them and we're not finished looking yet.' He turned to go. 'Any bloody nonsense, Nappe,' he called back, 'and you'll be hanging with the cavaliers before the day's end.'

Nappe waited until the Corporal had gone then spat on the nave floor. 'Pretty Corporal,' he sneered. 'Pretty bloody Corporal.' He wandered into the chancel, removed his helmet and sat down on the leaf mould.

Up the tower, Will sensed the immediate danger had passed and crawled away from the trapdoor. Snatches of an argument had drifted up the stairs but the church had fallen silent now and the voices he could hear in the clearing were growing fainter by the minute. A fragile ray of hope penetrated the dark horrors which had cast their long, black shadow across the day's proceedings. It appeared that the Roundheads had failed to find the crypt. What's more, no one had thought to search the tower, an oversight that made no sense to him but one for which he was deeply grateful.

He lifted the trapdoor an inch and listened for sounds of movement below. *What would I have done?* he thought. *Two men to stay behind, one up the tower and another covering the porch.* He lowered the trapdoor and crawled over to the parapet. He couldn't risk returning to the nave just yet. It would take just one pistol shot to bring the Roundheads pouring back into the clearing. No, he'd wait an hour, by which time Massey should have abandoned his search and be turning his attention instead to an undefended Whitecross. The men packed into the crypt would have to wait another hour.

Sitting on the chancel floor, slumped against the wall, Titus Nappe stared aimlessly at the carpet of leaves while dreaming a violent revenge on the corporal. Suddenly, he sat up. Something about the leaves wasn't right. He got to his feet and stood in the middle of the floor. The leaves around the edge of the chancel had settled into a compact layer but here, in the centre, they were loose and piled deeper as though they had recently been disturbed. Titus kicked the leaves aside with his feet and immediately his boot caught the edge of the flagstone. He knelt and brushed away the remaining leaves to reveal the stone with its iron ring and inscription. He'd never been taught to read in any language but it didn't take a Latin scholar to realise that the flagstone concealed some kind of chamber beneath the floor, a tomb most likely or perhaps a larger family vault. The slab was almost free of moss but of more interest to the Roundhead was the clear, razor-thin gap around the stone's perimeter. *It's not long since the stone's been lifted and lowered.*

Now the leaves began to make sense. He jumped to his feet and traced with his eyes the trail of disturbed leaves back into the nave.

The pretty corporal had missed it. They'd all missed it but now it seemed obvious. A substantial party of men had been in the church not long before the scouting party had arrived. Titus Nappe looked down at the flagstone again. It was the ring that puzzled him. Was the stone more than a simple gravestone, more like the entry to a void beneath the floor? Drawing his pistol from its holster, he tapped the butt on the stone. The tap resounded around the chancel. He shifted position on the floor before clearing more leaves and tapping again on another stone. The resonance was less pronounced but still unmistakeable.

Then it came to him.

He leapt to his feet. 'Bloody hell!' he exclaimed to no one. 'They're down there!'

He froze, wondering what to do next. He couldn't raise the stone on his own; he'd never have the strength to do it and, in any case, there was no way of knowing how many dragoons were hiding beneath the floor. He had little doubt their muskets would be primed, ready to blow his head off and yet, with their hideaway no longer a secret, they could emerge at any moment before he'd had a chance to summon help. His eye caught sight of a stone baptismal font standing beside the screen. 'Perfect,' he muttered. 'Bloody perfect.' He heaved at the massive stone basin and sent it crashing to the ground from its pedestal support. Glancing nervously at the rusty iron ring, expecting it to lift at any moment, Nappe wrestled the stone basin across the chancel floor and onto the flagstone. He straightened up and inspected his handiwork, a malicious grin spreading across his face. The men below ground were imprisoned now. He was tempted just to leave them there but quickly decided against it. No one would believe him when he boasted that he'd trapped Wintour's dragoons unless they saw it with their own eyes. *Pretty corporal's going to look a right bloody fool. He ain't gonna be corporal tomorrow.* He laughed out loud and then knelt low on the flagstone. 'You ain't going nowhere, slop suckers!' he shrieked. 'Not till Titus has arranged a little welcome party for you!'

Still chuckling, he slipped the helmet over his head and then made for the staircase up the tower. Three pistol shots should be enough to bring them running, he thought, and when the day's done, they'll be talking about Titus Nappe in every tavern in Gloucester. At the top of the staircase, he pushed open the trapdoor and stepped up onto the roof. A musket barrel rammed into the back of his neck and a voice snapped, 'Drop your pistol or you're a dead man!'

Titus froze, cursing himself. He should have guessed the cavaliers would post a man on the roof.

'I said drop it 'fore I blow your head off!' Will snarled.

'I'm doing it, I'm doing it!' Titus edged slowly away from the dragoon, removing his pistol from its holster and laying it down. Slowly, he turned around to face the dragoon, his arms slightly raised, watching to see what his enemy would do next. He didn't like what he saw. The musket pointing at his chest was a modern, short-barrelled flintlock. In skilled hands, it could kill a man from fifty yards. From ten feet, Titus reckoned, the musket ball would most likely remove a good part of his head. Stay calm, he told himself, and wait.

'Turn around,' Will ordered, 'and throw your sword over the edge.'

'So you're going to execute an unarmed man?'

'Do it!' Will yelled.

Titus hesitated for a moment, considering his options, and then unsheathed his sword and dropped it over the parapet.

'Shooting an unarmed man, 'tis the coward's way.'

Will was expecting a note of desperation in the man's voice, but there was none.

'I'll tell you what the coward's way is. It's tricking your enemy into crossing the river and then slaughtering them whiles they can't shoot back. *That's* the coward's way.'

'That weren't me,' Titus lied. 'That's them down there by the river. I'm up here killing no one.' He could read indecision in Will's face. The dragoon's finger was on the trigger but it wasn't tight. 'I'm thinking you ain't going to pull that trigger, are you?' He was growing more confident by the minute. "Cos if you do, there's two hundred muskets that'll be running here pretty quick and that won't help your friends down there, now will it?'

The merest of frowns passed over Will's face. The Roundhead had found the crypt.

'Oh yes, I knows about them down there, hiding with the dead. Now there's a thing.' His voice held a swagger now. 'You've got to fight me fair and square, dragoon, and you knows it.'

Knowing what you know, thought Will, *you've got to die; that's what I knows.* He tightened the grip on his musket. It would have to be quick and silent and that left him just one option. In a flash, he launched himself across the roof, smashing his musket into Nappe's breastplate, driving him backwards to the parapet. The Roundhead's arms flailed wildly, searching for solid purchase as momentum swept both men over the edge and into space before crashing heavily into the dense shrubbery forty feet below.

*

Beneath the chancel floor, the men had listened with dread to the sounds of someone striking the flagstone followed by something heavy being rolled across the floor above them. No one was in any doubt as to its purpose and the muffled insult yelled down through the stone had merely confirmed their worst fears – their refuge had become a prison.

Tom suffered his agony in silence, Grace's picture clenched in one hand. He longed to know if his suspicions were correct, that the man who had so callously sentenced his own company to die at the hands of the enemy was the same cold-blooded monster that had killed Grace and her unborn child. He longed to ask her out loud but the men would think he had lost his mind. He desperately wanted to hear her speak, to tell him what had happened. Had he really heard her voice or was he simply imagining it? Had he gone mad?

'I would have come back for you, Tom, if I'd not been a fool.'

There! His sister's voice, soft and melancholy.

'I begged Sir John to let you join me at Whitecross but he wouldn't have it. Said you were too young. I tried to persuade him as only a woman can and he encouraged me till… well, till I was with child. I loved him, see. But when he learned of my condition, he said I must leave and never return. I should have done as he asked but it weren't so easy to walk away, not with his child in my belly. I went to him early one morning on the shooting range, pleading with him to let me stay. There was another knight there with him – Sir Willoughby. Both men had pistols, primed and loaded. They were golden pistols like I'd never seen before. Sir John, he pointed his at me, threatening to shoot me dead if I did not leave. I hated him in that moment. I took hold of Sir Willoughby's pistol meaning only to frighten Sir John but in the struggle, the trigger was pulled and…'

'And Sir Willoughby was shot dead,' Tom whispered. 'I heard of it from the men. An accident on the shooting range, Sir John had told them.'

'It was an accident, Tom, I swear it. I never meant it. But Sir John aimed his pistol at my head – the very same pistol which lies with you in the crypt – and pulled the trigger.'

'I knew it!' Tom cried out. 'The man's in league with the devil.'

'Someone silence the boy,' a voice hissed from the darkness. 'He's losing his mind.'

'I'm sorry, Tom, but you got to know the truth. I'll never rest in peace, not till the man who killed us both is dealt the justice he deserves. He's evil right enough. I know that now. 'Tis too late for me to serve him justice but you can do it though I deserve nothing from you. 'Tis not luck that brought you here, rather 'tis fate and fate decrees that you should take from Sir John what he has taken from me and my child.'

'Yet he wore your picture around his neck,' Tom whispered as the tears flowed.

'You speaking to ghosts, Tom?' Hoskyns feared the boy had

indeed begun to lose his mind but got no answer.

'It reminds him of the time when he possessed me like some trinket that gave him pleasure. You're right – the devil dwells in his soul. He has no remorse for what he did. Will you do as I ask, Tom? Will you serve him justice and then give us a rightful burial so that I may live in peace with my ancestors?'

'I will do it. As God's my witness, Grace, I will do it, I swear.'

'There is something else I must ask of you, precious brother. My ancestors, they'll not receive my soul until the debt for the life I took is paid. Wintour carries the pistol that killed Willoughby. That very pistol must now save a life. How, I cannot say, but it is hidden at the top of Broadrock. Search for it there and somehow find a way. I ask so much of you when I gave you nothing but there's no one else can save us. Now be still and wait for your release.'

Tom waited for more but Grace had fallen silent.

Save a life? Pistols take lives so how can they save one? he puzzled. *Hidden at the top of Broadrock? If it's true, then Wintour must have passed that way. But why would he hide the pistol there?* Thoughts spun like a whirlpool inside his head as he struggled to make sense of what his sister had asked of him. Meanwhile, the embers of hatred for the knight were burning brighter inside him with every minute. But first, he had to escape from the crypt. As time passed, he became aware that his breathing was quickening – he could hear the same in the men around him – while a dull pain was growing behind his eyes. Inside his chest, his heart was racing as though he were wrestling hay bales into the stable loft and yet he was sat motionless on the cold stone floor of the crypt.

'Wintour was right,' a voice growled. 'Air's bad. Should never have come down here.'

'Air was good till we did,' Sergeant Hoskyns pointed out. 'We've been here too long.' He found himself pausing to suck in more air and yet no amount of breathing could quench his craving for it. 'Enemy's been and gone 'cos we ain't heard nothing for a while now.

I'm thinking that Master Whytton may have found trouble and he ain't coming back. We've got to lift the stone.' He got to his feet. 'I needs three of you.' Panting hard, the pounding in his head worsening all the time, he felt his way up the steps to the flagstone. 'On my word, push,' he commanded when the others had squeezed into position. 'Push!'

The four dragoons fought to lift the flagstone with all their strength but it wouldn't move.

'Need more men,' Hoskyns gasped.

'Ain't room for another on these steps, Sergeant,' a voice replied. 'We just got to do this and quick...' he paused, sucking at the air '...cos we're drowning down here.'

The four men tried again but failed.

'Rest!' Hoskyns slumped down, his head between his knees for he felt suddenly dizzy.

Tom's headache was growing steadily worse, as though someone was tightening a vice around his skull. He tapped the arm of the man sitting next to him. 'Are we going to die?' he whispered.

'If we don't lift that stone, then you got to prepare for it,' came the answer. 'Or, if the Lord's merciful, then he'll send Master Whytton back to do what he should have done an hour ago, and we can all go home, so maybe you best speak to the Almighty instead of me.'

Tom pondered this for a moment and then asked, 'You think Master Whytton is dead?'

'No way of knowing. Like I said, you got to pray he ain't.'

Tom had given up praying when his mother had died. God hadn't listened to him then, but instead had stood by while the witch had beaten him every day thereafter. As if that wasn't bad enough, Grace had been taken from him, and shot by the man she had loved. And now Will. He would not pray, not to a God who allowed such things to happen.

'Is this fate, Grace?' Tom whispered. 'To bring me here to die, so that my bones lie with yours forever.' He fell quiet, listening to the men wrestling once again with the flagstone, each effort weaker than the last. 'This way, I ain't going to serve justice on no one.' He was too tired to say more, too tired to care and simply lay down, curled into a ball and waited for the end to come.

Outside, the man who could free the dragoons from their slow and certain death lay broken and senseless at the foot of the tower, his own life slowly ebbing away.

CHAPTER 11

Almost four hours had passed since the bore wave had swept upriver when the mud-caked body of a man crawled from the fringe of reeds lining the English riverbank, a little more than halfway around the Lancaut Loop. He paused on the grassy bank a moment, shivering violently while the sun's meagre warmth sent steam rising from his sodden clothes. The enemy's muskets had fallen silent some while ago and the clamour of Roundhead search parties had receded into the distance. Even the tortured cries of dragoons, their bodies smashed by Roundhead musket balls, had faded to a deathly hush.

Slowly, Matthewe Bellamy rose to his feet, numb with cold. His boots had been sucked from his legs as he'd fought to escape the leviathan that had swept him from the ford, its murderous power hell-bent on drowning him. But the same leviathan had shown him mercy. A plank of wood, ripped by the wave from the boatyards at Chepstow, had drifted upstream with the current and saved his life just as he prepared to meet his maker.

He staggered forward into the cover of some low shrubs and looked about. Ahead, in the middle of the peninsula, lay the scattered buildings of a farmstead while over to his right, the tower of St James's church rose above the trees. He urgently needed a dry change of clothes and some food to restore his strength for the journey back to Lydney. The farm, he decided, was too risky. Massey had no doubt promised a handsome reward to anyone handing over the remnants of Wintour's company. No, he would make for the church and from there, search for the dead among the woods beyond. Dead men would have no need of clothes.

Fifty yards from the church, he bent low and listened. He'd spied no movement on the tower but knew that Massey might well have snipers concealed among the trees, ready to welcome any of Wintour's dragoons who came visiting. Moving silently, he began circling the church, stopping now and then to listen for a whispered snatch of conversation or the snap of a twig, but only the murmur of the growing river behind him disturbed the silence. Bellamy had almost completed the circle when his ears picked up a faint moaning sound. At first he thought it was the wind in the branches and yet it was coming from the foot of the tower. As he drew closer, expecting at any moment the crack of a sniper's musket, he caught sight of a body lying twisted in the thick tangle of brush. Two bodies! He scarcely noticed the thorns tearing at his bare feet as he pushed his way through the snarl of brambles and knelt alongside his friend.

'Merciful God, what's happened here?' Bellamy glanced up at the tower. 'Tell me you ain't fallen, you and this... animal.' The Roundhead lying next to Whytton was clearly dead, his neck broken.

'Master Bellamy,' Whytton croaked, his face twisting into a tortured grimace, the shards of broken ribs tearing into his lungs. 'You're alive.' He gestured with his hand for Bellamy to come closer. 'The men? Have you seen them?'

'Our men? I ain't see none of them.'

'Then they're still down there, in the crypt,' he whispered. 'Knock three times... then three more.' He groaned in pain while a trickle of blood seeped from one corner of his mouth.

'The crypt?' Bellamy frowned. 'But w-why...' He was shaking.

'The men.' The effort grew too much, the pain too great to bear. 'Three times...' He raised his arm and grabbed Bellamy's collar.

'Three times more.' His arm fell back and he closed his eyes.

'No, don't leave us, Will. It's not your time.' Bellamy gently lifted his friend's head. 'Will, d'you hear me?'

Will Whytton opened his eyes. 'Forrester. Fallen from Broadrock.'

'What's that? Wintour's horse? And Sir John?'

Will lay still for a moment, summoning the energy to speak.

'He's up there. Dead maybe.' Blood flowed freely from his mouth now, his face suddenly paler. He summoned up one final effort. 'The crypt. Go, my friend.' He emptied his lungs and lay motionless.

Bellamy closed the dead man's eyes and stood up. 'You were a good man, Will Whytton. God rest your soul.' He stripped off his sodden coat and shirt and, working as fast as his frozen hands allowed, pulled the same from his lifeless friend and struggled into them, throwing Whytton's bandolier and shot bag around his shoulder. 'Needs your boots too, Will. You'd understand, I'm sure.' When finished, he picked up Whytton's musket and looked down one last time. 'I'm coming back, Will, 'fore the crows come, I swear it.' He turned and hurried into the church, glancing nervously about him.

'Crypt,' he muttered. 'What's he mean?'

It didn't take him long to find the answer, although at first, the huge font basin lying on the ringed flagstone made no sense. The warmth returning to his limbs, he wrestled the font away and then hammered on the slab three times, then three times more. Putting his ear to the stone, he listened for the sound of movement from below but heard nothing. Had he heard Will right? If the men were down there like he'd said, surely they'd be pushing on the stone, eager to escape. He grabbed hold of the ring and pulled for all he was worth but it lifted no more than an inch before his strength failed him and it slammed down. Desperately, he looked around for something to wedge beneath it, something that would stop it from falling back. A piece of the wooden screen, that would do. Tearing at it, ripping away a length of its frame, he dragged it back to the flagstone. This time, when he hauled on the iron ring and raised the slab, he kicked the wood beneath it. Now he could curl his fingers under the flagstone's edge without losing them. Taking a deep breath, he hauled like a madman, his arms threatening to pull from their sockets until finally, the flagstone yielded.

'Oh, God in heaven!' He stumbled backwards. 'This can't be! Oh Lord, what have you let happen?' For a moment he was too dumbstruck to move. Piled high on every step and littering the floor below were the bodies of men he had known his whole life, their eyes staring out from ashen faces, lifeless corpses starved of air in a coal-black hell from which they could not escape. Their outstretched arms spoke of the futile struggle to lift the flagstone, for the christening font that had baptised so many souls into life had now taken theirs away.

Quickly he pushed aside the bodies on the top step, checking each for signs of life and started down the staircase. By the time he reached the floor of the crypt, he'd almost given up hope of finding anyone alive when, from the farthest reaches of the dark tunnel, he heard a cough.

'Who's there?' he cried out. Bending low, the tunnel being less than half his height, he stumbled forward until he felt something brush his legs. 'Thank God,' he muttered. 'There's one at least.' Reaching down, he seized a handful of clothing and hauled whoever was wearing it back along the tunnel and into the light. 'Tom!' he exclaimed. 'No more than a bloody arse-worm and yet you've outlived them all. Come on, let's get you some air.' He lifted the boy and climbed the stairs, threading a way through the stiffened corpses, before laying him gently on the chancel floor. Tom rolled onto his side, his lungs sucking violently at the cool, rich air, moaning all the while, eyes blinking in the bright sunlight. 'It's alright Tom, you're out now. Were a close thing, mind, for you that is.' Bellamy shot a glance at the bodies lying motionless on the staircase. 'Not for them poor buggers.'

Tom sat up, his face pale and purple grey. 'Master Bellamy?' he croaked. 'We thought you were dead. Drowned in the river. How's it possible...?'

'Nine lives, Tom, that's what I got.' Bellamy grinned. 'Mind, precious few left now. Listen, can you walk?'

'My head hurts bad but...' Tom struggled unsteadily to his feet, looking down in horror at the hole in the floor. 'What of the others? Surely they ain't all dead? Not every one of them?'

'Seems that way, Tom. Ain't no one else moving down there. 'Tis a terrible thing to see, for sure. But there's more you ought to know, though I don't know the best way of saying it.'

Tom braced himself.

'Master Whytton's dead. Fell from the tower. Took a Roundhead with him, mind. I'll wager it were him who trapped you in the crypt and Will killed him before he'd a chance to fire off a signal to the enemy. Saved your life, did Will.'

'But he never came back to lift the stone,' Tom sobbed as the tears flowed for the second time that day. First his sister and now his dearest friend. 'That would've saved every man down there.'

'He didn't know the men were trapped, Tom. He'd never have taken his own life if he'd known.'

'He didn't deserve this, Master Bellamy. He were good to me was Will.'

'None of them deserved this, Tom, 'cept the man who brought us here. Them in the boats, they were nothing but a bloody duck shoot for Massey's muskets. I watched 'em from the bank. A lot of the men just jumped into the river, preferring to drown than suffer a musket shot. Heaven help us, Tom, it's been a dark day.'

'You mean, we're all that's left? Just you an' me?' Tom could scarcely take it in.

'Looks that way.'

'And Wintour? What of him?'

'Master Whytton told me Forrester fell from the cliffs but Sir John himself, he reckoned he was still up there, dead or alive. There ain't no way of knowing.'

Tom's mind was made up. He'd sworn an oath to his sister and there was no going back now. 'There is a way, Master Bellamy. I've got to find out 'cos Wintour killed my sister, I'm certain of it. She's lying down there.' He nodded at the crypt. 'A bullet in her skull and she's wearing his picture round her neck. He was wearing hers when I found him on the Lydney road.'

'Your sister?' Bellamy shook his head. 'This gets worse by the hour. What's the girl's name?'

'Grace, but she called herself Emma.'

'Emma? I remember a servant girl called Emma. She were a pretty thing, for sure. I reckon every man had a thing for 'er. Thinking about it now, she didn't stay long. You say...' He stopped, seeing the anguish in Tom's face. ''Tis a bad business, Tom, I'm sorry. Would have been better if you and your sister had never set foot in Whitecross, but no matter what the man's done, you can't go looking for him up there. Place is crawling with Roundhead vermin. They'll shoot you dead even 'fore you see them.'

'I promised her and that's the end of it. If he's alive then I need the truth from him. He deserves to die, Master Bellamy. He's left his men to this, and every one dead save you and I.'

'*You* ain't dead yet, but sure as night follows day, you will be if you goes looking for Sir John.'

Tom ignored him. 'I need a musket and a powder cartridge.' There was a steely resolve in his voice Matthewe Bellamy had never heard before, as though suddenly the boy who'd hammered on the Whitecross gates two months before was now a man. Bellamy reached down into the crypt and lifted out a musket and bandolier.

'Here, if you must. Use them wisely and remember, don't over-prime the pan. It's an easy mistake to make but you'll blow your face off.' Tom nodded, taking the gun in both hands while Bellamy slung the bandolier of cartridges around his head.

'I promised her a proper burial,' Tom added. 'The men should have that too.'

'Yes, they should, but there's not much I can do for them now 'cept lay them straight. Stone needs putting back 'cos the foxes will smell them out if we don't. But we'll come back when it's safe and do what's right.'

'One thing more 'fore I go, Master Bellamy. There's a leather pouch down there. Wintour gave it to the sergeant 'fore he left us and inside, so Master Hoskyns said, there's a pistol made of gold.'

'You heard that right, Tom?' Bellamy stared at the boy.

'I swear it. Find the bag and you'll see for yourself. Better you has it than Wintour, if he's still alive. Mind, the sergeant said that Wintour's got another just the same.'

'Two golden pistols? That don't surprise me, mind. Man's got more wealth than the king, I'll wager. If the bag's down there, I'll find it. Meantime, you got to mind yerself. It'll be a sad day if all that's left of the company is an old relic like me.' He stretched out his hand and Tom shook it before sprinting out of the church, looking for the quickest route to the top of the Broadrock cliffs.

CHAPTER 12

A heavy silence had fallen on the river valley as Tom ran along the bank towards the cliffs, hugging the tree line so as not to be seen from above. The incoming sea tide had swelled the river, the mud slopes all but disappeared, while the current had lost its urgency. He had almost reached the rock fall, where earlier he had toiled to fill the carts with stone, when he turned left, away from the river, and began climbing the wooded slope. Bramble and wild rose grew thick beneath the stunted oaks, tearing at his legs, as steadily the slope steepened until, nearing the top, he was forced to climb over low rocky outcrops. He paused frequently to catch his breath and listen for sounds of Massey's men. When at last the slope began to ease, he traversed right towards the cliff top until he reached its northern edge. The faintest trace of a path led along the very lip of the precipice, partly hidden from view by a thick, thorny barrier of hawthorn. The tell-tale prints of massive horseshoes confirmed what Tom had suspected – that Wintour had passed this way, hoping to reach the southern end of the cliffs undetected. Had Forrester simply lost his footing and slipped over the edge? In places there was hardly room for a man let alone a charger. Alert, Tom set out on the path, constantly aware of the dizzying drop to his right. Here and there, vicious hawthorn branches overgrew the path, pushing Tom towards the very edge. Try as he might, he could not avert his gaze from the seemingly endless drop to the river far below, waves of giddiness washing over him.

Just as he began to think his quest a waste of time, he reached a platform of rock jutting out over the edge, the slabs of limestone spattered here and there with congealed drops of dark, red blood. At first, he thought the blood might have belonged to Wintour, ambushed through the hawthorn screen by Roundhead musketeers, but there were no signs of bloody trails where his body might have been dragged away from the cliffs. Whoever or whatever had been shot had gone over the edge. Bellamy had been insistent Will had not seen Wintour fall. Had he been taken prisoner then? It seemed the most likely outcome, and yet, nagging voices in his head told him he was wrong. He sat for a few moments on the platform, a safe distance from the edge, the sun warm on his back, watching the languid river almost three hundred feet below.

'Tom!'

He spun round, searching the bushes for the man who'd spoken his name. The voices in his head had been right. Wintour was still alive, hiding somewhere among the hawthorn, concealed so completely that he could easily have escaped the attentions of a dozen Roundheads. Working quickly, Tom primed his musket, eased the cock back as far as it would go and raised the musket, its butt firmly set into his shoulder. Wintour's head suddenly appeared from out of a crack in the ground that ran back from the cliff edge, just wide enough to accommodate a man. Covered in branches and dead leaves, it was almost invisible to anyone standing on the platform.

'God in heaven, put your bloody musket down!' Wintour panted as he struggled free from his hiding place. 'It's Sir John you're pointing at! Is it clear, Tom? Massey's bastards gone? If they have, then I need to retrieve something I've hidden down here.'

Tom backed away as far as he could, barely a foot from the void behind him.

'No you don't!' he shouted, fear streaming through his body. 'You come out of there nice and slow where I can see your hands.'

'What are you playing at, boy? Have you lost your senses? I haven't outplayed those Roundhead scum just to be...'

'I mean it, Sir John! You climb out now or I'll pull the trigger, I swear it. Don't think I won't for you got questions to answer, questions that every man you let die down there wants answering, d'you hear me?' He raised the musket, pulling its butt harder into his shoulder while his finger tightened on the trigger, the flint quivering in its vice. Wintour climbed out and slowly got to his feet, his dark eyes narrowing into a malevolent stare. 'You're making no sense, boy. The men who died down there, it were Roundhead shot that killed them; that and the bloody sergeant who's got no head for a fight.'

'Hold your tongue! You say another word 'gainst the men and I'll put a ball through your chest.' A raging anger burned inside Tom's gut, purging his fear and replacing it instead with a wild recklessness. 'Was it a Roundhead shot that killed my sister, tell me that?'

Wintour stalled for a moment, taken aback by the question. 'What d'you mean? Who's your sister?'

'Grace. She called herself Emma when you knew her. And don't go telling me you don't know her 'cos you was wearing her picture round your neck when I found you on the road, and she's wearing yours down there in the crypt. So tell me, who fired the pistol that took her life? And her baby's?'

Wintour stared at Tom's face for a moment as the past came back to haunt him. 'You!' he spat. 'I should have known it from the first.' He nodded, his mouth twisting into a cruel sneer. 'You stole something that belonged to me, Mundy. You'll pay for that.'

'I'm the one holding the musket, so if anyone's paying, it's you. I'll ask you again. Who pulled the trigger?'

There was a pause and then Wintour's face relaxed. 'Alright. You lower the musket, I'll tell you about Emma. Anyways, you pull the trigger, the musket's going to send you backwards off the cliff. Best you put it down, Tom.'

'You think I'm just a child, don't you? Well I ain't playing your game.'

'Have it your way, Tom, but Emma weren't no angel. When she came to Whitecross, she were eyeing up the men like she'd never seen one before.'

'Don't lie to me, Wintour, 'cos I'm pulling this trigger if you do. God help me, I will.'

'I'm not lying, Tom.' He stared at Tom's trigger finger, watching and waiting for the moment. 'She got herself with child and then she came blaming me.'

'You were wearing her picture round your neck. It was you that fathered her child, ain't that right?'

'Who told you that? You been listening to gossip, is that it?' The confusion in the knight's face was plain to see. 'Alright, I won't lie to you, Tom. She were a pretty girl and I was a fool to let her have her way, I grant you. There was no future in it, not a knight and a serving wench.' Tom's finger slackened on the trigger. 'But then she came one morning to the range, demanding that I let her stay. I couldn't agree to it.'

'You fathered her child. She had every right to stay.'

'I couldn't let her stay. You're only a boy. You don't understand these matters.'

'So you put a pistol shot through her skull?'

'That weren't me. Sir Willoughby was there and she grabbed his pistol meaning to shoot me dead but it fired in the struggle and shot her in the chest. I was sorry...'

'You're a liar, Wintour. That ain't how it happened.' Tom was shouting now. 'Willoughby's pistol killed *him* and then you shot her in the head. That's why you hid her body in the crypt so's no one would know you'd murdered a harmless girl in cold blood.'

This stunned Wintour into silence. A stable boy who'd lived at Whitecross for scarcely two months had described with unerring accuracy events which had taken place more than six months ago, events which could put the knight's head into a hangman's noose.

In an instant, Wintour leapt forward, his outstretched hand brushing the musket aside but not before the flint struck down on the frizzen sending a stream of sparks flying into an overfilled flashpan. The powder exploded with such force, it sent knight and stable boy hurtling over the edge. Tom's senseless body twisted and twirled through the air like a rag doll until it smacked into the stone-hard surface of the river, the collision shattering his bones, instantly draining the last remnants of life from his young body.

Projecting from the cliff, seventy feet above the river, an ancient juniper broke Wintour's fall. He smashed through it, the slender branches breaking the bones in both his legs while, at the same time, slowing his fall. Pain seared up through his body as he hit the river feet first, spearing through eight feet of water into the mud below. There, the mud held him until, with a violent thrust from both arms, he freed himself from its grasp and rose back to the surface. Floating on his back, barely conscious, he drifted slowly downstream on the turning tide, oblivious of Tom's body floating face down beside him.

So, too, was he oblivious of the haunting cry filling the valley, the cry of a young woman's soul trapped in a lifeless void far from her final place of rest.

'Tom, my love, what have I done? My dear, dear Tom. I've sent you to an early grave while the wicked man still lives. What will become of us?'

Grace's mournful voice fell silent. When she spoke again, her grief had vanished, replaced instead by a quiet resolve.

'Know this, precious brother, 'tis not over, not until justice is served. You will get another chance and when that day comes, I will guide you.'

PART II

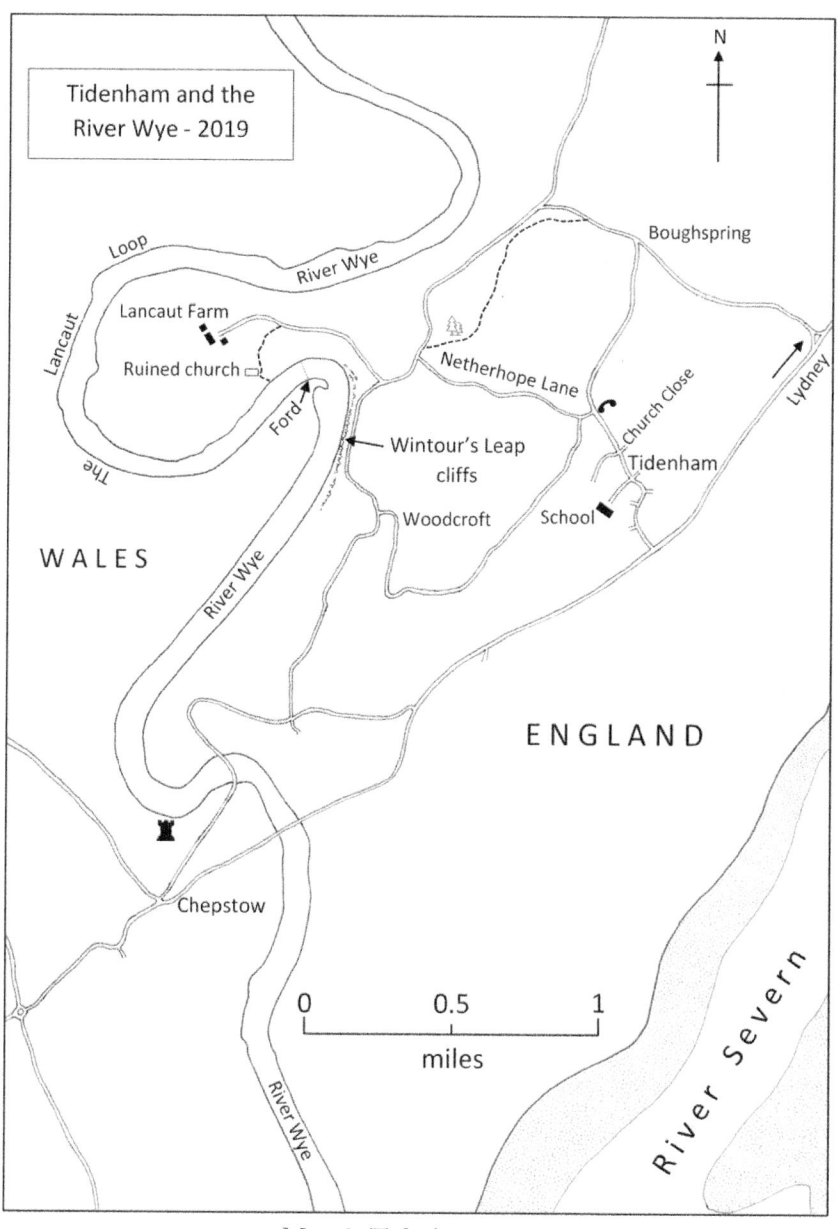

Map 3. Tidenham, 2019.

CHAPTER 1

Monday 2nd September 2019

Ezra Mear stepped out of his old Mercedes, locked the door and stood for a moment in the school car park, watching the children drift in through the main gate. How long could he put up with the little brats, he wondered? Becoming a supply teacher of history wasn't his idea. It was hers.

At first he'd been convinced he was losing his mind, that the woman's voice he could hear so clearly was nothing more than a figment of his imagination. After all, no one else could hear it. But the figment refused to go away. It seemed to come from nowhere and yet everywhere; sometimes loud and clear, at other times barely audible.

'You've got to get close to the boy, John.'

Right from the start, she'd called him John. Mistaken identity, he'd decided, and told her so, though she never replied.

'The boy will find a golden pistol, an antique worth countless thousands. If you want it, John, you'll need to get close.'

Getting close, she explained, involved becoming the boy's history teacher.

'Skinner will help you, John. Ask him. You'll get the job.'

Mear had met Jed Skinner, a fellow poacher, some months before on the banks of the nearby River Wye. Skinner had quickly proven his worth for his knowledge of the river and the bailiffs who patrolled it was impressive. Skinner's day job was site manager of Tidenham Academy. But when Mear asked him about a teaching vacancy in the school's history department, Skinner just shook his head.

'History teacher? There ain't no history teacher leaving, far as I know, but I'll ask around.'

It had taken him just twenty-four hours to discover that Mr Biddle, a member of the history department, had indeed been lured away by the BBC for a month's filming in Bath just when the new school year was about to begin.

'How'd you know about Biddle?' Skinner had asked him. 'You psychic or what? And anyhow, I thought you told me you were an English teacher. You ever taught history?'

'Subject's not important, Jed. Plenty of teachers teach outside their degree subject. Listen, I'll approach the school directly. Registering with a supply teaching agency is going to take too long. Chances are they might dig a little too deep, as well.'

'You got that DBS thing? You know – criminal record check and all that?'

'Of course I have and before you ask, it's clean.'

Skinner smirked. 'But you told me you'd been – how did you put it? – let go. So how many schools let you go, Ez?'

'A few but I never touched the little arseholes. Came close, mind, but it doesn't go on your record if they can't prove anything. I've got a couple of referees who'll say all the right things. Amazing what a regular supply of fresh salmon can do.'

In the end, it had all been so easy. He'd never taught a lesson of history in his life. His degree was in English but his application form said history was his specialism. Both referees stated that he'd taught a mixed timetable in their school – bit of English, bit of history – and in any case, Tidenham Academy were desperate to fill Biddle's shoes and time wasn't on their side.

The only fly in the ointment had been Biddle himself. At a meeting between the pair on the school campus, the old man had scythed his way through Mear's fabrication in less than ten minutes. It was obvious that Mear knew next to nothing about history and Biddle would have raised the alarm had he not been 'persuaded' to keep silent. As term approached, however, Ezra Mear began to suspect his threats were not enough. Something more potent was required to silence Biddle.

At precisely one minute past ten, with the term less than two hours old, a tall, gaunt figure appeared in the doorway of room 308 while Year 11 History Set 1 sat idly on the tables, feet on chairs, discussing the Premiership, Facebook gossip, and last Saturday's party at Gina's. Piercing slate-grey eyes surveyed the scene in front of him with cold contempt. His thick, black, wavy hair framed a long, narrow face with an angular, beak-like nose overhanging thin, downturned lips.

'Stand!' he barked. Twenty-six heads turned to stare at the stranger. Ezra Mear slammed the door shut and stood motionless; only his dark eyes moved, searching for the boy that he knew was somewhere in the room, the boy that would lead him to a fortune. The class fell into a shocked silence as they struggled to identify the unwelcome intruder into their social life.

'I asked you to stand. Now *do* it.' His voice had dropped by fifty decibels, yet was still laced with menace.

Arguments over who would win the Premiership would have to wait; exactly who kissed who at Gina's party would remain a teasing secret for at least another hour. Instead, the class slid off the tables while the object of their attention moved across the room, taking up a stance behind the teacher's desk. He opened a laptop to reveal the class register and paused, waiting for the voice to give him a name from the list, but she said nothing.

Meanwhile, the class brimmed with apprehension. This wasn't Mr Biddle who never raised his voice, never threatened menace. He shuffled and smiled and tut-tutted, often all at the same time. After forty years in the classroom, he'd mastered the art of cajoling teenagers without menace. So who was this dark stranger masquerading as a history teacher?

Mear addressed the class with the same low, sinister tone.

'When I enter the room in future, you will be sitting in silence with books open, ready to begin. *Is that clear?*' His gaze swept across the class, searching. If the class thought that a few mumbled replies would suffice, they were mistaken.

'I will ask you one more time.' Mear's rangy frame leaned across the desk. '*Is that clear?*'

This time there was unison. 'Yes, sir'.

'Sit and answer your names.' But before Mear could launch into the register, a clearly audible whisper came from the back of the class. 'This isn't right!'

For a few moments, Mear remained perfectly still, looking down at his laptop. Slowly, he raised his head to find the source of the remark. It wasn't difficult to locate for every eye was focused on a small, slightly built boy at the back of the room. The muscles in Mear's face tightened as he stared at him. *Is this the one? Surely not.* When finally he spoke, his voice seemed edgy.

'What's your name?'

But Merryn sat transfixed, unable to speak.

'You!' Mear shouted. 'You at the back! I asked you your name.'

Sitting beside him, Danny Field whispered behind a hand, 'For Christ's sake, just tell him your name.'

'Merryn,' came the reply.

Mear considered that for a moment and then looked down at the register on his laptop. 'Merryn MacIntyre?' There was no disguising the confusion in his voice while his eyes sank deeper into their dark hollows. When he spoke again, the menace had returned. 'And what *exactly* isn't right, eh? The rest of the class would like to know, I'm sure.'

'Where's Mr Biddle?' Merryn blurted.

Mear straightened. 'Where's Mr Biddle?' He paused a moment as though ambushed by the question. Then, making no effort to disguise the threat, he snapped, 'Keep your nose out of school business, MacIntyre. My name is Mr Mear. I'm your history teacher this year so get used to it.' Without pausing for breath, he turned to the rest of the class. 'Answer your names.'

When he'd finished the register, Mear closed his laptop and stepped into the middle of the room.

'Collect a laptop from the trolley and an exercise book. Google "Causes of the English Civil War". I want everyone on a useful website within five minutes. Make notes in your books. Move.'

For a few seconds, the class sat shell-shocked by the rapid-fire instructions. It was as though they were engaged in some military exercise and the sergeant had just barked out orders to advance. The contrast with a Biddle lesson could not have been starker. They couldn't recall a time when the class had used computers in a history class. Now twenty-six brains emerged from their summer hibernation to discover once again that there was more to the internet than Facebook, Snapchat and Instagram.

Mear kept mercifully silent for the remainder of the lesson, his thoughts entirely occupied with identifying the boy. The voice in his head that had plagued him for almost a year now had repeated it over and over again. A boy in the Year 11 History Set 1 at Tidenham Academy would find a golden pistol, an antique worth countless thousands. *Find the boy*, she had said, *and the pistol can be yours*. But there were twelve boys in front of him and without a name, how was he to know which one would lead him to the pistol? Damn the woman. She'd led him this far and now she was toying with him. No matter. He would find him and then the pistol would be his.

His dark eyes scanned the class until his gaze came to rest on Merryn's bowed head. *Surely not this scrap of a boy and yet...*

With just two minutes of the lesson remaining, Mear stood up and wrote on the board: "*The Causes of the English Civil War. Homework. Thursday. 800 words. Word processed.*"

He turned around to face the class. 'Log out, laptops away. Pack up. Essays without fail on Thursday.' And without waiting for the bell, Mear snatched up his laptop, flung open the door and disappeared. The class waited until he was a safe distance and then burst into a chorus of uproarious protest.

CHAPTER 2

Merryn was first out of the classroom. He was normally last, lingering long after the bell to excavate the treasure trove inside Mr Biddle's head. History with Mr Biddle appeared five times on Merryn's two-week timetable; five hours when the fifteen-year-old's imagination could really let rip. No one was better at feeding it than his elderly history teacher. He led Merryn's class on breathless journeys through time, fleeing from Viking berserkers, marching with Saxon kings, hauling sails on Norman ships. It seemed as if the very sounds and smells of medieval battle invaded the classroom as Mr Biddle launched his arrows high over the heads of William's charging cavalry into the ranks of Saxon housecarls. Merryn could hear the screams of King Harold's men as the lethal rain poured down on them, piercing their chain mail and massacring them where they stood. The battles of Hastings, Bannockburn, Agincourt, Bosworth Field – Merryn had witnessed them all, standing in the midst of the bloodiest action as it exploded around him. It was as if the real world suddenly dissolved away inside his head to reveal ancient landscapes on which Mr Biddle's stories could be played out by a cast of thousands.

Now all he wanted to know was when his old history teacher was coming back. The person who could answer that question was the

Head of History, Miss Grigoryev. She lived in room 309 so Merryn didn't have far to go. He found her handing out detentions to a gaggle of Year 8 pupils.

'Ah, Mr MacIntyre! Come in.' She waved him in from the corridor. 'My Year 8 class could learn a thing or two from our star pupil. Sadly, these little mishkins have not mastered the art of the homework. Excuses, yes. They are very good at the excuses. But homework, no. And how long have they had to do their homework? Six weeks. Six weeks of doing absolutely nothing. Hah! So, now they learn the art of detention. Very simple. Lunchtime. Here. With me. Good. Now go.'

The Year 8 pupils bundled out of the room, glad to be rid of Miss Grigoryev. Merryn, on the other hand, always enjoyed his conversations with the little old Russian woman. No one knew exactly how old she was. Sixty maybe, perhaps older. She had been in the school longer than anyone could remember and yet she had never lost her Russian accent. Merryn often wondered how a Russian had ended up in an English secondary school but he'd never found the courage to ask her.

'So, Mr MacIntyre, what can I do for you today? First day of your last year, yes? But no! You must stay into Year 12, of course. We cannot lose our finest history student, eh?'

Merryn blushed. If only every teacher was as complimentary about him as Miss Grigoryev. 'Actually, miss, I came to ask why we don't have Mr Biddle this year for history. He never said anything last year about leaving.'

Miss Grigoryev laughed. 'Mr Biddle leave the Academy? I think Prince William will be crowned king before Mr Biddle leaves this school! No, a few weeks ago, Mr Biddle received an invitation from the BBC Film Unit in Bristol to spend a month making a documentary about the Romans in Bath. Then, at the end of September, he comes back to Tidenham. I think he will enjoy being a film star, but it does not quite compare to teaching the likes of Mr

MacIntyre, eh?' She laughed but it wasn't her normal, songful laugh that danced along the treble clef like music. To Merryn it sounded cheerless and forlorn. Something was troubling her.

'So, Mr Mear won't be teaching us all year?'

'Not at all! Like I have been saying, four weeks.' The little old woman was reading the expression on his face. 'Ha, I know exactly what you're thinking.'

'Really?' Merryn looked alarmed.

'Of course. I understand. Mr Biddle is a very good teacher. Exceptional teacher. I wish I have his gift, but now you must give Mr Mear a chance. He is a little, er, fierce, perhaps, but I think maybe you can learn a lot from him.'

'Miss...' Merryn struggled to ask the question in a way that didn't sound impertinent. In the end, he just blurted it out. 'Who is he?'

Miss Grigoryev frowned. 'Mr Mear? I'm not sure what you mean?'

'Where did he come from?'

'I don't exactly know, Merryn; from a supply agency, I think. The Head didn't say. But...' A troubled look crossed her face. 'I shouldn't tell you this, Merryn. You're not to say a word, you understand.'

Merryn nodded, wondering what was coming next.

'The caretaker, Skinner – I do not like the man – he phones me to ask if there is a vacancy in the history department before anyone at the school knows about Mr Biddle's adventure with the BBC. And then he tells me he knows just the man to replace Mr Biddle. Well, how convenient. A history teacher just when we need one.' Seeing the confusion on Merryn's face, she added 'You find that odd, don't you?'

Merryn nodded. 'Maybe he knows someone at the BBC.'

'Skinner? Maybe. I should be pleased. We're lucky to have someone to fill Mr Biddle's shoes while he lives the good life in Bath. It's just...' She lowered her voice. 'Mr Biddle, when he comes back from his meeting with Mr Mear last week, he is not right.' She paused as though wanting to say more but then changed her mind. 'Never mind. I'm being silly, imagining things. Now then, you are starting with the English Civil War, am I right?'

'Yes. We have to write an essay for Thursday. The causes of the war.'

Miss Grigoryev forced a laugh. 'So, Mr Mear, he does not waste time, I think. Okay, here is your challenge. Use that extraordinary brain of yours and become an expert on the civil war. Show Mr Mear what you can do, eh? Then maybe he is less fierce. I think so.'

Merryn thanked Miss Grigoryev and made his way to the canteen for what remained of break. He sat on his own, lost in his thoughts, oblivious to the pandemonium that played out around him as five catering staff attempted to serve mid-morning snacks to a ravenous horde of five hundred in just twenty minutes.

Mr Biddle is not right. What did she mean? If he wasn't well, why hadn't he confided in her. After all, they'd been working together for years and seemed pretty close. There was something she wasn't telling him.

He turned his mind to more practical matters. *Become an expert on the civil war. Show Mr Mear what you can do.* Miss Grigoryev is right, he thought. An expert on the English Civil War in three days. How hard can that be?

The bell signalled the end of break and Merryn ambled down the corridor to his next lesson. The day dragged slowly towards ten past three when Tidenham Academy disgorged its six hundred pupils into the surrounding streets and Merryn made his way home to begin the task of becoming an expert on the English Civil War. Scuffing along the pavement on his own, a cold unease invaded his entire being as the face of his new history teacher stared into his mind's eye.

CHAPTER 3

Thursday 5th September

When Ezra Mear strode into room 308 at precisely eleven minutes past two on Thursday afternoon, Year 11 History Set 1, minus one, were all seated, their exercise books open in front of them. The class fell instantly silent as Mear opened his laptop and proceeded at pace down the register. He paused briefly at Merryn's name. There was something about the boy, something he couldn't put his finger on. *For God's sake, woman, tell me if it's him.* But, as ever, he got no answer. He'd barely finished the register when the door burst open and Zachary Luca-Hunt tumbled into the room, looking decidedly dishevelled. Standing at well over six feet, and topped with a mop of blond hair and startling blue eyes, he looked out of breath. If Merryn was addicted to history, Zac was positively obsessed with sport and rugby in particular. Right now, he was struggling with his tie which hung loosely around his neck, and his blazer into which he had thrust both arms but was now acting like a straitjacket. To make matters worse, he'd forgotten to tuck his shirt in and a sizeable lump of mud was firmly attached to one side of his face.

'Sorry I'm late, sir. Rugby training.'

Mear made no attempt at disguising his contempt for the latecomer.

'Name?' he snapped.

'Zac, sir.'

'Name?' Mear repeated, slightly louder.

'My name's Zac, sir,' Zac replied, also slightly louder.

'There is no *Zac* in my register, so either you're in the wrong class or your name is not Zac. Which is it?'

Zac glanced at the rest of the class. He sensed twenty-five pairs of eyes willing him on into battle. Instead, he just sighed.

'My name is Zachary Luca-Hunt but most people just call me Zac.'

'Well, Luca-Hunt, I'm not *most* people,' Mear barked. 'How dare you burst in like this, late, covered in filth and dressed like a tramp! Get out of my classroom and start again!'

Zac had forgotten that Mr Biddle was no longer running the history show. He wanted to say, 'What's the big deal?', but thought better of it. Instead, he shrugged and left the room. No sooner had he closed the door than a light switched on in some dark recess of his brain – a homework light. It illuminated a sign which read, "*History homework due Thursday, Causes of English Civil War, word processed.*" Zac swore quietly under his breath. He'd forgotten all about it. Through the door, Zac could hear Mear asking the class to put their names at the top of their essays and hand them in. There was nothing for it. He'd have to confess. What was the worst that could happen? A detention? As long as he didn't miss any rugby training, he didn't mind. He tucked his shirt in, straightened his tie and blazer and knocked on the door. No reply. He knocked louder. The door swung open. Mear stood in Zac's way, one corner of his thin mouth upturned in a sneer as he inspected the boy's state of dress. The lump of mud still decorated Zac's cheek.

'Be so good as to wash before you come to my lessons. Next time you're late expect an hour in the library after school. Essay?' Mear stuck out a hand, his dark eyes fixed on Zac's face.

Zac stared back. He was as tall as Mear and despite his meagre fifteen years, considerably broader. 'I don't have it.'

'*I don't have it,*' Mear mimicked.

'I mean, I forgot to do it.'

'*I forgot to do it*. Is this what I can expect from Luca-Hunt this year?' He moved one step closer to Zac but the fifteen-year-old stood his ground, meeting Mear's stare with his own. Rugby had taught him never to back down when the opposition gets in your face. Frequently, the opposition came in the form of eighteen-year-olds weighing in at fifteen stone. A teacher with the face and temperament of a vulture wasn't going to faze him.

'No, sir. I'll get it done.'

'You're right. You will. This afternoon at ten past three in the library. Now sit down.'

Zac glared at Mear and then turned and walked to his seat.

Mear picked up the pile of essays from his desk. 'Do I have twenty-*five* essays in my hand,' he demanded, 'or is Luca-Hunt going to have company this afternoon?'

A hand went up at the back of the class.

'You again, MacIntyre? Why doesn't that surprise me?'

Merryn held up a memory stick. He didn't have a printer at home and hadn't had time to print off his essay – all sixteen pages of it – in school.

'It's on memory stick, sir.'

'And what use is that? I can't mark a memory stick. Get it printed and in my hand before I leave at three-twenty. Understood?'

Merryn considered the logistics of getting his essay printed off by three-twenty, ten minutes after the end of school.

'Is that understood?' Mear's tone was threatening.

'Yes, sir.'

Normal service resumed with everyone engaged in internet research on the laptops, this time on the first great battle of the Civil War at Edgehill. Mear sat at his desk, still hopeful of a name, but getting nothing. He was beginning to think that he'd been led on some wild goose chase; that the boy and his golden pistol were nothing but a fantasy. And yet, from the beginning, almost twelve months back, every word she'd spoken had proven its worth.

'Ezra, there's money to be made on the River Wye. It's full of salmon and they're easy pickings if you know how. Let me show you.'

His poaching activities on the smaller Monnow, a Welsh tributary of the Wye, had given him several close calls with the bailiffs. It was only a matter of time before they caught him red-handed so he'd followed the woman's directions down to the Lancaut Loop on the Wye, to a ford that stretched across the river. She was right. The ford delivered sizeable catches of salmon, catches that grew ever larger as he refined his methods. It wasn't long before he'd teamed up with Skinner, a local poacher and together, they began to make serious money.

The more he listened to her – and at the ford, her voice was clearer than it had ever been – the more he began to believe. It no longer mattered that he couldn't explain it – a voice he didn't recognise speaking from God knows where. She was on his side. Why then should she suddenly feed him lies? Guiding him to a ford across the Wye, one that even Skinner had no knowledge of, had seemed miraculous so why not a golden pistol? But first, he needed to identify the boy, and for reasons he could not fathom, she was refusing to name him. Perhaps he'd not yet found the pistol. She had never said that he possessed it, merely that he would find it.

He cast his eyes across the bowed heads in front of him, searching for a treasure-hunter. Luca-Hunt was a prime suspect. Arrogance oozed from him like sweat from a boxer. He'd watch him closely.

At 3.08pm, he ordered the class to replace the computers in the trolley and pack away.

'Hunt, MacIntyre. Library, now. With me.'

He was gone before either boy had time to pack away. The bell went and a melee of children spilled out into the corridors, squeezing and jostling their way towards the exits, happy to have survived the fourth day of their prison sentence. Zac and Merryn fought their way up to the second floor against the mob tide, arriving at the library at precisely the same moment as Mr Mear. He stood by the door, motioning the boys to enter with a twitch of his head.

'Zachary, one hour. Use the notes you made on Tuesday. I want the finished essay tomorrow morning in registration. Merryn, there's a printer over there. Essay to the staffroom. I'm leaving in five minutes.' He left without waiting for an answer and the door of the library swung closed.

Zac threw his bag on the nearest table and kicked a chair in frustration. 'Scum-bag!' he burst out. 'Who the hell let *him* loose in our school?'

'Excuse *me*, Mr Luca-Hunt,' exclaimed a woman's voice from somewhere at the back of the library. 'I suggest you check your audience before mouthing off like that.' Miss Kelly stepped out from behind a bookcase, a look of severe disapproval on her face. She was a small, plain-looking woman in her mid-twenties with straight, shoulder-length ginger hair and a sea of freckles across her nose. Miss Kelly had taught the boys English in year nine and had grown fond of them both. 'So, what prompted that outburst?'

'Sorry, miss, I didn't know you were there. It's just…' Zac paused. How much could he say?

'It's just what, Zac? You're old enough to sort out your problems with other pupils without resorting to expletives.' She looked at him, shaking her head.

'It's not a pupil, miss. That's the problem. It's…'

'It's Mr Mear,' Merryn interrupted, switching on one of the library computers. 'He's a nightmare.'

'Merryn, you can't say that. In any case, it's only the first week of term.' Miss Kelly had had only the briefest of encounters with Mr Biddle's replacement in the staffroom. He'd managed only a mumbled, 'Mear, History,' in reply to her cheerful, 'Hi, I'm Sian Kelly, English.' After that, he'd retired to the far end of the staffroom where no one could disturb him.

'Actually, miss, he *can* say that.' Zac was impressed with Merryn's contribution. You could never quite predict how teachers would react when you confided in them, especially about other teachers. 'Mear's as bad as it gets. He makes the class work on laptops every lesson. He doesn't do any teaching.'

'And we've got him for four weeks while Mr Biddle is away,' added Merryn, as he opened his homework file from the memory stick and clicked print. '*Four weeks*.'

'Okay, so he's not Mr Biddle.' A hint of a smile crept onto Miss Kelly's freckled face. 'But you've got to give him a chance. It's not easy for new teachers.'

'Miss, *is* he new?' Merryn asked. 'I mean, has he taught here before?'

'Not to my knowledge. Maybe before my time, perhaps. Why do you ask?'

Merryn didn't know exactly why he'd asked. 'I'm not exactly sure.'

The English teacher shrugged and continued. 'New teachers have to make their mark early on. Get control of classes. Then they can relax a bit and have some fun.' She knew by the way Zac was looking at her that he didn't believe a word she'd said.

'Mr Mear having *fun* with our history class? I'll bet the most fun he's ever had is torturing kids with…'

'Thank you, Zac. I think that's enough. You know perfectly well I can't…' But Miss Kelly never got to the end of *her* sentence because without warning Mr Mear burst into the library.

'Merryn, where's the essay? And what are *you* doing?' He stared accusingly at Zac whose bag still lay unopened on the table. 'I thought I told you to start writing.'

'It's my fault, Mr Mear,' Miss Kelly intervened. 'Zac's been explaining to me why he's here. He's not made a very impressive start to his Year 11, it would appear.'

'Don't waste your time, Zachary,' Mear snarled, ignoring Miss Kelly. 'Get on with the essay. Merryn, where's yours?'

Zac shot a brief glance at Miss Kelly as if to say 'I told you so' while Merryn handed over his homework, all sixteen pages of it.

'What's this?' Mear looked at the bundle of paper in his hand. 'I said eight hundred words. How many's this?'

Merryn shrugged. 'I don't know. It's sixteen pages, so I guess about...sixteen times four hundred. Roughly.'

Mear shook his head. 'You weren't listening. The word limit was eight hundred. I'll take the first two pages. You can have the rest back.' He handed Merryn fourteen pages. 'Zachary, registration tomorrow without fail.'

'You see what we mean, miss?' said Zac, bristling with indignation after Mear had done his usual disappearing trick. 'He does that all the time. Gives out a whole load of instructions and then leaves before you can ask him a question. I can see you're not happy about it, either, are you?'

Zac was right. She was fuming inside but couldn't admit it. Instead she took a deep breath.

'Look, guys, I'll have a quiet word with our Mr Mear. Maybe he's had a bad day or something. I certainly appreciate the effort you've put in, Merryn. Mr Biddle speaks so highly of you and I can see why.'

'Miss, I asked him where Mr Biddle was and he refused to answer. All Mear said was that *he* was taking us for history for the whole year but that's rubbish because Miss Grigoryev said Mr Biddle's just gone to Bath for four weeks to make a film.'

'Miss Grigoryev is right,' Miss Kelly declared. 'He was invited by the BBC to make a documentary. I don't know what Mear – Mr Mear – is talking about.' For a moment she looked mystified but then recovered quickly. 'Anyhow, Zac, you'd better get on now. What's the essay title?'

'The causes of the English Civil War. Gripping stuff, eh?' Zac sat down disconsolately and pulled out his exercise book from his bag. 'I hardly wrote anything in Tuesday's lesson so at least I won't be breaking Mear's precious word limit.'

'You might as well have these.' Merryn held out the fourteen rejected pages. 'I'll print you off the first two pages, if you like. It doesn't make much sense without those.'

Zac looked up. 'Hey, are you sure? I mean, it must have taken you forever doing all that.' He'd never really taken much notice of Merryn before. The two boys were so different that their paths rarely crossed. They shared a few subject classes but that was about it. Merryn hated sport of any variety. He'd broken his collar bone playing rugby in the second week of Year 7 and from that moment on he'd employed a wide range of sport-avoidance tactics, none of them entirely successful.

'No, go on, otherwise I'll just have to bin it. It was Miss Grigoryev's idea. Become an expert on the civil war, she said. That'll impress Mr Mear. Waste of time that was.'

He printed off pages one and two, handed them to Zac and then turned to go.

'Look at the history books, Tom. There's one about Chepstow.'

Merryn spun round, startled by the woman's voice, no more than a whisper, expecting to find Miss Kelly behind him, but she was nowhere to be seen.

'Zac, where's Miss?'

Zac looked up from the pages of Merryn's essay scattered on the table in front of him. 'Library office. What's the matter?'

'Did you hear that?'

'What are you on about? I need to concentrate. You've written a bloody book, for God's sake.'

'So you didn't hear...'

'No. I didn't hear anything. Now hush.'

So I imagined it? Merryn put his bag down and wandered to the back of the library where a modest collection of history books occupied just two shelves. *Tom,* he thought. The name always made his heart race when he heard it out loud, something he had never been able to explain. Now here was some weird voice addressing him as Tom. All at once, the word Chepstow leapt out at him from the spine of a thin paperback on the bottom shelf. *A Short History of Chepstow*. He pulled the book out and flicked through its pages until, all at once, his gaze fell on an old ink drawing showing a line of tall cliffs rising straight up from the bank of a wide river. A soldier clad in armour standing at the very edge of the clifftop brandished a pistol while beneath him, plunging down to the river, a second soldier sat astride a leaping horse, his arms clutching the beast's neck. Merryn stood spellbound, staring at the drawing, his imagination transforming the image into a video.

'That's not how it happened.'

That voice again! Quickly, Merryn checked each alcove in the library just to be certain that no one had slipped unnoticed into the room but they were empty.

'Zac, are you sure you didn't hear her?'

'Will you just leave it, man. I'm trying to make sense of all this stuff you've written. Too much detail. *Way* too much detail.'

Then who was it? His thoughts were interrupted when Miss Kelly emerged from her office and, seeing Merryn holding a book, remarked, 'Ah, Mr MacIntyre has found a book worth reading. From the history section, no doubt,' she added, smiling. She looked over his shoulder and caught a glimpse of the ink drawing. 'Mr Wintour, I see. Now there's a civil war story you'll be familiar with.'

The blank expression on Merryn's face told her she was wrong.

'You've never heard of Sir John Wintour's exploits?' she asked, astonished that the Academy's history guru had never chanced upon the extraordinary events which, if the legend was to be believed, had taken place no more than a mile from the school. Merryn shook his head.

'Everyone round here's heard of Wintour,' Zac cut in, abandoning his efforts at paraphrasing sixteen pages. He wandered over to see what the pair were looking at.

'You mean it actually happened? In the civil war?' The video of the leap was still playing in Merryn's mind.

'No way!' scoffed Zac, examining the drawing. 'Like a soldier is going to ride off a cliff on his horse. I don't think so.'

'Slow down, mister cynic,' Miss Kelly retorted. 'According to the legend, that's exactly what Wintour did. So tell us the name of the river and the cliffs in the drawing?'

Without drawing breath, Zac answered. 'The river is the Wye and the cliffs are Wintour's Leap. Obviously.'

'How do you know?' Merryn was curious.

'Because, you idiot, the cliffs are just down the road.'

'Zac, that's a bit harsh!' and yet Miss Kelly was surprised that someone living so close to the cliffs had never actually seen them.

'So why did he jump, miss? Was he forced into it?' The legend was already clawing its way into Merryn's brain.

'All I know is what my dad told me when I was a kid. Bit younger than you. John Wintour was a Royalist – he fought for the king. He was ambushed beside the river and chased by a group of parliamentary soldiers. They surrounded him at the top of the cliffs and the only way he could escape was by jumping over the precipice on his horse into the river. My dad said that the horse drowned but Wintour survived and swam all the way down the river to Chepstow. Someone named the cliffs after his jump – Wintour's Leap.'

'So it's true, then?' The whispered words suddenly came back to him. *That's not how it happened.* 'The drawing in the book, I mean. Wintour really jumped over the cliffs on horseback and survived?'

'Oh my God, you haven't seen how high the cliffs are. There's no…'

'Language, Zac!' Miss Kelly interrupted. 'Anyway, fact is often stranger than fiction. I shouldn't think anyone will ever find out what really happened. My father goes fishing every week with an antiques dealer from Chepstow – Isaac Levi. They used to take me along with them when I was a kid. I'd sit and listen to Isaac for hours telling me all manner of legends – I'll bet he knows about the leap. Anyway, he used to say that legends could only live in the imagination. Trying to make sense of them was like taking a fish out of water. They suffocate and die. So maybe we should leave Mr Wintour in the water, so to speak.' She looked at the boys. Two more contrasting fifteen-year-olds she couldn't imagine. 'Right, Zac. You'd better get back to your essay. It's half three already and I've got to go. Don't forget to put the book back on the shelf when you've finished with it. Unless you want to borrow it, of course. You'll be the first if you do.' Miss Kelly picked up her bag and a pile of exercise books. She paused by the door.

'Remember, Merryn, it's only four weeks. It could be worse.'

'It's a pity we can't have her for history,' Merryn thought aloud when she'd disappeared.

'You fancy her, eh!' Zac grinned, keen to do anything but write an essay on the civil war.

'Don't be dull, Zac. I just mean she would be better than that animal we have to put up with.'

'Hey, you're calling *me* dull? You reckon that Wintour jumped over the cliffs into the River Wye and survived. Now *that's* dull! You've never even seen the cliffs. I can't believe that. Where do you live?'

Merryn pulled a face. 'Just up the road from the school, towards Cross Hill.'

'You could run to the cliffs from your house in about ten minutes. The road from Chepstow along the Wye Valley runs right along the top of them.'

'Go see them, Tom. You must see the cliffs.'

'What!' Merryn exclaimed, spinning round again, his eyes searching the room for the voice's owner.

'Hey, what's going on? You're acting weird.' Zac began to wonder if Merryn was a bit of a nutter, someone he should steer clear of.

'It's... some woman I keep hearing.' He slapped his head as if that would help. 'I mean, she says stuff.'

'Says stuff?' Zac grinned. He was right. Merryn *was* a nutcase. 'Like what?'

'I mean it, Zac. I know it sounds crazy.'

'Yep. It sounds crazy. So what's she saying?' The grin had morphed into a smirk.

'Go see them. The cliffs. That's what she said, I swear.'

'Yeah, right. Go see them. So?'

Merryn hadn't thought about 'so'. He just stood wrestling with the madness inside his head.

'All right, listen.' Zac decided to give the nutcase a chance. 'I've got an idea. If I get this stupid essay done by…' He looked up at the library clock. 'Say half four. Then I'll walk over to your place and we can go and check out the cliffs. Just look over the edge, I mean. Once you've seen the drop, believe me, you won't think that anyone could jump from the top on a horse and survive.'

Zac's plan took Merryn completely by surprise. He didn't mix much with anyone in school and certainly didn't go peering over cliffs to see if the drop would kill you.

'You're sure it's safe? At the top, I mean. It's not loose or anything?'

Zac laughed. 'Merryn, you're a wimp! Of course it's safe. I'm not suggesting we test out the legend and jump.'

'Ha ha.' Merryn wasn't amused.

'Now, what's your address?'

Merryn told him, wondering if it was already too late to back out.

'Give me your mobile number and I'll text you when I'm done here.' Zac took out his own phone to enter Merryn's number but Merryn just looked blank.

'I don't have a mobile so you can't. Just turn up when you're ready. Whatever you do, don't mention the cliffs to Mum. She's a bit paranoid.'

Zac looked horrified. 'You don't have a mobile? What's *wrong* with you? What do you *do* with your life?'

Merryn didn't answer. He picked up his school bag, replaced the book on the shelf and headed for the door. 'Don't mention the cliffs, Zac. I'll tell her we're going over to your place to do homework stuff. Okay?'

Zac nodded. 'Yeah, whatever. Now, any more voices?' but Merryn was gone.

On the short walk home, he tried to picture himself standing on the cliff top, looking down at the river far below. He'd heard stories of people standing on the edge of huge drops being suddenly overcome with an irresistible urge to jump. Well, that wasn't going to happen. He wouldn't go anywhere near the edge. He'd let Zac do that. Then they'd both go home and that would be the end of it. No more cliffs. No more voices.

CHAPTER 4

At home, Merryn kicked off his shoes and went straight upstairs. His mother, Donna, was changing the baby's nappy in the bathroom. Merryn's only sibling was six months old. Charlie had been a complete surprise to everyone, not least his parents. Donna had had a difficult time giving birth to Merryn, so much so they'd decided against having a second child. Charlie, however, had other ideas and decided that Merryn needed a brother.

Charlie had Down's Syndrome. Merryn loved the idea of having a baby brother and when Charlie arrived, Merryn spent ages googling Down's Syndrome, quickly becoming almost as knowledgeable on the subject as the hospital consultant who'd operated on Charlie to close a tiny hole in his tiny heart.

'Mum?' Merryn stuck his head round the bathroom door. 'Zac Luca-Hunt is coming round at about half four. We're going over his place to do some stuff.' Merryn hoped that keeping it vague would get it past the Spanish Inquisition that was his mother. He failed.

'Zac who? You've never mentioned him before.' Donna looked up from the changing mat where she was wrestling with her younger son who objected to having his nappy changed. 'Look, I forgot to tell you this morning. I've got to go out in half an hour. I'm trying to get some teaching hours again what with Dad's problems at the shop.'

Merryn frowned. Neither parent had mentioned 'problems' at his father's fruit and veg shop before. Donna could see the confusion in his face but decided this wasn't the time to explain. 'I need you to look after this hooligan until your dad gets in. Is it really important, this *stuff* that you're doing?'

Merryn sighed. He loved his little brother but all this babysitting was beginning to grate. It was like his parents were taking him for granted. They just assumed he'd look after Charlie because he had nothing better to do. It wasn't fair.

'No,' he replied glumly, 'it's not important. I'll go another day. If I'm not babysitting,' he added.

'Merryn, I'm not asking much. I need to get back to work.' But Merryn had closed the bathroom door and gone into his bedroom. This was his sanctuary, a space where he could indulge his obsession with the past. Every available square inch of wall space was occupied by photographs of Lancaster bombers and Sioux Indians, plans detailing troop movements at Bannockburn and Gettysburg, paintings of Viking longboats and Captain Cook's ship, *Endeavour*. A six-foot poster tracing the British royal line of descent all the way from Queen Elizabeth II back to King Alfred in 871AD had been stuck on the ceiling above his bed. From time to time, it peeled off during the night and floated down to cover him like a death shroud. He'd wake in the morning to have a close encounter with Ethelred the Unready.

In the far corner of the room, on a small, rather wobbly table, sat the computer that fed Merryn's insatiable appetite with an endless stream of facts about a hundred civilisations that had come and gone with the tide. It was the room he'd grown up in, the room where he'd spent more of his life than anywhere else, the room where he felt safe and utterly content. It never occurred to him that one day he'd have to leave it and start a new life somewhere else.

Donna knocked on the door. She knew better than to burst in uninvited.

'Yes, okay, I'll look after Charlie. It's just that I'd made arrangements to go over Zac's.'

Donna looked round the door. 'I'm really sorry, Merryn. I know I've messed things up. I should have told you earlier. So, who is Zac?'

'Just some boy in my history class. We're doing some stuff on the civil war. It can wait until tomorrow.'

The doorbell rang. Merryn glanced at the clock beside his bed. It was only just after four o'clock. Either Zac had written his essay in double quick time or he could run fast. Most likely, it was both.

'That's probably him. I'll tell him I can't go.'

Donna frowned. She should have given him advance warning. Just when it seemed he'd made a friend, someone who could coax him out of his hermit cell, she had to spoil it, but there was no one else who could look after Charlie.

It *was* Zac. He'd obviously sprinted the half mile from the school since he was breathing hard.

'Ready?' he asked.

'Slight problem. My mum wants me to look after my brother until she gets back from a meeting. What about tomorrow?'

Zac shook his head. 'No can do. I've got rugby trials in Chepstow straight after school. Anyway, why don't you bring your brother? We'll look after him.'

Merryn laughed. 'Charlie's only six months old. He might have trouble keeping up.'

Zac looked incredulous. 'You've got a six-month-old brother? Bet that wasn't planned.'

Merryn winced and pushed Zac away from the front door. 'Keep your voice down, will you? Listen, you could just go on your own. It won't take two of us to check out if Wintour could have jumped or not.'

'No way. It's no fun doing stuff on your own. In any case, you're the one who needs to see the drop. Listen, I've got an idea.' Zac paused, looking at the open front door. He moved further into the garden and lowered his voice.

'What d'you say we go out tonight, after your mum and dad have gone to bed? Wait till they're asleep then sneak out of the house. I'll meet you at the phone box up the road, at the junction with Netherhope Lane. Midnight. What d'you reckon?'

Merryn was quickly beginning to realise that having anything to do with Zac involved risk while Zac, on the other hand, had yet to appreciate that Merryn's life had been almost completely risk-free.

'It'll be dark so we won't be able to see the drop.'

'If the moon's out, we will. Anyway, by the time we get there, our eyes will be used to the dark. Stop making excuses.'

Merryn could still hear the woman's words echoing inside his head. *You must see the cliffs.* 'Okay. At the phone box. Midnight.' Before he could change his mind, Zac ran off down the Close.

Two hours later, Donna still wasn't back from her meeting at the Primary School. As for his dad, Malcolm, he seldom got in from work before seven in the evening. Merryn was sitting on the floor in the lounge explaining to Charlie why King Charles the First made such a mess of being king when the doorbell rang. 'Don't think we're done, Charlie. I'll be testing you when I get back. Multiple choice.'

Charlie just lay on his tummy and grinned while Merryn got up to answer the door. Molly, the MacIntyre's shaggy terrier with an insatiable appetite for mischief was already there, hammering the door with her front paws.

'Kitchen, Molly,' Merryn commanded. He could just make out the figures of two men through the frosted glass as he opened the door.

'Good evening, young man. I'm Mr Terry from TerryBaines Estate Agents,' said the older of the two men and by a factor of about three, the heavier. His dark, pin-striped jacket failed miserably to encircle his enormous pot belly while his trousers were only prevented from losing altitude by a pair of bright red braces. 'I'm here to show…' He paused, doing his best to shake off Molly's attentions. 'Would you mind removing your dog from my trousers.'

Merryn grabbed Molly's collar and yanked her back into the house.

'Thank you,' he sighed, eyeing the dog with disgust. 'As I was saying, I'm here to show my client, Mr Malik, around your property.' He spoke in short bursts between wheezy breaths. Walking up the steep driveway had been quite a challenge for his circulatory system. 'Perhaps your mother or father is at home?'

Merryn couldn't see much of Mr Malik. He was skulking behind the estate agent on the bottom step, looking intently at the front garden. In stark contrast to Mr Terry, he was lean and rather fragile with thick, black, shiny hair and copper-coloured skin.

'Did you say you're an estate agent?' Merryn asked, suddenly gripped by a terrible sense of foreboding.

'That's right, young man. Mr Terry from TerryBaines. I called your dad about an hour ago to say that Mr Malik was keen to inspect the property.' He paused to take a few more breaths. 'Your dad said he'd be here at six to show us round. Looks like he didn't make it, then?'

Merryn shook his head. 'I think you've got the wrong address. The house isn't for sale. Why don't you try next door?'

Mr Terry opened his folder. 'Number 14 Church Close? And your dad is Mr Malcolm MacIntyre?' His tone was patronising and laced with impatience. 'Am I right?'

Merryn's sense of foreboding suddenly evolved into panic. 'Yes, that's right. But I don't understand. My parents...'

'There's nothing much *to* understand, to be honest,' Mr Terry interrupted. 'Your father put the house on the market this morning. No details out yet but we've already got an interested buyer. We don't waste time, eh? Now all we need is your mother or father, or we *will* be wasting time.' He chuckled and turned to look at his client. 'And Mr Malik is a busy man, isn't that right, sir?'

Mr Malik stood in the middle of the small patch of lawn, surveying the front of the house. His large, black eyebrows were knitted into a deep frown and he began to shake his head.

'I don't think we need to take up any more of this young man's time, Mr Terry. The house is too small. I should have looked at some photos before coming all the way out here. Your description was rather exaggerated. A spacious semi-detached? I don't think so. It's more like a cramped end-of-terrace. You'll have to do better than this.' Mr Malik turned tail and walked back to his car.

Mr Terry muttered an obscenity under his breath that Merryn didn't quite catch. With Mr Malik gone, the panic subsided. Now he felt an overwhelming urge to push the estate agent down the steps but the laws of inertia made such an act almost impossible. Instead, he said, 'Oh dear, it looks as though you've lost your client. I think you're wasting my time,' and promptly closed the door.

Merryn paused for a few moments in the hall, looking out through the glass at the receding figure of Mr Terry negotiating the perilous journey back down the drive to his car. Merryn wasn't just angry. He was incensed. What did his parents think they were doing, selling the house without even telling him? And, in any case, why were they selling it? There was plenty of room for Charlie so what was going on?

No sooner had Mr Terry squeezed behind the wheel of his BMW and driven off back to Chepstow than Malcolm MacIntyre's elderly Ford transit screeched to a halt outside the house. Ever since he'd received Mr Terry's call at five o'clock, he'd tried desperately to ring Donna and tell her the news. Neither she nor Merryn had the slightest idea that he'd put the house on the market earlier that day, a decision thrust on him by his bank manager. He certainly hadn't reckoned on the estate agent turning up on the doorstep with a prospective buyer just eight hours later.

He found Merryn in the sitting room with Charlie on his knee. One look at his eldest son's face told him everything he needed to know. He took off his jacket and sat down opposite him.

'Okay, Merryn. We need to talk.'

Merryn didn't look up. His eyes were fixed on Charlie's face. Even

Charlie sensed something was wrong. He had stopped gurgling and sat quiet and still.

'No, Dad. *You* need to talk. You need to tell me why you decided to sell the house without saying a word to me. Does mum know or have you kept her in the dark as well?'

'I know you're angry. You've every right to be. I messed up. I should have told you. I only went to see the estate agents today. I never expected anyone to look at the house so soon. Terry's phone call just came out of the blue. I tried to get home before six but I was on the other side of Chepstow at the Charnley orchard and there are road works in the middle of town. That's why I'm late, Merryn. It's a complete mess and I'm really sorry.' A taut silence fell between them. Malcolm didn't know what else to say. He'd driven like a madman to make Terry's appointment in time, breaking every speed limit on the way and all to no avail.

Merryn listened in silence, still refusing to look at his father. Then, in a cold, quiet voice he asked, 'Why are you selling the house?'

His father sighed and ran both hands through his untidy curls of black hair.

'Let's wait for your mum to get back. Then we can talk about this together. You know she's gone to talk to Mrs Cartwright about going back to the school.'

Merryn nodded. He also knew that his mum had resigned from her teaching job when Charlie was born, so he couldn't understand why she'd gone back to talk to the head teacher.

When Donna came home a few minutes later, she looked tired and disconsolate. She'd been an attractive young woman when she'd met and married Malcolm. Her long waves of chestnut hair, huge brown eyes and warm smile had captured his heart on their first date. Now seventeen years later, worry lines had begun to etch themselves into her forehead and the first streaks of grey had appeared in her hair. Her smile hadn't changed; it was simply that she smiled less often.

She changed Charlie's nappy before putting a pizza in the oven and joined the boys in the sitting room. She wasted no time in trying to put things right with Merryn.

'I'm sorry about this afternoon. I should have told you this morning that I was going out. I hope you managed to rearrange things with...' Donna paused. She'd forgotten Zac's name.

'Yeah. Next week maybe,' he lied. 'So what happened at the school? Did you get your job back?'

Donna glanced at Malcolm and frowned. 'Not exactly. I need to register with a supply teacher agency and then I might get some short-term work – days here and there. The Down's Syndrome group in Chepstow say they can offer help looking after Charlie when I'm at work but...' She shook her head. 'I don't want just anyone looking after him so I'm not sure anymore.' Donna looked at her husband. 'We've got to find another way out of this.'

'Out of what?' Merryn looked puzzled. 'What are you not telling me?'

A heavy silence followed until Donna said 'He's got to know, Malcolm. It's only fair.'

Malcolm sighed. 'You're right. We should have had this conversation months ago.' He shifted uncomfortably in his seat, searching for a way to start. 'It's no secret that the shop hasn't been doing so well ever since the Superland store opened in Tidenham. They're buying fruit and veg in bulk at prices I can't compete with, stuff that looks perfect and at a ripening stage that gives it a week on the shelves to sell. The fruit and veg I sell comes from local producers, market gardens.'

'Malcolm,' Donna interrupted, 'we know all that. You don't have to apologise. It's not your fault that some money-grabbing farmer sells off a field to a faceless supermarket chain.'

'I should have seen it coming. It was in the planning stage for months.'

'And what could you have done? March up and down the High Street with a placard saying "No supermarket in our town"?' Donna was up on her soapbox. 'Trouble is people want it both ways. Cheap and convenient in a supermarket and at the same time high streets full of traditional shops, like a greengrocer selling local produce. Cheap is always going to win. It's a fact of life.'

None of that improved Malcolm's expression. 'Exactly,' he said quietly. 'I can't compete on price but I could upgrade facilities at the shop, broaden our range, offer a delivery service. It can be done, but it needs money upfront before we'd see any return on the investment and we just don't have that sort of money. I spent all morning with Mr Bairstow at the bank. He's not prepared to lend us any more cash. I get the impression that he doesn't believe the shop can survive with a supermarket less than a mile away.'

'That's ridiculous!' Donna was incensed. 'He's supposed to be supporting local businesses. That's what local banks are for, isn't it? We can't survive because Bairstow isn't prepared to do what's necessary to allow us to survive. So he's happy to sit back and watch Superland steamroll their way over all the local businesses in the town. Is that it? Five years from now, there'll be nothing left in the high street except charity shops. Oh, and banks, of course.'

Malcolm sensed that this wasn't helping Merryn understand why the house he'd lived in his whole life was up for sale. 'Well, I wish that was all the bad news, but it isn't.' He knew there was no easy way of disguising what came next, so he didn't bother trying. 'Our immediate problem is the mortgage on the house. We've been behind with the repayments for a while now, six months to be exact. Bairstow doesn't think we'll be able to afford them until the shop starts making serious money again and, like I said, he doesn't believe that's ever going to happen.'

Donna started rocking back and forward on the settee. Malcolm knew her fuse had been lit when she did this and it was only a matter of time before she exploded.

'Donna, we've got to face facts. Bairstow has given us two choices. Either we sell the house and give the bank back what we owe or the bank will repossess the house. It amounts to pretty much the same thing. They sell it, take what we owe and give us the rest. The problem either way is that because house prices have fallen over the last five years…'

'The house is worth less than we paid for it, right?' The fuse was getting shorter by the second.

'Borrowed for it,' corrected Malcolm.

'Of course, negative equity. So when either *we* sell it or the *bank* sells it, the sale price won't cover the mortgage and we'll still owe money. That's it, isn't it?'

Malcolm just stared at the floor and said nothing.

'That's it, isn't it?' Donna repeated quietly, close to tears.

Malcolm nodded.

Merryn had sat and listened in silence up to now. He didn't understand mortgages, repayments, negative equity, but he did understand losing his home. 'And then what do we do? Without a house? Live on the streets?'

'We're not going to live on the streets, Merryn.' Malcolm rolled his eyes in frustration. 'We'll rent a place until we can find somewhere permanent. It will all work out. We'll just have to get used to living somewhere else a bit smaller, a flat most likely.'

Donna stared at her husband thinking that she could no longer find the man she had married. The light in his eyes had grown dimmer these past six months as he slowly resigned himself to the collapse of the business, a collapse that would cost them their house as well. The fight had gone. In its place sat a crushing burden of shame and guilt. Malcolm was unravelling in front of her and she was powerless to stop it.

'So when do we have to move?' Merryn asked.

'Bairstow wants us to sell immediately but I told him that's not possible. Selling property takes at least two months and, in any case, we've got to sort out alternative accommodation. So he's giving us two months to get a buyer, three months to be out of here otherwise he'll push for repossession.'

Donna had stopped rocking. Malcolm waited for the detonation, but it never came. Her eyes blazed fury but her voice was steely calm. 'Let me look at the accounts. There's got to be some way out of this. Bairstow can say what he likes, but we're not giving up that easily. This house is not going on the market yet. Not until we've tried everything.'

Malcolm opened his mouth to explain that he'd already put it on the market but reading the expression on Donna's face, he decided against it. He'd ring TerryBaines first thing tomorrow and delay the inevitable. When Donna saw the accounts, she'd realise the house had to go.

The buzzer on the oven sounded. The only one with any appetite was Charlie but sadly, without teeth, the pizza base was out of his league. Merryn ate half a slice and then excused himself and went upstairs. He threw himself on his bed and stared up at the kings and queens of England. He wondered if any of them had ever lost their home. Edward II – murdered; Richard III – killed in battle; George III – went mad; Edward VII – abdicated. Ha! Found him. Edward VII. He was thrown out of Buckingham Palace because he refused to be king. It seemed like the stupidest of reasons for losing your house. Who wouldn't want to be king? More money than you could spend; more food than you could eat; more servants than you could remember the names of.

14 Church Close wasn't a palace. It wasn't even a spacious semi; but it *was* his home. Three months and it would all be gone, everything he'd ever known swept away and replaced with who knows what. They'd probably have to move town since he was sure there were no flats in Tidenham. Move town, move school.

Suddenly, Merryn sat up on the bed. The cliffs! He'd almost forgotten. He glanced at the clock beside his bed. It was nine o'clock. Three hours until midnight. How was he ever going to stay awake? He sat down at his computer and pressed *Enter* to wake it up. It was time to create a new shelf entitled 'Sir John Wintour' in his cerebral library, the vast trove of information which lay piled high on countless shelves inside his brain, deposited there without the slightest effort by its owner every time he opened a book or more often, a webpage. His photographic memory weighed heavily on him, however, for most of the facts and figures lay unclassified and often inaccessible, defeating his best efforts at retrieval. Anything historical, on the other hand, was a different matter. Merryn's brain had created an immense timeline dating back to the birth of human civilisations, a timeline divided into myriad shelves arranged in perfect chronological order. Information gleaned from the internet somehow found its way onto the appropriate shelf, one often already laden with the names, places and dates of kings, campaigns and conquests.

An hour later, however, he was no nearer to finding out exactly what happened at Wintour's Leap. In February 1645, Wintour and a small company of dragoons were attacked near the River Wye. That much seemed clear. But as to what happened next, the details were hazy. Some websites suggested that he simply rode straight into the Wye from the riverbank to escape the enemy. No leap, no cliffs, just a lot of mud. Others claimed he galloped at full speed straight over the three-hundred-foot cliffs and survived. Leap, cliffs and a lot of air.

Merryn gave up. He set his alarm for half eleven, crawled into bed fully clothed and turned out the light. As he lay in the darkness, his imagination got to work, just like it always did. Before long, he was astride a galloping horse, one of a small company of Royalist cavalry riding full-bore across open fields pursued not twenty yards behind by a much larger force of Roundhead cavalry. In the distance the ground rose gently before disappearing abruptly over a colossal limestone precipice. At the head of the Royalist force, the knight beckoned urgently for his men to sweep round to the left and yet showed no sign of doing so himself. Instead, he spurred his horse on, aiming directly for the cliff top. With only seconds left, he threw one final glance behind him and then, flinging both arms around the neck of his horse, disappeared from view. What disturbed Merryn as he lay suspended between reverie and reality was not the leap from the cliff top but, instead, that final glance, for it allowed Merryn the briefest glimpse of Wintour's face.

Dark. Thin. Malevolent.

CHAPTER 5

Four urgent notes, repeated over and over, penetrated Merryn's dream world. Moments later, the time machine raced back to the present and spat him out onto his bed. He sat up in a panic and switched off the noise coming from his wrist. Another button illuminated the watch face. Half eleven. It was time to go, but no sooner had he thrown back the duvet and got to his feet than he heard a whimper from the adjacent room – Charlie's room. He was crying. He often woke up around midnight. Merryn listened as his mother's footsteps crossed the landing. He sat back down on the bed. This was crazy. He should never have agreed to the plan. Now that Donna was awake, he was never going to get out of the house undetected; but Zac would be waiting at the phone box and if he failed to show, Zac would be furious. He'd never speak to him again.

He crept to the door and listened, hardly daring to breathe. Donna was singing a soft lullaby to the baby while she changed his nappy. Charlie fell silent while the seconds ticked by. Merryn checked his watch again. Eleven fifty. He was going to have to hurry. Then, after what seemed like an eternity, Donna's footsteps crossed the landing and Merryn heard her get into bed. After that, silence.

He counted to sixty, then slowly pulled open his door and tiptoed across the landing to the stairs. He knew the second stair creaked so he stepped past it. At the bottom, he paused and listened. Nothing. It took almost a minute in the pitch dark to fumble through the coats hanging by the front door and find his parka. He couldn't use the front door – it wouldn't shut unless it was slammed. It would have to be the back door, but that meant getting past Molly in the kitchen without waking her up and that was never going to happen. Merryn's eyes had adjusted to the dark now and he could just make out a twitch from Molly's ears as he crept past her basket into the scullery beyond the kitchen. For a moment, he thought he'd succeeded in escaping undetected but as soon as he opened the back door, Molly sprang to her feet and flung herself at Merryn, almost knocking him over.

'No, Molly! Back to bed, girl!' Merryn whispered, pushing the dog back from the door with one hand and quickly closing it behind him with the other, almost guillotining his left hand in the process. The click of the door's Yale lock as it snapped into place triggered an alarm bell somewhere inside his head. Frantically, he searched his parka pockets for a key, dreading what he was about to discover. They were empty. The key was in his school blazer. He'd locked himself out.

Merryn stood motionless in the cold September night air, furious at himself for being so stupid. Now what? There was no way of getting back into the house without waking his parents. He'd have to sleep outside and wait until morning when his father came down at six to let Molly out. Then, without warning, a sharp yelp came from the other side of the door. Molly wasn't content to wait until six. She wanted out now.

'You idiot dog! Go back to bed!' Merryn pleaded as loud as he dare. Sadly, to an excited terrier through two inches of back door, this sounded like, 'If you want to go for a walk, you'll have to batter the door down or bark loudly enough to wake Dad up.' Molly decided to play safe and execute both escape strategies simultaneously. Merryn sprinted down the drive and out onto Church Close. If he was anywhere near the house when the terrier got out, the dog would track him down him and follow him. That would be game over.

It was less than quarter of a mile from Church Close to the phone box at the junction with Netherhope Lane. Merryn ran the two hundred yards or so to the end of the street lamps where the scattered houses gave way to farmland. He checked his watch. Ten past midnight. He was late. Wreaths of mist were beginning to form above the dewy grass in the fields on either side of the road. Here and there, a finger of condensation slipped through the hedges onto the road and swirled ghost-like in the brilliant moonlight.

Before long, Merryn could make out the phone box but there was no sign of Zac. He hasn't bothered waiting, he thought. All that hassle getting out of the house and now I've got to go back and sleep outside for six hours. Brilliant.

Suddenly something moved on the roof of the phone box. A torch-beam flicked on and swept across Merryn's face.

'You're late,' a voice said.

'Zac! What are you doing up there?'

'Er, waiting for you, obviously. Where's your torch?'

'Torch? I didn't think of that. D'you reckon I'll need one?'

'Do I reckon you'll need one?' Zac laughed as he jumped down from the phone-box. 'It's dark and in about twenty minutes from now, you'll be crawling to the edge of a three-hundred-foot drop. Yes, Merryn, I reckon you'll need a torch.'

'Well, I can't...'

'Doesn't matter,' Zac interrupted. 'Mine's pretty bright. It'll do for both of us. Come on, we'd better go. Oh, before I forget. It's time you moved into the twenty-first century.'

Zac took an old Motorola phone out of his pocket, pressed the power button and waited for it to spring to life.

'Hey, would you look at that! It's still got some charge left.' He handed it to Merryn.

'It's my old one. You'll need to buy a new SIM card and put some money on it. It's easy. You might need to get a charger, though; I couldn't find the old one. Micro-USB.'

Merryn's parents had bought him a phone a year ago but after just two weeks he'd lost it and they'd refused to buy him another one. Since then, he'd survived without a phone. After all, social media assumed you had friends. 'Thanks,' he muttered, not sure what else to say.

'It's a bit of a fossil, I'm afraid. Come on, let's go.'

They set off along Netherhope Lane, heading west towards the River Wye. There was no pavement so they walked in the road. Without warning, Zac broke into a jog and Merryn did his best to keep up. His lungs were bursting by the time they reached the road running parallel to the river. Thick fog had begun to roll out of the river valley and when Zac turned left, heading for Wintour's Leap, visibility in the torchlight had dropped to less than ten yards. High metal railings topped with spiked finials lined both sides of the road.

'It's not far,' Zac called out over his shoulder. 'The top of the cliffs are just up ahead on the right. I'm pretty sure there's a missing railing along here somewhere. The gap's just wide enough to squeeze through. Once we're on the far side, we've got to be careful, mind. It's only about thirty feet to the edge.'

Merryn wondered how Zac could be so sure about the missing railing. What if it had been repaired or the gap wasn't wide enough? Zac might be able to climb over but he didn't stand a chance. Yet, the more Merryn looked through the railings into the black void beyond, the more he hoped that the missing railing *had* been replaced. What had he been thinking when he'd agreed to Zac's plan? This was insane. To make matters worse, Zac's torch lit up a large sign tied to the railings which read KEEP OUT – DANGEROUS CLIFFS. Underneath the bold red letters was the figure of a man plunging headfirst over a cliff, taking chunks of rock with him. Merryn stared past the sign. It was impossible to know exactly where the ground stopped and space began. Zac had lied when he'd said it was safe.

'Come on!' Zac urged, sprinting away. 'A car comes in this fog, we're roadkill.' Merryn followed until, sure enough, a gap in the railings appeared. 'Through here!' Zac called from the other side.

'No!' The woman's voice seemed to come from all around him. 'There's another gap but be quick!'

'What?' Merryn stared out into the darkness. 'Who are you?'

'Run!' she cried.

'What are you playing at, for God's sake. Get in here!' Zac yelled.

'It's the wrong gap,' Merryn called out. 'There's another further on,' and without understanding why, he took off along the road, his right hand flicking along the railings in case he should miss the gap. A ghostly glow lit up the fog around him. Merryn couldn't see the car but the growing gleam of headlights meant it wasn't far away and getting closer with every second.

'Hurry!' That voice again.

'But where is it?' he screamed back, sprinting like a madman towards the oncoming car. In seconds, it would explode out of the fog and slam into him. There'd be nothing the driver could do. Merryn's body would join the rabbits and badgers that littered the country lanes. As the fog around him lit up like an alien landscape, he found it – the second gap! The car shot out of the fog and in the same instant, a pair of hands launched him violently through the gap into the dense tangle of brambles whilst in the same moment, Zac's body tumbled on top of him.

'Have you lost your frigging mind?' Zac yelled, rolling off Merryn and sitting up, bramble thorns tearing at his clothes. 'Are you trying to kill us both, because that was a bloody good effort?'

'Gah! You hurt me, shoving me through the railings like that.' Merryn's shoulder throbbed where it had struck metal.

'What? I saved your bloody life! And mine. Why the hell didn't you just climb through the first gap? You said you'd never been here before so how did you know there was another one?' Zac pointed the torch at Merryn's face.

'She spoke to me again. I know you won't believe me.'

'She? Who's *she*?'

'Remember in the library, when I'd printed off that stuff for you? I asked you where Miss Kelly was?'

Zac thought for a moment and then nodded. 'Vaguely.'

'The same voice spoke to me then. Just now, she told me not to go through the first gap but keep running. There's another gap, she said, and she was right. There *was* a second one.'

Zac shook his head. 'I'm sorry, mate, but you've lost it. I mean, do you know how crazy you sound? You're hearing stuff in your head that isn't real. So where is she, this woman, and why is she trying to get us both killed?'

'I knew you wouldn't believe me but it was like how you're talking to me now. As clear as that. I didn't make it up. Why would I?'

'I have no idea. Listen, we didn't come here to argue about ghosts or whatever. We're still alive which is all that matters. It's time to check out the drop. Can't be much further, so we'll go careful from here.' Zac scanned the ground ahead with the torch, but the beam was growing dimmer by the minute. 'Batteries are running out.' Carefully, he edged forward on all fours, feeling the ground ahead with each hand. 'Stay right behind me. If your girlfriend tells you to stand up and run, just ignore her, okay.'

Patches of cold, hard rock began to appear beneath the thinning layer of damp leaves and twigs. Zac pushed aside a fallen branch. Beyond it, he could just make out a bare rock platform no wider than six feet. And then nothing.

'We've arrived!' Zac announced. 'There's a flat area in front of me. It kind of juts out like a diving board and then... empty space.'

Merryn pulled himself level with Zac. His eyes followed the beam of weak torchlight out beyond the rocky platform into black space beyond. For a few moments, he thought he was going to be sick.

'It feels like the edge of the world,' he gasped. 'It's what the ancient Greeks believed, that the Earth was flat and if you went too close to the edge, you'd fall off.'

Zac looked at Merryn for a few moments with a bemused expression. 'Okay, Mr Super History Geek, it's time to find out what's over the edge of the world, except we probably won't see a thing because of the fog.'

'No, look! Chepstow Castle! It's all lit up. The fog must have cleared.'

The walls of the castle, illuminated with powerful floodlights, were clearly visible, sitting proud on the cliffs above the Wye a mile and a half away. Zac crawled forwards onto the rocky prominence and peered over the edge.

'Hey! Check this out. The whole valley below us is full of fog. It's like an ocean.'

Merryn knew that he'd passed the point of no return. It was as though Zac had cast some spell over him, a spell that he had no power to break. He took a deep breath and inched forwards. As he came alongside Zac, his hands reached out and grabbed the cliff edge. One final effort and he peered over. He'd never seen anything like it. Fog filled the valley, its rippling surface shining in the soft moonlight. Only the highest points of the wooded hills to either side of the valley were visible, their slopes lapped by an endless sea of fog winding its way in sinuous curves above the river.

'It's like we're on some island in the sky. It's amazing.' Merryn had forgotten his fear of heights. Instead he lay transfixed by the magical landscape, his weary brain scarcely able to tell whether it was fantasy or reality.

'So, how far down to the river, d'you reckon?' Zac asked.

Merryn peered into the billowing fog rolling against the cliff face far below him. 'There's no way of knowing. Unless…' He paused and closed his eyes while he searched for a GCSE physics revision guide in his memory. He hated physics – it was all maths and none of it made sense. Nonetheless, a few pages – the ones he'd read – had found their way into his cerebral library.

'Unless what?' Zac was growing impatient.

Merryn opened his eyes. 'We need a stone.'

'A stone?' Zac looked perplexed.

'As big as possible although the actual size doesn't matter.'

'A stone? To throw over the edge?' Zac was catching on. 'Problem is...' He tapped the torch on the rock but only the faintest glow came from the bulb. 'Battery's gone and I'm not scrabbling about up here looking for a stone without a torch. We'll have to use something else.'

Merryn looked at the torch and then at Zac.

'What? You want me to throw my torch over the edge? You're having a laugh.'

'Not the torch. The battery. No point in keeping it if it's run out.'

Zac nodded. 'Oh. Okay. Smart thinking.' He unscrewed the back of the torch and removed the battery. At twelve volts, it was fist-size and heavy. 'So what's next? We're going to throw it off and time how long it takes to reach the river, yes?'

Merryn nodded. 'Exactly. But don't throw the battery down. Just let go gently and let gravity do the rest. I'll count the seconds until it hits the river. Ready?'

Zac sat up, held the battery over the edge as far as he dared and then let go. At the same instant, Merryn started counting. One little second, two little second, three little second, four little second. The faintest of splashes drifted up from the river below.

'Hear that?' Merryn turned to Zac. 'Just over four seconds.'

'Yeah, okay. Four seconds. Where does that get us?'

Merryn frowned while he rummaged in his head again for an answer. It was almost a minute before he found what he was looking for.

'Distance fallen equals half the acceleration of gravity times the time squared.'

Zac sniggered. 'And what the hell is that supposed to mean?'

'No listen. Acceleration of gravity is roughly ten metres per second per second. Don't ask me why. So we multiply that by the time squared. The time was four seconds. Four squared is sixteen. Sixteen times ten is…'

'A hundred and sixty,' Zac pitched in.

'Then divide that by two and you've got the distance that the battery fell in metres.'

'Eighty metres.'

'Three feet in a metre give or take, so three times eighty is…'

'Two hundred and forty.' Zac was beginning to enjoy himself.

'Actually, a metre is a bit more than three feet, so let's say two-sixty feet. And then we've got to add on some extra because the battery took just *over* four seconds. Two-eighty. So the cliff is two hundred and eighty feet high.'

For a few seconds, Zac just stared at Merryn, shaking his head. 'Are you serious? I mean, where's all that stuff come from?'

Merryn shrugged. 'Physics revision guide.'

'Oh Merry, Merry, Merry, you are one sad boy, sitting at home memorising your revision guide.' He laughed. 'So, two hundred and eighty feet. '

'You said three hundred.'

'So I wasn't that far out. Now look over the edge and tell me that a man and a horse could survive a jump from here into the river.'

Merryn went rummaging in his head again. He was cold and tired and his shoulder hurt so it took him longer than usual to find what he was looking for. 'According to the Guinness Book of Records, Harry Froboess, a German stuntman, jumped three hundred and sixty feet from an airship into a lake somewhere.'

'You're kidding me. So you just happened to memorise the whole of the Guinness Book of Records.'

Merryn smiled. 'No. Just the good bits.'

'I'm getting worried about you, MacIntyre. You really need to get out more. So what are you saying? If a German stuntman can jump three hundred and sixty feet, then Wintour can survive two hundred and eighty feet?'

'I don't know. Sounds crazy, but then why are the cliffs called Wintour's Leap? I looked it up on the net and everyone agrees that he and his men were ambushed here by Roundheads.'

'What, so he galloped over the cliffs to escape, like in that library book?'

'No one's certain how he escaped. It's all very muddled. But he definitely survived because he turns up later.'

'What d'you mean?'

'Well, at the end of the war, he was imprisoned in the Tower of London. Backed the wrong side, I guess, and paid for it. After that, it's hard to say. One source reckons he escaped to France and never came back because Oliver Cromwell wanted to hang him.'

Zac shuffled away from the edge and stood up. 'So that's it?' he said despondently. 'No one really knows what happened? I still reckon he didn't jump. A stuntman might survive but Wintour wasn't a stuntman. Come on, we'd better go.'

No sooner had Zac turned to find his way back through the railings than a wave of fog broke over the cliff top and engulfed Merryn, disorientating him. Without the moonlight and the torch, he could see nothing.

'Zac! Which way are the railings? The fog's come over the top. I can't see a thing.'

'This way. Just follow my voice. Don't stand up. Feel the ground ahead of you. You'll be safe when you get to the trees.' There was a sudden note of anxiety in Zac's voice. What if Merryn went the wrong way...

'Can you see the trees yet?' There was no answer. 'Just keep coming in this direction.'

But Merryn was blind. He could hear Zac's voice – it was only a few yards away, but he couldn't be certain from which direction it was coming. He inched forward on all fours, constantly feeling the ground ahead. Damp leaves began to replace the hard rock. Gingerly, he got to his feet. 'Nearly there,' he called out. 'I can't see the railings yet.'

'Move left.' The voice was unmistakable. She's looking out for me now, he thought. Taking one pace to his left, the ground suddenly gave way beneath his feet. He only had time to let out a startled cry before his head struck something hard and everything went black.

'Merryn!' screamed Zac. 'Merryn, what's happened? Merryn, for Christ's sake, say something!' But the ground between the railings and the cliff fell silent.

Silent and empty.

CHAPTER 6

The wave of fog washed back over the cliff leaving the top bathed once more in moonlight. Zac darted forward out of the shadow of the trees onto the rock platform, his eyes sweeping back and forth along the cliff top, desperately searching for any sign of Merryn.

'Merryn!' he screamed again. 'Say something!' He stood perfectly still and listened. The silence was terrifying. 'Merry, don't mess with me. This isn't funny. Make a noise. *Please!*' Zac was close to tears now as he crouched down on all fours and crawled to the edge. 'Please God you haven't gone over. Please God, please God, you can't have gone over.' He knew he was wasting his time peering over the edge. Even without the mist, it was too dark to see a body floating in the river almost three hundred feet below, but what else could he do? He stared down at the billowing clouds and, in his imagination, watched Merryn falling in slow motion, a look of terror on his upturned face as he disappeared from view, swallowed by the swirling mist. It was all his fault. He'd have to explain what happened to Merryn's parents, to his own dad, his friends, reporters, the police.

The police! He should phone the police. They would carry out a thorough search. They'd put boats out on the river. Maybe Merryn had survived the fall. Zac knew it was almost impossible. He'd said it himself – *a stuntman might survive but Wintour wasn't a stuntman.* Merryn wasn't a stuntman either, but Zac desperately needed a thread of hope, anything that challenged the terrible conclusion that had formed in his imagination. He pushed back from the edge, pulled out his phone and pressed it into life, his hands shaking uncontrollably. As the screen lit up an idea came to him. His old phone. He'd given it to Merryn. It still carried some charge and if Merryn hadn't turned it off, then it would ring when Zac called it. If Merryn had fallen into the river, it would be pointless. *But what if he hadn't?*

At first, Zac couldn't remember even the first digits of the number. Fear and panic strangled his ability to think clearly.

'Get a grip, Zachary, for God's sake!' he yelled at himself, wiping away the tears. He took several deep breaths. Slowly the number began to take shape. Finally, he punched in the eleven digits and then tapped the call pad. He held his breath, hardly daring to hope, and listened for the Motorola ringtone.

At first he thought he was imagining it. He wanted to hear the tinny jingle so badly that maybe his brain was creating the sounds, delivering the escape from his nightmare he so desperately craved.

But no! He wasn't imagining it. Somewhere between the edge and the railings a phone was ringing and yet it was barely audible. Zac stood up and began frantically searching through the undergrowth. The ringtone seemed to be coming from inside the cliff but how was that possible? Had Merryn dropped the phone down a hole?

'Merryn, where are you?' he yelled. 'Where in God's name are you?' A tiny ray of hope sparked into life. Merryn's phone hadn't fallen over the edge. Surely that meant Merryn was still alive. But if so, where was he? Suddenly, the ringtone was joined by another sound, a soft moaning. There! A few yards to his left, Zac could make out a narrow crevice running back from the edge of the cliff into the trees. At its cliff end, the crevice was no more than a foot wide, but as it ran towards the railings, it opened up. In places, its mouth was partly hidden beneath dead leaves and branches. Instantly, Zac realised what had happened.

The phone was still ringing – louder now. It didn't take him long to find the hole Merryn had fallen through into the bowels of the cliff. He was alive but how far had he fallen? Was he injured? Zac knelt down at the edge of the hole and peered into the depths. It was utterly black. If Merryn was down there, he couldn't see him. He cancelled the call on his phone and the ringing stopped.

'Merryn! Are you there?'

Fifteen feet down, pinned between two cold rock walls and buried in leaves, lay Merryn. The fall had knocked him out for a few seconds and now that he'd regained consciousness, the left side of his head throbbed angrily. In the pitch black of the crevice, he'd lost any sense of direction.

'Zac!' he croaked. 'Where are you?'

'Thank God! You're alive!' Tears of undiluted relief streamed down Zac's face. 'I thought you'd fallen over the edge. You gave me one hell of a scare. Are you hurt?'

'Where are you Zac?' A note of panic entered Merryn's voice.

'I'm up here. Just above you. You've fallen into some sort of crack. Are you hurt?'

Merryn worked one arm free and felt the side of his head. It was sticky where blood trickled from a gash in his scalp. 'My head. I must have banged it when I fell. I think it's bleeding.'

'Merryn, I can't see you. I'm going to clear some of these branches out of the way. That'll let some more moonlight in.' Zac worked feverishly at the top of the crevice, excavating as much of the opening as he could while leaves and twigs rained down onto Merryn.

'Okay, I can just about see you now. Can you move?'

Merryn scraped his legs hopelessly against the sides of the crevice. There was nothing for him to push against. The more he struggled, the deeper he sank into the bottomless bed of damp leaves. For the second time that night, he thought he was going to be sick. He lay still while the wave of nausea passed over him.

'Wait there. I'll get a branch.' Zac's mind was racing now as he sprang to his feet. There was sure to be a branch somewhere which he could lower into the crevice. If Merryn could grab hold of it then he might be able to pull himself out.

Merryn remained motionless, clamped between the rock walls. He twisted his head round to look up at the narrow slit through which he'd fallen. Far above, he could make out the twinkle of stars and the dark silhouettes of branches against the night sky. A few moments later, Zac returned dragging a long branch behind him.

'Merryn, are you still there?'

'Of course I am. Just hurry up and get me out of here. My head's pounding.'

Zac lay down and lowered the branch into the crack. Even with his arm at full stretch, the end of the branch dangled tantalisingly out of Merryn's reach.

'You need to get into an upright position to reach the branch. I can't lower it any further.'

Merryn began thrashing his legs around while his forearms, jammed across the crack, acted like a fulcrum. Slowly, his body began to turn.

'Right, try and grab the branch.' Zac leaned into the crack as far as he could but still Merryn couldn't reach the branch.

'Wait a moment. There's a lump of rock jammed in the crack just behind my head. I didn't see it before. I need to turn round... so I can use it... to get a bit higher.' Turning, however, required an almighty struggle since the crack held him like a vice and every movement sent pain shooting down his left arm. When, at last, he faced the jammed rock, he threw his right arm over it and hung there for a few moments, panting with exhaustion.

Reaching out, his left hand struck something metallic concealed beneath the rock. At first, Merryn thought it was simply a length of pipe jammed between the cliff walls, but the more he explored it with his fingers, the more curious he became. Something about the object – its shape and texture – felt very odd.

'Well done, Merryn!' Zac called down. 'If you pull up on the rock, you'll be able to reach the branch. Grab it with both hands and I'll try and pull you out.'

'Just give me a minute, Zac. There's something stuck beneath the rock. A bit of pipe. It feels really weird.'

'Forget it. It's probably a piece of rubbish that someone's chucked down there.'

'I'm telling you, Zac, there's something really weird about it. I just need a torch.'

Zac shook his head. What was Merryn playing at? 'Well I haven't...' Suddenly he remembered his phone. 'You've got one! We both have! How dull am I? Your phone is a torch. Have you still got it?'

Merryn bent both his legs and jammed them across the crevice, freeing up his hands. He grimaced as he twisted one arm to reach one of his parka pockets containing Zac's old phone and pulled it out.

'Okay, now what?'

'Slide your finger down the screen from the top. You'll see a set of tools. Find the torch icon and tap it. Got that?'

It took Merryn a moment to locate the torch icon but eventually a dull blue glow emerged from the front of the phone. With one arm around the rock, he pointed the beam of light at the metal pipe with the other. It was about eighteen inches long, straight and slender at one end, but thicker and curved at the other. The whole length of the straight section, perhaps twelve inches, was covered in a thick, flaky layer of rust but the other end – that was different. Very different. Merryn stared at it, scarcely able to believe what he was seeing.

'Hey, you should see this. It's some kind of gun. Been here a long time, mind. The barrel is totally rusted, but the other end – it's amazing. I'll try and get it free and bring it up with me.'

By twisting the wide end and tapping the thin end, Merryn worked the gun loose until suddenly, it fell free into his grasp.

'Wow! It's heavy!' he exclaimed. 'Like it's made of lead.' He pushed the gun into his parka and zipped it up. With one hand pushing against the rock, he reached up with the other and grabbed the end of Zac's branch.

'Hang on. Don't let go!' Zac hauled on the branch for all he was worth, raising his catch inch by inch from the darkness. Just when his hand could no longer grip the branch, Merryn emerged from the crack and into the moonlight, utterly spent. He lay gasping in the undergrowth like a beached whale, unable to move or speak. Using the torch on his own phone, Zac examined the lump on the side of Merryn's head. His left ear was covered in congealed blood which had run from the wound. It glistened ghoulishly red in the torchlight. Zac's euphoria at finding Merryn alive suddenly vanished.

'Your head doesn't look too good. You've got to get it looked at. I mean, it's bleeding pretty bad and there's a lump the size of a golf ball.'

But Merryn wasn't listening. He'd sat up and removed the gun from his parka. 'Shine the torch here,' he said weakly.

'That's got to hurt like hell. I know it's the middle of the night, but we ought… to…' Zac's voice suddenly tailed off as the torchlight fell on the curved handle of the gun – the butt. Unlike the barrel, it showed no traces of rust. The gleaming metal had been elaborately carved into the body of a leaping fox. Its back legs projected down below some kind of firing mechanism to form the trigger while its head and front legs stretched out in the curve of the butt to fit neatly into the palm of the firing hand. Gaping jaws revealed serrated rows of teeth while its eyes, two tiny inlaid jewels, sparkled in the torchlight. Neither boy spoke, as though the fox had cast a spell of silence. Merryn held the butt with his right hand, sliding a finger around the trigger, then lifted it with the other hand, aiming out into the darkness beyond the clifftop. The gun was so heavy, it took all his strength just to keep it still.

'At last, 'tis found. Now you can set us free, Tom. I took a life with it and now it must save a life.'

'There!' Merryn exclaimed. 'You must have heard that. Her voice. It's all around us.' He lowered the gun onto his lap and stared up at Zac but it was obvious his friend had heard nothing.

'We've got to stop the bleeding, Merryn. Your head doesn't look good.' Zac quickly removed his jacket and sweatshirt.

'You didn't answer my question. She just spoke to me – except she's got my name wrong again – and you're saying you didn't hear her?'

Zac had taken off his tee shirt and ripped it open. 'Hold still and I'll wrap this around your head. Should stop the bleeding. No, I didn't hear anything. I told you before, it's in your head. You've smacked it on the rock falling into the hole so no wonder you're hearing voices. Hold still, will you.'

'Ow, that hurts!' Merryn cried out as Zac tightened the tee shirt over the wound and tied the ends. 'She's talking to me, Zac. I'm not making this up but none of it makes sense. She keeps calling me Tom.' Merryn looked out across the valley at the billows of fog shimmering in the moonlight. 'Maybe you're right. It's all in my head.'

Zac wasn't listening. Instead he was admiring his first aid handiwork. 'I think the bleeding's stopped but you still need to get it seen to. If we get back on the road, I can call for an ambulance.'

'No way! They'll call my parents and Mum will go absolutely bonkers.' Merryn looked down at the gun. 'And we'll never see this again.'

'Okay, okay, but if you start rambling about voices again, I'm calling an ambulance. Now, please tell me you've read a book about old guns. You've read everything else.'

Merryn shook his head. He tried rummaging through the shelves in his head but drew a blank. 'I don't know. I've never seen anything like it. What d'you reckon? A hundred years old? I don't understand where the bullets go; and what's this for?' He pointed to a curious S-shaped piece of metal that slanted upwards from one side of the gun, just above the trigger. Like the barrel, it was badly rusted. At its upper end, clamped in a miniature, beak-like vice lay a tiny piece of stone.

'It's weird why only half the gun is rusted,' Zac remarked. 'Look at the barrel – it's a mess. But the fox looks like it was made yesterday. It's still shiny.'

'That's probably because it's made from stainless steel. It doesn't rust. Except I don't know when stainless steel was invented. In any case, why didn't they make the whole gun out of stainless steel?'

Zac checked his watch. It read one-thirty. 'It's pretty late. We ought to get back. If we get the gun cleaned up tomorrow and Google it, we should be able to find out how old it is.'

Merryn nodded wearily. 'Maybe. But it won't tell us how it ended up down the crack. Or who it belongs to.' *Or why a woman I can't see is speaking to me.*

'It belongs to us now.' Zac paused for a moment. 'Beats me why the person who dropped it down the crack didn't go looking for it. It's not like it disappeared into the leaves at the bottom.'

'Maybe they didn't drop it.' Merryn was finding it increasingly hard to ignore the pounding in his head.

Zac took the gun from Merryn. 'Bloody hell, you're right. It is heavy. Listen, are you all right to walk?' He pulled Merryn to his feet.

Merryn nodded. His vision was slightly blurred and his legs felt like jelly but at least he was alive. Using his phone torch, Zac guided him out through the railings onto the road. A breeze had picked up and thinned the fog but clouds had rolled in, obscuring the moonlight. A steady drizzle began to fall from the dark sky as they made their way back along Netherhope Lane. Without a decent torch, they could scarcely see ten yards ahead. Several times, Merryn felt overcome by bouts of dizziness and had to stop and crouch low until the world stopped spinning but, aside from this, the walk back to the phone box proved uneventful.

'You should come back to my house,' Zac suggested. 'I can clean the wound and dress it. You turn up at home looking like that, God knows what your parents are going to think.'

The night's events had sown such confusion inside Merryn's head that he completely forgot he'd locked himself out. 'No, I've got to get back before they find out I'm gone. I'll just wash the blood away in the morning before I go down. Dad leaves early and Mum is usually seeing to Charlie so won't notice.' He felt desperately tired and just wanted to lie down and say goodbye to his pounding headache.

Zac shrugged. 'If you're sure. Listen, I've got rugby training tomorrow after school and a game on Saturday morning, but I could bring the gun round your place in the afternoon. We can decide what we're going to do with it.'

'Okay.'

'You're sure you're all right on your own? I told you your head doesn't look nice.' He shone his phone on the tee shirt wrapped around Merryn's head. A dark red patch had begun to appear above the wound.

'I'll be fine. I just need to get some sleep.'

'If you're not in tomorrow, I'll see you Saturday. Sorry about your head,' Zac added, 'but you've got to admit, the gun is a seriously cool find.' With that, he was gone, sprinting away into the darkness.

Merryn turned and headed for Church Close. It began raining hard now, soaking the tee shirt and washing blood down his neck. By the time he reached the street lights, Merryn could have been mistaken for the victim of a horror movie, savaged by zombies yet somehow still alive. He turned the corner into the Close. His brain was operating in stand-by mode; he was too wet, too tired and too sore for anything requiring conscious thought. Number 14 lay dark and silent as he crept up the drive, through the latched gate into the covered passage at the side of the house. Instinctively, he dug in his parka pockets for the back door key. Something pressed enter on his keyboard and his brain flickered back into operational mode. No key! His parents were going to find out he'd been on walkabout after all.

Exhausted beyond care, he slumped down onto the step outside the back door and checked his watch. Quarter past two. Four hours until Malcolm unlocked the door to let the dog out. At least the passage was dry. He closed his eyes and seconds later, a fox leapt into his dreams.

CHAPTER 7

It came from the road through a gap in the railings with its tail held high and its nose to the ground. At first, it didn't appear to notice the crouched figure, perched above the abyss on the limestone platform. It was too busy sniffing out rodents from the tangle of undergrowth. Merryn stared, spellbound by the dark, vulpine shape that slid beneath the thorny snarl of hawthorn and bramble. Suddenly the fox lifted its head as though a sixth sense had warned it of the boy's presence. Its eyes blazed in the darkness like red-hot coals, fixing him with a demonic stare while its lips curled back to reveal long rows of dagger-like teeth. They glistened metallic-like in the moonlight as Merryn looked around desperately for somewhere to hide but he was trapped. Slowly the fox inched forwards, each leg stretching out in turn, its body stooped low against the ground. Merryn cowered back to the very edge of the world when suddenly, with a blood-curdling shriek, the fox launched across the rock platform with lightning speed, sweeping him backwards over the edge into space.

Boy and fox fell together. Merryn could feel the animal's paws pressed into his shoulders and its hot breath on his face. He wrestled to get free, arms thrashing wildly in an effort to push the beast away. Suddenly he was awake and Molly was standing over him, her tail wagging energetically.

'Molly!' Merryn was relieved to discover that he wasn't, after all, plunging into the Wye with a fox at his throat. 'How did you get out, for heaven's sake?' But it didn't take him long to figure out the answer. *You woke Dad up when I left and he came down and let you out. And now we're both locked out for the rest of the night. Unless, of course, you do your insane hammering at the door and barking thing which will wake Dad up again and he'll come downstairs… and open the door…*

Merryn got to his feet. He was wet through and shivering with the cold but he had an idea, one that Zac would be proud of.

'Molly, come here girl,' he whispered, leading the terrier out from the shelter of the passage and into the back garden and the rain. Midway down the weed-infested lawn grew an ancient apple tree. The remains of a tree house festooned its lower branches, scarcely ten feet from the ground. Only the rotting floor planks remained together with a rickety ladder that protested with creaks and groans whenever anyone attempted to climb its sagging rungs. Anyone human, that is. For reasons that only the terrier knew, but couldn't explain, Molly liked to teeter up the ladder on warm summer evenings and sit on the tree house floor, watching Mr Garfield mowing his manicured lawn over the fence. However, whilst Molly had inherited the gene for teetering up rickety ladders, her parents had failed to pass on the gene for teetering back down again. Consequently, she had to be rescued, a rather drawn-out and noisy affair. What bewildered Mr and Mrs Garfield more than anything was not why Molly kept repeating this act of canine stupidity – she was after all merely a dog – but why those MacIntyre numbskulls didn't remove the ladder from the tree, thereby preventing the dog from murdering the twilight tranquillity of Church Close.

'Come on, Molly,' Merryn whispered, as he tapped the bottom rung of the ladder. 'It's time to get stuck.' Molly, however, had absolutely no intention of climbing a wet, slippery ladder in the rain. Mr Garfield wasn't mowing his lawn and, in any case, it was pitch black. What could a dog see? Merryn was left with no alternative. He bent down and picked up the dripping terrier, carefully lowering her onto the middle rungs of the ladder.

'Go on, girl,' he encouraged, 'you can do it.'

At first, Molly's paws flailed hopelessly, unable to find any grip. Then, one by one, her feet found the rungs and Merryn let her go. For a moment, it looked as though the terrier was stuck, unable to climb up or down. However, Molly had never remained still for longer than thirty seconds in her waking life and with the stopwatch on twenty-five, she nervously stretched a front paw up onto the next rung and began the short climb onto the platform.

'Well done, girl!' Merryn exclaimed when Molly finally reached the relative safety of the tree house floor. 'Now bark your ears off!'

With that, he hurried back up the garden, along the side passage and out through the gate, closing it silently behind him. He huddled against the wall of the house, vainly seeking shelter from the hammering rain and waited. It didn't take long for Molly to realise that Merryn wasn't coming back. She filled her lungs and launched into a barrage of mournful yelps that rent the night air. To Merryn's delight, a second dog struck up a duet, its deeper tenor howls blending perfectly with Molly's soprano staccato. Two collies over at Pennington Farm added to the cacophony, curious as to what all the fuss was about.

Suddenly, light spilled out through the frosted glass of number 14's front door followed a few seconds later by the sound of the back door opening. Merryn's plan had worked. Malcolm stood looking out at the teeming rain, cursing softly under his breath.

'Bloody dog. I've had enough. Twice in one night.' A torch switched on and Malcolm hurried out into the garden to either rescue or strangle the terrier – he hadn't quite made up his mind – wearing nothing more than pyjamas and a pair of trainers.

Merryn opened the side gate, crept down the passage and slipped into the scullery through the open door. Once inside, he kicked off his trainers and wrestled out of his dripping parka, wincing at the stab of pain running down his left arm. Outside, he could hear his father shouting at the dog. There wasn't much time. Quickly, he hid his parka in a corner behind the washing machine, picked up his trainers and darted through the kitchen to the stairs. Despite the hall light, Merryn failed to notice the trail of wet sock prints that followed him across the carpet and up the stairs. Worse, he failed to notice Donna's slippers at the top of the stairs. Had they been empty, Merryn might have succeeded in reaching his bedroom undetected, although the sock prints made that unlikely. As it was, Donna's slippers were full of Donna's feet. As Merryn reached the fourth step, all hell broke loose. His mother screamed, his father slammed the back door and swore at the dog which barked, while his brother opened his mouth and howled.

Several minutes passed before the screaming, shouting, barking and howling stopped, several minutes during which the pounding inside Merryn's head grew steadily worse, and during which he vowed never to have anything to do with Zac's hare-brained schemes ever again. When everyone had calmed down, Donna took Merryn to the bathroom, removed the bloody tee shirt from around his head and inspected the golf ball.

'What were you *doing*?' she asked, struggling to keep control. 'In the middle of the night? Did someone do this to you?'

'No, Mum. I just went for a walk and... ow!'

'I'm sorry. I've got to clean this cut. It's still bleeding in places. You went for a walk and then?'

It's what Merryn had dreaded. 'Fell over.'

Donna called her husband. 'Malcolm, he needs to go to casualty right away. It's quicker for you to drive him. Ambulance will take ages.' Then she turned to her son and held his face in both hands. 'No more questions. We'll save those for later. The cut needs dressing at the hospital. But when you come back, you're going to have to do better than "I went for a walk and fell over". Now get changed quick.'

At the hospital, the duty doctor put six stitches in Merryn's scalp and kept him in overnight – or what turned out to be overday. Any illusions he'd harboured about catching up on sleep were soon dashed by a large, Irish woman with bulging eyes who, not content with shaking him out of his fathomless sleep every hour, proceeded to shine a blinding beam of light into each eye, sighing with satisfaction each time.

'Now then, Merryn, me lovely,' she said in her soft, Dublin lilt when she was convinced that her patient wasn't dead, 'Oi'm tinking you'll be wanting to get straight back off to the land of nod.' If he'd had the energy, he would have grabbed her two greasy pigtails and shouted 'Oi'm tinking I want to be left a-bloody-lone', but he was asleep before he'd even finished thinking it.

Later that afternoon, Malcolm came to rescue him from Nurse Fitzgerald. Merryn had never been more pleased to see his father in his life. Pleased and surprised. His dad never finished work before six o'clock, yet here he was at four. As he sat in the van on the short journey home from Chepstow, Merryn steeled himself for the inevitable cross-examination. It wouldn't come from his father. He'd leave that to Donna. She was so proficient at extracting the truth from her victims, usually Malcolm but occasionally Merryn, that both men in her life often wondered if she'd had a secret past gathering intelligence for MI5. At first, however, it appeared that there might not be a cross-examination. Instead, he was ushered into the living room, handed an overly sweet cup of tea and made to sit on the couch. Donna glanced nervously at Malcolm and then launched into her prepared speech.

'Merryn, we've been thinking about what happened last night and we both just want to say that we're sorry.'

If Merryn could have written his mother's script for the occasion, it would not have started with an apology. Instead, words such as 'irresponsible' and 'grounded' would have formed its main theme.

Puzzlement filled his face as Donna continued.

'We know why you went out.'

'You do?' How could they possibly know?

'Yes, of course we do. You were angry and you had every right to be. Your dad should never have put the house up for sale without telling you first.' She fired a disapproving look at her husband. 'Isn't that right, Malcolm?'

Malcolm had confessed in an earlier interrogation and now he nodded with an air of resignation. 'I should have told you both what was going on.'

'That's why you went out, isn't it, Merryn? You were upset.' Donna's voice was scarcely more than a whisper now. 'Where did you go?' She sat down beside him and slipped her hand into his. Merryn felt awkward. His parents hadn't the least idea why he'd crept out of the house at midnight and he certainly wasn't about to enlighten them. However, he had to feed them something that would keep MI5 at bay. A wicked thought suddenly torpedoed its way to the front of the queue and before he could assess its likely impact on his audience, he said, 'I went to the cliffs.'

'Oh my God, Merryn!' Donna spun round on the settee to face him. 'Which cliffs?'

'No, it's not what you think.' Merryn realised his mistake. He couldn't have his parents thinking he was suicidal. Now he'd have to reveal at least part of the truth. 'I couldn't sleep, so I went to do some homework. About John Wintour. We're studying the English Civil War at school and I just wanted to see if Wintour could have jumped, that's all. I fell over some railings in the fog and hit my head.'

'You went to Wintour's Leap? In the dark?' Donna shook her head in disbelief. 'Have you any idea how dangerous that was? The cliffs must be nearly two hundred feet high.'

Merryn was going to answer, 'Yes I do' and 'No they're not' but instead, he just sat and sipped his tea and wondered whether Zac would come round the next day. He wanted to see the gun in daylight.

'Your mum's right,' Malcolm added. 'In any case, Wintour certainly didn't jump. It's just a legend. Stuff and nonsense. A story blown up out of all proportion to turn him into a hero. No one could survive a two-hundred-foot jump into water. He'd break every bone in his body.'

'Harry Froboes survived. He jumped three hundred and sixty feet.'

'Don't tell me. *The Guinness Book of Records*?' Malcolm conjured a rare smile. 'Looks like your memory is still intact.' His son's memory never failed to amaze him. 'Mind you, I'll bet that Harry what's-his-name was a stuntman. Wintour wasn't a stuntman.'

'That's exactly what Zac said,' Merryn blurted out but regretted it as soon as he'd spoken. He shouldn't have mentioned Zac's name. Now the inquisition would start again.

'Zac? That's the boy who came round yesterday, isn't it? You said you were going over his place to do some homework, didn't you?' Merryn didn't like where this was leading. He needed to derail his mother's train of thought quickly.

'Look, I'm really tired. They didn't let me sleep at the hospital. Some big Irish nurse kept waking me up. I'm going to bed.' He got up to go.

'Merryn?' Donna didn't move. 'You know we'd be devastated if anything happened to you, don't you?'

Merryn looked down at the carpet. He just wanted to escape.

'You won't do that again, will you? Creep out of the house in the middle of the night and... fall over some railings?'

He could tell by the way she said it that his mother didn't believe a word of his story, but she'd given up looking for the truth and that was all that mattered. He nodded and retreated upstairs to his bedroom.

CHAPTER 8

Saturday 7th September

It was gone nine o'clock the next morning when Merryn awoke from a long and dreamless sleep. The lump on his head had deflated, the throbbing no more than a dull ache. At ten o'clock the house phone rang. It was Zac. Merryn took both handsets upstairs to his bedroom and closed the door. He didn't want his mum listening in on the conversation.

'Hey, how's the head?'

'Oh, apart from a night in Chepstow General, six stitches, a sadist called Fitzgerald and two antibiotic injections in my sore arm – the one with a huge, yellow bruise – everything's fine.'

'Six stitches?' Zac's tone suddenly took on a note of concern. 'No wonder you were covered in blood when you came out of the crack. I told you it needed looking at. What did your parents say?'

'Bit of screaming to begin with. Then Dad took me to hospital.' Merryn lowered his voice. 'I told them I went down to the cliffs to do a bit of research about Wintour and fell over some railings. I don't think Mum believes me. She suspects you were involved, I'm certain of it.'

'You didn't tell her it was my idea, did you?'

'No, of course not. It's just that she's got some sixth sense that tells her when someone's not telling the whole truth. What about your parents?'

'Oh, Sasha was a bit suspicious when I didn't wake up on Friday morning. She found my hoodie in the cloakroom – it was soaking wet. Dad didn't notice anything.'

Merryn wondered what kind of house had a cloakroom. And who was Sasha? His mother? But he never called her 'Mum'.

'Hey, any more voices?'

Merryn thought he could hear a snigger at the end of Zac's question, so he just ignored him. 'Are you bringing the gun round?' he asked. 'We've got to decide what to do with it.'

'I told you, I've got a rugby match in Chepstow at eleven. Should be done by one. Sasha will pick me up from the ground and I'll come straight over. See you about two.' With that, Zac hung up.

Merryn sat on his computer chair and stared at the blank screen. Maybe Zac was right. Maybe his imagination had grown so adept at recreating scenes from the past that now it was able to generate surround-sound voices speaking to him from out of the darkness. He tried replaying everything the woman had said from the moment she had guided him to the book in the library, searching for clues as to what it might mean. She had meant for him to find the drawing of the leap, he was certain. But then she had claimed the artist had made an error. *That's not how it happened.* How could she possibly know what had taken place over three hundred years ago? Was she a voice from the past, a woman who had actually witnessed the leap?

And then she had guided him to the pistol. What other explanation could there be for leading him to the cliffs, the second gap in the railings and finally, the crevice. *Move left.* She must have known the pistol was there and she needed someone to find it. What was it she had said to him when he'd first lifted the pistol. *At last, it's found. Now it can set me free.* Was that right? There was more, but no matter how hard he tried, he couldn't remember it.

And then there was the matter of his name. On the one hand, he was certain she was speaking to him and yet, three times she'd got his name wrong. That made absolutely no sense.

'Who are you?' he whispered aloud, feeling both foolish for speaking the question out loud and fearful that the ghost – after all, what else could she be? – might reply. 'Can you hear me? I'm Merryn so why do you call me Tom?' He sat quite still, waiting for answers but none came.

Switching on his computer, he decided to hunt the gun down on Google images. Of course, there would be millions of gun results in a Google search, perhaps tens or hundreds of millions. He needed first to remember exactly what it looked like. Taking a pencil and piece of scrap paper from his desk, he set about sketching the gun from memory. It took him several attempts to draw the complex firing mechanism since it had been swamped with rust. Getting a leaping fox to fit into the butt of the gun so that its back legs formed the trigger proved too much for him. How could his brain recall hundreds of pages of printed text that he'd read months ago and yet struggle to remember one object that he'd seen only two days before? Maybe the damage to his head *had* affected his memory. After a while, he gave up and resigned himself to trawling through pages and pages of Google images. He typed in *"old gun"* and pressed enter. There! One billion, one hundred and forty million results. Merryn groaned. This was going to take forever. He clicked on 'images' and began scrolling down. He'd barely started when an image at the bottom of the screen leapt out and grabbed his attention. It was a close-up photograph of the firing mechanism of an English flintlock pistol, dated 1710. Someone had added labels to the photo detailing the names of the various parts of the mechanism. Everything about it looked familiar. An S-shaped curve of steel – the cock – lay screwed at its lower end to the left-hand side of the gun, immediately above the trigger. At its upper end, a thin sliver of flint sat clasped in a tiny vice, held fast by a single screw. A flat, vertical, steel plate – the frizzen – lay immediately in front of the cock and its flint, while concealed beneath the frizzen lay the pan. The longer he stared at the image on the screen, the more convinced he became that the gun he'd found was an English flintlock pistol.

Quickly, Merryn clicked on the link to the source website. Five minutes later, he knew exactly how to load and fire a flintlock pistol. Ten minutes later, he knew when flintlocks had first been used in England and when they went out of fashion; and shortly before Donna called him down for lunch, he knew how much an original flintlock pistol in good condition was worth.

CHAPTER 9

Every Saturday afternoon, Donna attended a Down's syndrome support group in Chepstow. She would take Charlie with her and watch while the other Down's children, many of them older than Charlie, sat on the floor and played with him. Donna would marvel at how different her two boys were. Here was Charlie, always the centre of attention, entertaining a roomful of adults with his ceaseless giggling, whilst at home, her other son, shy and reclusive, shut himself away in his bedroom and rarely smiled, let alone giggled. She wondered if Charlie would ever become a teenage recluse. Studying the other Down's children, she doubted it.

When Zac rang the doorbell at two o'clock, Merryn had the house to himself. Malcolm was spending more and more time at the shop in a desperate bid to resurrect its fortunes so his family saw little of him at weekends. Little of him at all.

'Have you got it?' Merryn blurted out as soon as Zac stepped into the hall.

'You've gotta show me your stitches first.' He bent over to inspect Merryn's scalp. 'Oh, gruesome!' he exclaimed. The area around the gash had been shaved and the six stitches were clearly visible, neat black knots of thread. 'Actually, that's a serious fashion statement. The latest trend in piercing!'

'Actually, it's the latest trend in pain,' Merryn retorted. 'I distinctly remember you telling me that a visit to the cliffs would be perfectly safe. You didn't do a risk assessment.'

'You sound just like Mr McKenzie before a chemistry practical. "Now Year 11," he mimicked in his best Scottish accent, "have you carried out a rrrrisk assessment?" That's what makes school so boring. Risk is banned. Anyway, you're not dead, which I thought you were at one point. I'm keeping you on a lead next time.'

'There isn't going to *be* a next time,' Merryn said emphatically. 'You're the field agent from now on. I'm the online researcher. So, did you bring it?'

Zac held up his Nike grip bag.

'We'd better go upstairs just in case my parents come back. Mind you, Mum's probably bugged my bedroom.'

Safely installed in Merryn's room, Zac unzipped his Nike grip bag and carefully lifted out the gun as though he were holding a newborn baby and handed it to Merryn. 'The handle isn't made of stainless steel, is it?'

'The butt,' Merryn whispered, staring at it. 'You're right. It isn't. Whatever was I thinking?'

'So, who's going to say it because it sounds crazy.'

'I'll say it,' Merryn answered without hesitation. 'It's made of gold.' The boys sat in silence, staring at the fox, too overawed to say anything until Merryn added, 'Not gold plate. It's too heavy just to be plated. It's solid gold. Got to be.'

'Solid gold?' Zac shook his head and then burst out laughing. 'We've found a solid gold gun? It must be worth a bloody fortune. I mean, how many old guns have a butt made of solid gold? I'll bet there aren't any! We're going to be celebrities, Merry. Just wait till the press gets hold of this.'

'No one must know about this, Zac. Not yet. Not until we've made absolutely sure it is made of gold and we know how old it is and who it belonged to. You can't tell anyone.'

'Okay, keep your hair on. So, what do you know about old guns? I'll bet you've been swotting up on them.'

Merryn smiled. 'I know a bit.' He put the gun down carefully on the bed, sat at his computer and found his browsing history. He clicked on the link he'd found earlier. 'Have a look at this. Familiar?'

Zac picked up the gun and held it alongside the photo on the screen. 'That's it. It's exactly the same. This is the cock.' He pointed to the rusted S-shape projecting from the top of the pistol. He glanced at Merryn. Both burst out laughing. 'This plate must be the frizzen and somewhere under all this rust is the pan. Nice one. How long did that take to find?'

'About two minutes. It's an English flintlock pistol. Could date anywhere from 1630 to around 1820. After that, they went out of fashion.'

'So it's at least two hundred years old. That's crazy. No wonder the barrel's a mess. What do you reckon it's worth? Bet you didn't find that out.'

'I didn't think it was made of gold when I was searching. The butt just looked grey when you shone the torch on it at the cliffs. An ordinary flintlock pistol with a wooden butt in decent condition is worth around three grand. But this – there's just no way of knowing what it's worth. We need someone who knows about guns to have a look at it.'

'Okay, so we take it into Chepstow to an antiques dealer and say, "Hey, we found this gun. Can you clean it up for us?" Can you imagine what the guy is going to say? First question: where did you find it? Second question: what are your names because I'm phoning the police? Brilliant.'

Merryn knew Zac was right. Two teenagers with a golden gun wouldn't remain a secret for long. Then miraculously, as though their brains had been temporarily wired together, the two boys looked at each other and in perfect synchrony said, 'Miss Kelly.'

'Ha! I was right. You *do* fancy her.'

'What? *You* said her name as well,' Merryn protested.

'Yes, but I've already got a girlfriend. Anyway, what was the guy's name? The antiques dealer.'

Merryn shrugged. 'Can't remember.'

Zac looked surprised. 'But you can remember everything.'

'Only if it's on paper or a screen.'

'Doesn't matter. What do you say we take the pistol in on Monday and show it to Miss Kelly. Say we found it near the cliffs and that we don't want our parents to know until we've cleaned it up a bit.'

'Sounds risky. What if she goes straight to the head or the police? She's a teacher, remember. Teachers play by the rules.'

'Yeah, but Miss Kelly is still quite young. Maybe she hasn't got contaminated yet. We've just got to persuade her to keep it a secret.'

Merryn frowned and made a sceptical noise in the back of his throat. 'All right. We'll take it to the library. In the meantime, there are questions that need answering.'

Zac sat on the bed with the pistol across his knees as though he were about to change its nappy. 'Like what?'

'Like what was the pistol doing wedged in the crack?'

'Easy. The owner dropped it by accident and never went back to find it.' Zac thought about his answer for a moment and realised it was ludicrous. 'No, he dropped it and *couldn't* find it. After all, it was completely hidden from view.'

'Exactly!' Merryn returned. 'It *was* completely hidden from view. *So* well hidden that the only way anyone could find it was by climbing or falling down the crack and seeing it from below.'

'Yeah, but don't forget that it's been down there for a mighty long time. Hundreds of years. It's going to get covered up.'

'Listen. It's seriously heavy so if it was dropped down the crack, the butt would have suffered damage. There isn't any.'

Zac examined the butt. Merryn was right. There wasn't a scratch on it. Even where the fox's head had rested against the wall of the crevice, there was barely a mark to be seen. One of its ears had lost its fine point but that was all.

'Hey! Look at this!' Zac exclaimed. 'There's some markings on the fox's belly. Looks like writing of some sort.' On the underside of the fox, where the third, fourth and fifth fingers gripped the butt, four tiny shapes, aligned side by side, had been stamped into the metal. 'I can't make these out. We need a magnifying glass. Any luck?'

Merryn shook his head. 'I don't think we've got one. If we had a camera, though, we could take a photo and blow it up on the computer. Trouble is…'

'Merryn, you're a genius!' Zac took out his mobile phone, tapped it into life and selected camera mode. 'It's got a brilliant macro function for taking close-ups. Even better, why don't I email it to you and then we can magnify the image on your screen. Tell me you've got an email address.'

Merryn looked hurt. 'Of course I have.' What he didn't say was that no one ever emailed him.

Five minutes later, they were staring at the curious row of four symbols, magnified a hundred times on Merryn's computer screen:

'Okay, Mr Internet Freak. I bet you can't solve that in two minutes.'

But Merryn was already searching his memory, certain that he'd seen something like it before. Then a thought occurred to him. 'Wait here a sec. I've got an idea.' He hurried downstairs, returning with a small silver bowl, not much bigger than half an orange, supported by three ornately-carved legs. He handed it to Zac.

'My gran left it to my dad when she died. He says it's solid silver. Look at the bottom of it.'

167

Zac turned it over. There, stamped into the underside of the bowl were four symbols, similar to those on the pistol but large enough to read without magnification.

M^N&W^B ⚓ 🦁 Z

'Good effort.' Zac was impressed. 'Slight problem, though. None of the symbols match.'

'Of course they don't match. One's a gun made of gold – we think – and the other's a silver bowl for holding a tea strainer. What we need is a code-book for deciphering the symbols.' Merryn sat down at the computer and typed *"dating silver antiques"* into Google.

'Got it! The symbols are the hallmark.' He pointed at the first search result. It read *"Hallmarks – antique silver."* He opened the page and scrolled down. 'Look, it says there are usually four stamps in a silver hallmark. The maker's mark – that tells you who made it, obviously; the town mark tells you where the item was tested and hallmarked; the standard mark – how pure the silver is; and then the date letter – how old it is.'

Zac could scarcely believe the speed with which Merryn had extracted the information from the web. 'You're scaring me. That was less than two minutes.'

Merryn was in his element, his fingers at the controls of an information rollercoaster, twisting and spiralling its way through cyberspace. This was what he loved more than anything, feeding the machine with just a few, tiny pieces of an enormous jigsaw and watching, intoxicated, while it unfailingly began to generate the picture. He could never get used to the colossal power of the internet, the sheer immensity of its range and speed. It always left him dizzied, exhausted, but craving another ride.

'We'll crack the silver code first. Dress rehearsal. Right, got it. M^N

and W[B.] That's Mappin and Webb, the makers. The town mark is an anchor which means… that the bowl was tested and hallmarked in Birmingham.'

'Tested for what?' Zac interrupted.

'Purity. How much silver there is. The lion is the standard mark. That means the bowl is sterling silver. 92.5 per cent silver, 7.5 per cent copper. The more copper that's added, the redder the silver looks. Which leaves the Z. That's the date letter. Hang on. I need to do another search.'

'Tut, tut, Merryn. You're almost over your two-minute time limit.'

'Very funny. Here we go. Birmingham date letters. Every letter in the alphabet represents a different year.'

'That's dull. There's only twenty-six letters. They must have run out after twenty-six years.'

Merryn sighed patiently. 'It's not just the letter you've got to look at. It's whether it's capital or lower case *and* the shape of the box that it's written in. There's about ten different box shapes. Ten lots of twenty-six times two. Is that better?'

'Smarty-pants.'

'So, a Z in a square with rounded corners is… 1899. Let's work this out. Dad says that the cup originally belonged to his great-grandmother. Granny, Dad's mum, was born around… well, she's 71 now, so…'

'1948.' Zac's maths was one of his stronger subjects.

'Okay, so her mother would have been born maybe twenty-five years earlier.'

'1923 and her mother, your dad's great-grandmother in 1898.'

'So 1899 makes sense.'

'Right, dress rehearsal over. Time to get serious. Gold hallmarks.'

But Merryn wasn't listening. The rollercoaster had come to a grinding halt and he just sat motionless in his chair, wondering whether there was any point in carrying on. '1774' he said in a quiet voice.

'What d'you mean 1774?' Zac looked perplexed.

'1774. That's when the pistol was made. Look at the date letters. The letter B in a shield-shaped box; according to the website, that means 1774.'

Zac scanned down the list of dates on the screen. The years 1773 to 1798 were all represented by capital letters of the alphabet, A to Z, in a shield.

'So? The pistol was made in 1774. Why's that a problem? That's two hundred and something years old. Two hundred and forty-five to be exact. I mean, that's bloody old.'

Merryn spun round in his chair. 'You haven't been thinking what I've been thinking ever since we found it?'

'No one on the planet thinks like you. Your brain is too...' He paused, trying to find the right word. 'Weird. So what *have* you been thinking?'

Merryn hesitated. He felt stupid saying it, now that the hallmark proved beyond doubt that the pistol had been made in the late eighteenth century. 'I thought maybe the pistol belonged to Wintour but it can't have. All the websites and that book in the library – they all say that Wintour was ambushed in 1645.'

'Oh my God, you're fixated with Mr Wintour and his leap. Look, it's an amazing find no matter who it belonged to, so finish the job. If the butt is made of gold, it's got to be worth serious money.'

Merryn typed in "*hallmarks gold* and held his breath. He selected the first result that made any sense and clicked on it.

'I don't believe it!' exclaimed Zac, staring at the hallmark on the screen. 'It *is* made of gold. You don't need a field agent. You can do it all just by sitting at a computer.'

'Here we go. HvD. Must be the maker's mark but Google doesn't recognise it. It'll take a bit longer to track that down. 750 is the purity mark. It means that the butt is 750 parts gold out of 1000. Seventy-five per cent. Nowadays, that would be...' Merryn paused, scrolling down the page. '18 out of 24. That's 18 carat gold.'

'Seventy-five per cent? Is that all?' Zac sounded surprised. 'So what's the rest of it made of?'

'It just says "other metals". Pure gold is too soft on its own so they add other stuff to make it harder. Ah, found it. Equal amounts of silver and copper. So twelve and a half per cent silver, twelve and a half per cent copper. Now for the cat's head. It's a leopard. It means the pistol was made in London. If it was made before 1821, then the leopard wears a crown. After 1821, he loses his crown.'

'So the pistol was made before 1821. We know that. You said 1774.'

Merryn nodded. 'Capital B in a shield – 1774.'

'And silver and gold date letters are the same?'

'Yep. Before 1798, silver and gold hallmarks used the same date letters so…' Merryn never finished his sentence because the sound of a key opening the front door signalled Donna and Charlie's return. Zac swiftly wrapped the gun in his rugby shirt and laid it carefully back into his grip bag.

'You'd better go otherwise mum will tie you to a chair and beat a confession out of you.'

'I'll bring the pistol in on Monday. That gives you a whole day on the internet to find the answers to all the questions we haven't answered yet.' Zac thought for a moment. 'Actually, have we answered any questions?'

Merryn shrugged. 'We don't know who owned it or how it ended up down the crack. We don't know who it belongs to now or how much it's worth.'

'Looks like you've got your work cut out, then. See you Monday and I want answers.' Zac picked up his grip bag and hurried down the stairs. Escaping from Number 14 Church Close, however, was not going to be that easy.

'Ah, it's Zac, isn't it?'

Zac jumped. Donna appeared suddenly in the hall behind him. 'Oh, hello Mrs MacIntyre. Just came over to see Merryn because he wasn't in school yesterday and I thought I'd... er... check how he's getting on with his head, which looks pretty nasty, actually, what with the big lump, I mean.' Zac decided to stop talking before he said something stupid. And incriminating.

'That's kind of you, Zac. Merryn's head certainly does look pretty nasty. Has he told you how he got the injury?'

Merryn's right, thought Zac. She's going to tie me to a chair. 'Well, not really. He was a bit vague. Just that he sort of... er... fell over.'

'So it seems.' Donna paused and Zac wondered whether this was a signal that he could go now. He opened the front door and was about to say goodbye when Donna ambushed him for a second time.

'I understand you're a Green Day fan, is that right? I only ask because I used to listen to a lot of their stuff when I was younger.'

'Oh,' was all Zac could find to say as he struggled to make sense of the question. Had Merryn told her? Surely not. Then he said, 'Well, yes, as a matter of fact, I'm a bit of a ska-punk fan, Green Day in particular.'

'I thought so,' Donna said, a sly look on her face. 'Just wait there a moment, Zac. I've got something that I think belongs to you,' and she disappeared down the hall to the kitchen. Moments later she returned carrying a tee shirt ripped open along one seam. Printed on one side were the words *Green Day* together with the faces of three band members. 'I've tried washing out all the blood but it'll need another wash. Mind, it's not much use now that it's been ripped, eh?' She handed it to Zac who could think of no other response than 'Thanks, Mrs MacIntyre. Not much use, like you say.'

Merryn, who'd been crouched out of sight on the stairs, waited for Donna to return to the kitchen and then quickly came down and followed Zac out into the garden.

'See what I told you. MI5. I never told her you were a Green Day fan. Now she knows you were there at the cliffs.'

'Bloody hell, Merry, how do you ever get away with stuff? You know, like stealing food from the fridge or losing your footy boots?'

'I don't. There's no point in lying. She's got supernatural mind-reading powers.'

'But you're lying now. About Thursday night, I mean. What will she do if she finds out about the pistol?'

'She mustn't find out. She'll take it to the police and I'll be grounded for five years. We've just got to act normal like nothing out of the ordinary is happening.'

Zac looked over Merryn's shoulder. Donna was watching them from the front door. 'Okay, act normal it is, then. See you Monday,' and with that he turned and headed home.

CHAPTER 10

Sunday 8th September

Merryn spent most of Sunday tapping away at his computer keyboard, searching the information superhighway for something, anything that would tell him more about the pistol. Yet, the longer he sat staring at the screen, the more frustrated he grew. Google offered him nothing. Every search string drew a blank. By the time Donna called him down for lunch at one o'clock, Merryn was coming to the conclusion that the pistol he'd rescued from the crevice was unique. Golden flintlocks, it seemed, didn't exist anywhere outside of Zac's grip bag. He sat morosely at the kitchen table, a deep frown etched into his face and completely oblivious of Charlie's boisterous attempts to communicate with him. Donna ignored him. She would have got more response from a corpse.

After lunch, Merryn decided that there was little hope of tracking down the original owner of the pistol so he turned his attention to an equally intriguing question – to whom did the pistol *now* belong? He had already searched the miscellaneous shelf in his brain – the location of a vast store of unclassified trivia – and located the story of Mr and Mrs Casey who found a winning lottery ticket on a shop floor. They'd cashed it in for a £30,000 prize having made no effort to find its rightful owner. The couple had made an entirely understandable mistake, believing that the rules of the game they'd played as five-year-olds – Finders Keepers, Losers Weepers – applied just as much to a £30,000 lottery ticket as it did to the gob-stopper that fell out of Mandy's pocket in the school playground. Merryn dialled them up on Google and discovered, much to his horror, that they'd both received an 11-month suspended prison sentence. But that was a lottery ticket bought in 2009. This was a pistol made in 1774. Finding the owner of a mislaid winning lottery ticket seemed to Merryn a pretty straightforward task. Finding the owner of the golden flintlock was going to prove far more challenging. However, that didn't stop him wondering what the inside of a prison cell looked like.

He keyed "treasure" into Google and found an article on the Treasure Act of 1996. *"If you're lucky enough to dig up an item of gold or silver,"* it began, *"then your first task is to decide if the item is treasure or not".* [1]

Luck? thought Merryn. No, it wasn't luck that had led him to the pistol. He'd been guided by a woman from somewhere beyond the physical world, a woman who had known exactly where the pistol had lain since it was hidden there perhaps two hundred years ago, maybe more. He read on. There were five categories of treasure.

"Category 1: All objects, other than coins, which are at least 300 years old and contain at least 10% gold or silver."

Nope. The pistol was less than 300 years old.

Categories two, three and four referred to coins or prehistoric items. It was category five that made him sit up.

"Category 5: Objects that are less than 300 years old and made substantially of gold or silver, which have been deliberately hidden with the intention of recovery, and whose owners or heirs are unknown."

'Bingo!' he exclaimed aloud. *Deliberately hidden with the intention of recovery*. He was sure of it. *And whose owners or heirs are unknown*. He

---

[1] Contains public sector information licensed under the Open Government Licence v3.0. Sourced from http://www.legislation.gov.uk/ukpga/1996/24/contents

couldn't be so sure of that. The article continued;

"According to law, all finds of treasure must be reported to the local coroner within 14 days after the day on which the treasure was found. Failure to report a find without reasonable excuse is a criminal offence and carries a penalty of up to three months in prison."

He'd no idea who a coroner was, but the word "local" suggested that there were plenty of them around. As for "14 days", that meant there was no immediate rush to hand over the pistol. Yet, despite this, the prison cell that was taking shape in his imagination suddenly contained two inmates, both aged fifteen. His eyes fell on the next paragraph.

"All objects which qualify as treasure are deemed to belong to the Crown. However, the British Museum may wish to buy the item from the Crown at its market value. If so, then the Secretary of State will decide how much of this payment goes to the finder and how much to the landowner."

The Crown? Does that mean the queen? But if the pistol belongs to the queen, why would the British Museum buy it and pay the finder and the landowner? It made no sense. In any case, who was this Secretary of State? Was he or she a member of parliament? It seemed that a lot of people were suddenly involved and the only one that Merryn could be certain about was the finder. He sat motionless for a few minutes, reading and re-reading the paragraph on the screen. Then he turned his attention to the last of the people mentioned in the article – the landowner. Who owned that tiny sliver of land between the road and the cliff top? With Google up on the screen, Merryn's fingers hovered over the keyboard ready to launch another mission into the stratosphere but, before he could even begin the countdown, his mother's voice yelled up the stairs.

'Merryn! It's your father. He's waiting outside to take you to the hospital for your check-up. Have you forgotten?'

Merryn made a face and mouthed an obscenity. He was catching habits from Zac. He deleted his browsing history and shut down the computer. The landowner would have to wait.

CHAPTER 11

Monday 9th September

At half past eight the following morning, Zac was waiting for Merryn at the school gates.

'Hey, more fashion statements! Love it! How's the head?'

The hospital doctor had dressed Merryn's wound, wrapping an elasticated bandage several times around his head, leaving only a small crop of hair projecting from the top. It left him looking like a cross between a punk and a Native American Indian. The throbbing had finally subsided and he was given the all-clear to return to school.

'Take it easy,' his father had said to him in the van going home. 'No more midnight walkabouts, eh?'

But Merryn had no intention of taking it easy. A piece of history had dropped into his lap. It wasn't a painting from one of his bedroom posters or a webpage on his computer screen. Instead, it was solid and tangible with real life drama written into its golden butt and rusty barrel.

'Yeah, it's okay. Headache's gone. Don't know what the stupid bandage is for. The cut stopped bleeding on Friday.'

'Preventing infection, probably. So, tell me what you found out yesterday. I'll put money on you knowing everything about the pistol by now.'

But Zac would have lost his money. Merryn knew little more about the pistol's origins than when Zac had last seen him.

'It's treasure which means it belongs to the queen. The government will ask the British Museum if they want to buy it and then Secretary of State will decide if we get any money or if it all goes to the landowner. That's it.'

'The *queen* owns it?' Zac looked at Merryn as though two horns had just grown out through his bandage. 'Are you mad? There's no way we're handing the pistol over to the queen. She's got loads of antiques already. She'll probably stuff it in some glass cabinet in Windsor Castle and forget all about it. Anyway, she's never going to know we – actually *you* – found it.'

'Yes she will. You can't keep something like this secret for ever. And when she does, we'll both get three months in prison. You dragged me out of the crevice, remember, so you'll be just as guilty.'

'Rubbish. They don't send minors to prison. So, that's all you've found out? A load of gobbledygook about the queen and the government?'

'It isn't gobbledygook.' Merryn rolled his eyes. 'Zac, you don't understand. It's not that easy. There's nothing else like this pistol. It's been down a crack for nearly two hundred and fifty years. I reckon we're the first people to see it since its owner hid it there.'

'Dropped it there, you mean. Okay, you're the boss. Whatever you say. Remember, I'm just the field agent. We need an expert, though, so are we still on for plan A?'

'Plan A? You mean we show the pistol to Miss Kelly? We've got no choice. It's either that or take it to the police.'

'That's a choice, actually. At least Miss Kelly won't phone Buckingham Palace and tell the queen that...' Zac's voice tailed off. A small group of Year 11 girls on the far side of the school yard had caught his attention. They were gathered in a huddle and one of them was pointing animatedly at Merryn and Zac.

'Hey, Merryn, looks like you've got an admirer. That's Beatrice in the middle. Pretty girl, eh?'

'Yeah, not bad, I guess. Do you know her?'

'Not really, but I know some of her friends. She's from Kenya, apparently. Sara, that's the one on her right, told me Beatrice has never met her real father. Can you imagine that?'

Merryn couldn't. 'How come? Did he die before she was born?'

'Nope. Apparently, he vanished after a one-night stand with her mother. But, for God's sake, you didn't hear that from me, right!'

'Uh-huh. So how did she come to be here?' The longer Merryn stared at Beatrice, the more he wanted to know.

'I think her mum married some English bloke, a fridge salesman. That's what Sara said, but they've split up.'

Merryn frowned. 'Fifteen and she's lost her dad *and* a step-dad. How unlucky is that?'

'You're lucky, Merry. A lot of kids don't have both parents.' Zac paused as though he had something to add but the moment passed. Then he laughed and said, 'She's still pointing at you.'

'More likely pointing at my stupid bandage.' Merryn tried unsuccessfully to flatten the tufts of hair which projected up from the crown of his head. 'I knew this would happen. Anyway, how d'you know she's not pointing at you?'

'We could find out, if you like.'

The bell came to Merryn's rescue. Six hundred students melted slowly from the yard into either end of a long, three-storey, glass building. On the top floor, Merryn and Zac parted company since they registered in different forms.

'Library. Break time. Don't be late.' Zac patted his day sack with one hand and disappeared into room 301. Further down the corridor, Miss Grigoryev stood in her doorway waiting to intercept Merryn.

'Mr MacIntyre!' she exclaimed. 'Your head! I cannot believe it! What is happening? Have you been hit by a car?'

Merryn was rather taken aback. 'No, miss. I just fell over and…

hit some railings.' He didn't like lying to Miss Grigoryev but he couldn't tell her the truth. 'It's all right. Just a small cut, that's all,' he lied some more.

'I'm sorry. You gave me a shock. I am glad you are okay. Come in and close the door, Merryn. I have bad news, I'm afraid. So very bad.'

It was obvious from the woman's expression that something terrible had happened. The smile that normally creased her face with a myriad of wrinkles had vanished and in its place was a tight frown. There were tell-tale smudges of make-up down both cheeks and her lips, normally adorned with bright red lipstick, were grey and bloodless.

'Please sit.' She ushered him to a chair. Alarm bells suddenly started ringing inside his head. Only the worst kind of news required the recipient to be sitting down. Miss Grigoryev turned her face away from Merryn. When she spoke, her voice was almost a whisper. 'Did you watch the news yesterday, Merryn? BBC Points West?'

Merryn shook his head, dreading what was coming next.

'Mr Biddle has been hit by a car. He was cycling back from the centre of Bath, where he had been filming, to the guest house where he stays – it's not far, a little village called Monkton Farleigh. He is in Bristol Royal Infirmary now – intensive care. He has...' She was struggling to stay in control. 'He has broken bones in his left arm. Here.' She pointed at her forearm. 'Also broken ribs. Three. But worse, he has head injuries. Like you, but they are bad. He has been unconscious since the accident.' She went to her desk and pulled out some tissues from a drawer.

Merryn could scarcely believe what he was hearing.

'When did it happen, miss?'

'The headteacher, she phones me on Friday with the news but I know...' She stopped abruptly and turned her face to the window. It was a few moments before she continued. 'The head, she says that Mr Biddle has an accident on Thursday around eight in the evening. Someone at the BBC phones her early on Friday morning. It was a hit and run. The driver, he never stopped. The police, they appeal for witnesses. I tell him so many times that it is not good to cycle in the dark without lights but he never listens to me; and he does not wear a helmet. So now…' That was as far as Miss Grigoryev got. She sat down behind her desk and wept. 'I'm sorry, Merryn. You must go,' she said between sobs. Merryn picked up his bag and, unable to think of anything helpful to say, went to open the door. A thought suddenly occurred to him.

'Miss, do they allow visitors? In the hospital?'

She looked up, dabbing her cheeks. 'No. Family only.'

'Does he have any family?'

'He has a brother. That is all. I don't know where he is.' Miss Grigoryev blew her nose and stood up. 'They let me see him, Merryn. I will tell you if there is news. You register in 312, yes?'

Merryn nodded.

'Now you must go. I have made you late.'

*

When the bell went at eleven o'clock for break, Merryn could remember nothing of the first two lessons. He sat at the back, his mind in complete turmoil and tried to make sense of what Miss Grigoryev had told him. Hit and run, she'd said. Maybe Mr Biddle would be able to identify the car that had hit him when he regained consciousness. *If* he regained consciousness. He didn't want to think about it. Instead he thought about the little Russian woman. *They let me see him*. That didn't make sense. She wasn't family. He packed his books away and headed for the library.

'Good heavens!' Miss Kelly exclaimed when they pushed their way into the library against a torrent of Year 7's going the other way. 'This is getting to be a habit. And Merryn! What on earth have you done to your head?'

Merryn's well-rehearsed reply to that question, vague and wholly unconvincing, did little to quell the English teacher's curiosity. Zac interrupted before the questions started.

'Miss, we were hoping you could help us, actually.' Zac put his rucksack on a table and looked around furtively to see if there was anyone else in the library. There wasn't.

'And what exactly is it you want me to do?' Miss Kelly's voice was laced with suspicion.

'You mentioned that your dad – I mean your father,' Merryn corrected himself. 'You said that he used to go fishing with an antiques dealer. We've forgotten his name.'

'Isaac Levi. They still do go fishing together, every Sunday. What about him?'

'Well, we've found something that we'd like Mr Levi to look at. It's pretty old.'

'Seventeen seventy-four,' Zac chimed in.

'And we need someone who knows about antiques to look at it.'

'Would you like to see it?' Zac asked. He was reading the expression on Miss Kelly's face. Curiosity was written all over it.

'Okay. Show me. But be ready to answer some questions.'

Zac opened his rucksack and took out a thick bath towel. He laid it gently on the table, glanced at the library door, and then carefully began to unroll it until, suddenly, the pistol lay naked on the table, its golden fox gleaming brighter than ever.

Miss Kelly gasped. 'Oh my God! You *found* this?'

'At Wintour's Leap,' said Merryn. 'Last Thursday. We wanted to see if it was possible to gallop over the cliffs and survive.'

'You *what?*' Her voice suddenly rose by an octave. 'Because you found a picture of Wintour jumping into the river, you actually went to the cliffs? Your parents knew about this, didn't they? I mean, if anything had happened to you…' She stared at the bandage around Merryn's head. 'Oh, please tell me you didn't get that injury at the cliffs.'

It was pointless denying it. Guilt was stamped across his face and Zac's smirk just confirmed her worst fears. Miss Kelly buried her face in her hands and quietly shook her head in disbelief.

'Okay.' Her voice was back down to its normal register as she struggled to regain control. 'I want some answers to some pretty serious questions. First, how much do your parents know about this?' She motioned to the pistol.

The boys looked at each other, neither wanting to go first.

'Look, we haven't got time for this. It's ten minutes until the bell rings. Do your parents know what's going on here?'

'No, they don't, miss.' Merryn hadn't expected Miss Kelly to react like this. He'd imagined she would be as excited as he and Zac.

'And why not?'

Zac took over. 'Miss, it's not as bad as it seems. We were just curious about the legend. It's true, we went down to have a look – the cliffs are not that far from my house. Merryn just fell over some railings into a sort of crack. It was hidden by branches and stuff. That's where he found the pistol. In the crack under a rock. We haven't told our parents yet because they would take the pistol straight to the police. We wanted to do this ourselves. That's why we've come to see you.'

Miss Kelly sat quietly for a few moments, taking in Zac's account. 'How did you explain your injury, Merryn? To your parents, I mean. Like you did to me?'

Merryn nodded. 'Pretty much, miss.'

'And they know nothing about this?' She motioned to the pistol.

He shook his head. 'If I showed them the pistol, like Zac said, they'd take it straight to the police or Chepstow Museum or somewhere. It would be the last we'd see of it.'

Miss Kelly picked up the pistol and turned it over in her hands.

'Oh my goodness, it's heavy,' she whispered.

'The fox is gold, miss. Solid gold, we think. There's a hallmark. Look.' Merryn pointed at the four tiny symbols stamped into the butt.

'Solid gold? Are you sure?' The tone in her voice had changed. The pistol was working its magic. 'It *looks* like gold and yet the barrel is so rusty.' She gripped the fox in one hand and slid her finger around the trigger. 'It's amazing. The detail on the fox is so intricate. I've never seen anything like it before. Look at the teeth. You could count them. And the jewels for eyes. They look like emeralds.' She laid it down on the towel. 'Solid gold.' She looked at the two boys in turn. 'It must be worth an absolute fortune. And it was made in 1774? How do you know that?'

'The hallmark, miss. There's a date letter that tells you when it was made. We know it was made in London and it's eighteen carat gold.'

'That's very impressive, Mr MacIntyre. Doesn't surprise me, though.' The hint of a smile crossed Miss Kelly's face before she looked at her watch. 'Okay, this is what happens next. I'll speak to Mr Levi and arrange for you to take the pistol to his shop in Chepstow. Sometime this week after school, I suggest. That's my part of the deal. Your part is to tell your parents where you're going and why. Is that clear? You cannot keep something like this from them.'

The boys looked at each other again.

'Yes, miss,' declared Zac. He nodded imperceptibly at Merryn. 'I'll get Sasha – my mum – to give us a lift down after school. I've got a match on Wednesday but any other day is fine. Merryn?'

'Yeah, any day's okay with me.'

Miss Kelly nodded. 'I'll let you know later on today. In the meantime, Zac, you should get this locked away somewhere. As for Mr Levi, he is going to have an absolute fit when he sees it. He's bad enough when he gets his hands on a piece of plain Victorian china.'

The bell went. As the boys got up to leave, a thought suddenly occurred to Merryn.

'Miss, could I borrow that book on the history of Chepstow? It might have some clues about Wintour. Google isn't really helping.'

Zac sniggered. 'He's still convinced, miss, that Wintour jumped over the cliffs. He reckons that the pistol has something to do with Wintour as well just because he found it down a crack a few feet from the edge of the cliffs.'

'Zac, I don't want to hear where he found the pistol. I'm going to have nightmares about this. And Merryn, I'm afraid that a friend of yours beat you to it. The book's already been borrowed.'

'A friend of mine?' Merryn didn't have many friends, certainly none that shared his passion for history.

'Mr Mear. He came in looking for books on the English Civil War on Friday afternoon. The only one that even mentions the war is the book you're after.'

Merryn made a face. He wanted to read what the book had to say about Wintour and Colonel Massey's ambush. Now he was going to have to ask Mear for the book, not an encounter that he relished.

Once the two boys had gone, Miss Kelly fished out a phone from her bag and called Isaac Levi. She was about to hang up when an elderly voice answered. 'Who is it?'

'Isaac! It's Sian Kelly. Listen, are you sitting down?'

CHAPTER 12

Isaac Levi's reaction to Miss Kelly's description of the pistol was entirely predictable. For a seventy-five-year old, he was blessed with a bountiful reservoir of energy which in this instance was channelled into a series of unintelligible splutterings down the phone. Miss Kelly ignored his forceful insistence that the boys escort the pistol to him at once and instead, made an appointment for the following afternoon.

Merryn's attempts at extracting the history book from Mr Mear at lunchtime had a less predictable outcome. Summoning up his reserves of courage, he knocked at the staffroom door, already ajar. While he waited for a response, he read the notice pinned to the door which announced that staff would be in a brief meeting with the head until one thirty and, in the event of an emergency, pupils should contact one of the lunchtime supervisors. He was about to give up when he caught snatches of an agitated conversation between two men coming from inside the room. Clearly, they had boycotted the briefing. Mear's voice was unmistakable but Merryn couldn't place the other although he was certain he'd heard it before. He pushed the door open a fraction more and listened.

'I told you, Ez, I ordered it Friday morning, first thing. It weren't easy finding one, believe me. Next working day delivery means I'll get it today.'

'As soon as you get it, bring it round.' That was Mear.

'Don't know why you couldn't order it yourself.'

'It's safer this way, Jed. Hope to God you've ordered the right bloody side.'

'Nearside. I ain't…'

Suddenly, the door slammed shut. For a few seconds, Merryn just stood staring at it, wondering what to do next. It was obvious that the men didn't want to be disturbed so he abandoned his efforts at retrieving the book and instead wandered into the canteen and joined the queue. He was still some distance from the serving hatch when Miss Kelly slalomed her way across the canteen.

'I've made an appointment with Mr Levi at four o'clock tomorrow,' she told him. 'You should be back around half five at the latest. Do you know how to get there?'

Merryn nodded. 'Zac'll find out. His mum is giving us a lift down there.'

'And you'll tell your parents, yes?'

Merryn nodded again. 'Levi Antiques. Four o'clock. Back at half five.' He looked up. 'Are you going to be there, miss?'

Miss Kelly smiled. 'I think it's best if I'm there to introduce the pair of you. The old man can be a bit overwhelming at times. He has a habit of taking over without being invited so, yes, I'll be there as back-up, just in case.' She wondered if Merryn could see through her rather feeble answer. In truth, she was as excited about the pistol as they were. If Isaac Levi didn't have the answers they were after, then he certainly knew people who did. Of course she'd be there.

As she turned to go, Merryn said, 'One more thing, miss. I tried to ask Mr Mear for the book he's borrowed, the one on Chepstow history, but he closed the staffroom door so I never got the chance to speak to him. I was wondering…'

'You want me to ask him, is that it?' She no more wished to engage Ezra Mear in conversation than Merryn but that wasn't something she could admit to.

'Please. Do you mind?'

'I'll see what I can do.' She lowered her voice. 'Maybe he's had time to calm down a little.' She headed off down the corridor to the staffroom. Mear was sitting at the back when she entered, feet on a chair, hypnotised by the screen on his iPhone.

'Can't it wait?' was his initial response, spiked with a cold contempt that infuriated her.

'Actually, it can't. It's urgent.' Her temper had a short lead as some of her Year 10 pupils knew to their cost, and she resisted the overwhelming urge to let it run free. That wouldn't get the book. 'One of my students needs it for a project.'

'And who might that be?' he asked.

Bloody cheek, Miss Kelly thought. Why the hell should it matter *who* it is? 'One of my most promising students,' she replied. 'Merryn MacIntyre, if you must know.'

'MacIntyre?' Mear scoffed. 'Promising? Pain in the neck, more like. Anyway, I thought you taught English, not history.'

'The book is written in English.' Miss Kelly's temper was tugging frantically at the lead now. 'Have you finished with the book?'

Mear abruptly sat up, his eyes focused on some distant point in the room. For a moment, he remained quite still as though in a trance until he turned to look at Miss Kelly.

'You say MacIntyre wants the book?'

'That's what I said. He wants to know more about Wintour's Leap so if you've finished with it…'

'Wintour's Leap?' Mear's dark eyes narrowed as though he were deep in thought. Then he nodded. 'Okay. He can have the book but you'll have to wait while I make some notes.' He lifted a small black briefcase from the floor beside him, spun a combination lock and lifted the lid. 'Come back in five minutes.' He waved her away with a condescending sweep of his arm. The lead snapped and Sian Kelly's temper was free. She stormed out into the corridor before her vocal cords had a chance to voice what she was thinking. What was it Zac had called him? A scumbag? That was too kind. What was the school thinking of when they appointed him as a temporary replacement for Mr Biddle? Had there really been no one else? She paced up and down the corridor outside the staffroom, burning off her fury, desperately trying to regain control of her emotions.

The staffroom door opened and Mear stood, holding up the book.

'Something wrong, Miss Kelly?' he sniped.

She held his gaze but those dark, lifeless eyes frightened her. She stepped forward and snatched the book from his hand.

'Ezra – it is *Ez-ra*, isn't it?' She emphasized the first syllable, a mocking tone in her voice. She couldn't help herself. 'If you want to borrow books from the library, your name needs to be on the staff database on the library computer. Ten minutes from now, it won't be. Shame.' She made to step past him, but Mear blocked her escape with his outstretched arm against the wall. He leaned over the young woman's diminutive frame, his head tilted forward so that his dishevelled black curls almost brushed her face. 'Don't threaten me, Kelly,' he spat. 'I'm a member of staff, just like you, and I'll borrow any book I damn well please.'

He turned and disappeared into the staffroom leaving Miss Kelly seething in the corridor. She stormed off to the library, immediately opened the staff database and highlighted *Ezra Mear*.

'No you damn well won't,' she muttered under her breath and hammered the delete key so hard that she almost broke the keyboard. She sat motionless for a few minutes, trying unsuccessfully to get the spectre of Mear's face out of her mind's eye. It lingered there, staring at her, those two, cold, dark eyes drilling their way past her outer defences into her very soul. She shuddered, partly with disgust, partly with fear. She would take steps to avoid Mear from now on. What was it Merryn had said? *We've got him for four weeks.* She wasn't sure she could keep her mouth shut for that long.

When she returned to the canteen, Merryn was sitting on his own, stabbing apathetically at a plate of cold spaghetti.

'I think it might take a while longer for Mr Mear to thaw,' she said, handing over the book. Merryn read her expression perfectly and nodded.

'Thanks, miss.'

As soon as she was gone, he pushed aside the spaghetti, opened the book and turned to the drawing of Wintour leaping from the cliff top. He wondered if the artist had actually seen the cliffs since the scale was hopelessly inaccurate. The horse and rider were too large, the cliffs too small. Zac was right. No one could have survived such a fall on the back of a horse. Below the drawing, the author chronicled the events surrounding the leap, drawing upon what little evidence he could muster from parish records and oral testimony.

"Standing a mile and a half north of Chepstow on the Lancaut peninsula lies the ruined church of St James. It was the scene of a most bloody conflict in 1645 when the peninsula was occupied by a party of Royalists under the command of Sir John Wintour. His party arrived at low water to repair the ford which crosses the river at this point. Before they could complete the task, they were attacked by a superior force of the enemy. A number of Wintour's dragoons perished in the ensuing skirmish but Sir John himself escaped, reaching the cliff top which lies to the south of the peninsula. Being closely pursued, Wintour galloped in desperation over the precipice and escaped unhurt by swimming the river to Chepstow."

It was only after he had read the passage twice, consigning every detail to the Wintour shelf in his memory, that he noticed the thin pencil line that underlined one phrase in the passage: *"the ford which crosses the river at this point."* In addition, someone had scribbled notes along the page margin but, before he could read them, Beatrice Odoyo walked up to his table and stood, arms folded, glaring down at him.

'You're Merryn MacIntyre, aren't you?' she began, threateningly.

Merryn looked up in surprise. Beatrice was small compared to most of the girls in Year 11. Her jet black hair had been braided for half its length while the rest of it tumbled onto her shoulders in a mass of shiny curls. She wore brilliant-coloured clusters of bangles on each wrist and dazzling red varnish on her nails. None of this, however, was mirrored in her expression. Instead, she wore a dark frown, her eyes narrowed into slits and her lips tightly pursed together.

'I'm… er… yes. Merryn. Why?' He shifted uncomfortably in his chair. Like Zac had said, she did have a pretty face but right now it was obvious that Beatrice wasn't here to make polite conversation.

'You're Malcolm's boy, isn't that right?' She said it as though it were an accusation.

'Malcolm's my dad.' Merryn shrugged his shoulders. 'So?'

'Your dad owns a shop in Tidenham, doesn't he?' She didn't wait for an answer. 'My mum works there. She's worked there for two years. It was the only job she could get when we moved here. She's got no fancy qualifications – GCSEs and stuff. And now your dad's told her she's got one week left and then she has to go. Just like that. And then what are we supposed to do? If she can't get another job, then we'll have to leave. Do you know what that means?'

This time she did wait for an answer. All this was news to Merryn. To begin with, he'd never made the connection between Malika, who'd started working at his father's shop two years ago and the girl who was scowling at him now. On his last visit to the shop just ten days ago, Malika had been there, larger than life, teasing him with her wicked sense of humour just like she always did. He liked Malika. She made him laugh.

'I didn't know my dad had made her redundant.'

'You didn't know your dad had *sacked* her. *Sacked*, Merryn. That's the word. We'll have to go back to Kenya and live with relatives in Mombasa and my mum won't get the treatment she needs.' Tears had begun to well up in Beatrice's eyes. For a few moments, she couldn't speak. Then she lowered her voice and leaned over the table. 'You need to tell that to your dad because Mum won't tell anyone, especially him. She needs treatment and she won't get it in Mombasa. It's too expensive there, do you understand?' A fat tear slipped from her eye and rolled all the way to her chin. She wiped it away. 'Please.'

'Okay, I'll tell him. But I'm not sure it'll make any difference. The shop is...'

'Just tell him. It *will* make a difference. If your dad knows how much Mum needs the job, then he won't ask her to leave. Please talk to your dad.'

There was no point in arguing, Merryn decided. Beatrice clearly had not the faintest idea of the plight facing his father's business. Malika must know. How could she not? Fewer customers, less money in the till at the end of the day, more unsold fruit and veg spoiling on the shelves – she had kept it all hidden from her daughter and now Malcolm could no longer afford to pay her wages. Merryn knew that whatever misfortunes the Odoyu family were suffering right now, there was nothing his dad could do about it.

Suddenly he became aware that half the canteen was watching the encounter between the pretty Kenyan girl and the history geek, sensing that some drama was playing out that might escalate into a full-throttled dust-up. No one was in any doubt as to who would come off worse but sadly for them, Beatrice turned and walked back to her friends, leaving the geek fully intact.

*

There was no one home when Merryn arrived back from school. He went straight to his room, closed the door and switched on his computer. He took out *A Short History of Chepstow* from his bag, sat down at the computer and switched on the desk lamp. While Windows booted up, he found the page with the pencil notes in the margin.

LT 12/9 22:55 PeRi SpRing

His eye fell immediately on the capital R in PeRi and SpRing. They betrayed the author beyond any doubt. The last word in Mear's essay title – waR – written on the whiteboard seven days ago, was still fresh in his memory. He had thought it odd at the time that a teacher should be setting such a poor example, writing capitals instead of lower case. And no one else had borrowed the book from the library. Miss Kelly had said as much. It had to be Mear.

Extracting some meaning from Mear's jottings, however, proved taxing. The key to unlocking the puzzle, he decided, must lie in the phrase that had been underlined in pencil – *the ford which crosses the river at this point*. Ford? He typed the word into Wikipedia.

"A ford is a shallow place with good footing where a river or stream may be crossed by wading or in a vehicle. A ford is mostly a natural phenomenon." [2]

Merryn chewed this over for a while. According to the book, Wintour had taken his party of Royalist dragoons to the river at low water. Of course he had! Suddenly, it made sense. The sea invades the River Wye twice a day and the "shallow place with good footing" would become a very deep place with good swimming when it did. If anyone wanted to cross the river at the ford, they would have to choose their time carefully. LT – that must stand for low tide. So low tide was at 22:55 on 12/9 – the 12th of September. He Googled "Tide times Chepstow River Wye" just to make sure he was on the right track. He was. Merryn checked the date on his Windows calendar. The 12th was next Thursday. But why did Mear want to cross the river on Thursday night? Anyone who lived around the Wye could tell you just how treacherous its bottomless mud slopes were. Venturing anywhere near them at night was suicidal. It made no sense.

Merryn looked back at the text on the scrap of paper. PeRi SpRing made no sense. His Google search drew a frustrating blank so he returned to the website listing the tide times at Chepstow and scrolled down to the bottom of the page, searching for clues. Suddenly, he slapped his forehead. 'Idiot! How did I miss that?' He was looking at a graph of water depth in the River Wye at Chepstow plotted against the time of day on the 13th. A blue line ran across the

---

[2] Wikipedia Creative Commons GND: 4306851-0 desaturated from original: German National Library - From bank to bank by Konrad Droste – Nienburg/Weser 1992

graph from left to right, rising steeply and falling gently, then rising and falling again. High tide, low tide, high tide, low tide. Merryn read the lowest point of the line against the river depth axis. 0.2 metres at the 22:55 low tide. And the highest point: 12.3 metres at 05:10. That meant a rise in river level from low to high tide of 12.1 metres in just over six hours. He converted metres to feet using the computer's calculator. Forty feet. *Forty feet?* That couldn't be right. He did the maths again and got the same answer. All at once, the word 'Spring' made sense. It had been sitting on a miscellaneous shelf all along, filed there during a geography lesson in Year 5 at Primary School. Mr Evans had tried his best to explain, as simply as he could, how the sun and moon pull on the earth's oceans and cause the tides.

'When the sun and moon line up with the earth,' explained Mr Evans to a class of baffled nine-year-olds, 'the sea comes in a long way and goes out a long way. Big tides.'

He'd drawn a diagram on the whiteboard which had scored poorly on artistic merit and only slightly better on scientific merit. Merryn could see it now, a scrawl of circles and arrows. At the top of the board, having abandoned any attempt to link tides with lunar cycles, the increasingly harassed teacher had simply written "Spring Tides."

Quickly, Merryn typed in *"Peri Spring tides"* into Google. This time, Google obliged. 'Perigean Spring tides,' he read aloud. 'The highest and lowest tides of the year when: (1) the moon lies closest to the Earth on its elliptical orbit and (2) the sun and moon are in alignment with the Earth.'

If Merryn had interpreted Mear's notes correctly, then the River Wye at Wintour's Leap would be unusually shallow at five minutes to eleven on Thursday night and where it flowed across the ford, shallower still. The only water flowing over the ford would be fresh river water since the low tide would drain every drop of seawater from the river. There wouldn't be a better time to cross the ford if, that is, the ford still existed. Wikipedia suggested that fords were natural phenomena, geological features running beneath the surface of a river in which case, Merryn reasoned, three hundred and fifty years would make no difference. It would still be there.

But where exactly was 'there'? How could anyone know for certain where it was safe to cross if the ford was always hidden by water, even at low tide? He looked back at the passage in the book describing the leap. *"Standing a mile and a half north of Chepstow on the Lancaut peninsula lies the ruined church of St James."* Perhaps if I find the ruined church, Merryn thought, I find the ford.

With a few, rapid mouse clicks, he opened Google Earth and was soon staring at an aerial view of the river as it ran beneath the Wintour's Leap cliffs. Merryn had never heard of the Lancaut Peninsula, but using the ruler scale on Google Earth, he measured one and a half miles from the outskirts of Chepstow north along the river. At this point, the river took a sharp turn to the left, sweeping round to create a half-mile wide loop. This must be the peninsula, he decided. If it is, then…

'Found you!' he exclaimed out loud. Not far from the southernmost point of the loop lay the ruins of a rectangular building around a hundred metres from the river, at the edge of a clearing in the woods. The footprint of a square tower was just visible at its western end. He zoomed in still further and slid the image across the screen with the mouse so that the river came into view. If the ford still existed, it certainly didn't advertise itself. Merryn examined the banks on both sides of the river but could see nothing which suggested that the river could be crossed. Ten minutes later, he gave up the search and closed the computer down.

Despite the impressive resolution of Google Earth's satellite images, their pixels fell well short of revealing the small, square block of limestone that lay in the grass at the top of the ford, as it had done for several hundred years. As for the cross carved into the block, that would have taxed even the most advanced satellite imaging technology.

Ezra Mear, on the other hand, knew exactly where it was.

CHAPTER 13

Tuesday 10th September

Four years of trial and error had enabled Merryn to calculate the exact time required to walk from house to school at a pace that could be accomplished by a reluctant teenager whose brain was still some distance from full consciousness. This meant that he could delay the detestable act of throwing back the duvet on his bed until eight fifteen and still arrive thirty seconds before the registration bell sounded at eight forty.

On this particular Tuesday morning, however, Merryn arrived at school at eight twenty-one. Striding through the gates, his nervous system was up to speed and raring to go. The prospect of recounting his latest code-breaking efforts to Zac had sent the duvet flying even before his father had left the house at eight o'clock. The school yard would normally have been completely devoid of life at this hour. This morning, however, a tall blond-haired boy and a small, dark-skinned girl wearing a brightly coloured band around her braided hair were sitting at a picnic table on a small island of grass, their backs to Merryn. It was clear by her animated gestures that the girl was doing most of the talking.

Beatrice and Zac.

Merryn darted behind an oak tree growing on one side of the gates and took a deep breath. He'd promised Beatrice that he'd have words with his dad about Malika. But he hadn't. His father, it seemed, had been faced with a stark choice: pay the mortgage or pay Malika. In Merryn's mind, it was that simple. Malcolm had to look after his own family and if that meant that Malika and Beatrice had to return to Kenya, then…

He wondered what was wrong with Malika. She had seemed fine the last time he had seen her – smiling, laughing, joking, poking fun. Perhaps there was nothing wrong with her at all. Perhaps Beatrice was lying. She was using him to manipulate his father's conscience so that he'd make the wrong choice, the choice that would steal the MacIntyre's home. But the anguish in her face had not been a lie and neither had the tears.

Merryn stole a glance across the yard. They were still there, still talking. What was Zac doing? Passing the time of day? Asking her out? Didn't he already have a girlfriend? Whatever he *was* doing, Merryn wasn't about to march up to the pair of them and sit down on the bench. Beatrice would demand to know how successful he'd been at persuading his dad to keep Malika at the shop. No, he'd wait until break at eleven before updating Zac.

When the bell went for registration, he hung back, waiting until the pupil tide had receded before venturing across the yard and in through the south doors. There was no sign of Zac or Beatrice as he made his way cautiously up the stairwell to the top floor. He paused outside Miss Grigoryev's room, wondering whether he should ask her about Mr Biddle. He was desperate for news but the room was already full of Year 11 pupils. Perhaps he should wait until she was alone. After all, the news might be bad. He didn't want to think about it. The notion that Mr Biddle might never return to the school was...

'Mr MacIntyre!' His thoughts were ambushed by a familiar voice which reverberated along the corridor from the stairs. The tiny figure of Miss Grigoryev did her best to hurry but two sagging carrier bags full of exercise books coupled with a long, rather tight skirt and high heels made this impossible. When at last she arrived at room 309, she plonked the bags down outside the door and stood catching her breath.

'I think I retire soon, Merryn. Too much stairs, too much books. How is the head, eh? Still wearing the bandage, I see.'

'It's fine, really. I don't need the bandage. How is Mr Biddle?'

'I have news. Some good, some not so good. First good.' She leaned past Merryn and pulled the door to her form room closed. 'A scan shows no visible damage to George's brain. No bleeding. There is swelling and swelling can be bad, you understand. There is no room for the brain to swell inside the skull. But Doctor Strickland, he thinks the swelling is not so bad and it is subsiding now. So that is good news, Merryn, and we need good news.'

Merryn waited for the not-so-good news. The bad news. Miss Grigoryev took a deep breath and continued.

'George is still in a coma. That is four days and still he is in a coma. I ask Doctor Strickland why George is in a coma for so long if there is no damage to his brain. He says that he has given George a drug to keep him in a deep coma until his breathing and blood pressure are stable. When the brain is in coma, it does just enough to keep the body alive. It can rest, and rest for a damaged brain is good.'

'But Miss, you said the scan showed that there's no damage.' Merryn steeled himself for the bad news. It hadn't arrived yet.

'No, Merryn. I said there was no visible damage. George has received a big blow to his head where he hit the road. Doctor Strickland is worried about the damage that he cannot see, that the scan cannot see.' Miss Grigoryev paused as she struggled to stay calm. For a few seconds, Merryn thought that she was going to break down again but somehow she recovered.

'Tomorrow, the doctor will stop giving the coma-inducing drug. Then we wait for George to wake up. Maybe tomorrow, maybe next week.' Her voice dropped to a whisper. 'Maybe he never wake up.'

Merryn said nothing. His expression said it all.

'We must wait, Merryn.' She stretched out a hand and laid it gently on his arm. 'We must be patient.' She squeezed his arm and stooped to pick up the carrier bags. 'I am sorry, Merryn. I have made you late again but I must tell someone, you understand? It is better for me. We talk again, maybe on Thursday. Now please, can you open the door? My class will be climbing out of the window, I think.'

Merryn opened the door and Miss Grigoryev struggled in to face thirty noisy adolescents. It wasn't until he was sitting in his own registration class two minutes later that the full significance of what she'd said began to sink in. *Maybe he never wake up.* Did that mean that Mr Biddle would remain in a coma indefinitely? No. He would regain consciousness tomorrow when they stopped administering the coma drug. Doctors always painted the worst scenario, just in case.

An hour of maths followed by an hour of personal, social and health education gave Merryn a chance to try and make sense of the whirlwind that had engulfed him since the start of term. In the space of just seven days, the quiet, predictable life that he had led for fifteen years had suddenly and forcefully been sucked from the ground, spun around in some enormous vortex, broken up into a thousand pieces and spat out. Against the irritating drone of Mr Wessells' voice as he lectured Year 11 on the importance of factorising quadratic expressions, Merryn tried desperately to fit some of the pieces together into a picture he could understand. He started by trying to making sense of Mr Biddle's accident. He was still horrified by what Miss Grigoryev had told him earlier. Horrified and angry. How could a driver collide with a cyclist and then simply drive away? Miss Grigoryev had made no mention of the driver. Surely the police were hunting for him. Somewhere he'd read that hit-and-run was a criminal offence. It didn't matter that Mr Biddle had been cycling in the dark without lights. The driver should have stopped and reported the accident to the police and called an ambulance. Perhaps the driver hadn't realised that he'd hit a cyclist. That was unlikely, even in the dark.

But wait! Eight o'clock, Miss Grigoryev had said. It wasn't pitch dark at eight o'clock. On the contrary, it was easily light enough for the driver to know that he or she had hit a cyclist and left him lying unconscious at the side of the road. Merryn's anger was turning to rage. He could understand a driver hitting an animal and failing to stop, but another human being?

'Merryn? Are you with us?' Mr Wessells shook his head in exasperation. 'Does maths exist on the Planet Zardoz or is your new residence entirely devoid of numbers? And what about exams? I suppose they've been banned by the Zardons, eh?'

Merryn didn't like Mr Wessells or his sarcastic sense of humour. He had no idea whether to reply with a yes or a no, so instead he simply said, 'Sorry, sir,' and proceeded to copy down a few lines of algebra from the board into his exercise book. It might as well have been Mandarin. As soon as Mr Wessells became distracted by an argument in the front row, Merryn set to work on another piece in the puzzle. He had turned it over and over in his head but no matter which way he came at it, it made no sense. *I'm your history teacher this year so get used to it.* Why had Mear said 'this year' and not 'this month'? *Get used to it.* You wouldn't say that if you expected to stay for just four weeks and yet both Miss Grigoryev and Miss Kelly were adamant: Mear would be gone at the end of September. But there was something else about the man which disturbed Merryn, something he just couldn't put his finger on. Had they met before?

The bell went.

'Books in for marking, Year 11. I want to see good foundations being laid for a positive outcome at the end of this year.' Mr Wessells stood by the door collecting the class's exercise books. Merryn glanced at the three lines of hastily scribbled algebra that decorated the first page of his new book and wondered whether the outcome would be a short, sharp, verbal battering at the start of his next maths lesson or a more prolonged detention after school. He squeezed out of the room into the corridor and turned left before climbing the stairs to room 217 for PSHE.

Personal, social and health education was not normally a lesson that captivated Year 11's attention for a full hour on Tuesday morning. After all, what could wrinkling adults tell them about the challenges of being a teenager? All that was about to change, however, with the arrival of Mr Parrish, the school's youngest, and by common consent, best-looking teaching recruit. From the moment he launched a discussion about the evils of under-age binge drinking, the class were thoroughly captivated. Unhappily, his own exploits outside a Manchester nightclub almost twelve months earlier had recently been posted on Facebook. While the brief record of events left a lot to the imagination, the photographs accompanying the text did not and, by unhappy coincidence, one of Mr Parrish's five hundred and twenty-seven Facebook friends just happened to know a Year 11 pupil at Tidenham Academy. If Mr Parrish thought for a moment that his previous indiscretions in a student life two hundred miles away could be erased by moving to a small, sleepy town near the Welsh border, he was sadly mistaken. As a result, his problem was not *engaging* 11T on his chosen topic but rather *disengaging* them.

All except Merryn. He was wrestling with Mr Biddle's accident and getting nowhere. He closed his eyes and laid his head on the table, completely oblivious to Mr Parrish's increasingly futile attempts at fending off questions about *over*-age binge drinking.

Suddenly, Merryn sat bolt upright, staring straight ahead. *Hope to God you've ordered the right bloody side.* Had he remembered that correctly? A fragment from Mear's conversation with the other man in the staffroom the day before. And what was it Jed had answered? *Nearside.* That was it! The conversation had made no sense at the time though it appeared that the second man had ordered something that Mear needed urgently, something that wasn't easy to come by. And then that word: nearside. It sat on a trivia shelf tucked far away in the dark recesses of Merryn's brain, almost beyond reach. Almost.

Nearside – the side of a car nearest the curb. Nearest a cyclist.

'Merryn, are you feeling all right?' asked Mr Parrish. He held his hand up to silence the rest of the class.

'He's been drinking, sir!' a voice called out from the back. That brought a sudden burst of laughter but he ignored it.

'Merryn, what's wrong?'

Merryn suddenly felt an overwhelming urge to tell someone what was going on inside his head. He certainly couldn't share it with Mr Parrish or the class. He needed to get out and find Zac or maybe Miss Grigoryev.

'I need some fresh air, sir, that's all. Could I go outside for a few minutes?'

'Hangover, MacIntyre?' said the same voice again.

'Will the class be quiet, please,' Mr Parrish implored with little success. 'Yes, Merryn. Take a few minutes.'

Merryn needed no second invitation. He bolted for the door, slamming it behind him. Outside in the corridor, he stopped, uncertain what to do next. A terrible fury was growing inside him, making it impossible to think clearly. He looked at his watch. It was 10.40. Twenty minutes until break.

Zac. He'd find Zac. He'd know what to do. The whole of Year 11 had PSHE which meant that Zac must be somewhere on the same corridor. Merryn checked each classroom, peering through the narrow windows beside each door. At the third door, he struck lucky. Taking a deep breath, he knocked and went in. Mrs White, a silver-haired teacher whose reputation had a lot in common with Stalin's, was presiding over silent ranks of fifteen-year-olds whose views on binge-drinking were currently being aired on paper.

'Could Mr Parrish see Zachary Lucas-Hunt, please?' Merryn knew he was taking a risk but he couldn't think of another way of persuading Mrs White to release one of her pupils in the middle of a lesson.

'Why?' The question took Merryn by surprise. He should have known that the head of PSHE would require an explanation.

'Er...'

'Er *what*, Merryn?'

'I'm not sure, miss. He just wants to see him for a moment.'

Mrs White sighed. 'If he *must*. Zachary. Make it quick. Five minutes then back here. Go.'

Zac jumped to his feet and joined Merryn in the corridor, closing Mrs White's door behind him.

'What's going on?' he asked. 'Why does Parrish want to see me?'

'Sshh! Keep your voice down. He doesn't. I've got to tell you something. Come on. We've only got five minutes.'

He led Zac down the corridor looking for an empty classroom.

'Merryn, are you nuts or what? Mrs White will go mental if she finds out you're lying. You know she'll ask Parrish what he wanted to see me about? Then what?'

Merryn shrugged. It was too late. The only thing that mattered right now was the small section of the jigsaw that he'd pieced together and the shocking picture that it revealed. He pushed open the door to the boys' toilets at the far end of the corridor and slipped inside. He checked the cubicles were empty and then launched.

'It was Mear who tried to kill Mr Biddle. He knew Mr Biddle wouldn't be coming back to school at the end of September because on that first Monday he was planning on knocking him over with his car. And now he's doing Mr Biddle's job – or not doing it – while Mr Biddle is lying in a coma. We've got to do something.'

Zac stared at Merryn, shaking his head in disbelief. 'What are you on about? Biddle is working for the BBC in Bath. You had a conversation with Miss Kelly in the library, remember? You told her Mear was talking rubbish.'

'Zac, I'm not messing around, I swear. Mr Biddle is in intensive care in Bristol Royal Infirmary. He's in a coma. He was knocked off his bike last Thursday evening and I'm telling you, Mear was driving the car that hit him.'

'Okay, so how come you're the only one that knows about Biddle?

Something like that wouldn't stay quiet for long. And if Mear's guilty, why hasn't he been arrested? Sorry, but none of that makes sense.' Zac stared at Merryn, waiting for answers.

'It's been on the BBC local news so I'm not the only one who knows but the school's not going to broadcast it, are they? Miss Grigoryev told me. I think she just wanted to tell someone and she seems...close to Mr Biddle. I'm telling you, he's not good. His brain has swollen which is serious. If you don't believe me, look online at the BBC's Bristol news website.'

'Okay, I believe you. Biddle's been knocked off his bike but you're telling me that Mear did it deliberately. Why the hell would he do that? To get Biddle's job permanently? I don't think so. No one is that desperate for a job.'

'I don't know for certain, but...'

'Ah, that's a change of tune,' Zac observed.

'No, listen. If you want to knock a cyclist off his bike with a car, you drive up behind him and ram him with the passenger-side wing – the nearside. There's a good chance you'll damage something on that side. Headlight or indicator. And the wing will be dented, especially if you hit the cyclist hard.'

'Can you hurry up, please, because White is preparing a noose for my neck.'

'I overheard a conversation Mear was having with someone in the staffroom, a man called Jed. It was about damage to his car – Mear's car – because he asked the other man if he was certain that he'd ordered a nearside part. Do you see? And he wanted the part urgently, like you would if you had something to hide.'

'That's it? You're serious?' Zac shook his head. 'What is it with you and Mear? He's an evil git, I agree, but you're accusing him of attempted murder. Why would he do that? Why would he want to hurt Biddle, kill him, even? You've got no hard evidence and the police are never going to listen to some fifteen-year-old ranting on about a nearside part. Look, I'm really sorry about Mr Biddle. He's a good bloke and doesn't deserve this but there's nothing you can do to help him.' With that, Zac turned to go, but Merryn wasn't finished.

'I'll show you. Meet me outside the north doors when the bell goes.'

'You know I'm going to get eaten alive, don't you. What am I supposed to tell the White Witch?'

Merryn thought for a moment and then said, 'Tell her I'm having family problems and I needed to talk to someone. Teachers always fall for that.'

'Yeah, right,' and with that, Zac sprinted back along the corridor to face the music. He readied himself for the inevitable cross-examination, lacking any conviction that Merryn's suggestion would satisfy Mrs White's predatory instinct.

It didn't.

CHAPTER 14

It wasn't until ten past eleven that Zac emerged from the north doors into the school yard.

'She knew you were lying; didn't even have to ask Parrish,' he said as the two boys walked across to the car park. 'When I told her it was about your family problems, she asked me why it couldn't wait another twenty minutes. Sorry mate, but you're dead meat when she finds you.'

Merryn added Mrs White to his list of staff to avoid and then asked, 'Any idea which is Mear's car?'

'Just as well you've got a field operative.' Zac pointed. 'Over there, an old Mercedes.'

In a far corner of the carpark, several spaces from the nearest car sat a dark blue Mercedes 420SEL.

'He's obviously worried about kids damaging it. It's got to be worth a few quid.'

Neither of them noticed the CCTV camera pointing at the car from a lamp post thirty yards away. The Data Protection Act meant that very few people had access to the camera's recordings. The site manager was one of those, a short, stocky man called Jeremy Skinner, better known to his friends as Jed.

When they were within ten yards of the car, Merryn glanced

around to make sure no one was watching then quickly sprinted to the passenger door and ducked out of sight. A few seconds later, Zac joined him.

'Okay, show me. This had better be good.'

Merryn moved down to the front end of the car and examined the corner bodywork. It was, as far as he could see, flawless. No scratches or dents let alone broken headlights or indicators. Zac crouched beside him.

'You want to show me where the damage is because I don't see any?'

Merryn was beginning to have doubts. 'This is the nearside. There must be something here that needs replacing.'

Suddenly the bell for the end of break sounded. 'I'm going,' Zac announced. 'We've got you-know-who and he's not going to be too chuffed when we tell him we're late because we were inspecting his car.'

'Wait! I'm being dull,' Merryn announced. 'The other guy told him that the part would be delivered *yesterday* so the chances are Mear's already replaced it.'

Zac was losing patience. 'In which case you're looking for nothing.'

'How old d'you reckon the car is?' Merryn asked.

'I don't believe this. Now what?'

'Zac, just answer the question. Have you any idea?'

'I don't know. It's an old E reg so it's got to be at least, what, twenty years old, maybe older. Twenty-five.'

'Look at these screws on the indicator glass. They're definitely not twenty-five years old. I'd say they were more like twenty-five *hours* old. The screws holding the headlights in place are rusted but the ones holding the indicators are shiny *and* the indicator glass is brand new. Not a scratch on it. That's what Jed ordered.' He ran his hand across the nearside wing. 'And there's a slight dent in the bodywork. You can't see it but you can feel it. And the paintwork – it's not as glossy here as the rest of the car. It's been resprayed.'

'Now you're just imagining stuff. Looks exactly the same to me. Look, if we don't get our arses into 308 before Mear, then we won't be going anywhere after school.' Zac sprinted across the yard to the south doors and up the stairwell, taking the stairs three at a time. On the top floor, he was just in time to see Mear disappearing into 308 before slamming the door behind him.

'Bloody idiot,' he cursed, 'this isn't going to be pretty.' He waited until Merryn arrived, out of breath. The two boys paused, each waiting for the other to knock on the door and face the wrath of the demon within.

Suddenly Merryn turned to Zac and kicked him sharply in the ankle before rapping loudly on the door. 'You've twisted your ankle so you can't walk,' he murmured. Before Zac could protest, the door flew open.

'I could have guessed,' snarled the lank figure, his dark eyes blazing with anger. 'What time do you call this?' But if Mear thought he could intimidate the two boys, he was wrong. A cold anger was burning in Merryn's stomach, cold and calculating.

He stared straight back at Mear and said, 'Zac's twisted his ankle, sir. It's bad. I had to help him up the stairs.' Without waiting for Mear's response, Zac hung his arm over Merryn's shoulder and took one step into the room, wincing theatrically as he did so although in truth, his ankle *did* hurt. For an instant, Mear stood blocking their path, unable to compose a suitable verbal swipe. It was impossible to tell whether the two boys were lying without inspecting Zac's ankle. Had he done so, he would have found a small red weal, about the size of the tip of Merryn's shoe. Instead, he just snapped, 'Sit!'

What followed was predictable. Laptops and silence; and in the silence, Merryn found himself glowering at the man sitting alone at the front of the class, his fingers sliding endlessly across the screen of his iPhone. Zac was right. If he was going to get Mear arrested for the hit-and-run, then he needed evidence. Solid, incontestable evidence, not the circumstantial stuff that he had chanced upon. The police would have checked all the obvious lines of enquiry: eyewitnesses, glass at the scene of the collision, CCTV footage in the area. Mear wouldn't have been sitting in the classroom if they'd found anything useful. Clearly, then, they hadn't. His eyes returned to the laptop screen in front of him. There must be some way of finding out just how far the police *had* progressed. He Googled "Bath News" and clicked on a link to "Bath24", a local news website. Under Bath Crime News, he found what he was looking for – a brief article covering a hit and run accident that had left schoolteacher George Biddle unconscious at around 8pm on Thursday 5th September. He'd been found in a quiet country lane leading to the village of Monkton Farleigh, around five miles from the centre of Bath. The police were looking for eyewitnesses and asked anyone with information to come forward.

So that was it. They'd found nothing while Mear was busy cleaning up the damage to his car. Soon there wouldn't be any evidence.

'MacIntyre. Bring me your laptop.' Merryn's heart missed a beat. Quick as a flash, he closed the page.

'Now! Do it right now and get your hands off the keyboard.' There was a new menace in Mear's voice and even before Merryn could get to his feet, Mear was at his desk, snatching the laptop from his grasp.

'You've written nothing for the past ten minutes. I've been watching you. You were told to research Oliver Cromwell. Show me your notes.'

'I haven't put anything on paper yet,' Merryn answered. 'It's all in my head.'

'It's all in your head?' He leant over the desk, his face only inches from Merryn's. Their eyes met and in that instant, something intangible passed between them, a flicker of recognition that burned for a second and then was gone. 'Is that right? So why don't you stand up and tell the rest of the class what's inside your head? Tell us all about Oliver Cromwell.' Mear walked slowly back to his chair taking the laptop with him, a cruel smirk spreading across his face. 'I can't hear you, MacIntyre. Having trouble finding anything inside your head?'

The silence in room 308 was deafening as Merryn got slowly to his feet. He located the Cromwell shelf in his cerebral cortex, took a deep breath, and launched.

'Oliver Cromwell was born in Huntingdon on the 25th of April 1599 and baptised at St John's Church in Huntingdon on the 29th of April. He went to a free school which was part of St John's Hospital in Huntingdon where he was taught by Dr Thomas Bard, er... no, Baird and then he spent a year at Sidney Sussex College in Cambridge. He was good at sports rather than academic stuff. His father died in June 1617 and he went home to look after the family estate and his widowed mother and seven unmarried sisters.'

The smirk on Mear's face disappeared. The boy was reading – that much was clear – but from where? He had no laptop, his exercise book was closed and in any case, he was staring straight ahead at the empty whiteboard. What kind of trick was this?

'In August 1620,' Merryn continued at pace, 'Cromwell married Elizabeth Bourchier who was the daughter of Sir James Bourchier, a London merchant. They had nine children.' He closed his eyes to focus on the list in his memory. 'Er... Robert, Oliver, Bridget, Richard, Henry, Elizabeth, James – he died as a baby, Mary and Frances. I think that's the right order.' The class gave a concerted gasp, but Merryn took no notice. 'He was elected MP for Huntingdon in... 1626 and he joined the opposition to King Charles. Then in 1629, after he became ill and depressed, Cromwell had some sort of spiritual awakening...'

'Enough!' Mear bellowed. If this was the boy – she had finally told him it was – he'd take the pistol from him, but more than that, he'd make him pay for his trickery. No one made Ezra Mear look a fool and got away with it. He and Biddle. They were a pair and they'd get the same treatment. 'Sit down. Very little of that information is relevant to the civil war and none of it is written in your exercise book. Now get on with it.' He had no intention of returning the laptop. The boy might be able to recite Cromwell's life story, but if he couldn't write it, then he'd get what was coming to him.

Merryn didn't need a laptop. He simply sat down, opened his exercise book, rewound the cerebral tape and began to write. All around him, twenty-five teenage brains were mentally composing their Facebook posts which, later that evening, would broadcast to the world the defeat of Goliath by Year 11's David. Unfortunately for Year 11 History Set 1 and Merryn in particular, Mear's injuries were significantly less life-threatening than the hole in Goliath's skull. It took the history teacher less than a minute to recover his composure and devote his full attention to exacting revenge on the little runt who'd dared to humiliate him. He hadn't the foggiest notion as to whether Merryn's monologue was accurate since he knew next to nothing about Cromwell himself and yet the boy's delivery had been fluent and assured. No one could invent that much detail at such a pace.

Merryn's laptop sat open on the desk in front of him. Mear noted with some satisfaction that the boy had failed to log out which meant he could check his browsing history. Perhaps there was something there that would expose him as a fraud. He opened Internet Explorer and hit Ctrl+H on the keyboard. Merryn's browsing history flashed up on the screen. If Mear expected a clutch of sites detailing the life and times of Oliver Cromwell, he was disappointed. Only two were listed – Google and www.bath24.co.uk. Beneath the latter were links to three pages that Merryn had visited. Two dark eyes stared in disbelief at the third one down:

www.bath24/crime/MonktonFarleigh/hit-and-run/story.html.

CHAPTER 15

'Priceless! Absolutely priceless! And it's recorded on my phone!'

Zac and half a dozen others from the history class followed Merryn down the stairs and out across the yard to the computer block, a small two-storey building set apart from the main school.

'Did you see his face when you went on and on reeling off all that stuff about Cromwell? You could tell he was getting mad as hell but he just didn't know what to say. I don't know how you do it. I mean, I couldn't do that even if I'd spent all night memorising it. I might even forgive you for kicking me in the ankle.'

Zac was beginning to think Merryn had been the subject of some fantastical medical experiment in which doctors had downloaded a complete set of encyclopaedias into the terabytes of his newborn brain. The truth, of course, was rather less fantastical if no less impressive. In becoming an expert on the civil war, as Miss Grigoryev had suggested, he had read a short online biography of Oliver Cromwell. Some of the names and dates had faded beyond his reach so that on one or two occasions, he had had to invent them, but most of the detail still remained intact.

'I told you,' he replied, 'I remember stuff. Anyway, what do you mean it's recorded on your phone?'

'Voice recorder app. I just switch it on and go to sleep most lessons. I tell you, this has to go on Facebook!'

'Don't you dare! Mear will find out and run you over.'

Zac gave his friend a withering look. 'Run *you* over, more like.'

Merryn lowered his voice. 'Listen. Remember the book that Mear borrowed from the library. The one that Miss Kelly showed us last week with the picture of Wintour jumping off the cliff?'

Zac nodded. 'Yeah. What about it?'

'This is what.' Merryn took a scrap of paper from his pocket, unfolded it and gave it to Zac. 'Recognise the handwriting?'

'No. Should I?'

'If you stayed awake in history.'

The two boys stopped outside the computer lab and waited until everyone had gone inside. 'Why don't you skip all the super-sleuth stuff and just tell me what the writing means? I assume you've figured it all out.'

Zac handed the paper back to Merryn who wore a slightly hurt expression. 'If you insist.'

But before he could say any more, Mr Zammitt arrived from the staffroom carrying a steaming mug of coffee in one hand and a bag of doughnuts in the other. He took one look at Merryn's headgear and exclaimed 'Nice hat! How on earth did you do that?'

Merryn had almost forgotten about his bandage. 'Fell over, sir.'

'Likely story. Anyway, lurking in the corridor is a criminal offence carrying a minimum sentence of one hour with me.'

'Actually, fifty minutes, sir,' corrected Zac.

'Don't be impertinent, Zachariah Lucas-Huntworthy, or I'll make it two hours. In!'

Mr Zammitt very rarely addressed any pupil by their real name, preferring instead to embellish them with a sprinkling of extra syllables. Most pupils at Tidenham tolerated this gentle ridicule although Merryn, whom Mr Zammitt referred to as Meriadoc Brandybuck, was less amused. 'Sir,' complained Merryn on one occasion, 'why do I have to be named after a hobbit?'

'You should be pleased,' replied his ICT teacher. 'Meriadoc was the cleverest of all the hobbits. It's a compliment.'

If Mr Zammitt's compliments likened you to a small creature with pointy ears and hairy feet, Merryn pondered, what did his insults look like?

Once the two boys had squeezed into their adjacent seats, the population inside the computer suite, originally designed for a class of twenty, now rose to thirty-two. Once-spacious workstations with large screen desktops had been cleared to make way for smaller laptops. Even so, there was no room to swing a mouse, testament to the popularity of Mr Zammitt and, to a lesser extent, his subject. As a result, it was quite impossible to have a conversation with your neighbour without several other sardines overhearing most of what you were saying. The solution to this problem, Merryn decided, was a map. He glanced over at Mr Zammitt who sat staring intently at his laptop screen, alternately sipping coffee and demolishing doughnuts, several fragments of which were now lodged in his very ample beard. He rarely moved from his office recliner since, by tapping a three-digit code into his keyboard, he could bring up any one of the thirty-two screens in the class on his own laptop. This, together with a pupil-off-task sensor wired into his brain, made for a very easy life and a very large girth.

Merryn logged in and brought up his coursework – an interactive website detailing the pedigree of every royal family in Europe since 1000AD. That should keep Mr Zammitt happy. Then he took a pencil and proceeded to sketch out a map of the River Wye around Wintour's Leap on a blank sheet of A4. Five minutes later, he sat back to admire his handiwork before handing it to Zac. What it lacked in accuracy of scale, it more than made up for with a series of cryptic annotations that would have taken a GCHQ code breaker the best part of a day to decipher. Zac didn't stand a chance. He stared at the map for a full five minutes, making sure to shield it from prying eyes. The class had fallen quiet, the only sound the machine-gun staccato of laptop keyboards. He daren't risk whispering to Merryn so he took out a pen and circled *Mr M plans to cross here.* Beside it he wrote *Mear? How do you know?* and then *WHY?* before handing the map back to its author.

Merryn glanced up at Mr Zammitt who was still staring intently at his screen in between bites of his third doughnut. In answer to Zac's questions, Merryn took out the scrap of paper with the notes that Mear had made in the history book. He laid it alongside his map on Zac's keyboard and waited for a light to switch on inside his partner's head. Even if Zac could have found the light switch, which was unlikely, he didn't get the chance.

'Zachariah, bring me that piece of paper.' Mr Zammitt was no longer staring at his screen or eating doughnuts. 'I cannot for the life of me see how a rugby training website can benefit someone who is busy creating the world's largest online royal family tree. Perhaps the piece of paper that you and Merryn have been studying so keenly for the past ten minutes will enlighten me.' He dusted a considerable quantity of sugar from his hands before stretching one of them out. 'Advance to Go, Zachariah, with said piece of paper. Do *not* collect two hundred pounds.'

Zac gave Merryn a resigned look, stood up and weaved his way through a maze of smirks before handing over the map.

'And what, Mr Huntworthy, might this be? I see no mention of the word rugby. Neither, Mr Brandybuck, do I see any mention of King Leopold the nineteenth of Bavaria. Explain.' With that, he sat back in his recliner and took a swig of lukewarm coffee.

Merryn held his breath. He resisted the temptation to inform his ICT teacher that there had only ever been five King Leopolds.

'It's just some history stuff that me and Merryn are doing. Homework. We got a bit distracted, that's all.' And then he added, 'Sorry, sir.'

'Ah, history stuff. Of course. And your history teacher is…' He paused but then spotted *Mear* scribbled on the map. 'Mr Mear, it seems. I wonder what he would say if he came into possession of this... er... document?'

For the second time that morning, Merryn's heart underwent some very irregular contractions. If Mear ever got hold of the map, he and Zac were done for.

'On reflection, the spilling of blood does seem a rather harsh punishment for ten minutes of indiscretion on your part.' Somewhere beneath his doughnut-encrusted beard, Mr Zammitt was smiling. 'So shall we say instead that your lunch will be delayed by ten minutes?'

Zac nodded and Merryn's heart rate returned to normal.

'Sit.' Mr Zammitt screwed up the map and launched it across the room into the paper recycling box by the door. 'Does that get me a place on the rugby team, Zachariah?'

Zac didn't answer. He was too busy shooting disparaging looks at Merryn. Life had been plain sailing before he'd teamed up with the memory freak to solve the mystery of Wintour's Leap. Now, scarcely a lesson went by without deception, reprimand and detention, not to mention a bruised ankle. Both boys set to work on their ICT coursework, but neither had made much progress when the bell rang at one twenty.

'Ten minutes, boys,' Mr Zammitt reminded them as he left the room to replenish his supplies. The last pupil to leave was Beatrice Odoyo who paused briefly by the door to recover a crumpled piece of paper from the recycle bin. Without a backward glance, she headed off to the photocopier in main school reception.

CHAPTER 16

'Why didn't you stop her?' Merryn demanded.

'What?' Zac exclaimed. 'You're nearer the door. Why didn't *you* stop her? It's your map in your handwriting. Come to think of it, it's your blood that Mear is going to spill.'

'Not when he sees his name written in *your* handwriting. In any case, she can run. I'd never catch her.'

The two boys sat staring at their screens, knowing that there was nothing they could have done to stop Beatrice taking possession of the map. She'd had her eyes on it from the moment Zammitt threw it into the bin.

Zac broke the silence. 'She won't take it to Mear. She hates him as much as we do. She's going to use it as leverage, I'll bet you.'

'What d'you mean, leverage?'

'She'll blackmail you. She told me all about her mum and being made redundant at your dad's shop. She wants you to talk to your dad and persuade him to keep Malika on so that she can stay in the UK. She's worried because if her mum loses her job…'

'Then she'll have to go back to Kenya. I know. She told me all that. When did she tell you?' But Merryn knew the answer to that question already.

'Last night, she messaged me on Facebook to meet her at school really early this morning – quarter past eight. I thought she was… you know… coming on to me or something, but it wasn't that at all. She got it into her head – I don't know why – that the only person you had anything to do with in school was me and so she wanted me to persuade you to talk to your dad. D'you know what's wrong with her mum?'

Merryn allowed all of this to sink in before answering. 'Nothing, as far as I can see. I saw her about two weeks ago at the shop. She seemed fine. So what *is* wrong with her?'

'You mustn't breathe a word of this to anyone, you understand.'

Merryn nodded, wondering what was coming next.

'Malika is infected with HIV, the virus that causes AIDS. While she's in the UK, she gets anti-viral treatment free of charge on the NHS. If she goes back to Kenya, then she'll have to pay for the anti-viral drugs and, without a job, she won't be able to afford them. Beatrice said she won't live long without the drugs.'

Merryn hadn't read much about HIV/AIDS so he didn't know much. Like many people, he thought that once someone became infected with the virus, they didn't have long to live and yet Malika seemed perfectly healthy.

'Do you believe her?' he asked.

'Yes I do. She's not lying. She's desperate and she'll do anything to stop her mum having to go back to Kenya. If she loses her job at the shop, there's a good chance that she won't find another one. She's got no qualifications. She's only here because she married some guy with a British passport and now they've separated. Beatrice says they'll send her back if she has to claim benefits, so do you think you can persuade your dad to change his mind?'

'It's not that simple.'

Zac said nothing, waiting for Merryn to explain.

'Because Dad's business is going bust and the bank is about to take our house away and we'll have nowhere to live. My dad doesn't have the money to pay himself, never mind Malika. In any case, it looks like the shop is going to close. Most of his customers have gone to the new supermarket.'

Zac frowned. 'So why does Beatrice think that your dad might change his mind?'

'Because Malika hasn't told her what's happening to the business. Beatrice thinks my dad just wants to make more profit by getting rid of staff, but that's rubbish. Making her redundant is... well... I reckon it's his last attempt to save the shop. If he'd known she was infected with HIV, then...' His voice tailed off. There was no money to pay himself, so how could he pay Malika?

The two boys had been so immersed in their conversation that it was only now they noticed the figure standing in the doorway. They had no idea how long she'd been there or how much she'd heard. Beatrice threaded her way through the clutter of chairs and sat on the edge of a table. For a while she said nothing and just stared at the floor. Then, as though summoning up all her willpower, she took a deep breath and said, 'I'm sorry, Merryn. I didn't know any of that about the shop. You should have told me. I don't know why Mum hasn't told me. That's typical of her. She thinks about everyone except herself.'

She paused and turned her face away, desperately trying to hold back the tears. 'She's just got to find a new job. Simple as that. Zac's right, though. It won't be easy.' She stood up and walked over to the window, pulling out a tissue from her bag. The dam burst. 'I'm being so stupid,' she sobbed. 'I can't stop crying when I talk about it. She needs the drugs, every day for the rest of her life. You understand, don't you?' But neither of them understood. How could they?

Beatrice wiped her eyes and sat down again. 'There's a saying in Swahili: *Bahati mbaya haiji peke yake*. Bad luck doesn't come just once. For my family, it's true. Maybe it will change. But that's not why I'm here.' She took Merryn's map from her blazer pocket and spread it out as best she could on her knees. Her mood seemed to change and a faint spark of excitement flashed from her dark, brown eyes.

'What's this about? Some kind of treasure map?'

Merryn wondered if he could snatch the map from Beatrice's lap before she had a chance to react.

'No,' he began, but Zac interrupted.

'Yes, that's exactly what it is. A treasure map. Merryn thinks there might be something buried here from the Civil War.' He leaned over to point at St James's church but Beatrice quickly picked the map up and held it in both hands.

'Liar. You wouldn't tell me so easily if that was true. Come on, Merryn. What's all this stuff about Mr M. It *is* Mear, isn't it? And this: *pistol found here*. I'll give you it back if you tell me. I swear.'

Zac and Merryn looked at each other. Could they trust her? Zac shook his head but it was too late. Merryn's outer defenses had been breached.

'Alright, we'll tell you. But we want the map back. Agreed?'

'Agreed.' She liked Merryn. Zac was good looking but arrogant. Rugby players always were, but Merryn was different.

'There's not much really,' Merryn lied. 'John Wintour was a Royalist soldier who fought for the King in the English Civil War. He was ambushed by a company of roundheads — soldiers fighting for parliament — at a ford on the River Wye. He escaped by galloping off the cliffs at Wintour's Leap.'

'Says Merryn,' Zac scoffed.

'Anyway, we reckon Mear is going to cross the Wye at the ford on Thursday night. It's a Spring tide which will make it easier. The river will be low. That's about it.'

Beatrice stared at Merryn, wondering how he'd come by his head injury. She thought his head bandage gave him a rather dashing look.

'That's about it?' she said. 'The new history teacher is going to walk across the River Wye in the middle of the night? You expect me to believe that?'

Merryn had to admit that, put like that, it sounded somewhat implausible.

'And what about the pistol? Come on, if you want the map back, you'll have...' but before she had a chance to finish, Zac leapt from his seat and snatched the map from her grasp.

'Sorry,' he grinned, 'but we *do* want the map back. How else will we find the buried treasure?'

Beatrice smiled as though she had been half-expecting the boys to muscle the map from her. She leant forward and tapped Zac's arm and said 'brawn.' Then she tapped her head. 'Brain.' She picked up her bag and walked to the door just as Mr Zammitt came lurching back into the computer block carrying nutritional reinforcements in both hands.

'Ah, Beatrissimo,' he exclaimed, in a poor Italian accent. 'How are my two convicts coming along?'

'I'm not sure about their coursework, sir, but they're very interested in paper recycling.'

Mr Zammitt didn't need any further hints. One glance at the bin was enough.

'Map!' he barked. 'Now!' and for the second time in an hour, Zac handed Merryn's map to his ITC teacher. If looks could inflict unimaginable levels of pain, then Beatrice would have been in agony. As it was, her smile broadened, the brilliant white of her teeth lighting up her face like a beacon.

'I'm not sure you boys are getting the message. Perhaps another ten minutes will help. In the meantime, this stays with me.' Mr Zammitt opened a drawer in his desk and dropped the map into it. 'Beatrice, can I help?' She was still standing by the door, clearly waiting to say something.

'I just wanted to tell the boys that the new photocopier in reception gives really excellent results. In fact, you can't tell which is the original and which is the copy.' And with that, she vanished.

CHAPTER 17

'MacIntyre! You're late. It's nearly half-three. We're supposed to be in Chepstow at four. Which teacher have you upset now?'

Merryn grimaced as he climbed up into the back of the enormous black Range Rover parked a short distance from the school gates. 'Mrs White ambushed me.'

Zac sniggered. 'I told you she'd hunt you down. The old witch never forgets.'

This brought a disapproving tut from the front seat. 'Respect, Zachary. You need to show your teachers some respect. I never hear you say something good about them. Now, introductions please.'

Zac looked at Merryn and rolled his eyes. 'This is the Merryn that I told you about; and Merryn, this is Sasha. Will that do, Sash?'

'Pleased to meet you, Merryn.' A slim hand suddenly appeared between the massive front seats and Merryn shook it. It felt cold. 'Zachary has told me much about you. You have an amazing memory, so I hear.'

Her accent reminded Merryn a little of Miss Grigoryev. Similar but not the same. 'I can remember stuff, I guess,' he replied.

'I think you are being modest. Zachary says you can remember everything you read. That must be useful when it comes to exams.' Sasha laughed. 'I remember when I study for exams. Hours and hours I write out so many facts and test myself and then I forget them so quickly. What would I give for a memory like yours?'

Twenty minutes later, Sasha stopped the car outside Levi Antiques in a narrow lane just off the main street in Chepstow and the boys climbed out. She leaned her head out of the window. 'Five o'clock here. Don't be late. The wardens don't like me in Chepstow.' With that, she was gone.

'She's had five parking tickets this year,' Zac remarked. 'Traffic wardens don't like swanky cars.'

It is a swanky car, Merryn thought. His dad hadn't paid more than three thousand for his van at an auction. He reckoned the Range Rover was worth ten times that at least.

'What did you tell your mum?' Zac asked. 'About why we're here, I mean.' He expected Merryn to say that she'd beaten the truth out of him.

'I just told her that Mr Levi knows a lot about the civil war and that he could help us with a homework assignment. She seemed okay about it when I told her that your mum was giving us a lift. I'm worried in case she phones Levi up. I wouldn't put it past her.'

'Right, it's show time.' Zac patted his bag. 'Let's find out if your detective work is all it's cracked up to be.' He pushed open the heavy, oak-framed door that guarded the entrance to the antique shop's dark interior.

No one could accuse Mr Levi of wasting money on unnecessary window dressing. The entire shop floor lacked anything that could remotely be described as display. Items simply stood where sellers had left them, waiting for buyers to remove them. Centre stage, an enormous nineteenth century Welsh oak dresser rubbed its rough shoulders with slender-legged tables made from polished mahogany. Along one wall, a set of six ornately carved Queen Anne dining chairs were forced to sit facing a hideous, black leather, studded sofa, its seat bearing the polished cheek-marks of its long-dead owners. Bookcases crammed with mould-spotted volumes by authors Merryn had never heard of occupied the other wall, while above them, hung paintings of fox hunting, faded photographs of merchant ships docked in Bristol harbour, barometers forecasting everything from droughts to deluges, and clocks, most of which had long abandoned the effort of keeping time.

'Nothing is priced,' whispered Merryn, afraid that Mr Levi might be hiding inside a cupboard somewhere. 'And how are you supposed to know what anything is? There aren't any labels.'

'We're wasting our time. It's the wrong kind of antiques. I can't see any guns.' Zac's eyes were slowly adjusting to the gloom. He was right. There were no weapons of any kind to be seen. A grandfather clock struck the Westminster chimes announcing it was four o'clock. The shop door swung open revealing a rather dishevelled Miss Kelly.

'Merryn? Zac? Is that you? Oh dear, he's forgotten to turn the lights on again. Am I late?' She pushed the door closed just as the clock ended with its four chimes. 'Ah! What timing! Why is parking in Chepstow so difficult these days? So, you've told your parents where you are, yes?'

Both boys nodded.

'It's dark in here. Was that a definite yes?'

'Yes, miss. They know exactly where we are.' Zac wasn't lying. He was simply avoiding the whole truth since neither set of parents knew the real purpose of their visit to Levi Antiques.

'I'm glad to hear that. Have you met Mr Levi yet?'

'Er, no. We've only just got here. I don't think there's anyone in the shop. We could have run off with half the stuff by now.'

'You wouldn't have got far with that Welsh dresser, Zac. I'll go and find him. He's taken to having a nap in the afternoon without shutting the shop.' Miss Kelly disappeared into a back room.

'I've got a bad feeling about this.' Zac was beginning to lose faith in the English teacher. 'I know she's only trying to be helpful but look at the place. We need an expert, not a...'

Miss Kelly's voice cut him short. 'Come on through, boys.'

At the back of the shop, a dimly lit corridor led to a large office lined with dark oak panelling. Every inch of wall space was adorned with hundreds of framed photographs, some old in black and white, others more recent and in colour. Old or new, the subject of every photograph was the same – fishing.

In the middle of the room, a small and rather fragile figure sat hunched on an oversized leather armchair behind an antique wooden desk laden with piles of muddled paperwork. Thick waves of tousled white hair flowed in every direction from the old man's head while two enormous, bushy eyebrows bobbed up and down over his eyes like giant, noxious caterpillars. Most impressive of all, however, was the magnificent, untamed moustache that swept across his face from cheek to cheek. Sitting there, crouched over the desk, he reminded Merryn of an old photograph of Albert Einstein. Zac's first impression of Mr Levi was rather less complimentary and involved words like geriatric and decrepit. He wasn't the first person to make this mistake.

The old man's half-moon spectacles tumbled from his nose as he scrambled awkwardly to his feet. 'Gentlemen, come in, come in!' His voice was frail and croaky. He waved them in with an exaggerated gesture. 'May I apologise to my guests for the worst of welcomes. What must you think of me, fast asleep on such an important occasion. Rather too much tipple with my lunch, I fear. What can I say?'

Miss Kelly quickly intervened. 'Isaac, I think the boys are just very happy that you agreed to see them. Shall we get down to business? They have to be out of here by five.'

'Yes, of course, of course. Shall we clear a little space on the desk? Draw up some chairs, won't you. Sian has told me a little of your find, but I shall not believe a word of it until I see it with my own eyes.' He was transformed now, his eyes wide with excitement and his voice rising with anticipation. 'Let's see it.'

Zac pulled the pistol from his bag, still swaddled in the towel. Mr Levi watched spellbound as Zac carefully unwrapped the flintlock and laid it gently on the desk in front of him. Never in all the years Miss Kelly had known Isaac Levi had she ever seen him lost for words – until now. For sixty seconds the old man sat open-mouthed, staring at the pistol, unable to speak, until eventually he whispered, 'You found this?' He looked up in utter disbelief. 'You found this down some sort of *crack* by the cliffs?'

They nodded. They weren't sure how much Miss Kelly had told him but there seemed little point in holding anything back.

'We were doing some research about John Wintour,' Merryn began, 'trying to work out whether it was possible for anyone to jump over the cliffs and survive. That's when I fell into this crack and there it was, jammed between the walls about fifteen feet down.' Merryn paused, waiting for some response, but there was none. 'We had a bit of trouble getting it out. Actually, getting *me* out.'

'That how you injured your head?' Mr Levi asked, his gaze still fixed on the pistol.

Merryn nodded. 'Six stitches.'

'Well, Merryn, let me tell you this. Six stitches was a price worth paying because, put quite simply...' His voice began to tremble with emotion. He paused, scarcely able to believe what he was about to say. 'What is sitting on the table in front of me is the most extraordinary object I have ever laid eyes on. Have you any idea how long I have been in this business?'

Neither boy dared risk an answer though they guessed it was more than fifty years.

'I started here with my father in 1956. I was just eighteen years old then and I've been here ever since. Sixty-three years. And believe me, I've seen a lot of good stuff in those sixty-three years, but nothing like this. *Nothing*. Look at the detail. It's just extraordinary.' He dug into a pocket in his long, woollen cardigan and brought out a grubby handkerchief. 'And I haven't shed a tear over an antique for a very long time.' He wiped his eyes and blew his nose.

Zac was starting to reconsider his opinion of the old man. Maybe he knew something about antiques, about pistols even.

Mr Levi recovered his composure. He slipped one hand over the golden fox and picked up the pistol. 'Whoa!' he exclaimed, scarcely able to lift it for more than a few seconds. 'This cannot be happening. All that weight and yet, look how it balances.' He placed two fingers into the trigger guard and briefly held the gun aloft. 'See! The whole length of the barrel counterbalanced by the butt. It's perfect! Perfect!'

He put the pistol back on the desk. It was all too much for him. The handkerchief came out again.

'Most antique dealers will never see anything like this in their lifetime. They dream about it, but that's all it ever is. A dream. You know who I feel like right now?'

His audience waited for the answer since guesswork was pointless.

'I'll give you a clue. 1922. The greatest archaeological discovery of the twentieth century.'

Merryn didn't need to think. He just said, 'Howard Carter. Tutankhamun's tomb.'

'You know your history, young man. Well, this is as close as I'm ever going to get to holding a death mask made from solid gold. You understand what I'm saying? The butt is made from solid gold, I'm certain of it. It's just extraordinary.' He took a deep breath and shook his head. 'You are being very patient with an old man. Forgive me. It is a special moment, you understand. But we don't have much time, so let's get down to business. First, have you any idea what you've found?'

'Go on, Merryn.' Zac prompted. 'Do your stuff.'

Merry needed no persuasion. 'It's a flintlock pistol, made in London in 1774 by someone with the initials HvD and the butt is eighteen carat gold.'

Isaac Levi nodded. 'That's very impressive, Merryn. I can see you've been reading the hallmark. I know antique dealers who've been in the trade for donkeys' years who still can't read hallmarks. So, let's see how many points you've scored.' This time the pocket in his cardigan produced a magnifying glass. He pushed his half-moon specs back into place, switched on a desk lamp and peered down at the pistol butt through the magnifying glass, turning it over as he searched for the hallmark.

'There you are,' he said, locating the four tiny stamps on the underside of the butt. 'Now, let's see. HvD. You've got your first point. That is indeed the maker or at least, that's the initials of the goldsmith who made the fox. My guess is he's Dutch or German. H van D. H von D. We'll find him because this is magnificent work, which means he's almost certainly a master goldsmith. He'll have left his mark elsewhere.

'Next, seven hundred and fifty. Seventy-five per cent gold, twenty-five per cent silver and copper. That's eighteen carat gold. Two out of two. You're doing well, Mr MacIntyre. Next, the leopard. Leopard with a crown, made in London before 1821. Three out of three. Question is, are you going to get the full set? B in a shield. The date letter. I have to say, I'm surprised you even attempted this. Date letters are notoriously difficult to get right. You looked on the internet, is that right?'

Merryn nodded. 'We found a list of silver date letters and there was a B in a shield which stood for 1774. I couldn't find a list of gold hallmark date letters but I read somewhere that they were the same as silver.'

'And you were right. Until 1798, date letters in gold and silver hallmarks were the same. The question is, where did you get 1774 from because I can tell you this pistol wasn't made in 1774. The firing mechanism is typical of earlier flintlock designs. Seventeenth, not eighteenth century.'

Merryn looked puzzled. Had the maker stamped the wrong date letter into the hallmark?

'You used your dad's silver cup to work out the date letters, remember?' Zac suddenly found his voice. 'The cup's hallmark had a Z stamped into it. You found a website with a list of date letters and

Z meant 1899. The same list said that B in a shield was 1774.'

'And where was the cup made, if you don't mind me asking?' A note of mischief had crept into Mr Levi's voice. 'I'll bet it wasn't London.'

'Birmingham,' both boys replied in unison.

'And that's where you went wrong. Birmingham date letters are not the same as London date letters. Still, three out of four is a pretty good score for a beginner. I'd employ you. As an apprentice, I mean.' Mr Levi leaned over the arm of his chair and pulled out what looked like a telephone directory from a cupboard in his desk. 'Let's see when your pistol was made, shall we.' He thumbed through the pages while, for the third time that day, Merryn's heart rate leapt into treble figures.

'Here we go. B in a shield. My, my, you were a long way out with 1774,' he teased. 'It's a mite older than that.' He chortled into his moustache. 'The gold butt of this pistol was made in 1639.'

'I told you!' Merryn burst out. 'Didn't I tell you, Zac. It's Wintour's pistol. Made in London in 1639. Wintour jumps over the cliffs in 1645. It fits perfectly. I knew it was his.'

'No, you didn't tell me it was Wintour's pistol. You said you *wished* it was his pistol. And in any case, just because it *could* be doesn't prove it *was*.'

Isaac Levi raised his hand to quell the minor riot which his revelation had provoked. 'Zac is quite right. I can't hire an apprentice that jumps to conclusions based on circumstantial evidence. You've got to be more rigorous, discriminating, scrupulous when it comes to tying history and antiques together. Having said that, Merryn, I'm with you on this. I hope this is Wintour's pistol. Most people don't believe he actually jumped over those cliffs but wouldn't that change if we could prove that the pistol was his. Of course, we've no evidence to suggest that the pistol has been down the crack ever since 1645. Discovering who owned it might help us answer that and I know just the man for the job, but that can wait. Next on the agenda. Who does the pistol belong to now? Have you given that any thought, Mr MacIntyre?'

'Only what I read online. We've got fourteen days – actually, it's only ten days now – to tell an FLO about the pistol.'

'And for the ordinary humans here?' Zac cut in.

'Finds Liaison Officer. The FLO tells the coroner and the coroner holds an inquest. If it's treasure, which I think it is, then it belongs to the Crown – that's the queen – but she'll ask the Secretary of State to offer it to the British Museum. The TVC decides what it's worth and… now what?'

Zac's head was buried in his hands. 'TVC,' he muttered.

'Humour him, Merryn. And me,' Miss Kelly smiled.

'Treasure Valuation Committee. They decide what it's worth and who gets the money – the finder or the landowner – that the museum agrees to pay for it.'

'Or both,' Isaac added.

Merryn drew breath. 'I think that's it.'

'I'm not sure that an apprenticeship in a stuffy old antiques shop working for a stuffy old antiques dealer is the right career move for you, Merryn. You definitely need something a bit more challenging. You get full marks this time. Faultless. Tell us why you think it's treasure.'

Merryn was just about to recite treasure category five from the Treasure Act when, instead, he attempted some simple arithmetic inside his head and got stuck. '2019 take away 1639. Can someone help me out, please?'

Silence descended on the room while cogs turned. Miss Kelly got there first. 'Three hundred and eighty, I think.'

Isaac nodded.

'Three hundred and eighty? The pistol is three hundred and eighty years old?' Merryn sounded incredulous. 'No wonder it's so rusted. In which case, it's definitely treasure. Category one. Any object over three hundred years old which contains at least ten per cent gold or silver.'

'Do you memorise facts for fun, Merryn? I mean, how did all this get inside your head?'

'I was just thinking the same thing, Isaac,' added Miss Kelly.

Isaac glanced at his watch. 'The pistol was found on the English side of the Wye so it falls under the jurisdiction of the Bristol City Museum. The FLO there is a Miss Rosalie Edwards, a very dear friend of mine. She'll want to know every detail of the pistol's discovery. Then she'll take advice from me, or rather a friend of mine, and declare the pistol to be treasure. Finally, she'll contact the coroner who will arrange an inquest at which both you and the landowner will be present. And your parents, of course. The coroner will inform the TVC and they will determine the pistol's value and who gets how much of that sum. They'll offer it to the British Museum who will snap this up, I can assure you, regardless of its value.'

A stunned silence descended on the room. Three pairs of eyes fixed themselves on Isaac Levi, willing him to answer the question that no one dared ask. Isaac stared back, reading their minds until, unable to control himself any longer, he burst out laughing.

'Go on! Ask me! How much do I think the pistol is worth? That's what you're all thinking, eh?'

'How much do you think the pistol is worth, Mr Levi?' Merryn heard himself ask.

'Absolutely no idea!' Isaac laughed again. 'I'm no expert on flintlock pistols, but I know a man who is. Monsieur Pascal St Pierre. Lives in Montpelier in France. He's retired now but he's still one of the world's foremost experts on early modern firearms. He's also a wizard at restoration. The firing mechanism and barrel may look a bit rusty right now, but I promise you, once Pascal has worked his magic, the whole pistol will look, well, just like it did in 1639. And it won't take him long, either. He'll drop everything for this, believe me. I'll email him a photo of your pistol this evening, with your permission, of course,' he added, looking up for approval. 'Yes?'

Miss Kelly found herself nodding with the boys.

'Excellent. Then Pascal will be knocking at my door sometime tomorrow, I'll wager. He has a rather rapid form of transport.' He winked. 'I thought I was fanatical about antiques until I met Pascal. Anyway, once he's had a good look at it, he'll deliver it to Rosalie at the museum in Bristol. She will need a detailed, written statement describing exactly how, when and where the pistol was discovered, and I *mean* detailed. Leave nothing out. Can you sort that out for me, Sian? As soon as possible. Normally this process takes months but not this time if I've got anything to do with it.'

Miss Kelly nodded. She turned to the two boys. 'Library, lunchtime, Thursday. Be ready to cough up the ghastly truth, okay?'

The faint sound of a car horn floated into the room from the street outside. Zac checked his watch.

'That's Sasha. We've got to go.'

'Well, if you must.' Isaac shuffled reluctantly to his feet. 'But please know this, young treasure hunters. You have made me the happiest antiques dealer in the world this afternoon. Life is going to be pretty tame after this.' He extended his hand and the boys shook it in turn. 'I'll let you know what Pascal thinks about your pistol as soon as he passes judgement. Like I said, he won't take long.'

The blaring horn outside Levi Antiques sounded increasingly agitated as Isaac's visitors hurried out into the shop. Suddenly Merryn had a change of mind.

'Wait up, Zac. I won't be a sec.'

Before Zac could protest, Merryn disappeared back into Isaac's office.

'Mr Levi, sorry to bother you again,' he began rather awkwardly, 'but have you really no idea what the pistol might be worth? I mean, is it four figures or five figures?'

'Four figures or five figures?' Isaac shook his head. 'I told you, Merryn, I'm not an expert in firearms, but…' He paused, staring down at the pistol. The jewelled eyes of the golden fox returned his stare. Every one of his sixty-three years in the antiques trade was warning him to say nothing; to tell the boy to be patient and wait for an expert valuation. But Merryn had brought him an indescribable elation that he had so rarely experienced in all his long years, and he deserved an answer to his question, however inexpert it might be.

'If you insist, but you must understand that my valuation is not going to be accurate. It's a guess and a poorly educated guess at that.'

Merryn nodded. He daren't say anything that might change the old man's mind but the waiting was killing him.

'So, if the TVC values it at anything less than a hundred thousand pounds I will be astonished. If the butt of the pistol is solid gold – and the weight of it certainly suggests that it is – then we must be talking *six* figures. That much I do know. But you're not going to quote me, you understand. That's just between you and me. As to its exact value, I really have no idea. You'll have to wait until Pascal has seen it and then he'll tell you what it's worth to the nearest shilling.'

Merryn stood staring at the old man.

'The TVC normally splits the value between landowner and finder fifty-fifty. So that tumble at Wintour's Leap has earned you and Zac a few quid, eh?'

It was too much for Merryn to take in. He'd won the lottery simply by falling down a crack. Twenty-five grand. Maybe more. It might be enough to save his father's business. Enough even to save Malika's job, to save Malika. He felt his head might explode at any moment.

But Isaac hadn't finished. 'However, before you get too excited, there's just one thing I forgot to mention and it's important. There's a clause in the Treasure Act about trespassing. I expect you've read it and memorised it.'

The word *trespassing* landed on Merryn like a boxer's punch. He *hadn't* read the clause, a fact made plain by the expression on his face.

'Oh, I see.' The old man coughed awkwardly. 'Well, it says that if the treasure is obtained illegally because you knowingly went onto someone else's land without their permission, then the TVC will in all likelihood deny you any reward. So, Master MacIntyre, tell me you weren't trespassing.'

Merryn felt as though the air had been sucked from his lungs. 'How would we know?' he heard himself ask.

'How would you know?' Isaac chuckled. 'That's not difficult. If you failed to obtain permission from the landowner to be on his or her land. Let's say instead that you simply climbed over a fence that is clearly designed to keep you out or you ignored a sign saying Private – keep out. Please tell me you didn't.'

Merryn didn't need to speak the answer. It was written across his face. In a flash, his lottery ticket disappeared and no one, not even Mr and Mrs Casey, was ever going to find it.

CHAPTER 18

'Well, you certainly know how to keep a girl waiting, boys.' Sasha accelerated away from the antiques shop, wheels squealing as she hurled the Range Rover back onto Chepstow's main street and headed for Tidenham.

'Did you see him? The traffic warden? He's stalking me, I swear it. Let's hope he didn't recognise the car. Six tickets in one year would not be good. I think your father might ban me from driving, Zac.'

'It was Merryn's fault, Sasha. He'll pay the fine for you.' Zac grinned at Merryn who said nothing but simply glared back.

'Ignore him, Merryn. He can be an imbecile sometimes.' She laughed. 'So, tell me about your visit. Did you meet Mr Levi?'

After ten minutes digging for clues as to the real purpose of the boys' visit to the antiques shop, she gave up and concentrated on driving through the rush hour exodus. In any case, Merryn wasn't in the mood for conversation. The euphoria he'd experienced on discovering the pistol's value had lasted less than a minute, blown away by the certainty that he and Zac had been trespassing on the cliff top. They had, after all, ticked both of the boxes: squeezing through railings designed to keep people out and ignoring signs which said keep out. It was an open and shut case. The TVC would rule that one hundred percent of the pistol's value – a staggering one hundred thousand pounds, perhaps more – would go to the landowner. They could hardly reward two fifteen-year-old boys for breaking the law.

Merryn felt utterly crushed. What might have been would never be. He barely noticed when Zac pulled something out of his bag and dropped it on his lap.

'Hey, almost forgot. Found it in my sock drawer.' It was a phone charger. 'Plug your phone in when you get back and I'll call you tonight around eight. Remember to switch it on. We need to talk. About the *essay*, remember?' Zac winked at him.

Merryn nodded. They did need to talk. About a hundred grand disappearing down the drain. About a fortune that could have saved the shop and his home. A fortune that could have saved Malika. Maybe Zac had been right all along about the woman's voice since finding the pistol had come to nothing. He doubted he'd ever set eyes on it again. Secured by the British Museum, it would be displayed in some dreary glass cabinet for all the world to see while its story remained untold.

He made up his mind to forget about the flintlock and focus on finding the evidence to convict Mear of attempting to murder Mr Biddle. Mr Levi's words were still ringing in his ears. *I can't hire an apprentice that jumps to conclusions based on circumstantial evidence. You've got to be more demanding, discriminating, scrupulous.* If he took his meagre scraps of evidence to the police, they would say the same. The evidence had to be watertight and yet Merryn had no idea how to go about finding it. If the police had failed to find anything pointing the finger of guilt at Mear, what made him think that a fifteen-year-old could be any more successful?

He stared aimlessly out of the tinted windows as the Range Rover crossed the Wye bridge, heading north to Tidenham. The tide was out and scarcely two feet of muddy brown water meandered beneath the bridge to join the River Severn less than a mile to the south.

Ezra Mear was still in his thoughts when the car swung rather violently into Church Close and screeched to a halt.

'Nice to meet you, Merryn.' Sasha reached out her hand again. 'I hope we see you again. Maybe Zac will bring you over for a meal one evening and you can teach me some history, eh? The history of Romania, I think. That would be good.'

Zach rolled his eyes. 'You've probably worked out that Sash is from Romania. Don't forget to switch the phone on. Eight o'clock, remember.'

A squeal of tyres later and the Range Rover was gone. Merryn picked up the charger and headed indoors, praying that he wouldn't have to face a barrage of questions from his mother. Fate was clearly in a generous mood since Donna was fast asleep on the living room settee, allowing Merryn the luxury of a question-free passage to his bedroom. They would come later, he knew, but for now he was safe.

He put Zac's phone on to charge, then threw himself on the bed and stared up at the kings and queens of England. He lay there for almost an hour, a confusion of thoughts spinning inside his head. If he thought he could delete the shelf in his memory devoted to the pistol, he was sadly mistaken. Nothing short of dying was going to achieve that. What irritated him, however, was just how few facts sat on the shelf. For the first time in his teenage life, the awesome power of the internet couldn't help him. It couldn't tell him for certain whether the pistol belonged to Sir John Wintour, though now that it had been dated to 1639, he felt certain it did. Neither could it tell him why the pistol's owner had hidden the weapon fifteen feet down a crevice on the edge of such a precipice. Again, he was convinced that it had been deliberately placed there, carefully concealed beneath the jammed rock where it couldn't be seen from above.

The internet couldn't tell him if Wintour had jumped from the cliff top into the river. It had told him it was unlikely, that such a jump would normally smash every bone in the human body, yet without rewinding the clock back to that fateful day in 1645 when Wintour had been ambushed by Massey's Roundheads, there was no way of knowing whether or not the knight had leapt two hundred and eighty feet and survived to tell the tale. Someone had told the tale but was it fact or fantasy?

Merryn sat up and silently cursed his obsession with history. Without reliable eyewitnesses, so much of the past was mere speculation. Did King Alfred, the first great king of the Saxons, really forget that he'd put some cakes in the oven simply because he was sulking over a string of Saxon defeats by the Vikings? Was King Harold really undone by looking up at a passing seagull during the Battle of Hastings, thereby offering his eye as a target for one of William's arrows? And what of Robert the Bruce and his spider? Was the crowned king of Scotland really inspired by the heroic efforts of a small arachnid as, time and again, it rebuilt its web?

Kings Alfred, Harold and Bruce – what did it matter that their stories were part fact, part fiction? What did it matter that, when Merryn had finished turning over every online stone in his quest for the facts, he proceeded to fill in the gaps with his imagination. Even the sounds and smells were added to create a living, breathing canvas on which the triumphs and tragedies of history were played out. Isaac Levi had been right. Legends could only live in the imagination. It's where they belonged, where they flourished.

But now, for Wintour's leap, that simply wasn't good enough. Anyone could *imagine* a horse and rider galloping off the cliffs and plunging into the Wye below, just as the artist had done in *A Short History of Chepstow*. Merryn wanted the truth but, without a time machine, he was never going to find it.

'That's not how it happened,' he murmured to himself, repeating the words he'd heard in the library. 'If that's not how it happened, what *did* happen?'

'Come down to the river, Tom, and you will find the answer.'

Her voice was little more than the faintest whisper and for a moment, he wondered if he had really heard anything at all. Was his mind creating sounds inside his head, the answers to questions that he so desperately wanted to hear? But Tom – that was not his name though hearing it quickened his pulse as if somewhere in the darkest recesses of his memory there was a Tom with whom he had once been... close. A relative perhaps or a friend?

'Who are you?' he whispered, sitting perfectly still, his ears straining for an answer. When none came he tried again. 'Why do you call me Tom?' but still the only sound he heard was the distant drone of rush hour traffic.

He got to his feet, a growing sense of frustration building inside him. One last time and then that would be the end of it. No more talking to the wall. 'Come down to the river? But when should I come and where?'

'You have the answer. He wrote it in the book.'

'He? You mean Mear? The ford at five to eleven on Thursday night?' He stood waiting for confirmation but there was none. 'Mear? What is he to you? You've never spoken of him before.' Silence.

He gave up waiting and slumped down onto the bed again, excited and dejected at the same time. It was as if she was playing with him, holding out crumbs of information whilst never revealing anything that might betray her identity. *You have the answer. He wrote it in the book. A Short History of Chepstow.* She was still using it as a means of guiding him towards... where? At first, it had been the pistol at the cliff top. But now she was taking him down to the riverbank, to an appointment with Mear. She had known what Mear had written. Was he part of her scheme? Did she speak to him too? The thought that she might be conspiring with the man sent a cold shiver down his spine. Whose side was she on?

He cast his mind back to the moment when, sitting battered and bruised by the crevice, he'd lifted the golden flintlock for the first time. Instead of searching his memory for her words, he let them come to him.

At last, 'tis found. Now you can set me free, Tom.

No, not *me*. She had said *us*. Set *us* free. But free from what? And what part did the pistol have in all this?

Then what? *It killed a man.* Again, that didn't feel right. Pistols didn't kill people. Someone pulled the trigger. Surely…?

I killed a man.

There it was. A confession. She had led him to the weapon she'd used to kill a man. If that was true, then the voice belonged to a ghost from the distant past, from the seventeenth century. Merryn began to doubt whether the pistol had, after all, belonged to Wintour.

He longed to tell someone about the voice, someone who wouldn't simply dismiss it straight away as the wild imaginings of an adolescent with an obsession for myths and legends. But there wasn't anyone. He'd chosen his life of solitude, an island in the past buffered from the chaos and confusion of normal teenage life. Now, digging into the past had unleashed forces far beyond his powers of understanding and the island had become a prison from which the internet offered no escape.

Supper proved a tense affair. Malcolm had received an ultimatum from Mr Bairstow at the bank: pay twelve months' mortgage arrears by the first of October or face immediate repossession of the house. Malcolm knew that the chances of finding almost five thousand pounds by the end of the month were nil. Worse still, he was in debt to a short-term loan company whose interest rates were such that he now owed three times what he'd borrowed. The last resort, the one that had stalked him ever since Superland had tarmacked over Mr Barlow's farm now stared him full in the face – bankruptcy. Almost everything of value that his family possessed would be confiscated. Anything that he or Donna earned would be taken from them and the bare minimum handed back to feed and clothe the family. Then, after twelve months, their debts would be written off and they could start again. With nothing.

That's what he'd have to show for eighteen years of marriage.

Nothing.

The thought haunted him day and night, gnawing away at his

resolve to keep fighting. He had two boys of course, but he scarcely knew them; two boys who were growing up facing a harsh and unforgiving world without a father because he was too busy fighting the same world and losing. Losing the business that had been in the family for generations. In its current state, it was no more than a millstone around his neck, outdated, worthless, irrelevant. And with the business, went the home he had laboured so hard and so long to forge but which would now be snatched away by bankers who understood nothing of the trials and tribulations of running a high street business.

And so, as each day passed, Malcolm moved a step closer to the edge. He knew what lay beyond yet felt utterly powerless to stop himself from being dragged towards the abyss.

'Letter from Bairstow arrived today. He's given us a few more weeks to get things sorted.' The truth would have prompted hysterics from Donna and questions from Merryn, neither of which he could face. 'It's like I said, Merryn. Things will work out in the end.'

Donna shot her husband a look that said *I don't believe you.* His elder son just sat staring at his curry, wondering when Mr Terry's ample figure would make a second appearance through the frosted glass of the front door.

Later that evening, Zac called Merryn's mobile.

'At least you answered the phone this time,' he mocked. 'Last time, if I remember, you couldn't be bothered to take it out of your pocket.'

'Maybe that's because I was lying at the bottom of a crevice unconscious.' Merryn wasn't amused.

'Feeble excuse. Don't forget, you'd never have found the pistol if you hadn't fallen in, and fifty per cent of its value is coming our way. If the butt *is* solid gold, then that's got to be a serious amount of loot. Hundreds, thousands even.'

'It's worth at least a hundred thousand and none of it is coming our way.'

There was a moment of studied silence while Zac tried to make sense of both halves of Merryn's statement. 'A hundred thousand?' He was incredulous. 'How do you know?'

'Mr Levi told me. It's why I kept Sasha waiting. He said *at least* a hundred thousand. But he warned me that if we were trespassing on private property when we found it, then we'd get nothing.'

'And who says we were trespassing? You don't know that the cliffs are private property.'

'Think about it, Zac. Spiked railings and a sign saying Keep Out. Everywhere in Britain is owned by someone. Whoever owns the cliffs will point out to the coroner that we failed to ask permission to go on their land. Instead, we ignored a Keep Out sign and squeezed through a tiny gap in the railings. They're not going to let a hundred grand slip through their hands that easily.'

Zac struggled to take it all in. Maybe Merryn was right but it wasn't fair. The landowner would never have found the pistol, not in a million years. He didn't deserve *one* pound let alone a hundred thousand.

'You don't *know* that, though,' but the elation had gone from his voice. 'We'll have to wait till the coroner's meeting. So what do we do now?'

Merryn lowered his voice in case Donna *had* bugged his room. 'Did you understand the map? The one I drew in ITC? I'm pretty certain that Mear is going to try and cross the river on Thursday night.'

'Yeah, I got that, but it just doesn't make sense. Why would anyone walk across the river? And at night? That's just insane. Anyway, where's your evidence?'

'He wrote it in the book – *A Short History of Chepstow*. 10:55pm, Thursday night at the ford. There's going to be a spring tide so the sea will disappear from the river completely. The only water left flowing across the ford will be river water and there's not much of that at this time of year. If you were going to cross the river on foot, Thursday night would be the best time to do it.'

'You keep on about a ford. What ford?'

'It's mentioned in the book. There's a ruined church by the river about four hundred yards from the cliffs. St James's. I found it on Google Earth. The ford crosses the river not far from the church. Wintour and his men were ambushed there by the Roundheads in 1645. Mear underlined that bit and then wrote the tide times and the words "Peri Spring". Perigean spring tide – the lowest tide of the year. Wintour crossed there because the Royalists had destroyed the bridge at Chepstow to stop the parliamentarians from attacking the castle. Don't ask me why Mear wants to cross the ford but he knows the best time to cross when he does.'

'Maybe he's planning a robbery and needs a quick getaway. Escaping across the river on foot would be a pretty neat way of evading the police.' Zac waited for a response but got none. 'Yeah, alright. Bit farfetched. So why doesn't he just cross in a boat. That's got to be easier than wading across the river. My dad warned me a long time ago to keep out of it. He said people drown in the Wye every year. Mud and currents. Mear's an evil git but I just don't think he's that stupid.'

'Zac, we've got to go.'

'Sorry? Go where?'

'The ford. On Thursday night.'

'Excuse me? Is this Merryn MacIntyre speaking? What happened to the "there's not going to be a next time"?'

'Things have changed.'

'Like what?'

'Like…' There was no point in telling Zac about the voice.

'Yes, online researcher, I'm waiting.'

'Look, I can't get any further with the hit-and-run. You were right. We don't have any evidence that would stand up in court so maybe – just maybe – we'll find what we're looking for at the ford on Thursday night.' It sounded weak but it was the best Merryn could do.

'What *we're* looking for? You mean what *you're* looking for. But if you want to go the ford, then I'm up for it. Trouble is, your parents are never going to let you go down to the river in the middle of the night, not after last time. Come to think of it, Sasha would go nuts if she knew I was mucking around by the river in the dark. We need a plan.'

'You're the field agent,' Merryn reminded him. 'Planning is in your job description.'

Fifteen seconds later, a voice in his ear said, 'Okay, here's what we do. Thursday afternoon after school, you come over to my place. I'll ask Sash if you can stay over. I'll say we're working on some assignment together and we need to do some online research. You haven't got a printer, have you?'

Merryn didn't have a printer. According to his dad, it was too expensive to buy, too expensive to run.

'So, that's the reason you're coming over. We need to print off a whole load of stuff. Then we'll slip out of the house around ten. My dad will be in New York this weekend. Another conference. That leaves Sasha and she goes to bed pretty early. You just need to persuade your mum that you're coming over to do school stuff. Even *she* can't stop you doing that.'

'You don't know Mum. She could stop the Earth spinning if she put her mind to it. Anyway, sounds like a plan. What do I need to bring?'

'Torch and toothbrush. Look, I've got to go. Stacey – she's my girlfriend – she's trying to phone me. The girl is driving me crazy. I need a reason to dump her, Merryn. How's about you ask her out? You owe me one for saving your life.'

'Saving my life? Whose idea was it to go crawling about on the edge of the cliffs at midnight? See you tomorrow.' Merryn hung up.

CHAPTER 19

Wednesday 11th September

Wednesday dawned with a chill, autumn mist hugging the fields and woods around Tidenham, paling the sun's light and stealing its warmth. Nothing about the day encouraged Merryn to leave the cosy confines of his bed. Quite the reverse – everything persuaded him to play ill and take the day off. Of course, that was a flight of fancy since nothing short of smallpox would convince Donna that he was unable to attend school. Yet, the prospect of a verbal bashing from Mr Wessells and a lunchtime detention with the White Witch tested his willpower to its limits. He groaned as he rolled out of bed onto the floor.

At breaktime he sought refuge in the library from the teachers queuing to extract their pound of flesh. Miss Kelly was nowhere to be seen, so he replaced *A Short History of Chepstow* and scanned the shelves for anything else that might prove useful.

'I thought I might find you here.'

He spun round to face Beatrice.

'What… w-w-what are you doing here?' he stammered.

'I told you, I was looking for you. I wanted to talk about the map, the one Mr Zammitt chucked in the bin.'

'You mean the one you stole from the bin and photocopied.'

'Mmm. Sorry about that.' She flashed one of her dazzling smiles that had sorry written on it in the tiniest font. Beatrice read his mind and tried her best to look sincere.

'No really, I *am* sorry. I wanted to give you it back.' She pulled out the map from her bag and held it out.

'And this is photocopy number... ten?' Merryn took the map and stuffed it in his pocket.

Beatrice couldn't restrain herself any longer. 'Tell me about the pistol, Merryn. Why did you write 'pistol' on the map at the top of the cliffs? Something happened at Wintour's Leap, didn't it?'

Merryn had stopped listening. He was staring at her hair, mesmerised by the intricate patterns woven into each braid. It seemed that no two braids were the same, as if each one had been painstakingly created by a different artist, each trying to out-braid the others. How long, he wondered, had it taken? He could not begin to conceive of the patience required to sit motionless for hours while the braiders wove their magic.

'Come on, you can't keep something like this to yourself. I've seen the map so you have to tell me what it means. Please.'

Two large, brown eyes began to dismantle his outer defences. Something was happening to him, something that he was utterly powerless to stop. More than anything, he wanted to confide in Beatrice, to tell her everything so that they would have something in common, something to share, but he couldn't ignore the voices in his head telling him to say nothing. *You can't bring Beatrice into the loop without consulting Zac.*

'I can't tell you. I *want* to tell you, it's just...' He felt his face blushing and he turned away, terrified that Beatrice might guess what was going on inside his head.

'It's just what? You *can* tell me. I'm not going to go blabbing.'

'No, I can't tell you. It's complicated. And it's dangerous,' he added.

'What? Too dangerous for the little African girl, is that it?' Instantly, she wished she'd kept her mouth shut. Sometimes she sensed people didn't take her seriously because she was a girl and black but she knew that Merryn wasn't one of those people. She'd spoken without thinking, something that frequently got her into trouble.

'No, that's not it.' He turned to face her, incensed by the suggestion that he was treating her differently just because she was black. 'That's not it at all. I will tell you everything. Next Monday. It's just that right now there are people who are relying on me to say nothing. I can't let them down. I'm sorry.'

An awkward silence fell between them, then Beatrice spoke softly. 'No, *I'm* sorry. I shouldn't have come here asking about the map. It's got nothing to do with me. I just couldn't stop looking at it and thinking about...' She was going to say 'you' but the bell rang and the moment was lost. She turned to go. When the bell stopped, she said, 'I didn't mean what I said, about being a little African girl. You know that, don't you?'

Merryn nodded. At that precise moment, he would have nodded even if she'd invited him to go base-jumping. Having scaled the outer walls of Merryn's defences, Beatrice had fired a cannonball at the great oak door of the inner keep, reducing it to splinters. Now there was nothing to stop her from marching straight in. If she wanted to.

*

Merryn waited until supper before broaching the subject of staying over at Zac's the following night.

'We've a load of stuff to print. We're not allowed to print more than a few pages in school so Zac said we could do it at his place.'

'And you have to stay over to use Zac's printer?' Donna glanced at her husband to see whether he was as unconvinced as she was but he wasn't listening.

'No, I don't have to, but Sasha invited me for supper so I might as well stay the night. What's the problem?' Merryn played his ace card.

'You want me to babysit again?'

If he hadn't been lying then he might have felt pleased at outwitting his mother. Instead, he felt guilty. Lying to his parents had become the default setting. The backlog of half-truths and downright lies was now so large that he couldn't see a way back. Right now, he reasoned, with his father's business on the verge of collapse, the last thing his parents needed was the truth. Trespass, crevice, pistol, attempted murder, coma. It would push them over the edge. Lying was easier, kinder, safer until they were ready. Then he would tell them everything.

'Malcolm? Are you listening? Merryn wants to stay over at Zac's tomorrow. Is that okay with you?'

Malcolm looked up. 'Why not? I'll be home early tomorrow. I'm closing at four on Thursdays. Saves on bills. Who's Zac, anyway?'

Merryn rolled his eyes and got up from the table. 'You tell him, Mum. I've got homework.'

It was ten o'clock, however, before Merryn finally pulled his maths homework from his schoolbag but by then, he was too exhausted to factorise anything. Three hours scouring the internet for more pieces to the jigsaw had used up his last reserves of nervous energy, and all to no avail. Flintlocks with golden butts were nowhere to be seen online; the Bath-24 site had nothing new to report on the hit-and-run at Monkton Farleigh; and fords across the River Wye simply didn't exist south of Tintern in the tidal section of the river.

It was gone midnight when he finally fell into bed and switched off the light. Released from the boundaries of reality, his brain slipped almost at once into dream sleep, freed to wander at will along the corridors of his memory. Tapes of half-imagined happenings played in his mind, as vivid and animated as anything in his waking life. No sooner had he closed his eyes than a film began to play. An elderly man pedalling his bike along a narrow, country lane, the steepening gradient of a long, straight hill slowing his progress as he leaned over the handlebars, his eyes focused on the tarmac in front of him. He was determined to reach the brow of the hill without stopping. He'd never managed it before, but this evening he felt strong.

Behind him, unobserved, an old Mercedes began to climb the hill, moving no faster than the bike. The cyclist was out of the saddle now, panting hard as his bike lurched alarmingly from side to side. He didn't hear the sudden roar of the car's V8 as it accelerated like a rocket up the hill behind him. Too late, the cyclist looked round, shock spreading across his face as he glimpsed the driver just moments before the impact – sixteen hundred kilos of car smashing into fifteen kilos of pushbike.

The car squealed to a stop and the driver stepped out, walking quickly back to where bike and rider lay twisted and motionless in the road. He stooped to pick up fragments of orange glass and then, satisfied that the job was done, returned to his car and drove away.

CHAPTER 20

Thursday 12th September

The following morning, Merryn arrived at school early, before the duty staff could stop him entering the building and climbing the stairs to room 309. He knocked softly and Miss Grigoryev's voice answered.

'Come in. Ah, Mr MacIntyre. You arrive early, eh? And your head, it's good, yes?'

Merryn nodded. 'It's fine, thanks.'

'I'm glad. Well, I have no news, I'm afraid.'

'Have they taken Mr Biddle off the coma drugs yet? You said they might stop the drugs on Wednesday evening.' Merryn searched Miss Grigoryev's face for signs of hope, for anything that would keep the light alive at the end of the long, dark tunnel but he could find nothing.

'Yes, the consultant has stopped the drugs. I think he would like to keep George in a coma for a few more days to give his brain more time to rest but he is worried about his blood pressure. It is too low. He has tried more drugs to fix this but now he wants George's brain to fix it and that means waking him up.'

'So what happened when they stopped the coma drugs?'

'What happened? Nothing happened. It's like I say, Merryn, no news. It means that George is still in a natural coma. Remember, his brain gets shaken very hard when the driver knocks him from his bike. He is not a young man like you so it will take a little time. Maybe – like I told you before – a long time. We must be patient. We cannot hurry him back to life, you understand? He will come back to us when he is ready.'

He nodded. Miss Grigoryev made it sound simple but he could read the agony in her face. There was something else there, too. Something that he hadn't seen before in the bubbly little Russian woman.

Anger.

Shock, pain, anger. He had read it somewhere – the stages of grief. The little Russian woman had reached the anger stage. What would she do when she discovered that the man behind the wheel of the hit-and-run was a man she worked with every day? A man whose application form she must have read and whose appointment she must have sanctioned?

'Miss, have the police made any progress? Do they have any idea who hit Mr Biddle?' The question left his lips before he could stop it.

'I spoke with them yesterday. No, they have made no progress finding whoever did this. It happens on a quiet lane with no traffic and no witnesses.'

There was no question that Miss Grigoryev had reached the anger stage. It was seething beneath the surface.

'The car must have been damaged, miss. Where it hit the bike. Maybe scratches and broken lights. What if the police found the car?'

She stared at him for a few moments, curious as to where his questions were leading. Was he trying to tell her something?

'And where would they look for the car, Merryn? Bath is a big city with many cars. I think the police, they know about this. It's what they do. All they say to me is that no witnesses have come forward and until they do, then…'

'Then he gets away with it. But he won't, miss. They'll find him. And when they do…'

'And when they do, Merryn...' It was Miss Grigoryev's turn to interrupt. Her voice fell to a vicious whisper. 'When they do, God help him.'

Merryn felt his head was about to explode. He could tell her now. Right there in her room. *It's Mear. The man you appointed to cover for Mr Biddle. He's the one who drove the car – a Mercedes. Look in the car park. It's got a dent and brand new indicator glass.* But if he told her, what then? She would never last the day without confronting the animal and that would warn him off his late-night appointment at the ford. Mear would deny everything, of course. He would have an alibi. His sidekick – Jed – would vouch for him and then he would be beyond reach.

Miss Grigoryev, however, wouldn't see it like that. She had confided in him about Mr Biddle and in return he had told her nothing.

'I've got to go, miss. You'll tell me if Mr Biddle wakes up, won't you?'

'No, I'll tell you *when* he wakes up. You'll be the first to know. And Merryn.'

He stopped by the door. 'Yes?'

'You're right. They'll find him.'

*

The lunchtime appointment with Miss Kelly in the library proved to be a masterpiece of selective recall. Merryn, who did most of the talking, avoided lying – he'd already dug that hole as deep as his conscience would allow. It was as well that he did for what remained was more than enough to make the English teacher feel physically sick.

She unfolded a 1:25,000 scale map of the Wye Valley and asked the boys to point out the exact location of the crevice where the pistol had been found. It wasn't hard to find. Merryn's finger traced the road running south along the top of the cliffs from Netherhope Lane. After only a few centimetres, he stopped at a point where road and cliff top seemed to merge on the map.

'Here.'

Miss Kelly looked at him. 'Absolutely certain?'

'He's right, miss,' Zac cut in. 'There was only about thirty feet between the road and the edge. That's the spot.'

'Okay, if you're sure.' She circled it in red. 'And you've no idea who owns the land, is that right?'

'Merryn has let us down there, I'm afraid.' Zac grinned. 'We could always go back and ask around. Someone must know.'

'You'll do no such thing. I don't want you anywhere near those cliffs. Either of you. One set of stitches is enough so you can wipe that stupid grin off your face. I'm already an accessory to a near-death-by-misadventure. Any more shenanigans and I'm going straight to the head. Just remember, my job could be on the line. You're going to play by the book from now on, do you understand?'

The grin disappeared from Zac's face and he nodded. Merryn groaned inwardly and said nothing. He was fairly certain that a night-time stake out on the banks of the Wye could be classified as a shenanigan. The hole he was digging just got a little deeper.

Miss Kelly continued; 'Now, before you go, I have some news.' Her voice had softened again and the excitement was back in her eyes. 'Mr Levi phoned last night. At ten to midnight, to be precise.' She smiled, shaking her head. The boys held their breath. 'Monsieur St Pierre touched down at Bristol Airport yesterday lunchtime. Isaac was right. He does indeed have his own transport – a private jet. Anyway, he spent the afternoon examining the pistol in a state of considerable excitement, during which time he made several phone calls to a private collector in New York. Isaac is keeping his cards pretty close to his chest but he's fairly certain that St Pierre knows who the original owner of the pistol was.'

'Did he tell you?' Merryn asked, barely able to contain his excitement.

'No, he didn't, I'm afraid. St Pierre is flying over to New York today to examine a similar pistol in some private museum. Isaac said that when he returns, he'll divulge the full story. In the meantime, you'll just have to be patient. The pistol has been transferred to Miss Edwards at the Bristol Museum. She'll contact the British Museum to see if they're interested in buying it. The coroner has already set a date for the inquest. Tuesday October 1st at eleven in the morning. It's being held at the function room in the museum. Do you recall Isaac saying it normally takes months? He clearly has some pretty serious clout in the world of antiquities.' She paused for breath. 'Are you following all this?'

The boys nodded.

'Since you're both under eighteen, your parents will receive a formal request by letter to attend the inquest. Have you told your parents about the reward that's coming your way?'

Merryn looked depressed. 'Actually, we haven't because it's not going to happen.'

'Oh, and why's that?'

'After you'd gone, miss, Mr Levi told me that if we were trespassing, then we'd get nothing. I've checked it online and he's right. The Treasure Act 1996 says that we are eligible for a share of the pistol's value only if we obtained permission from the landowner. We didn't, so according to the law we get a reduced share or nothing.'

Miss Kelly thought for a moment. 'Yes, but a reduced share of thousands is still a lot of money.'

'But nothing isn't. We ignored a Keep Out sign and squeezed through iron railings that were designed to keep people out.'

Miss Kelly frowned. 'That's the first I've heard of a Keep Out sign. Why didn't you tell me about it before?'

Merryn looked at the table while Zac's eyes bored holes in his partner's head.

'No, Zac. Don't go blaming your accomplice. Omitting to tell me stuff is just as bad as lying. Why do I get the feeling that I've only heard half of the story? Now, Merryn, what exactly did the sign say?'

'Keep out – dangerous cliffs.'

'And the railings? How did you get through them?'

'There was one missing. If we hadn't squeezed through, we'd have been run over by a car. It was foggy, you see.'

Miss Kelly winced. 'This just gets worse and worse. Squeezing through railings in the fog above three-hundred-foot cliffs.' She scribbled it all on paper before looking up. 'Anything else you've omitted to tell me?'

'That's it, miss.'

Zac was too ready with the answer, she thought. 'Merryn? Anything to add?'

He shook his head.

'Okay, meeting adjourned. I'll get this typed up and email it to Isaac and the FLO. How about you call in at break tomorrow and I'll update you on what's happening?'

When the boys had gone, she sat quietly at the table for a few moments and asked herself for the hundredth time why she had not reported the whole matter of the pistol to Mrs Bowden-Lees, the head teacher. Anything which happened on the school premises was a school matter. She knew that. It had been drummed into her at college. *Never get so close to pupils that their secrets become your secrets.* But for four days, she had thought of nothing else but the secrets of two fifteen-year-old boys, the secrets they had shared with her. And those she was certain they hadn't.

That's it, she decided. Enough was enough. She had been a fool to let matters run this far without informing the head. She would make an appointment to see Mrs Bowden-Lees at the earliest opportunity and tell her everything. Then her conscience would be clear. She would step back from the whole affair and get on with her life.

She went into the library office and phoned the head's PA.

'Sorry, Sian. The head's out at County Hall today. Tomorrow at twelve-thirty. That's the earliest I can do, I'm afraid.'

Damn, she mouthed silently. She wanted to talk now. She might change her mind by tomorrow. A lot could happen in twenty-four hours.

'Tomorrow at twelve-thirty,' she heard herself say. 'Thanks, Natalie,' and she put the phone down. When the boys came over to the library for a news update on the pistol, she would tell them that the head had to know everything. Their secrets would no longer be her secrets.

CHAPTER 21

'You live *here*?' Merryn gaped at the high wrought iron gates guarding the entrance to a long, gravel driveway. It curved out of sight through an avenue of lime trees and rhododendron bushes.

Zac nodded. 'It's a bit of an epic, really. I don't know why Dad doesn't find somewhere a bit smaller. Come on. Sasha's very excited about meeting you again. I can't imagine why. I tried telling her you were actually pretty dull and unsociable but she wouldn't listen.'

Merryn wasn't listening. Walking up the drive, the house slowly came into view – an eighteenth-century Georgian manor. It was a wide, three storied, stone building with large, white-framed sash windows set in perfect symmetry around a columned porch leading to an enormous front door. Surrounding the house on three sides, manicured lawns stretched out to a fringe of dense woodland. At first glance, it seemed to Merryn that the garden was larger than the public park in Tidenham.

'How many people live here?' he asked, scarcely able to believe that someone as normal as Zac could live in such a place.

'Just the three of us. Dad should sell it but he won't. He's always lived here. It's been in the family for years, centuries actually. My great-great-grandparents lived here, apparently. We'll go round the side. Front door's always locked.'

Merryn crunched across the gravel behind Zac to a door at the side of the house. Before they reached it, the door opened and Sasha appeared. She was much taller than he'd imagined since he'd only seen her sitting in the car. He guessed she was a few years younger than his mum. The likeness to Zac was uncanny. If she wasn't his mother, then who was she? An older sister? Surely not. The age difference was too great.

'Merryn with the magic memory,' she exclaimed. 'I'm so glad you accepted my invitation.'

Zac put an arm around Sasha as if restraining her. 'I told you she gets excited. She's from Romania. Did I tell you that?'

'Ignore him, Merryn,' she said, shrugging off Zac's arm. 'He has the manners of his father. Now, we shall eat at seven. Zac can show you around the house.'

Merryn never got the conducted tour. Instead, Zac led him up an enormous, creaking staircase to a first-floor landing stretching the whole length of the house. At one end, narrow stairs led up to Zac's bedroom on the second floor.

Zac pushed open an old wooden door, threw his grip bag on the floor and collected his iPad from a table beside one of four beds in the room. 'So, what time do we need to leave?'

'Wow!' Merryn stood in the doorway, gaping at the sheer size of the room. 'It's massive! You could play cricket in here.'

'Or rugby. It used to be the attic. That's why it's so long. Anyway, you're not listening. What time do we need to leave? You said ten fifty-five at the river, right?'

'Yep. Five to eleven. That's low tide. But we should be there before that. The problem is we don't know where the ford is. There's no sign of it on Google Earth.'

'If you don't know where it is, then why did you draw it on your sketch map?' Zac opened Google Earth on his iPad and zoomed in to Wintour's Leap.

'Because I found the ruined church and, according to the passage in the book, the ford is close by.'

'Show me.' Zac handed Merryn his iPad. Merryn had never used a tablet touchscreen before but it didn't take him long to get the hang of it.

'There's the church,' he said, pointing at the rectangular shape a short distance from the river. 'The ford must cross the river somewhere…' – he slid the river into view – '…here.'

'I don't want to ruin the party, but there's nothing there. It's just muddy water running between two muddy slopes; and you're basing the existence of this ford on a description taken from some moth-eaten history book, the same description that has Wintour galloping off three-hundred-foot cliffs and surviving.'

'Two hundred and eighty, actually. So why did Mear underline the bit about the ford in the book? Why did he write tide times in the margin?' Merryn glared at Zac, waiting for an answer. 'I'm not saying it's definitely there. In any case, it's not the ford we're really interested in. It's Mear.'

Zac shrugged. 'You still haven't answered my question. What time do we need to leave?'

'I reckon we should get to the ruined church at about ten. That'll give us time to check out the river and then find somewhere to hide before Mear turns up.'

Zac took his iPad back and zoomed out from the church to look for the best way of reaching it from the road. 'It may have escaped your notice that it's going to be dark at ten. How exactly are you going to find the church in the dark? There's no road to it, just a vague path which leads downhill through the woods.'

It was obvious from Merryn's expression that he hadn't given this any thought. 'We need a map and a torch,' he suggested.

'Luckily for you, your field operative can do better than that.' Zac took out his smart phone and tapped the screen a few times. 'Check this out.' Merryn leaned over the phone to watch as Zac positioned a 1:50,000 OS map on the screen showing Boughspring at the top and the ruined church not far from the River Wye at the bottom. Using a short pointer-pen, he double-tapped on his house and then again on the ruined church. 'That's start and destination. Now I select mode of travel – walking – and there's the route.' A green line appeared from Zac's house, along roads to the footpath that led downhill to the ruined church. 'And because it's GPS, it knows exactly where we are at all times. If we stray off route by more than ten metres, it sounds an alarm.'

'Can you ask the app to avoid roads?'

'Why?'

'Just in case.'

'Just in case what? Mear drives past and tries to run us over?' Zac laughed. 'Yeah, okay, you're in luck. There's an 'avoid roads' option.' A couple of taps later and the app had recalculated the route. 'There's still about four hundred metres of lane. It's unavoidable unless we trespass across people's gardens.'

'Nope. We've done enough trespassing. We'll just have to run that bit. How far from your house to the church?'

'It says one point three miles. That'll take about fifteen minutes or half an hour at your speed.'

'So we leave here at half nine.'

*

It was just after nine when two dark shapes emerged from the door at the side of the house. Neither had scored high marks for patience. A gleaming full moon made brief appearances through legions of dark clouds sweeping across the sky, driven by a brisk wind. Merryn thought he could feel rain in the air as he followed hard on Zac's heels across the lawn and out through the gates into the road. Once they were a safe distance from the house, Zac slowed the pace and took out his phone.

'The battery only lasts for about an hour when the GPS app is running, but that's more than enough.'

'Unless we get lost,' observed Merryn.

'We can't get lost, you big numpty. Look. All we have to do is keep the red arrow – that's us – on the green line – that's the route to the church. Watch what happens if we stray more than ten metres from the route.'

They'd reached a point on the edge of Boughspring where a small cul-de-sac led off from the main road. Zac sprinted into the cul-de-sac and his phone gave off a series of high-pitched bleeps. Almost immediately from somewhere in the cul-de-sac, a dog began barking.

'See what I mean? As soon as I'm back on route, it'll stop.'

'I'll bet the dog doesn't stop when you're back on route.'

'That's because my phone is smarter than the dog. There. Back on route.' The bleeps stopped while the dog continued howling into the night.

A few yards beyond the cul-de-sac, the GPS took them over a stile at the side of the road onto a wide footpath leading southwest across fields. The clouds were thinning and the moon provided all the light they needed.

'This is the Offa's Dyke path,' observed Zac. 'It crosses two fields then veers south through a conifer plantation. The Wye Valley road is just beyond that.'

Ahead, the path disappeared into a dark conifer plantation and they switched on their torches.

'In about two hundred metres, we'll come out the other side and turn left onto…' Zac's phone vibrated. 'Oh, now what? Someone's giving me grief on Facebook.' He minimised the GPS app, opened Facebook and stared at the message, struggling to make sense of it. He held out his phone to Merryn. 'Tell me I'm imagining that, will you?'

Merryn read the message on the screen. It said simply: *"What's wrong with the road?"* It wasn't, however, the message which made his pulse quicken. It was the sender's name, displayed at the top of the screen in large bold font.

Beatrice Odoyo.

'What the hell does she mean – what's wrong with the road?

Which road? I tell you, she is one strange girl.'

'She knows where we are.' Merryn's tone was quiet and matter-of-fact but his brain was racing. 'She's asking why we're not walking on the road.'

'What? She knows where we are? How can she?' said Zac, increasingly rattled.

'Maybe she can track your phone with hers,' Merryn suggested.

'No way. There *are* tracking apps on the market but the person you're tracking needs to have the app on their phone as well, and I certainly haven't got any tracking apps on my phone. They are seriously bad news. Can you imagine what Stacey would do if she could track my every move? Nightmare.'

'I've just had a thought.' Merryn's brain was still racing. 'She's got a copy of my map. The one I drew in ITC. She knows about Mear's appointment at the ford – I wrote the time on the map.'

'I knew it was a mistake telling her anything. But that still doesn't explain how she knows that we're not walking on the road. Unless…' Zac turned and shone his torch back along the path, sweeping the beam left and right, searching for signs of movement among the rows of Sitka spruce. 'Unless she's following us.'

'Does she know where you live?'

'No. Well, maybe. Loads of Year 11 know where I live. I have parties in the summer. Not so much this summer, mind, but in Year 10. Beatrice never came; we weren't really friends, but she knows people who did.'

'That's a yes then. So maybe she *is* following us. Send a reply. Ask her…' He thought for a moment. 'Ask her: *When shall we three meet again?* See if she takes the bait.'

'Macbeth? I thought you said Shakespeare was a waste of time.' Zac typed it in and tapped "Send". The boys waited, staring at the brightly-lit screen, willing the phone to vibrate. It wasn't long in coming. "*When the battle's lost and won.*"

'Oh my God. That's Macbeth as well, isn't it?'

The message made Merryn smile. 'The witches scene at the beginning. Clever. She knows her Macbeth and at the same time, she's told us nothing. She's not going to, either. We're wasting time. If she's following us, we'll soon find out.'

'I still don't get it.' Zac brought up the GPS map and resumed walking, his pace more urgent now. 'Why would she follow us? It's got nothing to do with her.'

'Maybe three is better than two,' Merryn suggested.

'No it isn't. Three is someone being nosy. Come on, we've got to lose her.'

It wasn't long before the path emerged from the eeriness of the wood into the brilliant moonlight. It turned sharply right and met the main road.

'Two hundred yards along the road, then a right turn into Lancaut Lane. We'll sprint this bit.'

'Remember, my legs are only...' But Merryn never finished the bit about his legs being only half as long as Zac's because Zac's legs had vaulted the stile onto the road and were racing away towards the turning.

'Great teamwork!' Merryn shouted while at that very moment, the brakes on a pushbike squealed as it pulled up alongside him.

'Looks like you need a lift. Use the saddle and I'll stand.'

'Beatrice! You frightened the life out of me. What are you doing here? I mean, how did you know…?'

'No time to explain. Get on the bike quickly before a car comes. We'll catch Zac up. Nice of him to wait for you. Oh, and don't call me Beatrice. It's Bee.'

Merryn had never ridden tandem before. Having squeezed onto the saddle behind her, he couldn't figure out where to put his limbs.

'Keep your feet away from the wheels and hold on to my waist otherwise you'll fall off. Like this,' and she pulled his arms tight around her waist. She pushed off and accelerated away, her legs pumping hard on the pedals. To Merryn's astonishment, the bike gained speed quickly despite a slight incline in the road. He knew of Beatrice's running prowess – everyone did – but he'd no idea she was a crack cyclist as well. From out of nowhere, a car approached from behind, sounding its horn as it swerved around the bike. The driver lowered his window, stuck his head out and shouted, 'nutters!' before accelerating away.

Merryn heaved a sigh of relief. Neither head nor voice belonged to Mear. Ahead of them, a narrow lane forked away to the right.

'Turn here, is that right?' gasped Beatrice, glancing behind her to check the road was clear.

'Yeah, I think so. It should say Lancaut Lane.'

There was still no sign of Zac as Beatrice swung the bike off the main road and pedalled hard down the lane. Dense oak wood pressed in from both sides so that rider and passenger could see nothing beyond the bike lamp's narrow beam. To Merryn, Beatrice seemed possessed, her body swaying violently from side to side with each turn of the pedals, the bike gaining speed rapidly on the downhill. Merryn's whole being burned with a wild exhilaration.

'There he is!' she called out.

Merryn grinned. He was going to enjoy this. Beatrice skidded to a halt a few yards from a startled Zac.

'Hi Zac,' she beamed. 'Looks like we three meet again.'

Zac just stood, shaking his head in disbelief but, before he could say anything, Merryn nudged him and pointed down the lane.

'He's here.' He played his torch beam over the back of a car parked in a shallow layby. Mear's Mercedes. It sat dark and menacing like its owner, the rear reflectors flashing red in the torchlight like the eyes of a demonic beast. 'Get off the road!'

Darting into the woods, they crouched in the darkness, listening for the sound of a car door opening.

'Mear?' whispered Beatrice.

'Maybe,' replied Zac.

'How do you know it's him?'

'Because very few people own an old E-reg Mercedes 420.' A trace of impatience had crept into his voice.

'So, why is he here, and please don't give me the "crossing the river" story? No one is dull enough to try crossing the river at night.'

'Actually, Bee,' Merryn whispered, 'that's exactly what he's going to do. There's an old ford near a ruined church. At low tide – that's at five to eleven tonight – he's going to cross the river. Exactly why, we've no idea. That's why we're here.' Merryn wanted to tell her more, that they were there because a woman's voice had led him there, but he could feel Zac's eyes on him.

'Oh, it's *Bee*, is it? How nice and friendly. And how come we're suddenly three? What are you doing here?' Zac made no effort to conceal his resentment. This had been his and Merryn's show and now she had somehow muscled in, acting like she belonged.

'Buried treasure, you said, Zac. There's no way I was going to miss out on that.'

'Oh, funny girl. So tell us, *Bee*, how did you know where we were?'

'Stick with rugby, *Zac*. You'll never get a job with the secret service. You're too easy to follow. Mind you, the cross-country bit threw me. Why didn't you just walk along the road?'

Zac searched in vain for a knockout punch but he couldn't find a way through the girl's defences. She wasn't just a pretty face. She was smart. Too smart.

Merryn interrupted the boxing match. 'Come on, we've got to go. How far to the path?'

Zac checked the GPS on his phone. 'It starts exactly where Mear parked his car. Makes sense. He's using the path to get down to the river.'

Cautiously, they approached the Mercedes, half-expecting a door to fly open and Mear to step out, but the car was empty.

Yelping in disgust, Beatrice suddenly sprung back from the rear of the car. 'Oh yuk! I just trod in something weird. What *is* this stuff?' Her torch beam picked out a pile of white, translucent chips. She bent down and grabbed a handful. 'Ice!' She held it up for the boys to inspect. 'He's dumped a load of ice on the ground. Why would he do that? Unless . . .' Suddenly, Beatrice was on a beach, watching fishing dhows coming home after a morning out on Lake Victoria.

'Unless what?' Zac looked mystified.

Merryn looked at Beatrice. 'Are you thinking what I'm thinking?'

'Depends what you're thinking,' she replied.

'I'm thinking fish.'

'Then I'm thinking what you're thinking.'

'What? So we've come all this way just to watch Mear fishing?' Zac still looked mystified.

'No, Zac,' Beatrice sighed. 'We've come all this way to watch Mear *poaching.*'

CHAPTER 22

'Poaching? How can you be so sure? Maybe he's just into night fishing.' Zac resented the girl's interference in a plan that he and Merryn had conceived. More than that, he resented the approval that his partner was radiating towards Beatrice.

'She's right. He's poaching.' Merryn twisted the knife. 'The only reason anyone would risk fishing the Wye at night is if they were breaking the law.'

Beatrice looked at the ice in her hand again. It was melting quickly. 'Back in Kenya, I remember the women always had baskets of ice like this ready on the beach when the fishing boats came back. Fish go off after about three hours if they're not kept really cold. Then you can't sell them. Mear's expecting to catch a lot of fish and he wants to sell them.'

'So why's he dumped all this ice on the ground?' Zac asked, looking for a hole in Beatrice's logic.

'Think about it. He comes back to the car with… I don't know… say, twenty good-sized salmon. He's got cold boxes in his boot full of ice ready for the fish, but he needs to make room for them. So what does he do?'

Zac said nothing. He knew she was right.

'So you're saying he's already brought a load of fish up from the river?' Merryn's voice dropped to a whisper.

'Must have. And looking at the ice, I'd say he's not long gone. It's only just starting to melt.'

Instinctively, they ducked behind the car and switched off their torches, straining to hear voices but the only sounds were the faint rustling of leaves and the far-off bark of a fox carried up from the river on the breeze.

Merryn checked his watch. 'It's nine-forty. A little more than an hour to low tide. River will be pretty low by now, low enough for a man to cross the ford with a net.'

'I read somewhere poachers use poison to stun the fish upstream of a net.' The other two looked at Zac wondering if he was bluffing. 'Then they just wade into the river and pick them out of the net.' He met Beatrice's stare and tapped her arm. 'Brawn.' And then his head. 'Brain'.

'You should use it more often,' Beatrice whispered. 'Listen, we should call the police.' The poise in her voice was disappearing. 'You don't know how many men he's got down there with him.'

'Bugs me to say it but you're right,' Zac conceded, minimising the GPS on his phone. 'You wanted to nail him, Merry, and now you have. He'll get a pretty heavy fine for poaching, if that's what he's doing.'

'That's what he's doing, but...' From out of nowhere, a switch flicked on inside Merryn's head which replayed a conversation he'd had with the Head of History.

Zac winced. 'Here we go. There's always a but.'

'Because things aren't always as simple as you make out, Zac. I went to see Miss Grigoryev after our first lesson with Mear and she said something a bit... well, weird. That Mr Biddle wasn't right after his meeting with Mear.'

'What meeting?' Zac asked.

'Before term started. A handover meeting. You know, getting Mear up to speed. Which classes he was going to teach, what he was going to teach.'

'Okay, but "wasn't right?" What did she mean?'

'She didn't say, but she was upset about it, I could tell.'

'And what's this got to do with Mear poaching on the...' Zac's voice tailed off.

Merryn turned to Beatrice. 'You see where I'm going?'

She shook her head. 'Not the foggiest.'

'Ha! Not so smart after all,' Zac scoffed. 'What if Mear accidentally let slip at the meeting that he was into a bit of poaching on the side. Maybe he asked Biddle if he'd like some fresh salmon now and then. And Biddle, being a decent sort of bloke, threatened to report Mear to the police. So Mear, being a nasty sort of bloke...'

'Yes, go on. Finish the sentence.' At last, Merryn thought, he's on my side.

'No. He wouldn't. Just because Biddle threatens him. Attempted murder? No way. He'd warn him off first.'

'What are you talking about, attempted murder?' The last vestige of poise in Beatrice's voice sprinted away into the darkness. Now she was afraid. 'Mear tried to murder Mr Biddle?'

'So Merryn reckons,' Zac answered. 'But the evidence is pretty thin.'

'That's it *exactly*!' Merryn protested. 'That's why you can't call the police. Come on. I'm going down to the church.'

'Merryn, wait!' But it was too late. Beatrice watched as the online researcher melted into the darkness of the oak wood while beside her, the field agent swore under his breath.

'Is he always like this?' Beatrice asked. 'I'd got him down as kind of timid.'

'Mear's got to him. He's obsessed with this hit-and-run thing. He just won't let it go.'

'Well we can't let him go alone.' She stood up. 'If Mear finds ...'

'Yeah, alright, but I'm ringing the police as soon as we get to the river. They can sort it out, whatever *it* is.'

The path through the woods was steep from the start and clearly little-used, in places overgrown and difficult to follow. Despite the patches of dappled moonlight between the oak trees, Merryn kept losing the path, ending up knee deep in a tangle of brambles and broken branches. As the gradient began to ease, they reached a clearing. Thirty yards to their right in the middle of the clearing, the ruins of an ancient church stood grim and desolate. Nothing of its roof remained, the stone tiles and timbers long since looted. The tower, too, had been dismantled, stone by stone.

Zac checked the GPS. 'The path goes straight across the clearing to the left of the church. The river isn't far beyond that.'

'I don't like this.' Beatrice's voice was taut. 'We're using the same path that Mear is using to get to his car. Any minute, we're going to bump into him. Then what? You said he's already tried to kill Mr Biddle.'

'It's the only path down to the river from here,' Zac insisted. 'We can't just hack our way through the woods in the dark. We'll get ripped to pieces by brambles. We've got to stay on the path.'

'But the moon; it's like a spotlight.' Beatrice began to wish she'd stayed at home.

'Then we'll run like hell. As long as we stay close.' Zac gave Merryn a meaningful stare.

'It's not my fault you keep losing me,' Merryn protested. 'Run at the speed of the slowest. That's me.'

'Okay slowest. Are you ready?' Without waiting for an answer, Zac launched into the clearing. Before Merryn could follow, he felt a hand on his arm. Beatrice pulled him closer so that she could look straight into his eyes.

'I'm frightened,' she whispered. 'You won't do anything stupid, will you?'

Ambushed by the girl's sudden intimacy, Merryn lost control of his mental faculties and before he could think of a reply – or even think at all – Beatrice leaned across and kissed him gently on the lips. 'You'd better not,' and with that she was running. 'Come on,' she urged. 'Stay close!'

Beatrice's kiss had unleashed pandemonium inside his head, so much so that he failed to notice the small, stocky figure crouched in the moon shadow at one corner of the church, an empty sack on the grass beside him. Doing his best to keep pace with Beatrice, he reached the far side. There, Zac checked his phone and, without a word, turned and headed off towards the river.

'At last, Tom, you will keep the promise that you made so long ago.'

Merryn spun round and stared back at the church.

'Did you hear that?' he whispered.

'Hear what?' Beatrice tugged at his arm, urging him to move.

'It's her, the woman, speaking to me. From the church, I think. So much louder than before. It's like she's right here.'

'It's just the wind.' She stared at him, wondering what drew her to this boy who was so different from the rest. 'Come on, we've got to move.'

'But take care for he means you harm. I will guide you, Tom. Listen and I will guide you.'

'There, again. She's in the church, I swear it. She's spoken to me before. It's the same voice.'

'Come on!' Beatrice urged, tugging harder. 'You're just imagining it.'

Merryn hesitated, his ears straining to hear more but she was silent now. 'What is it you want me to do?' he whispered, following hard on Beatrice's heels.

Ahead of them, an old dry-stone wall ran along the edge of the wood, parallel to the river. A wooden gate, set in the wall, marked the point where the path spilled out onto the riverbank – the end of the green line. Keeping low, Zac approached the gate, scanning the riverbank left and right for signs of life. He turned to the others. 'Get down!' he mouthed, gesturing wildly with both arms.

Merryn and Beatrice dropped to the ground, hearts racing with a sudden rush of panic. Zac pointed downstream. No further explanation was needed. Mear was approaching rapidly along the bank, a bag slung over his shoulder. They had to move quickly, but where? To the right, the stone wall had collapsed in several places but to the left of the gate it was still intact. In less than a minute Mear would reach the gate. Then came the ominous sound of heavy footsteps on the path behind them. If they didn't move now, the game would be over.

'This way!' Zac hissed, one finger to his lips, the other hand motioning for them to keep low. As fast as he dared, he weaved his way left through the undergrowth, heading for the wall. Reaching it, he dropped to the ground, wriggling into the deep drift of leaves at its base until he was completely hidden. Quickly, the others joined him. No sooner had they buried themselves than they heard the click of the gate latch opening followed by a sharp clang as the gate swung shut.

'Ez, did you see 'em?' Merryn stiffened as he recognised the voice, the same one he'd heard in the staffroom. It came from the other side of the wall, no more than twenty feet away. Something moved in the leaves beside him. Beatrice's hand was searching for his. He moved closer and took hold of it, sensing the fear in her fingers.

'See who?'

'Three kids. I heard 'em coming down the path from the car. Watched 'em cross the clearing. Running they was, like they was being chased.'

'Three? I was expecting one. Where are they now?'

Merryn's heart missed a beat. What did Mear mean "I was expecting one?" Was he the 'one'?

'Dunno. If they didn't come through the gate, then they're in the woods somewhere. You wanna be worried, Ez, 'cos I reckon two of them were the pair messing about round your car last Tuesday. Caught 'em on the CCTV. '

'You what!' Mear barked. He lowered his voice, struggling to control his temper. 'And you didn't think to tell me?'

'I only looked at the tapes this morning.'

'Messing about? What does that mean?'

'They was looking at the indicator. The new one.'

'MacIntyre.'

'Yep, Merryn MacIntyre. How d'you know that? Can't remember the other's name. Tall lad with blond hair, plays rugby.'

'Luca-Hunt,' Mear spat. 'Arrogant brat. You said there were three of them. Who's the third?'

'Dunno. It were a girl. Didn't recognise her.'

'So, MacIntyre swallowed the bait. He solved the clues, the clever little git, just like she said he would. Well that's just perfect, except I didn't reckon on him bringing anyone with him.'

'What d'you mean *bait*? You didn't tell him we were down here, did you?'

'Calm down, Jed. He's exactly where we want him. He knows where the pistol is. Forget the fish. According to her, the pistol's worth more than all the bloody fish in the river.'

'Don't start with that pistol stuff again, Ez. You're doing my head in with all your mumbo jumbo talk. We got more important things to worry about.'

'Mumbo jumbo? Why do you think I'm here instead of dodging the bloody bailiffs on the Monnow? And what about the job, eh? You think that was just a coincidence? I just happened to turn up at the school when Biddle was leaving?'

'You're scaring me, Ez, 'cos you ain't been making any sense recently. None of this makes sense. I thought we was just poaching down 'ere, like always.'

'Sense? Of course it doesn't make sense. You think I don't know that, listening to that bloody woman in my ears all the time? But that doesn't matter, now. All that matters is that MacIntyre's here and he's going to tell us exactly where the pistol is. Then we'll deal with him nice and quiet.'

'Wotcha mean "deal with him"? Like you dealt with Biddle?'

'We'll do what needs to be done.' Mear's voice was barely audible now. 'Simple as that. Do you understand?'

'I don't like it, Ez. It's not right, hurting kids. In any case, there's three of 'em. '

'You don't like it, eh? Well that's just too bad because you're in this up to your neck, just as deep as I am.'

'I didn't have nuffin' to do with the old man. That was your idea, Ez. We should have just…' Behind the wall, the hideaways heard a sharp groan and then Mear's voice, scarcely a whisper now.

'I told you to keep your bloody voice down.' A pause, then, 'You've got to understand, Jed, the boy's been doing his homework. If he takes it to the filth, it could get awkward. Awkward for *both* of us.'

'But there's *three* of 'em.' Skinner had found his voice again but it was shaking.

'You leave your shotgun by the ford?'

Behind the wall, Beatrice's grip on Merryn's hand suddenly got a lot tighter.

'Christ, Ez, I ain't using…'

'Listen. Just listen, okay? I'm not asking you to use it but the kids won't run with a twelve-bore pointing at them, loaded or not. We've got to find out what they know and to do that, we need to find them and shake them up a bit.'

'I'm sorry, Ez, I ain't doin' it. Gun's only here as a decoy; you know that, in case the bailiffs come snoopin'. I start threatenin' kids with it, I'm gonna get myself locked up. They'll recognise me straightaway. In any case, we gotta get the net off the ford. The bore will be 'ere in around twenty minutes. It's goin' to be a big one, Spring tide an' all. We got no time for kids.'

Mear had forgotten about the bore. Skinner was right. Once it passed, the ford would be inaccessible. 'Have it your way. We get the net off the ford and bag the fish, but I'm not leaving till we've found them.'

A minute's silence passed before Beatrice lifted her head from the leaves.

'Oh my God, this is crazy,' she whispered. 'That's Skinner, the school caretaker, I'm sure of it. I can't believe he's doing this. I always thought he was an alright bloke.'

Merryn sat up, brushing leaves from his hair. 'Did you hear that? *She's* talking to him too. How else could he know about the pistol?'

"No, Merry, I heard a nutter talking about a shotgun, so stop all this crap about some woman. It's like Skinner said – mumbo jumbo. Someone's told Mear about the pistol. Miss Kelly, probably, since they both teach in the same school. We should never have trusted her. We've got to get back to the road and call the police. This isn't a game anymore.' Zac sprang to his feet. 'Beatrice?'

'Zac's right, Merryn. We've got to go. It's not safe here.' She tugged on his hand, urging him to his feet.

"But you must believe me now about Mear and the hit-and-run.' Merryn didn't budge. 'It's what I've been saying all along, Zac. He was driving the car. You heard Skinner. *"Like you dealt with Biddle."'*

'Okay, I believe you now. It's just...'

'It's just what? You still think I've made all this up?'

'No, but seriously, with a good lawyer, he'll wriggle out of it. Neither of them actually *said* they knocked Biddle off his bike. Think about it. There was almost nothing incriminating in that conversation. Just stuff about you knowing too much, but knowing about what? The poaching? In any case, it would be their word against ours. Their word against three kids.'

Merryn said nothing and yet inside him, a battle was raging. Lying there, buried in the leaves, he'd felt utterly vindicated. Now, listening to Zac, he realised the evidence they needed, *he* needed, eluded them. *Dealt with Biddle*. It wasn't enough.

'I don't know what all this car stuff is about and right now I don't care.' Beatrice interrupted his thoughts. 'You've got to call the police. *Now,* Zac. I mean *right* now. They've got a shotgun.'

Zac nodded. He tapped his phone back into life. The GPS app was still open so he minimised it. 'Bugger! No signal. What about yours?'

Beatrice shook her head. 'Nope. Mine's useless. Lost signal ages ago. Try moving.'

Warily, Zac crept along the wall, willing a signal bar to appear on the screen.

Twelve thousand miles above the Wye Valley, four Navstar satellites were bouncing Zac's precise location back to his phone as the flashing red arrowhead moved further and further from the green line. Seven metres, eight metres. 'Come on, for God's sake,' Zac whispered. 'Don't let me down.' Nine metres… Suddenly, without warning, high-pitched beeps screamed into the night air.

CHAPTER 23

Zac sprinted back to the others, caution thrown to the wind. The alarm fell silent but it was too late.

'We've got to go! I can't get a signal down here.' Zac was already moving back to the path but, behind him, Merryn crouched by the wall intent on going nowhere. He had an idea.

'You go. I'll stay. I'll only slow you down – you know I can't run fast.'

'Have you lost your mind? You're not sitting at your computer now. This is for real. You heard him. *We'll deal with him nice and quiet.* He knows we've sussed his poaching game. Don't be a bloody hero! We've got to go.' He ran back and grabbed Merryn's parka sleeve, dragging him away from the wall.

'No, Zac! You *still* don't understand!' He ripped his arm free and glanced over the wall. He could just make out a solitary figure running along the bank towards them. 'Skinner's coming. If he sees you running back up the path, he'll follow but there's no way he'll catch you. I'll hide here. Mear will never find me. He'll think we've all gone. I'll just watch him until the police get here.'

'Merryn, don't do this!' Beatrice pleaded. 'We should stay together. *Please!*'

'I'll be alright. You need to get a signal and phone the police.

You'll be faster without me. Just go.'

For a second, Zac stared at his friend, utterly baffled by his motives. Merryn was brewing a plot, he was certain, but there was no time for an interrogation. Fifty yards away, Skinner had slowed to a stumbling jog. Every few steps, he glanced nervously over his shoulder but there was no sign of Mear.

'I don't know what you're playing at, Merry boy, but you're taking a hell of a risk.' Zac handed Merryn his torch. 'It's more powerful than yours but whatever you do, keep out of sight.'

'Do what he says,' Beatrice pleaded, a tortured expression on her face and with that, she and Zac sprinted to the path and were gone. Skinner reached the gate, breathing heavily. Merryn lay motionless, his head just clear of the leaves, watching as the stocky figure passed through. He paused to stare back downstream and mutter something inaudible. Then, with a shake of the head, he turned and continued slowly on up the path.

Merryn got to his feet and peered over the wall. Downstream, he could make out a dark shadow striding back along the bank towards him. There was no time to lose. He took out the phone from his parka pocket and switched it on. He waited while it searched for a signal and finding none, settled silently into offline mode. Everything now depended on Zac having loaded a voice recorder app like he had on his current phone. Merryn swiped left and scanned the list of apps. There! Voice Recorder Plus. Quickly, he tapped the icon. When a green 'record' button appeared in the centre of the screen, he slipped the phone back into his pocket.

Primary sources. Mr Biddle had drilled it into him from the very first lesson all those years ago in Year 7. Trust nothing except primary sources. A good historian will drill back through the confounding layers of fables and folklore, massaged and mutated by countless generations of retelling, until finally he reaches bedrock evidence – an autobiography, diary, news film. Better than that, Merryn reflected, as he watched Mear approach, was a digitally recorded confession.

"'Tis time for justice, Tom. This time, it will be served. Listen and I will guide you but remember: he means you harm.'

He spun round, half-expecting to see a woman standing among the trees. 'Justice? Justice for Biddle? Is that why I'm here?'

'He still lives.'

'But he's lying in a coma. You must know that. Does that not deserve justice?' Merryn's frustration was reaching boiling point.

'He has done worse. Far worse.'

'Mear? You mean... he's killed someone?'

'He killed me, Tom. And my baby.'

Her words struck like a hammer blow but a click and clang wrenched him back into the here and now as Mear arrived at the gate. Merryn scrambled up and over the wall, before putting some distance between them.

'Merryn MacIntyre!' Mear stepped back through the gate, shotgun in one hand. 'Solved the clues, eh. So where's your two mates?'

Merryn slid a hand into his pocket and tapped the middle of the screen. A single note indicated that the recording had begun.

'I'm on my own.'

'We both know that's not true. You were speaking to someone.' He edged along the wall, peering over. 'They've gone, have they, and left you here?' Mear's tone was ice-cold. 'It's not safe at night, you do know that, don't you? Not for little boys.' He held the shotgun in both hands now, one finger curled around the trigger.

Merryn backed away, unable to take his eyes off the gun, its long barrels gleaming in the moonlight. *Bee's right. We should have stayed together.*

'It's not loaded. He won't harm you till he knows where the pistol is.'

'But why did you tell him about it? About me?' *Is she plotting with Mear to steal the pistol? Is all this just some trick, some evil deception?*

'The woman. You're talking to the woman, aren't you?' Mear

began to close the gap to his prey. 'Well I'll be damned. She told you where to find the pistol, didn't she? And now you're going to tell me.'

'No. *You*'re going to tell me what you're doing here, you and your friend Jed?' Merryn switched on Zac's torch and aimed the powerful beam directly into Mear's face.

'That's none of your business, boy.' Mear ducked out of the beam. 'But then you've been sticking your nose into my business for a while now, haven't you? You shouldn't have done that.'

A rising tide of anger took hold of Merryn. 'I don't like what you did to Mr Biddle. You shouldn't have done *that*.'

Mear stopped, the merest frown passing across his face. 'And what exactly did I do to Mr Biddle?' he asked, his voice almost a whisper, as though the trees might be listening. 'You think you're a clever little shit, so go ahead and tell me.'

An avalanche of fury swept the fear from Merryn's head. 'You ran him down with your car!' he yelled. 'You left him for dead! But he isn't dead and when he wakes up, he'll identify your car. And you. You won't get away with it.'

Mear's grip tightened on the gun. 'And you've got evidence, have you? Why don't you tell me about the evidence?'

Merryn could tell Mear was rattled.

'Old car but a brand new indicator. *Nearside* indicator. It didn't fool me and it won't fool the police.'

'And that's it? That's all you've got? A new indicator.' He laughed mockingly, then all at once, he was charging. Merryn turned and ran for all he was worth along the bank towards the cliffs, looking desperately for a path, any path, leading up the steepening, wooded slope to his left. He might have outrun Mear, badly hampered by waders and the weight of a shotgun but, possessed by a blind panic, Merryn failed to notice the shin-high length of rope stretched taut across the bank. Tripping over it, he somersaulted through the air like a rag doll sprawling helplessly in the grass beside a slab of limestone. Before he could recover, Mear was standing over him, holding the gun by its empty barrel, ready to bring the butt down on his head. Instinctively, Merryn curled up, covering his head with both hands, quaking with terror as he waited for the blow to strike. Mear's attention, however, was distracted by a faintly glowing object lying on the grass beside the boy.

'So, what do we have here?' He stooped to pick up the phone and peered at the screen. 'So that's what you're up to, eh?' and with that, he threw the phone into the river. 'And now, MacIntyre, it's your turn to get wet.'

He dropped the gun and took hold of Merryn's parka with both hands, wrenching him violently back to his feet before wrapping an arm around his throat and dragging him backwards towards the top of the mud slope.

'You and Biddle. You're a pair, aren't you? Sticking your big noses where they don't belong.' He put his mouth to Merryn's ear so the boy could feel his hot breath. 'Well now, you're going the same way as the old man, except this time I'll do the job properly.' Merryn moaned, his whole body convulsing in an attempt to wriggle free but Mear's grip was vice-like.

'It's no good, MacIntyre. Like I told you, the river isn't a safe place for little boys at night. But I'm going to give you a chance to save yourself. One chance, so make sure you take it.'

Scarcely able to breath, Merryn clung to the faint ray of hope Mear was offering.

'You can hear the woman, can't you? She's been talking to you, telling you things. I'm right, aren't I?' He pulled Merryn's head back by his hair. 'Aren't I?' he shouted.

Merryn squealed in pain, nodding frantically.

'She told you where the pistol was hidden, didn't she?'

Merryn nodded again, all the while trying to speak, trying to explain that it was too late, that he didn't have it anymore.

'I knew it. And you found it, you and Zachary.'

The pressure on Merryn's windpipe relaxed a fraction allowing him to suck the cool air into his lungs.

'Yes, we did. Now let me go and I'll tell you where it is,' he croaked, all the while panting for air.

'You'll tell me now or you're going for a swim.'

'I don't have it. It's in the Bristol City Museum.'

'Bristol City Museum?' Mear's arm suddenly tightened around Merryn's neck again so that his airway was almost squeezed shut. 'You've handed it over to a museum like a good little boy? Well, there's a pity because I might have let you go if it was still in your possession but now you're surplus to requirements. Your chance has gone.'

'The lamp, Tom, the lamp!' There was desperation in her voice now. A shaft of light danced in front of Merryn's eyes, stabbing at the darkness. The lamp? *The torch*! He could feel it in his right hand. There wasn't much time left – a few more seconds – his vision was fading. Merryn grasped the handle with both hands and with as much strength as he could muster, swung the torch up and over his head. The sharp crack of glass shattering on bone was followed by a groan. Mear staggered backwards, clutching his face. The pressure around Merryn's neck had gone and he was free.

Mear wiped the blood streaming from his broken nose. 'You're going to regret that, you little shit.' Reaching into the pocket of his waders, he took out a short handle and with practiced precision, squeezed a tiny trigger at one end. A blade snapped into view, flashing in the moonlight. 'Game's over.'

Merryn stared at the knife in terror. In desperation, he turned and looked down the mud slope. The line of the rope was clearly visible, running across the gleaming mud until it disappeared into the river. Beyond that, he could just make out three dark objects in the moonlight – buoys – equally spaced across the water, tracing the rope's path to the far bank. The ford! *A shallow place with good footing.*

'Follow the rope, Tom, but be quick. It's coming!'

It's coming? Did she not mean *he's* coming? In an instant, his mind was made up. This had to be the ford. He launched down the slope, praying that he was right. If he wasn't, the game would be over. He grabbed the rope, hauling himself down through the mud towards the water. Behind him, the sound of laboured breathing grew steadily closer as Mear, blood gushing from his nose, swung his long, bony legs down the slope in giant strides, his waders sliding easily through the mud.

'Bad mistake, boy,' he gasped. 'A bad, bad mistake.'

Merryn looked round. Mear was gaining on him, his bloody face contorted with rage.

'It's coming, Tom!' She sounded almost hysterical now. 'You won't get across so be ready when it strikes.'

'What's coming?' he cried. Immediately, he felt something solid beneath his feet and a glimmer of hope catapulted through his brain. With exhaustion paralysing his legs, he struggled to drag them clear of the mud until finally, pulling for all he was worth on the rope, they broke free and he staggered up onto the glassy-smooth surface of the ford. Almost at once, he lost his balance and crashed into the foot-deep water, the cold stealing his breath. He half expected the current to sweep him downstream from the causeway but, to his astonishment, the river appeared to be flowing *up*stream and he found himself pinned against the rope and beneath it, hidden from view, the poacher's net. Out of the corner of his eye, Merryn caught the flash of Mear's knife drawing ever closer. Instantly, he was back on his feet and moving across the ford, past the first buoy and on towards the second.

Mear suddenly stopped and stood motionless, listening. He gazed downstream towards the bend, to where the river vanished out of sight beneath the cliffs. A gentle crescendo of sound like distant thunder had begun to fill the valley.

Merryn lurched on across the causeway, unaware Mear had stopped. His arms and legs, numbed by the river, felt alien and detached, while his clothes, sodden and heavy with mud, weighed him down like chains. Again and again he lost his balance, stumbling forwards into the shallow flow. Ahead of him, the second buoy floated just out of reach. With one final heave on the rope, he grabbed it.

'Stay where you are and hold tight! Don't let go!'

Beneath the surface, Merryn felt the net twisting and writhing against his legs as the salmon fought to escape the mesh. Now he was just one more fish, trapped in the net, waiting for the knife.

Mear stood fighting the current, midway between two buoys, staring at the wall of water hurling itself around the bend and rushing towards him, its foaming crest sparkling in the moonlight. Skinner had been right. The bore wave was a monster. Could he stay where he was and let it wash over him like a child playing in the sea? No. The bore, he knew, was only the advance guard. What followed, a huge surge of sea water, would instantly raise the river's depth to above his head.

He glanced at Merryn, clinging to the second buoy. There was no time to deal with him. In any case, the wave would finish him off. Mear turned and started back but realised he'd delayed too long. Before he could reach the first buoy, the air around him roared and the bore struck.

Drawing a deep breath, Merryn felt himself soaring upwards to the crest of the immense wave, its ferocious power threatening to tear his grasp from the buoy. For a few moments, the swell was too much even for the buoy. It disappeared below the surface, taking Merryn with it. As suddenly as it arrived, the wave was gone and the buoy, with Merryn still attached, exploded back to the surface. He hung there, spewing out saltwater, struggling in vain to make sense of the maelstrom around him. He could no longer feel the smooth rock of the causeway beneath his feet and he tightened his grip on the buoy.

The colossal force of the wave picked up Mear's gaunt frame and drove it into the rising net, thrusting his arms and legs deep into its mesh. Snared in the net and without a buoy to ride the wave, Mear vanished below the surface. His hands clawed the water like a madman and it seemed to take forever until suddenly, his head broke through the surface and he was sucking air.

Six feet of seawater now flowed across the ford and only by standing on tiptoe could Mear gain access to precious air. There was no time to lose. He could feel the rope pressing hard against his waist and below it, the net. They were all that stopped him from being carried away upstream. Quickly, he grabbed the rope with both hands and pulled himself towards the second buoy. He'd dropped the knife when the wave had struck but no matter. He'd wrest Merryn from the buoy, force him under and watch him drown.

But something was wrong. His left foot had tangled in the net. The wave had forced his wader's left boot through the mesh and now, like the wriggling salmon, it was trapped. He tried desperately to pull his leg free but each frantic tug merely pulled the heavy net towards the surface leaving the boot snared. He was going to drown. The thought overwhelmed him. The river level would rise quickly, way above his head and the net, midway between the buoys, would hold him under. If he could only remove his chest-waders, then he'd be free for boots and waders were one piece. Removing them, however, required both hands and as soon as his arms stopped their frantic sculling, he sank below the surface. He would drown, he realised, long before he could remove the waders.

Suddenly the net quivered. Merryn was moving, clawing his way along the rope towards the far bank. Leaving the relative security of the buoy, he drifted round until his legs faced upstream, the current threatening to sweep him away. Between the buoys, the rope looped down below the surface. Each time he hauled his way along it, he had to fight to stop himself from being pulled under. Seawater forced its way into his mouth, choking him. It seemed to take forever to reach the third buoy and then, slowly, the mud slope on the far bank drew closer, inch by inch. Finally, with what felt like his last ounce of strength, he pulled himself from the river and collapsed, exhausted, on the soft, cold mud.

'You're safe, Tom. Thank God you're safe. 'Tis almost done.'

Then another voice pierced the still night air. 'Mer... Merryn!'

Mear! Merryn rolled over and peered out across the river.

'For Christ's sake, unclip the...' Silence, then again, 'Unclip the rope!'

'Don't listen to him. This is what he deserves.'

Merryn spotted Mear's head, a dark shape buffeted by the powerful upstream current. He watched as it slipped below the surface before reappearing again.

'I never meant...' The dark shape disappeared, this time for longer. In the silence, Merryn could sense the water lapping around him as slowly, inexorably, it crept up the mud slope. He stood and took hold of the rope. It twitched as though it were alive. Wearily, he dragged himself up onto the grass bank. Safety, at last!

'Listen to me!' Mear was screaming now. 'I'm drowning! Unclip...' Violent spasms of coughing erupted as water slipped into his lungs. 'Unclip the rope!' he gurgled. 'I beg you!'

Merryn shivered violently. In front of him, growing in the middle of the bank stood a small willow sapling and around the base of its trunk, someone had looped a nylon sling. Attached to it by a climber's karabiner was the rope.

'Merryn!' Mear shrieked, water retching from his mouth. 'I don't want to...'

Merryn slumped to his knees beside the willow and stared at the sling. 'You doan wanna die,' he slurred. His face was numb with cold and he could barely speak. 'But Mr Biddle, you wan him to die so w-why should I l-let you live?'

'He killed us both, me and my baby. Now he deserves to die.'

'An eye for an eye,' Merryn murmured. He leaned forward and tried to take hold of the karabiner but his hands had lost all feeling and shook uncontrollably. His fingers wouldn't bend.

'Leave the rope! You swore an oath that you would do it, serve the man justice. I need it, Tom. My baby, too.'

He glanced back at the river but there was no sight or sound of Mear. He slapped his hands together and tried again. This time, he managed to unscrew the ring locking the gate of the karabiner but the powerful upstream current had pulled the rope taut and, without slack, it wouldn't slide out of the gate.

An eye for an eye – you'll never rest in peace. There must be another way.

Merryn worked on the karabiner with two, lifeless claws, twisting it round by ninety degrees. He scarcely noticed one of his fingers becoming crushed between rope and metal and then, suddenly, the rope snapped out through the open gate and snaked its way down the mud slope before disappearing into the river. Almost immediately, a head broke the surface midstream.

In that same moment, a mournful, harrowing cry flooded the valley. 'Noooooooooooo!'

Across the river, Wintour's Leap gleamed eerily white in the moonlight. The noise of police sirens travelling at speed drifted on a faint breeze from somewhere beyond the brow of the valley but Merryn paid them no attention. Neither did he heed the unmistakable drone of a helicopter sweeping up the valley from Chepstow. Instead, he lay down beside the tree, curled up into a tight ball and closed his eyes. His body began to shake less violently as his core continued to cool. 36 degrees, 35, 34, 33...

CHAPTER 24

Friday 13th September

Merryn's left eye opened a fraction.

'Oi'm tinking y'er coming back now, eh?' whispered a familiar voice. She had been studying Merryn's face for almost an hour, watching the flicker from his eyelids getting stronger by the minute until it seemed impossible that they could remain closed any longer.

The eyelid slammed shut while its owner struggled across no-man's-land towards waking. At first Merryn was convinced he was dead; that for some unspeakable misdemeanour in his early life he had been consigned to hell where Nurse Fitzgerald would forever deprive him of sleep.

'Welcome back to Chepstow General, Mr MacIntyre. Oi can't say oi'm deloighted to see you, but at least you're in ICU and not downstairs in... somewhere else, eh?'

With both eyes open now, he tried to focus on two bulging eyes staring down at him. He hadn't focused on anything for twelve hours while the medical staff had gently caressed his temperature back to normal.

'Don't get me wrong now, my lovely. It's sweet of you to look in and see us every Friday morning, but oi'm tinkin' that maybe you could give us a break next Friday.' She checked the computer screen by his bed and nodded approvingly. 'Voitals looking good. Oi'm getting the doctor, a hot drink and your mum and dad, so don't be going anywhere, d'you hear me?' Halfway through the door, she stopped. 'Oh, and the noice policeman who's bin waiting to speak to you since one o'clock dis morning.'

Merryn desperately wanted to go somewhere – anywhere – where Nurse Fitzgerald wasn't, but every part of his body ached as though he'd been run over by a tank. His throat felt like sandpaper and an odious taste hung in his mouth. He looked down at his right hand. The forefinger was heavily bandaged. He tried to bend it and immediately wished he hadn't.

The nurse returned with a full complement of extras. Donna got to him first, flinging her arms around his neck and bursting into tears.

'I told you, Merryn,' she murmured between sobs, 'if anything happened to you, what would we do?' She leaned back and held his head with both hands, staring achingly into his eyes. 'You mustn't do this to us anymore. It's too much. You understand? It's too much.'

Malcolm lifted her gently back from the bed. 'It's alright, Donna. He's okay now. We can talk later. Here, the nurse has brought you tea, Merryn. You look like you could do with it.'

'Oi'm tinking he could do widout the monitor, Doctor. Voitals are good.'

Doctor Bhatia smiled. 'Your vitals *are* very good, Mr MacIntyre. Rather better than they were twelve hours ago. Let's give you a little time with your parents and then maybe we'll unplug you. I'm sure DI Parker can wait a few minutes longer.'

DI Parker stifled a yawn and nodded. 'Five minutes.' The detective's night shift had already drifted into a day shift as he'd waited for the boy to regain consciousness. It seemed to him grossly unfair that his colleagues were busy unveiling a catalogue of serious crime – failure to stop after an accident, attempted murder, actual bodily harm, possession of a firearm with intent to cause fear of violence, poaching, fraud – the list seemed endless – while, since one in the morning, he'd been sat in the waiting room outside intensive care, waiting for the victim to show some interest in life.

Left alone with their son, Donna and Malcolm pulled up a couple of chairs and sat down, scarcely knowing where to begin.

'How are you feeling?' Donna's voice sounded tired and thin.

'A bit sore. What time is it? Actually, what day is it?'

'It's Friday. Half twelve. You've been here since about midnight. The police knocked on our door sometime after eleven. Said they'd had a report that you were down by the river. Dad went with them to the police station. Zac and Beatrice were there. Next thing we knew you'd been picked up by helicopter from the riverbank suffering from hypothermia and were brought here. One of your fingers got squashed somehow and you've bruised your shin but no serious damage, thank God.' She put her hand on his forehead. 'You're warm now. You were so cold when they brought you in, Merryn. Thirty-two degrees. The doctor said you were found just in time.' She stared into his eyes, trying to understand what had happened to her fifteen-year-old son. The truth was that she didn't know him any longer. She'd left him to flounder through adolescence on his own, devoting her time and energy instead to Charlie. Now her teenage son had drifted away into a world of his own, a world to which neither she nor Malcolm belonged, a world they didn't understand.

'We're not angry with you,' she said, 'just confused and scared. Why didn't you tell us what was going on? Don't you trust us?'

Merryn didn't answer. When Donna was angry, she often said she wasn't.

'I'm not blaming you. It's mostly our fault. We haven't made time for you. We used to talk before Charlie came along, before the shop... had problems. Now we don't talk.' She looked at him, wondering if it was too late, if he'd remain beyond their reach forever.

'Helicopter?' For a moment Merryn felt baffled. 'I don't remember that.' He paused, trying to recall the events of the previous twenty four hours. 'Actually, I don't remember anything.'

'Police helicopter from Bristol.' Malcolm pulled his chair closer. 'I can think of better ways of getting a free ride in a helicopter.' For a brief moment, his face wrinkled into a smile but it quickly faded. 'The doctor told us you might not remember much at first but it will all come back in time and when it does, then we want the whole story. No more secrets, eh?'

Merryn nodded. It was the moment he'd been dreading, explaining to his mother that since the start of term, the little he had told her was nothing more than a fabric of lies or at best, half-truths. From the moment that Mear had...

'Mear!' he blurted out, sitting bolt upright in the bed. 'What happened to him?'

'Hey, calm down, calm down.' Donna leant over him, a restraining arm around his shoulders.

'No Mum, you don't understand.' He gently shrugged her arm off. 'I need to know. He was drowning. I remember. What happened to him?'

'Donna, it's okay.' Malcolm eased her back into her seat. 'You're right. He was drowning. When the police pulled him from the river, he'd stopped breathing. They thought he was dead but the defibrillator on the helicopter got his heart going. He hasn't regained consciousness. He was colder than you when they fished him out.'

'But he's alive, isn't he?'

'Yes he's alive. Just. They've taken him to the Gloucester Royal. The further the better, as far as I'm concerned.'

'What about Zac and Bee... Beatrice?'

'They're fine. They rang the police just before eleven last night and were taken to the station in Chepstow. They were there when I arrived.'

'It wasn't easy for us, you understand,' Donna interrupted. 'I mean, they were standing there right as rain and all they could tell your dad was that they'd left you down by the river with… with that man.' She was working up a head of steam now. 'Can you imagine how we felt?'

'Donna, he's not ready for this. In any case, they were both very upset. Beatrice was distraught. They had to take her home.'

'Not as upset as I was. I was going out of my mind with worry.' Tears streamed down her face now. She dug in her coat pocket for a tissue.

'It wasn't their fault, Mum. It was all my idea. You can't blame them.'

Malcolm stood up. 'I think you'd better go now, Donna. Charlie will need rescuing. I've got to stay while the detective interviews Merryn. I'll get a taxi home when he's finished. You can come back this afternoon.'

Donna leaned forward and hugged her son tightly. 'We love you,' she whispered, 'and we're going to spend more time together, I promise.'

Merryn nodded without much enthusiasm. 'More time' probably meant 'more interrogation'. After Donna had left, DI Parker stuck his head round the door.

'Just when you thought it was safe to get some kip, eh? Oh, look out.' Nurse Fitzgerald pushed past him carrying a tray of food.

'Food,' she announced. 'Oi'm tinkin' you moight be a tad hungry.' He was ravenous and for the first time in their brief relationship, Merryn smiled at her. She sat him up and set the food down on a tray across the bed. 'Now you can eat yer lunch while the noice detective hears yer story. Wish Oi could stay.' She uttered a sharp guffaw.

DI Parker closed the door behind her and sat down. 'Have a seat, Mr MacIntyre. We may be here some time.' He turned to the patient. 'Bet you'll be glad to be out of here,' he grinned. 'Oi'm tinkin'.'

Merryn laughed. He'd been expecting a Donna-style interrogation with reprimands for dessert but the DI didn't appear to be heading in that direction.

'So, young man, how did you damage your finger?'

Merryn shook his head. 'I don't know. I mean, I can't remember. Everything's just a blur. Have you spoken to Zac and Beatrice?'

'Your accomplices? Yes, they provided a statement last night; at least Zac did, but they're in again this morning having a more thorough interview. They should be done by now.'

'And Skinner, the caretaker? Have you found him?'

'Hey, your memory's not so bad.' The DI smiled. 'As it happened, we didn't need to find him. He found us. Walked into the station last night around one o'clock.'

'He gave himself up?'

'That's right, he gave himself up. Happens sometimes. Decent folk can't carry the burden of guilt for ever. He's been very helpful, has Mr Skinner. No doubt you'll want to know what's happened to *his* accomplice, your history teacher.'

'Except he isn't my history teacher. Mr Biddle is my history teacher. Dad said Mear's in a bad way.'

'Certainly is. He's on life support. That's what happens, Merryn, when your body temperature drops.' The point wasn't lost on him. 'As for Mr Biddle, I understand he's also in a coma. We've spoken to Miss Grigoryev who tells us that she's been keeping you in the know about Mr Biddle. It seems you haven't been keeping her in the know about Mr Mear. You might want to avoid her for a while when you go back to school.' The DI grinned and shook his head.

Merryn shuddered. Miss Grigoryev? He'd forgotten all about her. 'So there's no change to Mr Biddle?'

'Not as far as I know. When there is, we'll let you know. Now, we'd better get started. My boss is calling me every half hour to ask if you've given a statement. Let's rewind the tape back to the beginning. That's the *very* beginning when you first got involved in all this. It helps sometimes to walk through events along a timeline; put everything in order. Remembering one event triggers the brain to remember the next in the sequence.'

Merryn nodded. He glanced at his father sitting at the end of the bed. He looked shattered.

'But don't stop eating. Your brain's going to work hard for the next hour so you'd better feed it.' DI Parker took out a voice recorder and switched it on. 'Interview commenced in Chepstow General ICU room 4 at twelve-fifty. Present are D.I. Parker, Merryn MacIntyre and his father, Malcolm MacIntyre.'

An hour later, the DI called time on the interview and switched off the recorder. Merryn's account was littered with loose ends but he was exhausted. By the time he'd recounted his desperate escape across the ford, the DI was ready to admit that never in his eighteen years on the force had he heard a story like it. He couldn't make up his mind whether to recommend the boy for a George Cross or reprimand him for taking the law into his own hands.

'Mr Biddle would be proud of you. It's just a pity that Mear got to him before he could be stopped. From what I gather, you saved Mear's life. If you hadn't unclipped the rope, he would have drowned. Saving the life of someone who's trying to kill you; that takes guts, Merryn. A lot of people would just have left him to drown.' That was the George Cross.

Merryn shrugged. Both men were in a coma which meant their lives were on hold. They could go either way.

'And *you're* a lucky man. D'you know why?'

Merryn knew what was coming. He was only surprised it had taken so long.

'Because you nearly died. Thirty-one point eight. That's how cold you were when they found you. Not everyone survives that. In fact, it was a miracle that we *did* find you. Everyone was searching the left bank because that's where they found Mear. The heli went up with searchlights and the pilot spotted you on the other bank. Without the heli, you'd be dead right now.' He paused for a moment to allow Merryn to take it all in. 'You've got to let the police do their job.

Playing detective with men like Mear – it could've got you killed. You understand?' That was the reprimand. 'One last thing. You're fifteen which means the press aren't allowed anywhere near you.' He glanced over at Malcolm who had been silent for the last hour. 'Section 45 of the Youth Justice and Criminal Evidence Act 1999. If Mear regains consciousness and is shown to be of sound mind, then he'll almost certainly be prosecuted and that means you'll be asked to testify. You following?'

Merryn nodded.

'Now, my colleagues have this afternoon obtained an order which restricts anyone from naming you or publishing any personal details about you. Same for Zac and Beatrice. Name, address, school – anything that could lead to your identification. No video or stills either. So as far as the public is concerned, three young people were involved in an incident last night and that's it. Obviously, the media are hungry for details of exactly what went on down by the river but any information will come from us, not you or your parents. We've arrested and charged Jed Skinner and his name has been released but the law is very specific about under 18s. So, no one's allowed to knock on your door or come up to you in the street and start asking questions. If they do, say nothing and contact us immediately. Got it?'

Merryn nodded again and then asked, 'Have you found any glass on the road where Mr Biddle was knocked down?'

'You haven't heard a word I said, have you?' The DI sighed deeply while Malcolm just closed his eyes and shook his head. 'I shouldn't tell you but... yes, we have. This morning. We were looking in the wrong place before.'

'And CCTV footage of Mear's car?'

Billy Parker laughed. 'Enough! I'm off now. Get some rest.'

Malcolm got up and ran both hands through his hair. He felt at that moment a greater sense of failure than at any time in his life. Here was his older son, someone he scarcely recognised, lying bruised and battered in a hospital ICU ward, fighting for justice when his father had just rolled over and allowed Superland to trample all over his business until it was worth next to nothing.

'The detective was right. What you did took a lot of courage. I'm so proud of you – not of your methods, you understand, but of your... well, doggedness. Like Molly when she gets her teeth around a stick. The harder you pull, the tighter she bites.' He paused, frowning. 'But, I've listened to you for an hour and yet I still can't understand why you went back to the river. What did you hope to achieve?'

'I don't understand myself, Dad. It's just something I had to do. That's it. I'm sorry.'

'Hey, don't be sorry. Maybe once you've had some rest and your head is a bit clearer, then it'll make more sense. I've got to go now but Mum will be back later. Do you want us to bring you anything?'

Merryn wanted to say Beatrice but instead shook his head.

After Malcolm had gone, he lay back and stared at the ceiling. He'd learnt almost nothing new from D.I. Parker save that Skinner was now in custody and being 'helpful'. He should have been ecstatic. If Skinner was dishing the dirt on Mear, then there'd be no need for his phone recording. Of course, that was lost. Skinner was the primary source now. He knew about the attempt on Mr Biddle's life; he might even have been in the car at the time. If he was talking, then Mear was finished. *That's what it's all been about – justice for Mr Biddle.* But lying there, Merryn felt no sense of elation. He wondered what justice would look like. Mear in a prison cell for the rest of his life? Or a coffin? No, a coffin would not be justice but rather escape. *She'd* wanted him dead. That much was clear. *He killed me and my baby.* She was talking about Mear but that just wasn't possible. If she had used the pistol to kill a man, then she was from the 17th century in which case Mear couldn't have killed her.

He closed his eyes. The puzzle was far bigger than he'd first imagined. The background hadn't changed but Mear's attempt on Biddle's life wasn't the main event; it was a side-show, a few pieces tucked away in one corner. Something else, far more terrible, occupied the gaping hole at the centre of the puzzle. The young woman belonged there, he was certain, trapped, longing to be set free.

He lay there, going over and over the events by the river, each time trying to remember the exact words she'd spoken until finally exhaustion pulled him into a dreamless sleep.

CHAPTER 25

The room was almost dark when Merryn resurfaced from the deep, lit only by the ghostly glow from a monitor above his bed. For a few moments he was disorientated, staring up at the coloured traces streaming across the screen. Almost a minute passed before he noticed the figure sitting motionless in a chair at the foot of the bed. He could tell that she was watching him. The screen's glow sparkled in the brilliant whites of her eyes.

'Hey.' She stood up and moved the chair closer. 'You're awake. You've been asleep for ages.'

'Bee!' She'd ambushed him again.

'Do all the girls have this effect on you?' she asked, noting the sudden rise in Merryn's heart rate on the monitor.

'You keep surprising me, that's all. How long have you been here?'

'Zac's mum brought us down about four. Zac had to go at five. Rugby training. I think he was getting bored just watching you sleeping. He said he'll be back tomorrow but I think you're being discharged in the morning. Your mum was here too, but she had to rescue your brother from a babysitter. Visiting hours finished at six but the staff nurse said I could stay for a while. Mum knows I'm here.'

'What did she say last night when you got home?'

'What do you think? She went ballistic and I mean *ballistic*. The police went round after we phoned them – Zac's phone picked up a signal just before we reached Mear's car. They woke her at about midnight and explained where I was. Of course, she didn't know I'd left the house. They were going to bring her in to the station but I had to go home. I was in quite a state. I couldn't talk to the police. Zac did instead.'

'Dad and I – she must hate us both.'

Beatrice had promised herself she would stay calm when Merryn awoke but talking to him now, her resolve crumbled and the tears flowed. 'Why did you stay?' she sobbed. 'Idiot. You should have listened to Zac.'

For a while, Merryn lay still and watched the little African girl, her shoulders shaking as the anguish slowly ebbed away. Finally he spoke.

'I should have listened to Zac. You're right. But I couldn't.'

Beatrice took out another tissue and blew her nose. The worst seemed to be over. 'What do you mean you couldn't? That rubbish about slowing us down – that was just an excuse, wasn't it. Skinner would never have caught you. So why did you stay?' She moved her chair to the side of the bed and sat down. 'Because of the voice you keep hearing?'

Merryn took a deep breath. 'You're going to think I'm nuts. Like Zac. He thinks it's all in my head because he can't hear her, but it's not. *She's* not. She's been talking to me for a week now.'

Beatrice leaned forward. 'You can't blame him. It does sound crazy.'

'I knew that's what you'd say.'

'I didn't say I don't believe you, but you're the only one who can hear her. How is that possible?'

'No, you're wrong. She's been speaking to Mear as well. You heard what he said. "Listening to that bloody woman all the time." She's been leading him just like she's leading me until…'

'Until what?' Beatrice asked quietly.

'Until we met. At school. Then down by the river. Except I'm certain we've met somewhere before. Something happened in that first history lesson. I could see it in his face, like he recognised me. It scared him, I'm certain of it. He certainly scared me. I couldn't explain it at the time. I still can't.'

'And the pistol? Did you really find a pistol?'

'Didn't Zac tell you?' but Merryn already knew the answer to that.

'No, he didn't. I asked him why you'd written it on the map and he told me to mind my own business, like he always does.' She reached out and took hold of his left hand.

With his defenses now fully breached, Merryn quickly succumbed and by the time he'd finished describing the flintlock, Beatrice was speechless, a state she very rarely experienced. Finally, in a small voice, she said, 'Okay, time to rewind back to the start. Tell me everything this woman has said to you from the moment you first heard her voice. Can you remember?'

Merryn wondered if she was just humouring him but there was a fervour in her eyes which said she wasn't. 'Okay, I'll try but she's spoken to me so many times.'

Day by day, starting with the library, he recalled as best he could everything he'd heard the woman say.

' "At last, 'tis found. Now you can set us free, Tom." That's what she said when we found the pistol. Set *us* free, not *me*.'

'She called you Tom? Why would she do that? Your middle name's not Tom, is it?'

Merryn shook his head. 'That's the name she uses every time.'

'Okay, this just gets crazier by the minute. So, keep going. What else did she say?'

He continued, reliving every moment of the past eight days until the walk down to the river. 'Remember when I stopped after we'd crossed the clearing? I asked you if you'd heard her speaking.'

'Yes. I told you it was just the wind. I'm sorry.'

'Doesn't matter. You believe me now, don't you?'

Beatrice hesitated and then said 'I'm starting to believe though it's not easy. So, go on. What did she say?'

'"At last, Tom, you will keep the promise that you made so long ago." And then she warned me that Mear wanted to harm me. Her voice was coming from the church. That's where she is, I'm certain. Whoever she is. Or whatever.'

'The ruined church? You think she's maybe buried there, speaking to you from her grave?'

'Maybe.'

'Okay, go on.'

Slowly, he stepped through the events on the riverbank, then into the mud and the frigid waters of the Wye until finally, he hauled himself up onto the far bank.

Beatrice leant closer. 'This is going to sound like a heartless question, but from what you said, it's obvious Mear wanted you dead.' She paused while she struggled to stay in control. 'And *she* wanted Mear dead. All that stuff about him getting the justice he deserved for killing her.'

'And her baby.'

'Yes, and her baby. If it's true, that's just dreadful. He's a monster. And yet, you saved his life. You ignored her. Why did you do that? Why did you untie the rope?'

Merryn sat quietly, saying nothing, searching his own mind for an answer to the girl's question until finally he said 'Killing someone – anyone – it's not right. I only had her word for it, a voice speaking to me from who knows where? If I knew who the woman was and why it's me she's speaking to, then maybe it would make more sense.'

Beatrice took out a tissue and wiped her watery eyes. 'You know, where I come from in Kenya, a lot of people believe in the supernatural. I mean spirits and stuff. My mum grew up in a small village not far from the Maasai Mara National Park in Kenya. You've heard of it?'

Merryn nodded.

'She got a job there in a safari lodge – nothing fancy, just cleaning out guest bedrooms. That's where she met my father. Anyway, she was brought up like all the other children to believe in a mixture of traditional religion and Christianity. It wasn't until my grandad died – that's Mum's dad – that any of it made sense. Even then, I had a lot of questions. Mum told me that he hadn't really died at all; his soul was just passing from this world into a place closer to God. She said he had to leave his body behind since it had grown old and useless but his soul was still alive. When he was buried, the men in the village collected acacia branches – they have huge thorns on them – and laid them along the path from our house – that's where Grandad lived – all the way to the burial ground. I remember every time we went to visit his grave, mum made me collect the branches that had blown away and put them back along the path. I used to hate going because the thorns made my hands bleed.'

Merryn listened in silence, painting the scene in his imagination.

'She explained that Grandad had entered the spirit world as a soul and the thorns would stop him returning to the village. It was better for him to leave the village and find his ancestors than return to the pain and suffering of his old life. I asked her where he lived now but she couldn't tell me. She said that no one really knew for certain and the only thing that mattered was that Grandad was at peace with his ancestors.'

'But what's this got to do with the voice I'm hearing?'

'Well I may have got this all wrong, but…'

'Go on.' Merryn had fallen under Bee's spell. How could anything she said be wrong?

'Grandad died peacefully. He was old – at least old for someone in Kenya – and he got a proper burial. My mum made sure of that. There were people in our village who died very young or died out in the bush. Hippo attacks were common at night. Sometimes the body was never found.'

'So their soul never reached their ancestors.'

'Or if it did, it was rejected, forced to live apart from them. My mum called that hell – a soul imprisoned *here*, where they'd lived their earthly life, unable to reach the spirit world of their ancestors.'

Outside in the corridor, a nurse pushed a rattling trolley past the glass partition to an adjacent room.

'Do you believe it? That the soul lives on beyond death?'

Beatrice slipped her hand from his and looked away, lost for a moment in her thoughts. 'Do I believe it?' She turned back to face him. 'To be honest, I don't know. Mum believes it but no one here seems to believe anything. It's so different in Kenya, at least in the rural areas where I came from. But what if it's true? The woman who is speaking to you died when she was young, murdered and buried without a funeral. Her baby too. So when she says "you can set us free" she's talking about her and her child. It's her soul speaking to you, asking you to free her so that she can join her ancestors.'

'Yes, but her voice comes from the church. Doesn't that mean she had a proper burial?'

'You don't know that she was buried properly. Maybe someone just dug a hole and threw the body in. Or bodies.' Beatrice thought for a moment. 'You said that, at the beginning, she was guiding you to the pistol. I mean, you'd never have found it without her directions.'

Merryn nodded. He wondered where this was leading.

'And the pistol was made in 1639. When did Wintour jump over the cliffs, assuming he *did* jump?'

'1645.'

'A gap of just six years. Coincidence?'

'I don't think so. I'm certain it belonged to him. There's this French expert in old firearms who's gone to New York to look at a similar pistol so we might know for sure when he returns.'

'And she needed someone to find it. She needed *you* to find it. "Now you can set us free."'

'And then, like I told you, she said that she'd taken a life with it. She murdered someone.'

'And that's why she can't reach her ancestors,' Beatrice suggested. 'She's a murderer. They would reject her.'

Merryn sat up with a start. 'That's it! They would. Until she set things right.'

'But she can't.' Beatrice frowned. 'Time has moved on. It's too late.'

'No, she can. "Now it must save a life." I remember it now. It's what I've been trying to remember ever since I woke up. The pistol must save a life. She's trying to make amends for what she did all those years ago. It's why I had to find it though I don't know how an old pistol can *save* a life.'

Beatrice sighed. 'It's like a dream, a crazy, crazy dream with so many unanswered questions.'

'It is crazy. Why was the pistol that she used to kill a man hiding down a crack at the top of the cliffs? And why is she so certain that Mear killed her and her baby? That's just not possible. Mear isn't that old. And what do I have to do with any of it?' Merryn slumped back on his pillow, exhausted.

'I think we've just got to wait until she speaks to you again.'

'If she does. I broke my promise, so she says, so maybe she won't.'

They fell into a silence until Merryn changed the subject.

'Did you go to school today?'

'You must be joking. Mum insisted I stay home and answer a million questions. Then the police came round at ten this morning to take a statement. I was shattered anyway. I hardly slept last night. Zac messaged me at lunchtime. Wanted to know if I was okay. Told me the police had been round his house – same reason. Have they interviewed you yet?'

Merryn never got a chance to answer since the door to the room flew open and Doctor Bhatia stepped in followed closely by a nursing assistant carrying a tray of food. Beatrice jumped to her feet as the lights came on.

'I'd best be going,' she said quickly. She turned to the doctor. 'Will

Merryn still be here tomorrow?'

'We're moving him to a general ward after he's had a bite to eat. He seems to have made a good recovery, shall we say.' Beatrice detected a faint smirk on Doctor Bhatia's face. 'How's the finger?'

Merryn refrained from testing it again and simply answered, 'Sore.'

'It will be. There's a bit of soft tissue damage but nothing serious. You'll have to use your left hand for a week or so.' He turned back to Beatrice. 'We'll keep him here overnight and then hopefully, all being well, he'll be discharged tomorrow morning. Why don't you phone the hospital tomorrow about ten?'

She nodded. 'See you tomorrow then.' She gave him a look that he couldn't decipher and then disappeared.

Doctor Bhatia interrupted his thoughts as he stripped away the sensors that had been monitoring his vitals. 'I almost forgot. A Miss Kelly came to see you this afternoon. She wasn't allowed up on ICU but she said to pass on her best wishes and hopes you'll be back in school soon. She wrote a note which she asked me to pass on to you.' He dug in the pocket of his white coat, fished out a folded piece of paper and handed it to Merryn. 'Wish I'd had teachers like that. Mine certainly wouldn't have taken time off to visit me in hospital.'

When Doctor Bhatia and the nurse had gone, Merryn sat up in the bed staring at the paper while his shepherd's pie went cold. Finally, he plucked up the courage to unfold it. It wasn't hard to imagine the blazing rant which Miss Kelly had surely penned on the paper when she'd learned of the boys' latest shenanigan, one that they'd omitted to mention at Thursday's meeting. Hardly daring to breathe, he read Miss Kelly's message written in her immaculate script:

"So glad you're on the mend but not so glad that you needed mending. Some good news to hasten your recovery. Your convictions regarding the pistol's ownership appear to have been well founded. I'll let you break the news to Zac!"

CHAPTER 26

Merryn's custodial sentence at Chepstow General was cut short by twelve hours owing to a serious rush hour accident on the Severn Bridge that urgently required hospital beds, including the one he occupied. So at nine o'clock that evening, he climbed into his father's van and settled back for the twenty minute journey home. His mind had been racing ever since reading Miss Kelly's note. He wanted to tell someone, anyone, everyone that he'd been right all along. The news must have come from New York, he guessed; someone there must have recognised the pistol.

'Tired?' Malcolm asked, as he swung the van out onto the main road.

'I'm okay. Been sleeping all day.' He would tell Zac first. After all, the pistol was as much his. It wasn't difficult to imagine Zac's response. A smug smile began to crease his face.

'So, are you ready?'

'Ready for what?' The smile vanished. He knew what his father meant and Malcolm knew that he knew.

They had almost reached Church Close when Merryn broke the silence.

'I'm sorry.'

Malcolm said nothing, sensing that there was more to come.

'You didn't need all this when you're having to deal with the business and the house and everything. I don't know how it all happened. It's like I wasn't in control. I mean, it wasn't Zac making me do stuff. He was trying to stop me. It's hard to explain.'

The van drew up outside the house and Malcolm switched off the engine.

'I appreciate the apology. You're right. It's bad enough trying to keep the shop afloat without my son trying to kill himself every Thursday night. As for the other bit about not being in control, don't mention any of that to your mother. That's red rag to a bull. You didn't have to sneak out of the house at midnight and then lie about going over to Zac's. You made those decisions, Merryn. No one else. You've got to accept responsibility when you make a mistake. Your mum will want to hear that, you understand?'

Merryn nodded. Maybe his dad was right. He could have said no right at the start when Zac suggested going to the cliffs at midnight, but if he had, Mear would still be on the loose. And what of Skinner? Would he have walked into the police station if three pupils from the Academy had not suddenly appeared on the riverbank to watch him poach salmon? Merryn liked to think not. But his parents would never understand what had driven him to pursue Mear. He scarcely understood himself.

It was almost eleven o'clock when Merryn shut his bedroom door and collapsed onto his bed. Donna's interrogation had been surprisingly gentle for her. For the first time he could remember, she'd let him talk uninterrupted for almost thirty minutes. He did his best to mollify the more perilous episodes, omitting minor details such as the precise location of the cliff-top crevice, Mear's impressive collection of weaponry and the colossal size of the bore wave. As for the voice, Merryn couldn't remember either parent expressing an interest in anything remotely supernatural. They were here-and-now people, concerned only with the terrestrial struggles of everyday life. Voices emanating from ruined churches would probably have sent his mother into one apoplexy too far.

He lay, staring up at the poster, his eyes focused on a point far beyond the royalty of Britain as his mind wandered back to his conversation with Beatrice. She'd come out of nowhere to breach his guileless innocence, running riot with his emotions as no other girl had ever done before. What was this madness that possessed him now, that raged inside him creating such euphoria that he could not imagine life without it? He could still feel the soft warmth of her hands as they'd toyed with his fingers. Were they an item? Was it official? Nothing had been spoken. Had she expected him to say something, to ask her out? Was that what her expression had implied when she had left? *Why have you said nothing, Merryn? Don't you care?* He would tell her how he felt when he saw her next... if he could find the right words... at the right moment... and his courage didn't fail him.

'It won't happen,' he muttered, angry at himself for being so feeble. In any case, she wasn't interested. He'd misinterpreted the signs. He was the class geek for heaven's sake. What could Beatrice – or any other girl – possibly find attractive about him? He swung his legs off the bed in disgust, crossed the room to his computer and switched it on. It was over before it had begun. He'd remove all traces of Beatrice from the keep, repair the damage and redouble its defences. He glared impatiently at the screen while the BIOS chip went in search of an operating system. He wouldn't allow another invasion. It was too painful. Drawbridge up, portcullis down. When Google finally flashed up on the screen, Merryn typed in *"soul"* and pressed enter. Immediately, he was offered one and three quarter billion results. Here we go again, he thought, too much clutter. Fortunately, Google had headlined the results with a definition taken from Wikipedia: *"Soul – the incorporeal and immortal essence of a living thing."*[3] Incorporeal and immortal? A few clicks later and it made sense: *"bodiless and everlasting."*

---

[3] Wikipedia Creative Commons GND: 4054146-0 desaturated from original: German National Library - various

A few minutes later and it became evident that in almost all the world's great religions, the human soul sat centre stage. For most, it was the spiritual energy which breathed life into a frail and mortal body, navigating the perilous path through the trials of human existence; and when the curtain fell on earthly life, the soul departed on a journey into the afterlife. Before Beatrice had mentioned it, Merryn had never given his soul a moment's thought and yet now it seemed to him that understanding this essence and its role in his existence was far more important than all the Shakespeare, supernovas and simultaneous equations which the Government had deemed essential knowledge for human survival.

He glanced at the computer's clock. It read 23:35. He wanted to ring Beatrice. The notion that he could keep her out of his head was ludicrous. She'd taken up residence in the Keep's Great Hall and had no intention of leaving. Then he remembered that his mobile – Zac's mobile – lay in the mud at the bottom of the Wye where Mear had tossed it. He considered using the house phone but it wasn't safe. He was convinced that his mum sometimes eavesdropped on the other handset. Curiously, he had neither seen nor heard anything of his parents since coming upstairs. Had they gone to bed without looking in to say goodnight? Was this the new regime – give Merryn space to be himself? If so, he wondered how long it would last.

He typed in the word *"afterlife"* into Google and discovered it was here that the world's religions parted company. Beatrice had made it sound so simple – the departure of the soul from the body in search of eternity with one's ancestors. But the great faiths, it seemed, could find little common ground as to the final destination of the departed soul, other than the unshakeable belief that it did not die. A link took him to a page on reincarnation. *The soul begins a new earthly life in a new body.* Is that what happens, Merryn wondered, when relatives of the dead fail to line the path to the grave with acacia branches? The soul is drawn back into the body of a newborn? Or perhaps the ancestors of the deceased send the soul back to live another life, displeased with the nature of the owner's death or the short-comings of the burial. And yet the soul of the woman at St James's Church, if a soul could be pinned down to a particular location, seemed trapped in a no man's land without a body and with no escape to her ancestors.

Suddenly a knock at the door startled him. He minimised the page.

'Yeah?'

The door opened and Malcolm's head appeared. 'Still awake? You must be shattered. Can I have a word before you crash?'

Merryn ignored the un-Malcolm-like language and swivelled round in his chair. 'Okay.'

His dad sat on the bed – there was nowhere else. Merryn thought he suddenly looked much older for his eyes seemed to have sunk into dark hollows and the two frown-furrows ploughed between them were deeper and more permanent than he remembered.

'I thought we could strike a deal. If I'm completely up front with you about our financial situation, then you can fill me in on a few missing details that your memory might have overlooked.'

Mum's put you up to this, I'll bet, thought Merryn, but he said nothing.

'I'll start, if you like. There's never a good time for bad news but you're going to...'

'Dad, you can say it. It's about the house, isn't it?'

Malcolm nodded. The furrows were deeper than ever. 'Yes, it's about the house. And the business. We're putting both on the market. There's no point in delaying the inevitable so we're looking for somewhere to rent. We might have to wait a while; there isn't much out there, but the Council will find us emergency accommodation if we have to move out before we can find a flat.'

'So, Mum didn't find anything when she looked at the finances?'

'No, she didn't. She wondered if we could convert the shop into accommodation but Grandad's will stops us from doing that. In any case, we only own the ground floor and it's not big enough.'

'But we're not going to be homeless, are we?'

'No. Absolutely not. Like I said, the council will find us somewhere. Then we'll get help with the rent until I can find a new job.'

'You've made Malika redundant, haven't you?' It sounded like an accusation although it wasn't intended to be.

'You've been talking to Beatrice. I can understand how she feels but what choice do I have? There's no money to pay her. It's as simple as that. Believe me, I wish it wasn't.'

'I'm sorry. I didn't mean it like that. I know you haven't got a choice. So does Bee.'

'Is there something going on between you two? She was certainly very upset at leaving you down by the river.'

'No, there's nothing going on.' In truth, Merryn didn't know the answer.

'So what about your part of the deal? What about this gun? The account of that night at the top of Wintour's Leap that you gave to DI Parker was pretty short on detail. You fell into a crack and found an old gun. I didn't believe you so I'm sure the detective was having doubts. And then you never told us what the antiques dealer said about it.'

Mum definitely put you up to this. That's where you've been all evening, planning the latest information extraction technique. Merryn decided that his parents might as well know sooner rather than later. It would soften the blow when the inquest found the boys guilty of trespass. So for the next fifteen minutes, Merryn recounted in lurid detail the discovery of the pistol, the visit to Levi Antiques and the content of Miss Kelly's note confirming that the golden pistol had belonged to Sir John Wintour. Malcolm sat and listened in silence.

'A hundred grand?' he whispered when Merryn had finally finished. 'You found a gun worth a hundred grand?'

'But we'll get nothing, Dad. We were trespassing. The law says you get nothing if you were trespassing when you found the treasure. There was a Keep Out sign and spiked railings. Mr Levi reckons the

British Museum will buy it and the full amount will go to the landowner. Every penny. Never a good time for bad news but there it is. I'm really sorry. The money would have changed everything for you. For us.'

Malcolm's face creased into a cheerless smile. 'It doesn't matter,' but the despondent tone in his voice said it did. 'What matters is that you're alive after two near misses in one week. Family's more important than anything. *And* what matters is you've found Wintour's pistol. I seem to remember telling you that the legend was a load of nonsense.'

'You did. Zac thinks it's nonsense as well.'

'So do a lot of people, I'll bet, and you've proved us all wrong. At least, you've proved he was up there, on the edge.'

Merryn chewed that over for a while. 'You're right. It doesn't prove he jumped. And it doesn't tell us *why* he jumped, if he did.'

'That's for you to find out, using your computer and that amazing brain of yours. We don't want to stop you being a historian; you know, searching for clues. You've got a gift. I'm proud of you. We both are.'

Merryn was taken aback. He couldn't remember his father making such a long speech and certainly not one with so many compliments.

'So you're done with the river now, are you? No more Indiana Jones impressions?'

Ah, thought Merryn, the nub. This is where it's all been leading. No more fieldwork. No more nights away with friends. I'm going back to being an historian in front of a computer screen where no one gets hurt, living off secondary source scraps, never proving anything, never answering the questions that matter.

'Yes, I'm done with the river.'

'So, it's all over. I mean, if Mear regains consciousness and pleads guilty, you won't need to give evidence in court. The police reckon the case is watertight. He'd have to plead guilty.'

'And if he doesn't regain consciousness?' Merryn could almost hear the woman's voice in his head – *It's what he deserves.*

'If he doesn't, then he won't be pleading anything. He tried to kill Mr Biddle and he tried to kill you. The world's probably a better place without him.'

'Maybe.' He wanted to add 'maybe not' but his father wouldn't understand. Everyone wanted Mear dead but death evades justice. Earthly justice. Merryn wondered what would happen to Mear's soul if his body died. His ancestors would surely reject it. Perhaps it would suffer the same fate as the young woman's, locked in no-man's-land until it could find redemption. But how was that possible? How could it amend the evil it had perpetrated during its earthly life?

'Get some sleep, Merryn. You look pretty out of it.' Malcolm stood up and walked across to the door. 'It's over, isn't it? No more surprises, right?'

Merryn nodded because his father wanted him to, but it wasn't over. A few pieces had been added to the gaping hole in the puzzle but still the picture eluded him.

CHAPTER 27

Monday 16th September

At seven o'clock on Monday morning, Donna gave Merryn the all-clear to return to school. Aside from a slight limp, a sore and bandaged finger on his right hand and a set of fast-dissolving stitches on his scalp, barely visible now through a lawn of oddly-blond hair, you would never have known that Merryn had recently fought off an attempt on his life and survived a near-drowning in one of Britain's most dangerous rivers.

The short walk to school gave him time to ready himself for the inevitable barrage of questions. His mother had suggested that she escort him to the school reception just in case he should require a bodyguard to fight off a deluge of pupils all demanding to know the precise details of his heroic encounter with the wicked Mr Mear. Merryn declined the offer. Firmly. In the event, the school's other inmates ignored him completely, just as they did on any other day. The court's banning order had clearly been effective. While the names of Mear and Skinner had been widely reported on both local and national television, the three teenagers who had alerted the police had remained just that – three, anonymous teenagers from the local area.

Merryn had scarcely made it through the school gates, however, when Zac and Beatrice pounced and dragged him to a vacant picnic table away from the madding crowd. Zac slung his school bag on the table, looked at his watch and sat down.

'Ten minutes, online researcher. So, cut to the chase. Spill the beans. What the hell happened down there after we left?'

'Zac!' Beatrice protested. 'How about "Good to see you, Merryn," or "Glad you're still alive." That would be nice.'

Zac ignored her. 'Come on, Merry, sit down. Nine minutes now.'

In the event, it took Merryn just five minutes to relate his encounter with Ezra Mear. Beatrice couldn't help noticing that there was no mention of the woman's voice in his account. She understood why.

'Bloody hell!' Zac blurted out when Merryn had finished. He looked up to make sure no one was listening and then in a hushed tone, added, 'He almost killed you!' He sat for a while, shaking his head. 'And you saved his life. You untied the rope. I don't think I would have done that. Honestly. After he tried to stab you? Christ, Merryn, when they said you'd been taken to hospital, we thought... well, you know. Second time in a week! Your parents must have gone nuts.'

'Well, if they did, I wasn't awake to hear them,' Merryn answered ruefully.

'Mear's on life support in the Gloucester Royal.' Zac paused for a moment and then said, 'Go on, say it.'

'Say what?' Merryn wasn't on the same page.

'I told you so. Don't tell me you haven't been dying to say it ever since Thursday night. Mear's guilty, just like you said he was. The police are going to charge him with attempted murder and a whole lot else besides when he wakes up.'

'How do you know that?' Merryn asked.

'Haven't you watched the news? It was on BBC Breakfast. The police have got enough evidence to charge him with the hit-and-run. Looks like Skinner's told them everything. God knows how he got mixed up with that creep.'

Merryn sat down, quietly absorbing the news. Then a smile spread across his face. 'Actually, I *should* be saying I told you so. For another reason.'

The others looked at him quizzically, waiting for him to expand.

He pulled out a crumpled piece of paper from the inside pocket of his blazer. 'Like me to read you Miss Kelly's note, Zac?'

'Miss Kelly? Wrote you a note?' Zac sniggered. 'I'm gonna love hearing this. I knew you had something going with Miss Freckles.'

'No, you're *not* going to love hearing this.' Merryn cleared his throat and read. '*Your convictions regarding the pistol's ownership appear to have been well founded.*' He paused while the arrow found its mark. 'I think that deserves an "I told you so."'

Zac's grin evaporated. 'And what's that supposed to mean? Your convictions regarding...'

'Ha!' Beatrice burst out. 'The pistol belonged to Wintour. That's what she's saying, isn't it?'

'No, that's not what she's saying.' Zac was clearly rattled. 'Is it?'

"Fraid so.' Merryn was enjoying himself. 'Someone in New York has identified it. Wintour's pistol at the top of Wintour's Leap. Now, what does that tell us, I wonder?'

The registration bell smothered some choice expletives in Zac's reply. When they got up to go, Beatrice pulled Merryn back.

'I need to talk.' She waited until Zac was a safe distance. 'My mum wants to see you. I mean, she wants to talk about the woman's voice. She asked me loads of questions but I said she should talk to you.'

'You told her about the woman?'

'Not to begin with, but she kept asking questions and in the end... well, I just told her everything. You don't mind, do you?' She grabbed his arm and looked directly into his eyes. He shook his head because any other response was impossible. 'You haven't got a phone, have you?' she asked. He shook his head again. 'I'll get my mum to phone yours and tell her you're coming over my place after school.' She slipped her hand into his and pulled him towards the North door. 'Come on, we'll be late.'

When they reached the top floor, she disappeared into her form room and left Merryn to walk the plank on his own. Miss Grigoryev had surely prepared an ambush, lurking by the door of 309, ready to beat him senseless. He'd kept his suspicions about Mear from her – even lied to her – while she had confided in him. She wouldn't forgive him for that.

The corridor was empty. Her class, like the others, had been called in. If the door was closed, he was safe, at least for now. It was ajar and he caught the sound of an unfamiliar voice – a man's voice – taking the register. Merryn sighed. Miss Grigoryev, it seemed, was not in school. Perhaps she's visiting Mr Biddle, he thought. She'd want to be there when he woke up.

He'd almost reached his form room when the head's PA caught up with him. 'Merryn, Mrs Bowden-Lees wants to see you. I'll let your form teacher know you're in school.'

Merryn wasn't in the least bit surprised. The head would have a thousand questions for him. He wondered if she'd answer any of his. Minutes later, he knocked on her door and pushed it open, apprehensive as to what might follow.

'Ah, Merryn, come in and have a seat. How are you feeling?' Her voice was warm and welcoming but her eyes were the temperature of liquid nitrogen.

'Bit sore, miss, but otherwise, I'm fine.'

'I'm somewhat surprised that you've returned so soon after your ordeal.' She leaned back in her commodious leather chair and held both hands together beneath her chin as though in prayer. 'From the start, I must say that the school owes you a debt of gratitude for exposing Mr Mear for exactly what he is. Of course, I cannot condone your methods which were somewhat unconventional, to say the least, but thank heavens you've made a quick recovery and we must just hope and pray that Mr Biddle too is soon restored to full health.'

Merryn suspected immediately that this was just a polite *hors d'oeuvre* to something rather more sinister that was to follow. He was right.

'In view of the fact that this is an open case under investigation, I'm not at liberty to question you. However, I would like some clarification regarding events which have nothing to do with Mr Mear, events which I understand from the police took place at the top of Wintour's Leap on... er.' She looked down at a notepad on the desk in front of her. '...Thursday 5th of September.' She looked up at him expectantly and then, getting no response, she said 'The gun. You found a gun, I believe, is that right?'

Merryn nodded, wondering where she was taking this. 'Yes, miss, an old flintlock pistol.'

'How extraordinary. An old flintlock pistol.' Her voice was no longer warm and welcoming. 'And you took the firearm to the police the following day, is that right?' The trap was set.

'Not exactly. The law states that treasure – the pistol's butt is made of solid gold so it qualifies as treasure – must be reported to the local coroner within fourteen days. It hasn't been fired for at least three hundred years so we didn't think the police would be interested.'

'Solid gold? Good gracious.' For a second, she was thrown off the scent but quickly regained it. 'So apart from the coroner, did you show the pistol to anyone else? I mean, you must have needed help in identifying it.'

Merryn was about to answer when suddenly the penny dropped. Mrs Bowden-Lees had no interest in the pistol whatsoever. Instead, she was digging the dirt for evidence of unprofessional behaviour by a member of staff.

'Yes, we took it to an antiques dealer in Chepstow, Isaac Levi. He contacted a friend of his to...'

'I'll stop you right there, if I might, Merryn. You said "we took it". Who's *we?*'

Merryn swore silently inside his head. It was clear that the head had attended the same interrogation course as his mother.

'Zac. That's Zachary Luca-Hunt. He was with me when...'

'Zac and...?'

Merryn had reached the end of the blind alley. There was no escape. 'Miss Kelly,' he mumbled.

'Sorry, was that Miss Kelly, an English teacher at the school?'

You know damn well who she is. 'Yes. She knows Mr Levi.'

'Merryn, it would be helpful if you could tell me exactly when Miss Kelly became involved.' She glanced at the clock on the wall. 'I don't have a great deal of time, so brief and to the point, please.'

Sixty seconds was all it took to implicate Miss Kelly and when Merryn had finished, Mrs Bowden-Lees stood up, thanked him for being so co-operative and showed him the door. He was about to leave when she added,

'Next time you have any concerns about staff at this school, I'd be grateful if you would share them with me first.'

To Merryn, that sounded like an accusation, a shifting of the blame for the events of the last two weeks from whoever appointed Mear onto him. For a split second, he hesitated, fighting the temptation to ask, 'Why? Have you appointed any more psychopaths?' but decided against it.

Had he been a fly on the wall in Mrs Bowden-Lees' office, he would have heard the head asking her PA to send Sian Kelly down to see her the moment the bell rang for break.

'And Natalie, perhaps you could remind Sian that I'm a busy woman who can ill afford to waste time waiting for staff to turn up to meetings.'

CHAPTER 28

'Ah, Sian, come in. I'm glad you could make it this time. Take a seat, won't you.'

Miss Kelly had never warmed to the head. She found her sarcasm deeply irritating.

'Now then, Sian, where to begin?' The head pushed the reading glasses that were hanging around her neck onto the tip of her nose and leaned forward to inspect the notes she had made during her meeting with Merryn. 'Well, let's start with the gun, shall we? A three hundred-year-old flintlock pistol with a handle made from solid gold.' She looked up, peering over the top of her glasses. 'That's a good place to start, don't you think?'

Miss Kelly cleared her throat and launched into the speech she'd had only fifteen minutes to prepare. 'Well, Merryn MacIntyre found this pistol at the top of Wintour's Leap a little over a week ago, and he and Zac – that's Zachary Luca-Hunt – brought it to the library, believing that a good friend of mine, an antiques dealer, might be able to shed some light on its origins and value.'

'And you reported this meeting to me, to the police, to the boys' parents? I mean, we are talking about a firearm, are we not? A weapon which, if discharged, could result in serious injury or death?'

Miss Kelly's worst nightmare was unfolding before her ears. She had pulled the plug on her meeting with the head the previous Friday when neither Merryn nor Zac turned up at breaktime. It didn't take her long to discover they were both absent from school. That set off alarm bells. Another phone call told her Merryn MacIntyre had been flown by police helicopter to Chepstow's intensive care ward. That set off an air raid siren. Twenty minutes later, having triggered the speed camera on the A48 into Chepstow, she was listening to an encouraging progress report from a Dr Bhatia. When he'd finished, she'd wanted to kiss the man but then decided a hug would do instead. Now she had to figure out a way of defusing the grenade that the head was holding in plain sight, one that could blow her fledgling teaching career into a million pieces and she had to do it fast.

'No, the pistol was harmless. It was a rusty antique, nothing more. I agreed to help the boys on the condition that they informed their parents about the pistol. They both assured me that they had done so when we visited an antiques shop in Chepstow.'

'Was that a school visit, Sian?'

Miss Kelly wondered where the hell Bowden-Lees was going with this. She could sense her blood pressure rising. Attack was the best form of defence but finding a chink in the head's armour wasn't going to be easy.

'The visit had nothing to do with school otherwise I would have filled out all the relevant paperwork. The boys travelled in their parent's car so...'

'That may have been so,' the head interrupted, 'but I take a very dim view of teachers who fraternise with pupils outside of school.'

Sian Kelly's blood began to boil. Fraternise? What the hell was she insinuating?

'I can assure you there was no *fraternising*.' She was edging ever closer to the cliff edge. 'I was *about* to say that the boys' parents were entirely happy with the arrangements. The pistol has since been handed over to the relevant authorities as the boys were legally required to do. I'm not sure I can add anything more.'

'Oh, but I believe you can.' Mrs Bowden-Lees' nose had turned puce, a sign that every member of staff had learned to read. 'I understand that the information which led to the boys' nocturnal misadventures, some of which almost cost Merryn his life, originally came from you, is that right?'

My God, Miss Kelly thought, this cow has subjected Merryn to the Spanish Inquisition. And over the cliff she went. 'How *dare* you imply that I am to be held responsible for Merryn's injuries simply because I gave him a book from the library. It's my job to foster curiosity through reading. What the boys did with the information in that book has nothing whatsoever to do with me.' She was tumbling out of control now, unable to stop herself regardless of the consequences. As she stood up to leave, her eye caught sight of a sign hanging beneath a mirror on the office wall. THE BUCK STOPS HERE. There it was, the chink in Bowden-Lees' armour. Sian lowered her voice. Her words would do the shouting. 'Merryn's injuries were not the result of a library book. They were inflicted by a supply teacher; and every member of staff at this school, every parent and, I should imagine, most of Year 11 are asking the same question, one that only *you*, as the head teacher of this school can answer: how the hell did Ezra Mear get through the vetting procedures which are there to protect the likes of George Biddle and Merryn MacIntyre?' And with that, she turned and left the room, striding furiously past a rather startled Natalie in the anteroom. She made her way directly to the staff toilets, locked herself in a cubicle and promptly burst into tears. However much she resented the head's accusations, the unavoidable truth was that she should never have agreed to the boys' requests without first informing the woman. The tears flowed unabated until the bell rang for the end of break.

Two hours later, when the corridors suddenly filled with voracious children, Miss Kelly had regained full control of her mental faculties. If the head was going to caution her – or worse – over her dealings with the boys, well, what the hell. Let her try. She'd come this far with the pistol and she wasn't going to let go now. With her mind made up, she went in search of Merryn. It didn't take her long to find him, sitting at a computer in the library. Occupying the same chair was Beatrice whom Miss Kelly had never taught but had heard a great deal about. At first she presumed that the girl was sitting on Merryn's lap simply because she wanted a closer look at the screen but revised that premise when she saw her arm draped over his shoulder.

'Oh, sorry, miss!' Beatrice hastily disentangled herself from Merryn and the chair. 'Didn't see you. We're just, er, you know…'

'Doing some research. Wintour and all that.' Merryn stood up and braced himself for yet another pasting. He suspected, from what he knew of the English teacher's reputation, that this might be the loudest tongue-lashing yet.

'Where's Zac?' she asked.

'We don't know. Probably with the rugby lads,' Beatrice offered.

Miss Kelly nodded and motioned for the pair to follow her into the library office. She closed the door behind them and as soon as they'd sat down, took a deep breath and launched. 'It's a pity Zac's not here because he needs to hear this. I'm so proud of you. All three of you. I know it almost cost you your life, Merryn. You nearly gave me a heart attack when I found out you'd been taken to Chepstow hospital. Again! God knows it could have turned out differently but, in the end, Mear and Skinner got their just desserts. You did what the school failed to do, exposing Mear for the psychopath that he is.'

'How much do you know, miss?' Merryn asked. 'About Thursday night?'

'Enough. Maybe too much.' She shuddered. 'I received a visit from PC Carrington on Sunday morning. I expect you can guess why.'

Merryn winced. 'I'm really sorry, miss, but the police wanted me to tell them everything, right from the start, and I couldn't leave the stuff about the pistol out. They would have found out later.'

'And Mrs Bowden-Lees, I guess she would have found out later as well.'

'Miss, I swear, she had me sitting in her office and...'

'Stop, Merryn. Enough. It doesn't matter. All that matters is Mr Mear is no longer trying to kill people at this school. PC Carrington told me a little about Thursday night. They haven't charged Mear yet – obviously, they can't – so a lot of the evidence against him can't be revealed. And there's a court order protecting your privacy so I'm not allowed to ask you anything. To be honest, I'm not sure I want to know the gory details. I'm just glad you're here. And, of course,' she added quickly, 'I'm hoping – everyone's hoping – that Mr Biddle recovers quickly. I know you're his greatest fan. The feelings are mutual from what I hear, so you'll be as worried as anyone, I guess.'

Merryn nodded. He was worried. Almost two weeks had passed since Mear had knocked him down and still there were no signs of Mr Biddle emerging from his coma. He changed the subject.

'Thanks for the note, miss. Made me feel a lot better. Bet you were pretty excited when you found out.'

'Oh yes,' Miss Kelly's face lit up, 'I most certainly was. You were right about the pistol. It belonged to Wintour, no question. But there's something else.' She sat staring at them with a face full of childish mischief until she felt like bursting. 'There's two of them!'

'What? *Two* of them?' Merryn could scarcely believe what he was hearing. 'Where's the other one?'

'In a private collection in New York. According to Isaac, as soon as St Pierre saw the one you found, he knew it was the partner of an identical pistol in a private collection in New York, one that has a full provenance; you know, a documented history. Wintour, it appears, owned *two* golden pistols.'

'I can't believe this. They must have got separated somehow. Zac's going to love this.'

'No, you're going to love telling him,' Beatrice corrected. 'Actually, he should be here. He's going to be mad if he hears all this second hand. Can you wait five minutes, miss, and I'll go find him?' Beatrice was gone even before the English teacher could reply. Three minutes later, slightly out of breath, she returned with Zac in tow.

'Two pistols?' he gasped, panting hard. 'Is that right?'

Miss Kelly nodded. 'Two pistols and, according to Monsieur St Pierre, they were given to Wintour by Charles I as part payment for cannons.'

'Cast iron cannons,' Merryn pronounced. 'Now it all makes sense.'

'Here we go.' Zac's contribution received a black look from the teacher.

'The king needed cannons to fight parliament in the civil war. Cannons are made of cast iron and cast iron comes from iron ore. But getting the iron out of the ore isn't easy. You need...'

'A blast furnace,' Zac interrupted.

'Yes, of sorts. The furnace needs loads of fuel to heat the ore. Now Wintour just happened to live next to the Forest of Dean, thousands of acres of oak trees.'

'Okay, so the oak trees are the fuel. Where's the ore?' Beatrice asked.

'Chemistry field trip last summer. Where did we go?' Merryn was enjoying himself.

'Nowhere,' Zac sniped. 'I was on a rugby tour.'

Beatrice ignored him. 'The caves in the Forest. Clearwell Caves.' The penny dropped. 'Ah ha! They were originally iron ore mines. The iron ore came from the forest too.'

'Exactly, and Wintour owned the mines. So most of the cannons in Charles' army were made from iron supplied by...'

'Wintour.' Perfect synchrony.

'So, don't tell me, Charles paid for the cannons with two golden pistols.' Zac's manner had changed. He was starting to believe.

Merryn looked expectantly at Miss Kelly. 'Is that right, miss? Is that what St Pierre said?'

'No,' she replied, still reeling from Merryn's deductive powers. 'He didn't say any of that, but I'll buy it. Actually, what he *did* say is something that you're not going to like.' Miss Kelly's tone had changed. 'Ready for the bad news?'

'Bad news?' Merryn frowned.

'Yes, very bad news. The pistol in New York was bought at auction by an American millionaire for – wait for it – just over half a million dollars. That's around four hundred thousand pounds.'

Zac was the first to react. 'No kidding. *Four* hundred thousand?' He looked at Merryn, sitting with his mouth open. 'I thought you said it was worth *one* hundred thousand.'

'Mr Levi was guessing. At *least* one hundred thousand was what he said. But he's not a firearms expert. Four hundred thousand. Four. Hundred. Thousand. Oh my God. Bad news? It's worse than that. It's way, way worse.'

Seeing Merryn's disconsolate expression, Miss Kelly felt guilty. Maybe she should have said nothing and let him find out the pistol's value at the inquest. 'Look, Merryn, you don't know for certain that you won't get at least part of its value. You're going to have to wait until the inquest.'

'I do know for sure, miss. I went back and double checked online. The law is clear. Trespassers get nothing. Owners get everything. It's as black and white as that.'

'So you keep saying,' Zac remarked. 'Do we know who the owners are? Can't be that hard to find out. Maybe we could go round and... work out a deal or something. You know, fifty-fifty.'

Miss Kelly smiled inside. She loved his cavalier attitude. 'That's got to be illegal, Zac, so please don't do that. Alright, forget the valuation. According to Isaac – I should tell you he was absolutely beside himself with excitement – you've made the archaeological find of the decade. You should be immensely proud of yourselves. It's only a matter of time before the media gets hold of this. No restraining order this time, I'm afraid. Wouldn't surprise me if the BBC are knocking on your doors the day after the inquest.' She paused for a moment to let it all sink in and then said, 'Mr Biddle would be so proud of you. All three of you.'

'It's so wrong that he can't be a part of this,' Merryn said quietly, shaking his head.

'He'll wake up.' Miss Kelly tried to sound convincing. 'We just have to be patient.'

'Six months to two years for the brain to rewire itself,' Merryn found himself saying. 'But if the damage is too severe, then…'

Zac stood up abruptly. 'Miss is right. He's going to wake up. We've got to stop all the negative stuff; it's seriously doing my head in. Mear's where he should be but Mr Biddle belongs here. Thanks Miss for the update. I've got to go.'

The others sat speechless, somewhat bewildered by Zac's sudden departure until Merryn broke the silence. 'Miss, there's something we haven't told you about… well, the pistol and Mear and the river. We dragged you into this and you deserve to hear it.'

He shot a furtive glance at Beatrice who nodded imperceptibly.

'You know I can't promise confidentiality, Merryn.' There was a no-nonsense tone in the teacher's voice. 'I'm not keeping your secrets anymore, you understand?'

'It's not like that, miss. I don't think anyone would believe you if you told them. I'm not sure you're going to believe it.'

'Oh dear, this sounds ominous. Alright, I'm all ears.' Miss Kelly steeled herself for more revelations. Merryn took a deep breath and launched. 'Ever since I found that book about Chepstow in the library, I've been hearing a woman speaking to me.'

Miss Kelly sat in stunned silence as Merryn recounted each occasion that he'd heard the voice. 'And Mear could hear her as well. She's been speaking to him. We think – Beatrice and I – that the woman's soul has been trapped between life and death, unable to reach her ancestors. Now, because I found the pistol, she believes that I can free her.'

Miss Kelly stared at the boy, her mind a turmoil of disbelief and wonder, of fear and joy, longing on the one hand to believe every word of his unearthly tale, yet on the other, terrified of its implications. 'Are you certain that you heard this voice? I mean *absolutely* certain?'

'Absolutely certain, miss. Like I said, she's been talking to Mear as well – for weeks, maybe months – so I know my head isn't making it up.'

Miss Kelly sat quite still, saying nothing. These two adolescents were asking her to renounce her entire belief system, one which had always rejected the supernatural as nothing more than a muddled distortion of reality.

'I know it sounds crazy and I don't expect you to believe any of it, but I wouldn't have found the pistol without her, or gone down to the river. She planned everything from the start.'

'She's responsible for almost killing you twice, is that right? Are you sure you should be listening to this voice?'

'I've thought about that a thousand times. Whose side is she on? And why is she using me to set her free?'

Miss Kelly stared at the boy, fearful that the voice – be it real or imaginary – was leading him down a treacherous road. 'So is it over now?'

'No, it's not over. She told me that the pistol we found is the one she used to kill a man. Now it has to save a life if she's to be free.'

'Save a life? How's that possible?

Merryn shrugged and looked at Beatrice. 'We've no idea.'

'Has she spoken to you since your exploits at the river?'

'No. She wanted Mear dead but I saved him from drowning.'

'You think you've let her down, is that it? Because you didn't let him die. But what's Mear got to do with any of this? It makes no sense.'

'I've got to go back,' Merryn whispered. 'To the church by the river. It's where her voice is coming from.' He looked at Beatrice, waiting for her reaction.

She nodded, and then seeing the anguished expression on Miss

Kelly's face, she said 'My mum will come down with us, too, miss. She comes from a country where people are comfortable with the supernatural.'

'And you're going to do what, exactly? Search for a grave because her voice seems to come from somewhere around the church?'

'I don't know. Maybe she'll speak to me there. Tell me exactly what I've got to do.'

'And when exactly are you going? Just so's I can book my visitor's appointment at Chepstow General.'

Merryn smiled. 'Not exactly sure but we'll let you know. Nothing's going to happen this time.'

'And Zac, is he going with you?'

Before Merryn could answer, Beatrice said 'Yes, I think he should. He's been in this from the start. What about you, miss? Do you want to come?' In that moment, Beatrice felt the veil of age and rank between them dissolve away and a silent bond begin to form.

'I can't. It wouldn't be right.'

'But you want to, don't you?'

Miss Kelly nodded. The veil had disappeared. 'Of course,' she whispered.

The bell for afternoon registration brought them rudely back to the present.

'We'll let you know when we go, miss, and then you can decide.'

The teacher watched them both leave and then sat quietly for a moment while her form group filed noisily into the library. She was hurtling down the slope now like a climber without an ice axe, unable to check her slide and yet overwhelmed by a sense of euphoria, of freedom that had been denied her for so long. Of course she would join them and to hell with the consequences.

CHAPTER 29

'We'll take a short cut across the fields.' Beatrice took Merryn's hand as they passed through the school gates at the end of school. 'Woodcroft's not far, maybe a mile.' She waited until they'd left the road, climbing over a stile onto a footpath before she turned, wrapped her arms around Merryn's neck and kissed him. For the next minute, or maybe two, Merryn thought he'd gone to heaven. When finally she stepped back, letting her hands fall into his, she stared up at him. 'So, we're going out?' she murmured.

He nodded. 'I'd like that.'

She laughed. 'I'd like that too.' She reached up and kissed him again, then turned and pulled him along the path.

They fell into a comfortable silence, dodging the frequent brambles and nettles crossing the path until Merryn finally spoke. 'Will you tell me about your mum? I mean, when did she come here?'

'It's not a happy story. You mustn't tell anyone, promise?'

'Of course not.'

'I told you before that Mum worked at a safari lodge. She had a one-night stand there with some guy and got pregnant.'

'With you?'

'Yep, with me. Heavens knows where he is now, not that I care. My grandparents looked after me while Mum worked. Then she met

Darren, a catering fridge salesman. He stayed at the lodge in the Maasai Mara for almost a month. He and Mum got friendly – not like before – Darren seemed okay. I think he really loved her in the beginning. He and I got on pretty well, too. After that, he would visit the lodge regularly, maybe every couple of months and in between they Facebooked a lot until one time, he asked Mum if she and I would move to the UK with him and, of course, Mum said yes. She worried about my education in Kenya. She could barely afford the fees and she didn't want me to turn out like her, cleaning toilets in some tourist lodge. That sounds bad, but you know what I mean.' She looked up at him and smiled. 'So we moved to the UK in 2015 when I was eleven, to a little flat in Enfield and six months later, Mum and Darren were married. Mum got a family visa and a job in a local supermarket.'

'What about you?'

'Me? I went to the local comprehensive. It was alright. Made some good friends.'

Merryn sensed that the good times were screeching to a halt.

'Darren used to spend a lot of time abroad, like a month away then just a week home before he was off again. He didn't seem bothered by it, the fact that he spent so little time with us but, after a while, Mum began to get worried. It was like we were just tenants living in his flat. Then Mum got ill and was diagnosed with HIV. Darren spent a lot of time away in Kenya and it wasn't hard to work out how Mum got infected.'

'Darren?'

Beatrice nodded.

'Do you think he knew he was infected before… you know?'

'Before he slept with Mum? I don't think so. He got himself tested as soon as he found out about Mum and sure enough, it came back positive. He blamed *her*, can you believe that? Said she'd infected *him*, that she'd brought the virus back from Kenya.'

'Was that possible?'

'Possible, yes, but Darren was the only person she slept with after her one-night-stand. Anyway, he became abusive after that. Physical as well as verbal. It was… a nightmare. Waiting for him to come home.'

Merryn scowled. What kind of a monster could do such a thing?

'That's when Mum decided we had to leave. She's got very distant relatives who live in Gloucester – an elderly couple – and they agreed to take us in while we got sorted. So, one day when Darren was away, we packed everything into a couple of suitcases and left. Nekesa – that's the lady who took us in – she found an advert in some local newspaper that your dad had placed for an assistant. She's very persuasive is Nekesa and Mum got the job. We moved down to Woodcroft so that she could walk to work.'

'What about her condition?' Merryn asked. 'I mean, I thought it was, you know, serious, but she seems fine.'

'Yes, she's fine as long as she keeps taking the drugs that she gets from the NHS. HIV isn't the death sentence it used to be unless you live somewhere where drugs aren't available or they're too expensive.'

'I don't get why you will be sent back to Kenya if your mum can't find a new job. Surely if she's still married, then you still have a visa.'

'They're divorced. It came through last year. Darren applied for it the moment we left and Mum didn't contest it. She just wanted rid of him but now we don't qualify for a visa. Mind, the Home Office can make exceptions, like if going back to Kenya means Mum will develop full blown AIDS. The government there are working with charities to provide antiviral drugs free to people with HIV.'

'So your mum will be okay if she goes back to Kenya. I mean, she'll get the drugs she needs.'

'Mum has a very aggressive form of HIV which is okay as long as she gets the right combination of antivirals. Up until recently, Kenya were offering something similar to what she gets now free of charge but there's evidence it causes miscarriage and now they won't give it to women under forty. So, no, Mum won't be okay. Mum's case worker has written to the Home Office explaining the situation but because she no longer has a full-time job earning enough to support me, the chances are we'll be sent back. I think even with a job, they'll send her back.'

'When will you find out?'

'Not sure. Maybe next week.'

'I'm sorry, Bee.' Merryn didn't know what else to say. 'I shouldn't have asked.'

'No, *I'm* sorry.' Beatrice stopped and took hold of his blazer sleeves. 'Ever since I first spoke to you in the canteen, remember, I've been blaming your dad, but it's not his fault. Mum has never blamed him. There's nothing he can do. She knows that. Anyway, this was going to happen whether she lost her job or not.'

For a few moments, they just held each other. Finally Beatrice pushed back, wiped away her tears and said, 'Come on, we'd better go. Mum is so excited to see you.'

Twenty minutes later, they emerged onto the road not far from a terrace of old, limestone cottages. As soon as Merryn appeared at the front door, Malika came rushing out of the kitchen and threw herself at him, wrapping both arms around his meagre frame, squeezing the air from his lungs and exclaiming, 'You crazy boy! Trying to get yourself killed. What were you thinking, Merryn MacIntyre? Lord knows! But you're here now.' She slackened her grip and pushed him back so that she could inspect his stitches. 'Eeeeehhhh! Look what he's done to you, that cruel man.'

'Mama!' Beatrice intervened. 'Merryn did that to himself. In any case, he's okay now.'

'Crazy boy.' She held his face in her hands and hugged him again. 'If anything happened to Merryn then what shall we do, eh? Oh Lord, your Malcolm and Donna must have been sick with worry about you, poor things. Come, take off your coat and sit. We got a *lot* to talk about, oh my goodness, surely we got a lot. I'm getting some tea. We're going to need a lot of tea. And you gotta be hungry after all that, so maybe some cake.' She disappeared into the kitchen closely followed by her daughter. Merryn shed his blazer, sat down on a shabby sofa and looked around him. He'd expected the house to be full of Africa but instead, the room was devoid of anything but the sofa, an old table and two chairs. No pictures, no ornaments, and yet, he reflected, the two people who lived here seemed so full of life, bubbling with a wonderful mischief. Sometimes, he wished Malika was his mother. Her methods of interrogation were never cunningly disguised. They were quite blatant, noisy and always full of fun. Sitting in one corner of the threadbare sofa, listening to the musical chatter in the kitchen, Merryn felt a deep contentment. Then he noticed a photo frame sitting on the windowsill, most of it hidden behind a curtain. He glanced at the kitchen, then stood up and pushed back the curtain to take a closer look. The frame held a faded black and white photo. He instantly recognised the young woman standing on an empty beach that seemed to stretch into infinity behind her. She wore a broad smile and Merryn marvelled at how little it had changed down the years, despite the hardship and misfortune that had dogged her life. In her arms, fast asleep, she held a tiny baby. He guessed that must be Beatrice. Next to Malika, standing no taller than her shoulders, stood a wiry figure who leaned forward on a wooden stick that he clenched with both hands. The camera had caught him with his head thrown back in the midst of a howl of laughter.

The kitchen door opened and before Merryn had a chance to retreat back to the sofa, Beatrice was standing beside him. 'Recognise mum?' she asked. 'That was taken fifteen years ago when I was a baby. That's me of course, and that – she pointed – is Grandad, mum's dad. He was always laughing, mainly at his own jokes. He died when I was eleven. I still miss him.'

Malika came in carrying a tray of tea and slabs of chocolate cake. 'Now we're gonna talk,' she announced. 'Beatrice, she has told me all about the voice you heard but you can tell me again. I mean, if you don't mind, that is.' She handed Merryn a steaming cup of tea and a plate with the largest slice of chocolate cake he'd ever seen.

'In case you hadn't figured,' Beatrice explained, motioning to the cake, 'that's a bribe.'

'Bee, hush yourself. I'm embarrassed now.' Malika laughed, then waited for Merryn to begin.

She listened spellbound, her eyes fixed on Merryn's face as he unfolded the series of events leading to his confrontation with Mear. When he'd finished, she sat deep in thought, and then said, 'Tom? She calls you Tom, never Merryn?'

Merryn nodded.

'And that evil man, she has been speaking to him also.'

'For quite some time, I think. We heard him tell his partner that she'd persuaded him to move from Wales because the poaching was better in the River Wye.'

'And how did she refer to Mr Mear? Did she call him by name?'

The question took Merryn by surprise. He'd never given it any thought and yet now, he couldn't recall the woman using any name. 'No, she didn't. Just "he".'

Malika sat quietly as if in a trance. Suddenly, she came to. 'The woman claims that Mear killed her and her baby, and that you promised to serve him justice for the crime.'

'That's right.'

'But she confessed she has killed someone herself with the pistol you found. How old is it?'

'It was made in 1639 and hidden down the crack in 1645 – I think.'

Malika paused for a moment and then said, 'Time you ate some cake and I'll tell you what's in my head; although from what Bee told me, you've already made some good progress.'

She waited until Merryn's mouth was full of cake. 'What you're hearing, you and that bad man, it's the woman's soul, I'm certain of it. She's speaking to *your* soul. Your ears can't hear it. That's why Bee and Zac heard nothing.'

'Why then do I use my voice to speak to her?' Merryn asked. 'If my soul was speaking then no one would hear what *I'm* saying.'

'Your body and soul are one whilst you're alive so that while your soul hears her, it's your body's voice that replies.' Seeing the confusion in his face, Malika added, 'In this life, Merryn, we can never hope to understand how body and soul connect with each other. Perhaps when we die, it will become clear. My father, the man in the photo...' She motioned to the frame on the windowsill. 'He heard a voice like the one you heard. It was his mother's. She died very suddenly of malaria when she was so, so young, just twenty-five. Her husband – my grandfather – he buried her the same day in an unmarked grave, somewhere out in the bush, beyond the village.'

'Mama, you've kept that a secret,' Beatrice protested. 'But I've seen her grave. It's in the village cemetery with everyone else. You've taken me there. And it's got a stone with her name on it.'

'But she wasn't buried there when she died.'

'Why would your grandfather do such a thing?'

'Why? My father, he never told me but there were rumours in the village of course. Plenty of rumours.' She sighed. 'Anyways, her soul was left in torment, somewhere between the body she had left behind and the place where she could join her ancestors. A soul never rests until it reaches that place.'

'Do you think she ever reached her ancestors?' Beatrice asked.

'I believe she did. My father, he heard his mother's voice when he was out in the bush searching for her grave. He was only a young boy, scarce nine years old. She begged him to give her a funeral since without one her ancestors would have rejected her. There's a path which every soul must follow and it always begins with a funeral.'

'How was that possible without a body?' Beatrice looked perplexed.

'It isn't possible. You see, my father found her grave.'

'But you said it was unmarked.' It was Merryn's turn to look perplexed.

'Yes it was. He told me that his mother had somehow guided him there with her voice. He marked the place with stones and then he waited until my grandfather died. Well, that wasn't until the year after I was born, 1984. My father, he must have been, what, thirty-three by then.'

'All those years, your grandmother's soul, wandering around in...' Merryn couldn't imagine where.

'And then he moved her?' Beatrice was shocked that such a thing could happen in her family.

'Yes, he did. The day after his father died, he dug up her bones, for that was all that was left of his mother's body, put them in a casket and gave her a traditional village funeral like she should have had all those years ago. Then he buried the casket with our ancestors, but as far away as possible from my grandfather. I wonder if you noticed that, Bee. She's been silent ever since. You see, I believe that the soul only speaks to someone if that someone can help them reach their ancestors. The woman whose voice you've heard, she's chosen you because she believes you can help her make the journey.'

'But she spoke to Mear as well, so you're saying that he can help her reach her ancestors too? I just don't see how that's possible.'

'You said she guided him to the river, close to the ruined church where you say her voice comes from.'

Merryn nodded.

'Maybe she asked him to dig up her bones and give them a proper burial. When he refused, then she turned to you for help.'

Merryn sat for a while, taking it all in. Malika had added a few pieces to the puzzle but the burning question that was driving him mad still lay unanswered.

'Mear and I. Two people living in the twenty-first century with no connection to something that happened in the seventeenth century. Why us?'

Her audience watched as a strange look came over Malika's face. 'There are some truths that you must hear from this woman, Merryn.'

'Mama, what do you mean?' Beatrice asked. 'Do you know something?'

'It's not my place to say any more. You're going back to the church, Bee tells me. That's good. And you would like me to come, Merryn?'

'Yes, of course.' Then he added 'Actually, Mum doesn't trust me to go anywhere by myself now, so having you there would make things a lot easier.'

Malika laughed, instantly defusing the tension in the room. 'I can understand how she might react when she hears you're going down to the river again. Let me speak to her first. Malika's magic. That's what your dad used to call it, when I was sent out to deal with awkward customers at the shop. It never failed.'

But it has failed. Just like Bee said, bad luck doesn't come just once. It failed to protect you from the monster you married, from his HIV. It failed to persuade the Home Office to let you stay. And the shop. It failed there, too. There is no magic, Malika. Instead, there's only injustice for the people who least deserve it.

'Merryn, are you alright?' Malika asked. 'You look a bit lost.'

'Sorry, I'm okay. I… er… you know, it's a lot to take in. But I'm fine. I'd better go. Thanks for the cake. It's the best I've ever tasted, seriously.'

CHAPTER 30

Beatrice's somewhat extended goodbye meant that by the time Merryn reached Church Close, it was getting dark. He caught a glimpse of his mother's anxious face peering out from the sitting room window as he walked up the drive past Malcolm's van. He'd scarcely had time to find a back door key in his pocket before the front door flung open.

'There you are. I was getting worried.'

'Why? You know where I've been.' He struggled to hide the irritation in his voice.

She gave him an awkward hug. 'Come down when you've got changed. We've had a letter.'

Malcolm appeared from the kitchen. 'Hey,' was all he said and disappeared again.

So this is how it's going to be, thought Merryn as he wearily climbed the stairs to his bedroom. Hugs and heys. It won't last long. A week or so and it'll be back to normal: Mum devoting all her time to Charlie and Dad wrestling with the business and the bank. Except there'd be nothing normal when the house was sold and the business folded. Normal would disappear over the horizon. Then he thought of Malika and immediately felt guilty. After all, what was normal for her?

Ten minutes later, the MacIntyre family sat around the kitchen table, Charlie wriggling for all he was worth on Donna's knee as he tried to grab the letter in her hand. 'It's from someone at the Bristol City Museum, a coroner called Mrs Frampton-Burnett. She's holding a meeting about the gun you found.' Donna tried to sound casual, pushing the letter across the table to Merryn. 'There's a receipt for it in the envelope from the man who owns the antiques shop. Isaac Levi.'

Merryn knew where this was going.

'The man you went to see with Zac about...'

'What *matters*,' Malcolm interrupted, 'is that the gun – the pistol – is officially treasure. But you already know that, I suspect.' Merryn nodded. 'So we have to attend an inquest in Bristol on Tuesday October 1st. I'm guessing Zac's parents have also had a letter. Have you any idea what the coroner's going to ask you?'

Merryn sat for a few moments reading the letter and then looked up. 'Pretty much,' he answered.

'Do you think you could maybe fill us in?' Donna's efforts at indifference were proving too much for her.

'The pistol is treasure, like Dad says. The coroner,' – he looked down at the letter – 'Mrs Frampton-Burnett is going to ask us how we found it. Did we ask permission from the landowner before climbing through the fence? Did we see any signs telling us not to go on his land? We've already sent that information to a woman at the museum, the Finds Liaison Officer, and she's sent a report to the coroner. But I guess she needs to hear it from us. That's about it. She'll send a report to a committee somewhere that values the pistol and they decide who gets a reward which, in this case, will be the landowner.'

Merryn looked down at the letter again. The British Museum had registered their interest in purchasing the pistol but there was no mention of the private collection in New York who already possessed its twin. The last remnants of Donna's indifference evaporated and, ignoring her husband's calming hand signals, she asked, 'Since you found the pistol, why won't you get part of the reward? I mean, you almost died finding it, for heaven's sake.'

Merryn sighed. 'We were trespassing, Mum. That's breaking the law. You don't get rewarded for breaking the law.'

'So you'll get nothing.'

'Nothing.'

'Have you any idea how much its worth?'

Merryn was dreading this question. 'A rough idea,' he lied. 'When Mr Levi first saw it, he told us it was worth at least a hundred grand but he doesn't...'

'What?' Donna shrieked. 'One hundred thousand pounds? How can that be? A rusty, old pistol? Merryn, why haven't you told me this before?' She looked at Malcolm. 'Did you know?'

Malcolm's face provided the answer. 'You both knew and you didn't think to tell me? What the hell is going on in this family? Is this some kind of conspiracy? Keep Donna out of the loop? I thought we'd agreed Merryn, no more secrets.' Charlie began to cry, frightened by his mother's outburst, his mournful wail adding to the tension in the room.

'Okay, okay, it's my fault.' Malcolm held his hands up. 'Merryn told me the pistol's value last week but I didn't want to get your hopes up because... because, like Merryn said, he and Zac were trespassing when they found it. That's the truth, Donna, I swear.'

Donna stood up and bounced Charlie up and down to calm him. When he was quiet, she asked 'How can an old pistol be worth that much?'

'Actually, it's worth a lot more. Miss Kelly told us today that there's another identical one in New York that's worth...' He could hardly bring himself to say it. Even Charlie stopped his wriggling in anticipation.

'Four hundred thousand.'

Donna's eyes opened as wide as tennis balls. 'This had better not be a joke, Merryn. Tell me this isn't a joke.'

'It's not a joke, Mum, I swear. That's what a private collector in New York paid for an identical pistol. Wintour had a pair of them, given to him by Charles I around 1640. The handle is solid gold. You'll understand when you see it. Isaac reckons it's the biggest find of a single piece of treasure this century.'

'Solid gold? You found a gun with a solid gold handle? Oh my God. And it's worth four hundred thousand?' And then, with an air of resignation, she added, 'And you'll get *none* of it.'

'I'm so sorry, Mum – and Dad – but the land is private. We don't know who owns it but whoever it is isn't going to be happy about two kids crawling around above the cliffs. Once they find out that the pistol is worth a fortune, they'll get their lawyers on the case and that will be it.'

'Makes you sick.' Donna began swaying back and forth. 'There wasn't a cat-in-hell's chance of the owners finding the gun and yet you say they'll get every penny of its value. There's no justice in this world.' She sat down again to regain control. 'Anyway, doesn't matter what the coroner decides, I think you're a star, Merryn MacIntyre, a bloody dangerous one but a star nonetheless.' Charlie sensed that the mood of the room had changed and promptly giggled. 'We'll all go. Make it a family occasion.' Donna looked across at Malcolm, who nodded. 'If that's okay with you,' she added, turning to Merryn.

He shrugged. 'You have to go. I'm under eighteen. But you won't say anything, will you.'

Donna smiled. 'As if I would. I just can't wait to see it. Will it be there, do you think?'

'I'm not sure. Mr Levi has taken it to the museum in Bristol, same place where the inquest is being held so maybe it'll be on display. Mind, it needs a lot of work on the barrel and the firing mechanism, but the butt – it's just unbelievable. I still can't believe it was down there, waiting to be found for all those years.'

Donna sat gazing at her teenage son, trying to remember the last time she had heard him speak so freely and with such passion. She wanted the moment to last forever but she knew it wouldn't. He'd recede back into his shell and shut them out but, now at least, she knew the boy she had nurtured for so many years was still there. That was enough.

CHAPTER 31

Monday 23rd September

The Critical Care Unit at the Bristol Royal Infirmary occupied much of the sixth floor, the windows of its single rooms looking out over the vast, glittering sprawl of the city. In room 608, Miss Grigoryev leaned forward in her chair across the tangle of cables connecting her husband to a myriad of monitors and slipped her hand into his.

'George, I know you can hear me so I will not be speaking bad things today. Yesterday, I am angry, you understand, but you don't want to hear that any more, so I shall speak good things only.' She paused as if to allow her words to soak through the injured tissues in George's brain to a deeper place in his subconscious.

'Today, I am trying to return to school but Mrs Bowden-Lees, she will have none of it.' She squeezed his hand. 'I must return so that I speak with Merryn. I have a hug waiting for him, big like a Russian bear. Mrs Bowden-Lees, she tells me he has returned, none the worse for his adventures.' She leaned closer. 'Darling, you must wake up for Merryn is waiting for you. Fight, do you hear me? You must fight. I am tired of watching these machines with their bleeps and buzzers and their flashing digits and tracing graphs. It is time to come home, to come back to me.'

She quickly wiped away the tears in case George woke up suddenly and found her crying. 'Tonight you must make a big effort so that tomorrow we celebrate. If you can do that, then I will bring Merryn MacIntyre to see you. I think he knows our secret, George. He's a smart boy but you know that, don't you? I wonder if he knows about your first meeting with that *zloy ublyudok*. Even that does not describe him. No, I don't think he knows but I will tell him. He deserves to know. You had Mear measured from the start, didn't you? A dirty, lying fraud. History teacher? Pah! I should have seen it, the head too, but we were blind.'

She wiped away another tear. It was the same every time she sat with her husband; the rage lying buried between visits spilling out into the open, triggered by the sight of the man she adored lying silent and spiritless.

'Why did you confront him, George? Mr Skinner, he tells everything to the police and the police, they tell me.' She paused, waiting for an answer. 'Of course I know why, my dearest.' She leant forward and kissed his pale cheek. 'Because you are everything that Mear is not. He threatens you, that's what Skinner says, threatens to hurt you if you speak a word of his deception. But Mear can see your virtue for it shines like a bright light. Evil cannot tolerate such light, my darling. That is why he tries to kill you. But he will not win. Evil will not win. You will come back to me, I know it.' Miss Grigoryev gently laid her head beside her husband's and let the tears flow.

*

Thirty miles away in Gloucester's Royal Hospital, PC Mike Spence sat outside room 117 in the Acute Medical Unit reading a copy of *Homes and Gardens*, a clear sign of just how desperate he was for something, anything, to break the mind-numbing monotony of his four-hour shift. Inside the room, Ezra Mear's life hung by the thinnest of threads, a life sustained only by the hiss of a ventilator as it pumped air into his lungs through a trach tube in his neck. No one heard the voice that spoke to him for even if she had screamed, PC Spence would have heard nothing.

'Look how far I've come,' she said. 'The chains that bind me are looser now. Does that vex you, John? Frighten you, even?' She paused as if waiting for an answer. 'I know you can hear me, lying there betwixt life and death, stripped of the power you once possessed over me. Your ancestors sent you back to atone for your sins but the evil in your soul would not do it, would not lift the stone and set us free.' She fell silent, wondering why she had come so far when there was nothing to be gained by doing so.

'In all the lives you have lived, all the bodies you have possessed, I have wished upon you torment and grief, the same that you have brought to those around you. But more than that, John, I have wished you a violent death like the one that sent me and my child to this desolate place. Why do you think I brought you to the school, to the boy? He promised me long ago he would serve you justice. I longed for it at the river, watching you drown. But he saved you, John. The boy released the rope and saved you. Do you know why? Is it within your power to understand such mercy, one human saving another? I think not. And me? I was a fool to think that the life which would set us free was your life. But revenge is not our path to freedom. I know that now. There is another way and God willing, we shall find it. But for you, I fear, the path to freedom is still many lives away. Yes, I fear it, because in those lives, your soul will practice the evil which possesses it and I may not be there to stand in your way.'

CHAPTER 32

Tuesday 1st October

Merryn woke to the sound of rain hammering on his window. He snatched a glance at his alarm clock through one eye – ten past seven – and dropped back to the pillow, pulling the duvet over his head. The day he was dreading had dawned, the weather matching his mood perfectly. A call from Isaac Levi the previous evening had done little to lift his spirits for it transpired that the appointed coroner, Mrs Frampton-Burnett, enjoyed a reputation for adhering categorically to every letter of every law.

'Forewarned, forearmed, Merryn,' Isaac cautioned. 'She's a bit of a battle axe and doesn't suffer fools, so you and Zac had better get your story straight before you arrive at the museum. If she suspects for one moment that you were treasure hunting, then she'll deny you both any claim to the reward. She's done that in the past, referring metal detectorists to the police when they'd failed to seek permission from farmers. Just stick to the truth, young man, and maybe she'll show you a little clemency.'

For the first time in his life – at least as far as Merryn could remember – Donna phoned the school to say her son would be absent until lunch. Then at nine o'clock, the phone rang.

'Hey, where are you?' Zac asked. 'Tell me you're not ill.'

Merryn had hardly spoken to him since the meeting with Miss Kelly, spending every spare moment with Beatrice instead.

'There's something wrong with Donna.' He lowered his voice. 'She's given me the whole morning off.'

'Lucky you. Dad said the same but Sasha wouldn't have it. So, are you ready for this?'

'Ready? There's not much we can do except turn up, is there?' Merryn wondered what Zac was plotting.

'You get a call from Isaac last night?'

'Yes, but it didn't help much. The coroner is someone you don't mess with, apparently. Doesn't like trespassers.'

'That's what he told me, but we weren't treasure hunting, were we? The discovery was accidental. Pity you don't still have the bandage on your head. You could put one on just for the inquest.'

'Zac, she'd see through that straight away. Isaac said stick to the truth. If she suspects we're making stuff up, then she'll refer us to the police. She'll probably do that anyway, in front of my parents. Mum's going to go ballistic.'

'That's not going to happen. We've discovered the antique of the decade. Dad's really fired up about it. Says he can't wait to see the pistol. Pity Isaac's not going to be there – didn't get invited, apparently.'

'Beatrice and her mum are being sent back to Kenya,' Merryn announced abruptly. 'They got a letter yesterday from the Home Office.'

'What? No way. They can't do that. They've been living here for... how long?'

'Since 2015 but Malika divorced her husband in 2018. She thought she could apply for Indefinite Leave to Remain but it turns out she doesn't qualify. Her case worker tried to persuade the Home Office to let her stay because she needs the NHS drugs for her HIV, but now that Kenya are providing treatment free of charge, she's got to go. They don't seem to understand that the drugs she'll get won't be the right ones. Nothing she can do about it. No money, no prospect of a decent job, no passport and a dependent child who was born to a Kenyan father. It doesn't get worse than that.'

There was a long pause and then Zac said quietly, 'See you at eleven.'

*

The tables in the City of Bristol Museum's function room had been arranged into a square. Sitting on one side were Zac and Merryn together with their fathers while to their left sat an elderly bearded gentleman in a tweed jacket next to a younger man in a black suit who shuffled papers back and forth on the table in front of him. Sitting facing the boys were two women either side of a vacant chair, one of them tapping feverishly at a laptop keyboard, the other checking emails on her phone.

The British Museum contingent entered the room from the back, an elderly lady with round-rimmed glasses accompanied by two much younger men. They'd scarcely got seated when a rather severe, middle-aged woman carrying a black briefcase in one hand made her way to the front, settled into the vacant chair, removed a number of folders from the briefcase and looked up.

'Good morning and thank you all for coming at such short notice. It would appear that the normal timetable for an inquest of this nature has been somewhat accelerated, against my better judgement, I might add. Now, I should make it clear to all present that, whilst our modest surroundings today bear no resemblance to a court of law, be under no illusions that the evidence given today in relation to the item of treasure is subject to the same exacting requirements as that given in a court of law. In short, gentlemen,' – she looked directly at Merryn and Zac sitting opposite her – 'I expect nothing less than the truth, the whole truth and nothing but the truth, is that understood?' Her words hung ominously as Merryn nodded while Zac answered, 'Yes, miss. Understood.' Mrs Frampton-Burnett made a mental note: *watch the tall, blond one.*

'The inquest this morning has been called to establish the facts surrounding the discovery of a seventeenth century flintlock pistol in a crevice at the top of the Wintour's Leap cliffs in the Wye Valley. I'm sure that some of you present today were hoping to see the pistol but for security reasons, I'm afraid, it cannot be displayed here.'

This brought murmurs of discontent from a number of those present, most audibly from Donna who sat at the back of the room with Charlie on her lap. The coroner rolled her eyes and continued.

'I have in my possession a letter and photograph from a Monsieur Pascal St Pierre, an antique firearms expert who comes highly recommended by the British Museum.' Avid nods from the Museum trio confirmed this. 'Monsieur St Pierre indicates that, from the hallmark on the pistol's butt, it was cast in London in 1639 by the eminent Dutch goldsmith Hugo van Diercksen. Furthermore, he claims that an identical pistol resides in a private collection in New York, one of a pair given to Sir John Wintour by King Charles I, information gleaned from a detailed provenance. From work carried out on the New York pistol, it is clear that the butt is solid gold. Miss Edwards, our FLO' – she glanced at the little, grey-haired woman who sat to her left with a look of intense excitement on her bespectacled face – 'has examined the pistol and assures me it qualifies as treasure under Section 1(1)(a) of the Treasure Act 1996. Furthermore, the British Museum has expressed an interest in purchasing the pistol although its value has not yet been established. I understand that there are a number of other parties who have registered their interest in acquiring the pistol. We'll leave that matter to the Secretary of State. Our business this morning is to ascertain the exact circumstances of the pistol's discovery and to that end I will call upon Merryn MacIntyre and Zachary Luca-Hunt to describe the events which took place between midnight and one a.m. on Friday, the sixth of September at the top of the Wintour's Leap cliffs. Merryn, will you stand please.' She sat back in her chair and folded her arms. 'Take your time. Unlike certain antiques dealers, we are in no hurry.'

Merryn stood, took a deep breath and launched. His account was brief and to the point and some way short of the whole truth. When he'd finished, the coroner leaned forward, her eyes narrowed beneath a puzzled frown. 'And why exactly *were* you squeezing through railings in thick fog at midnight? I assume that neither sets of parents were aware of your nocturnal exploits?'

'Research,' Merryn answered. 'We wanted to find out if Wintour could have jumped.'

Mrs Frampton-Burnett stared at him incredulously for a few seconds. 'Research? At night? Explain, please.'

'Simple, really. You drop something into the river and time how long it takes to hear a splash. Then you calculate the drop height.'

'And you can't hear a splash in daylight when you stand a better chance of avoiding falling into cracks and knocking yourself out? Or worse still, falling over a three-hundred-foot cliff?'

Donna sat fuming at the back of the room, barely able to restrain herself from aiming a few choice words at the woman she judged to be a pompous, self-important cow. She was a coroner, not the bloody queen.

'We wouldn't have found the pistol if I hadn't fallen into the crack. If we'd gone there in daylight, we wouldn't be here now.'

'That's my boy,' Donna muttered under her breath.

Mrs Frampton-Burnett uttered a theatrical sigh. 'I don't think anyone present approves of your midnight escapades, Merryn, least of all your parents. And, you ignored a Keep Out sign, am I right?'

Merryn nodded.

'That's a yes, is it, just for the record?'

Merryn's answer was rather louder than he'd intended to which the coroner gave him a long stare and then said, 'That'll be all for now. Zachary Luca-Hunt, please stand.'

Zac counted up to five and then stood.

'Your account, Zachary, if you will, please.'

'Same as Merryn, except there are two points which he didn't make absolutely clear. Number one: the wording on the sign. Keep Out – Dangerous Cliffs. Nowhere on the sign did it say *Private* and therefore at no time on the night of September sixth did we deliberately trespass on private land. As far as we knew, the land was as public as the road. Second…'

'Zachary, I must stop you there.' Mrs Frampton-Burnett raised one hand. 'I asked only for your account of how you came to find the pistol. I have no interest in your interpretation of the law of trespass. That's my job. So, I will ask you again. What took place – in your words, not Merryn's – between midnight and one o'clock on the sixth of September?'

Zac exchanged the briefest of glances with his father. 'It was foggy. We could hardly see two yards in front of us. We ran past the Keep Out – Dangerous Cliffs sign until we came to a gap in the railings where one of the metal posts had rusted so bad it had fallen off. It was just as well no one had thought to repair it,' – he shot a glance at the bearded gentlemen before continuing – 'because Merryn would have been run down by a car that came along the lane. I pushed him through the gap to save his life. That's when Merryn fell down the crevice and found the pistol.'

Mrs Frampton-Burnett interjected at this point. 'According to your co-conspirator, your intention from the start was to squeeze through the railings and crawl to the edge of the cliff to undertake' – she cleared her throat – 'research. The sudden arrival of a car merely hastened your progress through the fence, am I right?'

'Yes, I suppose so, but without the gap, we would have been run over.'

'No Zachary. You would have been run over because you were running along a narrow country lane at midnight in dense fog. Please continue. Merryn falls into the crevice. What happened next?'

The coroner was right. Car or no car, they'd have squeezed through the railings anyway. Instead, he tried a different tack.

'So, Merryn fell into the crack. He must have been about fifteen feet down and there it was, hidden beneath a rock, totally invisible from above. There was absolutely no way anyone would have found the pistol if he hadn't fall in. No way.' He glanced over at the bearded gentleman again just to underline the point.

'And there you go again.' The coroner let out another audible sigh. 'Assertions. I think that's enough, thank you. You may be seated.' She turned to her clerk and waited until she'd finished typing.

'Mr McGregor.' The elderly man got slowly to his feet. 'No need to stand, Mr McGregor. Just a few questions for the record. Your full name is Rodger MacIntosh McGregor, is that correct?'

He nodded. 'It is.'

'And you represent the Wye Valley Wildlife Trust.'

'I do.'

'Could you confirm your position in the Trust?'

'Chief Executive.'

Merryn felt a cold chill run down his spine at this. The landowners had sent the big guns to the inquest. They must know there was a lot of money at stake.

'And the gentlemen seated alongside you is your lawyer, is that correct?'

'He is. Mr Billings of Billings and Chowder Law.'

'And am I right in saying that the Trust owns the land at the top of Wintour's Leap?'

'It owns the Lancaut SSSI nature reserve of which Wintour's Leap is a part. That includes the narrow strip of land at the top of the cliffs.'

'A simple yes would have sufficed. Are you also responsible for maintaining the fence that runs between the road and that narrow strip of land?'

Mr MacGregor turned to his lawyer who shook his head vigorously and mouthed 'no comment'.

'I'm afraid I can't answer that question at this time.'

'You can't? Because you don't know or because it's inconvenient for you to do so?'

Mr MacGregor shifted uncomfortably in his chair while his black-suited lawyer whispered something to him. Then he said, 'I would need to check that with our legal team.'

'You just have, Mr MacGregor,' Mrs Frampton-Burnett stated acidly. 'Can I remind you both that it is an offence for a person to withhold evidence from an inquest of this nature. Mr Billings, you of all people should know that.'

The lawyer found his voice. 'To be perfectly honest, ma'am, we don't know. I can find out quickly enough.'

'I'd like the answer before my office closes today, thank you. Now, let me ask you a question that perhaps you can answer. Do the public have a right of access to the thin strip of land at the top of Wintour's Leap? A simple yes or no will suffice.'

A brief exchange between the two men was followed by, 'Yes and no.' Mrs Frampton-Burnett groaned but Mr MacGregor ignored her. 'We have an access agreement with the British Mountaineering Council which states that climbers reaching the top of the cliffs may attach themselves to bolts placed in the rock a few feet back from the edge and bring their partners up. However, they must abseil back down the cliffs from these bolts for there is no access to the road from the cliff top. Neither is there access to the clifftop from the road.'

'Unless, of course, the people responsible for maintaining the fence fail in their duty to do so, is that not right, Mr MacGregor?'

'Absolutely not, ma'am. Just because there's a hole in a fence does not give anyone the right to climb through it.' He glanced at his lawyer who nodded his approval.

'Very good. Now, humour me, Mr MacGregor, but if I was to parachute onto the clifftop, would I be trespassing? This time, I shall have my yes *or* no.'

The chief executive looked askance before once again seeking guidance. Everyone in the room, with the possible exception of

Charlie, understood exactly where the coroner's line of questioning was leading, no one more so than Mr Billings.

'I must press you for an answer, Mr MacGregor. We don't have all day. Is that a yes *or* no?' Mrs Frampton-Burnett began tapping her pen on the table in front of her.

'Well, ma'am...'

'No, not *well, ma'am*. Yes or no. Would I be trespassing?'

'No.' Mr MacGregor's answer was barely audible.

'Just to be clear, that was a no, am I right?'

'It was. But…'

'No buts, thank you. Your assertion is – correct me if I'm mistaken – that the boys had every right to *be* on the clifftop but they had no right to *access* it through a hole in the fence.'

'That may well be correct. However, it needs checking.'

Zac stretched out his hand beneath the table for a low five with Merryn, but it was met with a brief shake of the head. The fat lady wasn't singing yet.

The coroner waited until the clerk had finished typing into her laptop before clearing her throat ceremoniously. 'I'd like to consult with our legal team in London before making a decision regarding who is eligible for the reward in this case. Given the value of the pistol and the somewhat unusual nature of its discovery, it would be imprudent of me to make a hasty judgement. I propose therefore that we reconvene tomorrow at nine sharp when I will deliver my verdict. In the meantime, I would be grateful if you would refrain from talking to the media. We'll release a press statement after tomorrow's announcement.' With that, the coroner rose to her feet, gathered up the papers into her briefcase and hurried out of the room.

Zac turned to Merryn. 'So, mister doom-and-gloom, we *weren't* trespassing after all. Serious money coming our way.'

Merryn glanced over at Mr MacGregor who was deep in conversation with his lawyer. 'Keep your voice down,' he whispered. 'We're not there yet otherwise she would have delivered a verdict today.' He dared not believe, but for the first time since leaving Isaac Levi's antiques shop, Merryn's eyes were fixed on a glimmering light at the end of a long tunnel. Was it possible that, after all, they would be rewarded with a substantial portion of the pistol's value?

CHAPTER 33

Wednesday 2nd October

The following morning found the same assemblage once again gathered around the square in the museum's function room, the atmosphere heavy with nervous anticipation. At precisely nine o'clock, Mrs Frampton-Burnett, with an expression no less severe than the previous day settled into her chair and surveyed the scene in front of her. Satisfied that all relevant parties were present, she extracted a file from her briefcase and laid it decorously in front of her.

'Thank you once again for your prompt attendance, somewhat miraculous given the morning rush hour traffic in this God-forsaken city. I will endeavour to keep you for as short a time as I can. So, let us proceed. Can I start by thanking Mr Billings and his client for emailing me the document detailing the ownership of the fence through which the boys gained access to the cliff top. It would appear to be the property of the local authority, who erected it some years ago, prior to the Wye Valley Wildlife Trust purchasing the reserve, in order to keep the public safe and to stop climbers from accessing the cliffs from above. The sign warning pedestrians of the cliffs was also erected by the local authority. Since that time, there has been no change in the law regarding access from the road. In other words, it is illegal to do so. What's more, access to the cliff top area itself is restricted to climbers who are members of the British Mountaineering Council and no one else, provided they reach the top from the ground below. So Mr MacGregor, you were incorrect in stating that parachutists landing on the cliff top, heaven forbid, would not be trespassing because the documents you have provided state quite clearly that they would be, as would anyone squeezing through the fence from the road.' She paused to let this sink in, only too aware of the increasingly despondent expressions on a number of faces around the room. Those belonging to the chief executive and his lawyer were not among them.

'It is my duty, therefore, to inform you of the findings of this inquest. Firstly, that the pistol recovered from the crack by Merryn MacIntyre is treasure. Secondly, that in recovering it, both he and Zachary Luca-Hunt were trespassing on an area of the Wye Valley Wildlife Reserve whose access is restricted to BMC climbers from the ground only. Thirdly, it is clear that the two boys did not knowingly trespass although they failed to heed a sign warning them of the dangers of passing through the fence. Neither did they visit the cliff top with the intention of treasure hunting; in other words, the discovery of the pistol was entirely by chance. It is now my duty to inform the Treasure Valuation Committee at the British Museum of these findings. They will work towards a valuation of the pistol prior to restoration and determine whether a reward should be payable to the finders and landowners, and if so, how much. This concludes the inquest. I shall prepare a press release which will go out tomorrow. Can I reassure those present that details of finders and landowners will not be disclosed; neither will the location of the find, nor the manner in which the pistol was found. You are under obligation to do likewise.' Without another word, Mrs Frampton-Burnett slipped the folder back into her briefcase and hurried out of the room as though she had a train to catch.

Zac turned to Merryn. 'Did not *knowingly* trespass. That's got to be worth something.'

Merryn shrugged. 'But we *were* trespassing. That's all that matters.'

Zac's father stood up. 'Come on boys, I'll drop you back to school. Is that okay, Malcolm?'

Malcolm nodded. 'Appreciate that,' he replied, mustering as much enthusiasm as he could. The pistol might well have been the find of the decade, but the last flickering candle of hope that his business might be saved, his mortgage arrears paid, had just been snuffed out. He knew he was wrong to imagine for a moment that a reward for something he'd had no part in might atone for his own business inadequacies, but ever since his son had spoken of the pistol's value, the flame had been lit. He had imagined himself sitting in Bairstow's office at the bank, a smirk across his face, handing over a cheque for every penny he owed and then announcing that he was taking his business elsewhere. But it wouldn't have been his money, not a penny of it. And now, with the trespassing verdict, there wasn't going to *be* any money.

'Mr MacIntyre?' A voice nudged him from his thoughts. 'My name is Winifred Khatri. I'm Curator of Seventeenth Century English Antiquities at the British Museum; quite a mouthful, I know.' She laughed and stretched out a hand. Malcolm shook it, not quite sure how to respond. 'I just wanted to say how much I admire your son's spirit of adventure, falling into a crack like that and yet having the wherewithal to recover the pistol. Like his friend said, without Merryn's tenacity, it would have spent another three hundred years undetected. Remarkable, quite remarkable. You must be very proud of your son.' The diminutive old woman stared up at him through her round-rimmed glasses, beaming a smile which said she meant every word.

'Yes, he's history mad. Obsessed, you might say. Talks about nothing else.'

'That's wonderful, when so many young people spend their days in front of screens. It's just such a pity that the boys were trespassing when they found the pistol. It'll fetch a very high price when it's sold and they'll not get a penny. Still, the law is the law. Well, it's been nice meeting you.' With that, she turned and hurried out of the room to join her colleagues since she *did* have a train to catch. Malcolm watched her go, her words echoing inside his head. *You must be very proud of your son.* He wondered if his son was proud of him. Within twenty-four hours, he'd be discussing bankruptcy with Mr Bairstow and within forty-eight, selling the house with Mr Terry. No. His son wouldn't be proud of him.

CHAPTER 34

Thursday 3rd October

It took the jungle drums less than twenty-four hours to beat the news of the discovery of Sir John Wintour's pistol by two schoolboys at the top of the cliffs bearing his name. Shortly after five o'clock on Thursday evening, Beatrice rang Merryn's landline.

'Are you watching the news?' Beatrice could barely contain her excitement. 'BBC One!'

Merryn turned on the TV just in time to see a reporter standing on the bank of the Wye looking up at the cliffs, describing in some detail the events which led to the discovery of a seventeenth century golden pistol belonging to Sir John Wintour. Merryn stared at the screen, scarcely able to believe what he was hearing.

'How the hell did they get hold of all that?' he muttered.

'Merryn, what's wrong?' This wasn't the response she'd expected.

'The coroner, she said she wouldn't release any details of how the pistol was found. Well, someone's blabbed.'

The reporter looked straight into the camera: 'Worth as much as £400,000, the pistol is one of a pair, the other residing in a private collection in New York. It's doubtful that the boys who found it will be eligible for any reward since an inquest held in Bristol yesterday determined that they were trespassing on part of the Wye Valley Nature Reserve with restricted access to the public. This is Ellie Stanford, BBC News, the Wye Valley.'

Merryn turned the TV off and stormed upstairs to his bedroom. 'Bee, she promised not to release any of that. I can't believe it. Someone at the inquest has leaked everything to the media.'

'But the BBC are pretty good at digging, aren't they? They could have found all that stuff just by talking to the right people.'

'The right people? Yeah, like the chief executive of the nature reserve who stands to get 100% of the pistol's value. He's making absolutely sure that everyone knows we were trespassing. And now they do.'

Beatrice waited for a break in the storm. 'At least they haven't revealed your names. I'll bet that would have been breaking the law. Merryn, are you still there?'

For a few moments, Beatrice thought he'd ended the call, but then a voice said, 'Yes, I'm still here.'

'Tell me what this is really about. I mean, you should be dead chuffed that – what did the antiques dealer call it? "The find of the decade" – is all over the national news.'

'Bee, did you hear what the woman said? No reward. Nothing. My dad won't be able to save the shop. He won't be able to give Malika her job back.'

'Listen, I don't think that would make much difference. Job or no job, she doesn't have a passport or a visa. She's appealed against the Home Office decision and maybe they'll change their mind. They've got up to sixty days to respond. Meanwhile, she's tried the new supermarket, last resort and all that. They've only got part-time work with minimum wage. She'll have to take it, just to pay the bills. There's nothing else we can do. Nothing else *you* can do so stop beating yourself up about it.'

'But what if they don't change their mind? What if you have to go? Your mum…'

'It's what it is, Merryn. We've just got to make the best of it.'

'Is there a best? It's not brilliant here, either. Dad's at the bank right now. He didn't say why but it's not going to be good.'

'Listen, let's not talk about bad stuff. My mum is meeting yours in town tomorrow for coffee, to talk about going back down to the river; did she tell you?'

'Nope. She would have if she knew what it was about. Your mum hasn't told her yet. I can't believe she'll let me go.'

'Wait and see. Listen, I've got to go. Speak tomorrow. Love you.'

Merryn sat down on his computer chair and stared at the blank screen, in two minds about switching it on. He tried to remember when it had all started, when Google images had morphed into tangible objects, Google Earth into tangled bramble woods and stinking mud. All at once, he spun round on his chair. 'You're here,' he whispered.

'I'm always here.' To Merryn, her voice seemed much louder than when she had last spoken to him in his bedroom.

'Then talk to me. Tell me where you've come from, why you call me Tom; and Mear, how could he possibly have killed you?'

'When you come to the church, I will tell you everything, I promise.'

'Then at least tell me who you are. Don't I deserve that?'

'You deserve so much more. It's I who deserve nothing, for my foolishness brought this all about. Who am I? I'm Grace Mundy, your sister.'

CHAPTER 35

Saturday 12th October

Sasha stopped the Range Rover where Mear had parked his car a month before and its four passengers spilled out.

'One o'clock back here. Ring me if you're going to be late.' With that, Sasha performed a hasty three-point turn and roared back towards the main road.

'Where's Miss Freckles?' Zac asked. 'Thought she was supposed to meet us here.'

'Zac, don't call her that,' Beatrice reprimanded. 'Miss Kelly. I told her nine-thirty. Maybe she's had second thoughts. I think she's nervous about being involved – you know – being a teacher.'

'Bit late for that,' Zac grinned. 'Ha, talk of the devil.' An elderly Peugeot 208 drove down the lane and pulled up alongside them.

'Sorry I'm late. Engine wouldn't start.'

When Miss Kelly had parked her car, Malika wandered over and stuck out a hand. 'Miss Kelly, lovely to meet you again. I'm Bee's mum.'

'Mrs Odoyu. Yes, I remember. We spoke at a parents' evening last year. You've brought up a remarkable young lady. You should be proud of her.'

Malika smiled. 'She's the best thing that ever happened to me.'

Beatrice blushed. 'I think it's time we got moving,' and with that, she set off at pace down the path. The boys waited until the two women had started after her and then followed at a safe distance. 'You know why I'm here, don't you,' Zac called over his shoulder. 'Your girlfriend is pretty persistent, I have to say.'

'I'm not sure she *is* my girlfriend, actually,' Merryn replied.

'What d'you mean? Of course she is. She's nuts about you. Can't imagine why.'

'Thanks.' There was a pause, then he said, 'She's been a bit weird this week. Feels like she's pushing me away.'

Zac didn't answer though he knew what his friend meant. Instead, he changed the subject. 'So, what are you expecting to find down here? By the church, Beatrice said.'

'Maybe *in* the church, I don't know. I can't explain, Zac, because you didn't hear anything.' He paused. 'Except you did. You heard Mear talking about the same voice. His sidekick, Jed, thought he was nuts, too.'

Zac said nothing.

'Alright, I'm not expecting you to believe any of this. If I was you, I wouldn't. It's not easy for me hearing this woman's voice all the time. Last Monday, she spoke to me at home. She hasn't done that before. She told me her name was Grace.' *And she's my sister. How is that possible? How is any of this possible?*

Zac suddenly ground to a halt and turned to face Merryn. 'Listen. I know it all sounds real to you. Beatrice thinks it's real but like I said, she's nuts about you so she would, wouldn't she. But there's millions of people out there, billions probably, who believe in God and God is just as supernatural as this woman you keep talking about. Everyone's free to believe what the hell they like so I'm not going to try and persuade you that it's a load of nonsense. It's up to you. I don't believe in God and I don't believe this woman is any more real than Father Christmas, but I'm cool if that's what you want to believe. Okay?'

Merryn had never heard Zac talk reason like that before and he sensed that the barrier which had grown between them was being dismantled.

'Yeah, okay.'

'High five?' Zac held up his hand and Merryn slapped it, thinking it was the first time he'd high-fived anyone. With that, they set off down the path to join the others.

'Feels odd to be back here in daylight,' Beatrice reflected when the two boys arrived at the clearing. 'The church doesn't look so... I don't know... sinister. More like sad.'

'So, what do we do now?' Zac looked at Merryn. 'We're looking for a gravestone belonging to a Grace somebody, is that right?'

'Grace?' Miss Kelly asked, astonished that the woman suddenly had an identity.

'She told me her name a few days ago. Sorry, miss. I should have told you.'

'No, that's okay. It's just I'm having difficulty getting my head around all this.'

'You're not the only one, miss,' Beatrice said.

Searching for gravestones in the thick tangle of vegetation surrounding the church proved an ordeal, wicked bramble thorns and tall nettles prompting cries of pain as they pricked and stung. It quickly became apparent that there weren't any gravestones.

'Maybe the ground was never consecrated,' Malika suggested when they'd convened again by the church entrance.

'It looks that way,' Merryn said. 'The church was used by monks who walked down the valley from Tintern Abbey. It's more likely they buried their dead in the Abbey grounds than down here. But, in any case, I don't think Grace was buried.'

'And we've just spent ten minutes ripping our jeans looking for her gravestone.' Zac was looking at an ugly tear in one leg of Miss Kelly's jeans.

'Zac, hush!' Beatrice swatted him with the ends of her scarf. 'Don't make it any more difficult than it already is.' She turned back to Merryn. 'So what do we do now? Look inside?'

He nodded and led the way through what was once the porch into the nave. Nothing remained of the nave roof but in the chancel, a pair of huge oak beams still spanned the walls.

'Merryn.' Miss Kelly could read the disquiet in his face. 'Do you know what you're looking for?' she asked gently. He shook his head and then pushed his way through the vegetation towards the chancel. A few steps lead up through a gap in a low stone wall, the intricate wooden screen that it had once supported long since thieved for firewood. The chancel floor was covered by a shallow layer of grass and ferns rooted in ancient leaf mould. Malika sat on the steps facing the others in the nave and put a finger to her lips, sensing that Merryn needed space and silence. He stood quite still, bathed in the sunshine pouring through the empty chancel window.

'Grace.' He whispered the name as one might to someone asleep. 'I'm here.' His gaze moved across the stone walls, decorated here and there with hart's tongue fern. In places, patches of plaster still clung to the stones, fragments of centuries-old graffiti scratched into their surface.

'Lift the stone, Tom.'

He spun to face the others. 'She spoke.' He waited in vain for her to say more.

Getting to her feet, Malika asked 'What did she say?'

'Lift the stone.'

'That's it? Lift the stone?'

'That's what she said.' Merryn shrugged. 'But which stone?'

'In the floor?' Beatrice suggested. 'We can't lift stones in the wall.'

Miss Kelly kicked her boots into the ground. 'The stones have gone. It's just soil now.'

'Here maybe, but there's not so much vegetation where Merryn's standing.' Zac took the steps up into the chancel in one bound and immediately fell to his knees, digging away the leaf mould with both hands. 'See, I was right. Flag stones.' He looked up at Merryn. 'Okay, so which one?'

Merryn frowned. 'I haven't a clue. She didn't say.'

'We need to clear the floor.' Zac looked round at the other three and grinned. 'Come on, time to get your hands dirty.'

After less than five minutes of frenetic activity during which leaf mould flew across the chancel floor in all directions, Miss Kelly suddenly exclaimed, 'Ow! What was that?'

The others dropped down beside her and finished clearing away the leaves from a huge, raised flag stone with a massive iron ring embedded in its centre.

'This must be it,' Beatrice announced. 'There must be a tomb down there.'

'A crypt, I think it's called. Do you remember reading *Moonfleet* in Year 7?' Miss Kelly couldn't help herself. 'The crypt beneath the church floor where the smugglers hid their booty?' To her dismay, this drew a blank from both boys.

'There's something carved in the stone. Letters.' Merryn scratched away the moss which concealed the writing. 'It's too faded. Must be hundreds of years old.' He got to his feet. 'The stone has got to weigh half a tonne. At least. We're never going to lift it.' He stood up, wondering why she would ask him to do something that was clearly impossible.

Zac looked up at the two oak beams stretching across the roof above their heads. 'Rope. We need a rope. Any ideas?'

'I could go into town and buy some, if you want,' Miss Kelly offered.

'No need, miss!' Merryn suddenly had a thought. 'Mear and Skinner stretched a rope across the ford. The net was attached to it. If the police haven't taken it as evidence, then it's still there.'

Zac got to his feet. 'The rope you fell over when Mear was chasing you? No wonder you remember it.'

'Zac, you're a pig sometimes.' Beatrice joined the two boys as they hurried out of the church to retrieve the rope.

When they returned, Zac's head protruded from a mass of blue nylon rope coils strung about his shoulders. 'It's not often the victim of attempted murder makes off with evidence from the scene of the crime.'

'I hope you're not being serious.' Miss Kelly clicked back into teacher-mode.

'It was just lying there on the bank, miss,' Merryn replied. 'No sign of the net.'

'It can go back there when we're done.' She frowned theatrically. 'Now, I think we're on the same page, Zac. Rope over the beam, one end tied onto the ring, we pull the other. Am I right?'

'We've enough rope to do that twice, miss. Means we won't get in each other's way when it comes to pulling. The beams aren't directly over the slab, but that's good. Means it'll lift like a trapdoor on a hinge. We won't be lifting its entire weight.'

Zac threw the rope on the floor and started gathering a collection of coils in one hand. Then he threw them over one of the beams and pulled the end down before tying it securely to the rusty ring on the slab.

'Mind out, guys, I'm testing the beam.'

The others moved clear as Zac hauled with all his strength on the rope but they needn't have worried. The beam, despite its age, would have held an elephant. He repeated the process with the other end of the rope, thrown up and over the second beam.

'Right. Two teams. Once it gets to about forty-five degrees, Malika and Miss, can you help me pull it up on end. Bee and Merryn, keep hold of your rope so it doesn't flatten us. Make sense?' Everyone nodded, impressed with Zac's sudden enthusiasm for the task.

Beatrice and Merryn grabbed one rope, Malika and Miss Kelly the other.

'Okay, pull!' shouted Zac.

At first the slab refused to move, welded into place around its perimeter by centuries of detritus. Then, as muscles began to tire, a crack appeared along one edge.

'Come ooooon! It's moving!' Zac shouted. 'Give it welly!'

Slowly but surely, three sides of the flagstone parted company with the floor. Released from its bed, it began to rise more easily.

'Come on, Zac. I can't hold this much longer,' Miss Kelly gasped.

'Okay, I'm going to try and prop it open with my back. As soon as I've got it steady, you two drop the rope and help me get it vertical. Ready?'

He let go of the rope and flung himself into the hole in the floor, wedging his back against the leaning stone, both feet braced against the rim. 'Got it! Now let go and help me. Merryn, Bee, don't stop pulling, whatever you do!'

One final gut-wrenching effort and the flagstone stood up on one side.

'Well done, guys,' he panted. 'God knows how they… Jesus!' he screamed, leaping back from the hole. 'It's full of skeletons! Oh my God, what are we doing?'

The others peered into the crypt, uttering horrified cries as their eyes fell on a row of skeletons laid out on the floor at the bottom of the steps, their muskets lying beside them.

'Lord have mercy on them.' Malika stepped forward, her voice calm and quiet as though she had seen the bones of men many times before. 'It's alright. We needed to find this for something terrible has happened here. These were soldiers I am certain – see their guns. They were wearing clothes when they were laid here; see the shreds of leather jacket and boots, what's left of them. Someone carried them here, perhaps from the battlefield where they died. They've not had a proper burial, none of them. Merryn.' She turned to him. 'You will know better than I. Why are they here? And so many.'

'Soldiers,' Merryn whispered to himself. He turned to the others, their gaze fixed on the horrors that lay below. 'These are Wintour's men; dragoons. See the short-barrelled muskets and no armour.

Cavaliers fighting for the king. They were ambushed at the ford just like the legend says they were.'

'And Colonel Massey, he's thrown them down there? Like a mass war grave?' Zac's mind was in turmoil, unable to process what he was seeing.

'They weren't thrown in. They've been laid out in a row. There's so many.' Merryn knelt down, peering into the darkness. 'The crypt goes back a way. There's more as far as I can see.' He looked round. 'I've got to go down.'

'You can't go down!' Zac insisted. 'It's full of bodies, skeletons. It's not right, disturbing the dead. We should just leave this to the police.'

'The police? Again?' Beatrice shook her head. 'They're not going to be happy.'

'We will tell the police, of course. These men deserve a proper burial.' Merryn looked at Malika who nodded. 'But before that happens, I must go down. She said I'd understand everything if I came to the church. She's guided me to the entrance of the crypt just like she guided me to the pistol, and now she wants me to go down, I'm certain of it.'

Zac looked away, a tortured expression on his face. A battering ram hammered on the door of reason inside his head, the timbers splintering with each blow. 'You won't find anything down there, Merryn, just dead bodies, bodies that should be left alone.' With that, he wandered into the nave.

'Does anyone have a torch?' Merryn asked, breaking the awkward silence.

'Take my phone.' Beatrice held it out. 'No signal but there's plenty of charge for the torch. And for God's sake, be careful. The roof might not be safe.'

'It's okay, Bee. She won't let anything happen.'

Merryn took the phone, tapped the torch icon and, with his heart thumping in his chest, stepped down into the crypt.

CHAPTER 36

Reaching the last step, Merryn played his torch across the skeletons lying side by side on the floor in front of him, each with a musket laid neatly by its side. Here and there, thin strips of rotting leather hung around their ribs, the remains of powder cartridges still attached.

'This is history, Mr Biddle,' Merryn whispered. 'You should be here, not lying in some bed between life and death. Look at these muskets. Flintlocks. They were only invented around 1630 but every soldier here has one. No, I'm wrong. There's an old matchlock! Just one. Maybe belongs to an old timer who doesn't like new technology. Just like you, Mr Biddle, eh?'

He stepped down onto the floor, taking care to avoid standing on bones and called out softly, 'Grace, I'm here,' but there was no reply. The cool air carried the fusty smell of decay. Here and there, the torchlight fell on long-legged spiders, transfixed in the centre of huge webs. A narrow tunnel led a short distance beneath the floor of the chancel towards the nave and here, still more skeletons lined the floor, each carefully stretched out with their musket beside them.

'Something isn't right,' Merryn muttered, brushing away cobwebs from his hair. 'No sign of damage to the bones. No holes, no breaks. How did these men die?'

On either side, niches hewn from the solid limestone lay empty like open mouths waiting to swallow the dead. Bending low beneath the dipping roof, Merryn crept along the tunnel, half-expecting at any moment to hear her voice. Then, at the end of the tunnel, the torch beam suddenly fell upon a skeleton much smaller than the others, stretched out in a niche.

'Grace?' he whispered.

'What's left of my body, Tom. I've no use for it now. It was never much of a body even while I lived.'

Merryn's gaze came to rest on the ugly hole in her skull immediately above her left eye socket.

'You were shot!' The words tumbled from his mouth as the mystery stalking him ever since Mear walked into his history class began to unravel. 'By Mear? But how?'

'By John Wintour, the man I loved.'

'But you told me it was… Mear.' In a flash, several pieces in the puzzle tumbled into place. Merryn let out a stunned gasp as he dropped to his knees, scarcely able to grasp the full magnitude of what had finally been revealed. 'Mear is Wintour,' he whispered.

'Mear's soul once possessed Wintour's body just as your soul once possessed my brother's body – Tom Mundy. To me, you will always be Tom.'

'You…' The words stuck in his throat. 'You really are my sister? From another life? You mean, I'm reincarnated from someone in the seventeenth century?'

'Few believe in such a thing where you live. If you don't believe in something, then when it's there in front of you, you cannot see it.'

Merryn shook his head, all the while thinking he must be dreaming. 'I couldn't see it. Neither could Mear, though we both knew that we had met sometime in the past. You're saying that in some past life, I knew John Wintour? Did we fight? Did he kill me too?'

'Listen and I will tell you everything.'

And so she did, starting at the Black Horse. Tom, kneeling beside the remains of his once-sister and her unborn child, listened spellbound. His passion for history had taken him to the past so many times in his short life, and yet the events he recreated in his imagination – animated, embellished, exaggerated – flickered only briefly before returning to their lifeless state: words on a page, pictures on a screen. But now, sitting in the crypt, the sights and sounds and smells of history invaded his whole being, soaking through his flesh and blood until they reached his very soul. The hole in Grace's skull, her sweet voice recounting their troubled life together at the inn, the dank smell of death that still hung in the air. *This* was history.

'He shot you when you were pregnant?' he exclaimed when she described the events at the shooting range. His torch picked out the remains of a tiny skull and spine, nestled below her ribs. 'How could he *do* that?'

'He was a violent man with a terrible temper. I went to him at the range, demanding that he let me stay at Whitecross, since the baby in my belly was his, but he would not have it. Another knight was there with him, Sir Edmund Willoughby. I grabbed the pistol he was holding, loaded and primed – 'tis the one you found – meaning to threaten John with it. Such foolishness, Tom, you cannot imagine. I was desperate beyond reason. In the struggle, the pistol fired, the shot killing Willoughby right there in front of me.'

'But you didn't mean it. It was an accident.'

'I would have hung for it if John had not killed me first.'

'And he meant to kill you?'

'Most certainly. When he saw Willoughby, still and lifeless on the ground, he lost all control. I knew there was nothing I could do. Part of me *wanted* to die for a young woman with child would not have lasted long on the streets.'

'I wish I'd not released the rope that let Mear live. I see now why you wanted him dead.'

'No, you were right to save him for revenge gains nothing. Only another life that had to be atoned for. I know that now but back then, when John was alive, I spoke to you in this very place just as I am speaking to you now. I made you promise you would take his life just as he had taken mine and my unborn child.'

Before Grace could continue, Beatrice called down from the entrance to the crypt. 'Merryn, are you alright?'

'I'm fine,' he called back. 'I won't be long. Best you don't come down. There's not much room.'

Grace recounted the events at the ford and Hoskyn's fateful decision to hide in the crypt. 'You were the only one left alive when Bellamy raised the stone. Neither of you survived long after that. Bellamy was caught by Massey's men, and you...'

'Go on. How did I die?'

'You fell from the cliffs, you and John both. You forced the truth from him and when your musket fired, it took you both over the edge. He survived but you did not.'

'We fell?' Merryn gasped. 'And Wintour survived?' He shook his head, scarcely able to believe what he'd heard. 'The legend has it all wrong, then. I remember you telling me that in the library. "That's not how it happened." Wintour wasn't escaping from the enemy but from the truth. And Mear, he was the same, trying to wipe away the truth by killing Mr Biddle. And then me.'

'Yes, but truth always finds a way. In this life or the next.'

'Tell me about the pistols, Grace. I know there are two of them.'

'The golden pistols. Like I told you, I killed Willoughby with the one you found at the cliff top. Wintour concealed it there while he was hiding from Massey's men. The other, the pistol he shot me with, he gave to his sergeant to hide here in the crypt. When Bellamy, the last of John's dragoons, lifted the stone, he pulled you out alive and took the pistol, but he was captured by the enemy soon after and the pistol fell into their hands.'

'Why did you lead me to the one hidden down the crack? To set you free? But how?'

'I killed a man, Tom. My ancestors will not receive me until the pistol has saved a life. You are my only hope, your soul returning at last to a body born so close to the cliffs as if drawn to the place where you died all those years ago.'

'But you led Mear to the river. I heard him speaking to Skinner, telling him how you promised him better poaching if he came to the ford. And then the history job. He faked his application to get it. Why did you bring such evil back to the river? Back to me?'

'I was a fool as I have been a fool so many times before. I believed we could not be free unless you kept the oath that you swore to me, to take John's life. Everything I said to you both had but one purpose – to bring you together here by the river. I told John that you would find the golden pistol and if he got close to you, then he could take it from you. It was bait, Tom. I knew he would swallow it.'

'But he almost killed Mr Biddle. His life still hangs by a thread.' Merryn's angry words reverberated around the crypt. 'He meant to kill me too, chasing me across the ford with a knife. Did you not realise that such an evil man would do anything to possess such a treasure?'

'You are right to be angry with me. My plan was witless from the start. When John set out to kill your teacher, I pleaded with him to stop, to think again, but I was dealing with forces beyond my control. The power of evil cannot be reasoned with. As for you, I believed you would not come to harm if I could guide you.'

'I'm sorry. I don't mean to be angry. If I hadn't struck Mear with the torch, he would have killed me for certain. I should be grateful to you for that.'

'I should never have brought him to the river, to the school, where he could cause so much suffering. You must understand, Tom, I was desperate to be free from the prison that has been my home since John laid me here, condemned to spend eternity separated from those I love. Hatred consumed me. Hatred of the man who tossed me aside. I wanted justice.'

'No, you wanted revenge, and like you said, revenge gains nothing.'

'I know it. I cannot defend what I have done and I deserve no mercy from my brother. When I abandoned you at the inn, I promised I would come back and take you away with me, but I never did. For that, you can never forgive me, and that is my punishment. I shall gladly endure it for eternity.'

'Why should I harbour a grudge for something that happened in another life? I just want to help you escape but you must tell me how. What have I got to do?'

'You are the same boy I knew all those years ago, the brother I never deserved. If I am to escape, then these bones must receive a rightful burial in consecrated ground. Indeed, every man here deserves the same. And the pistol that you found, it must save a life. I cannot tell you how but you will find the answer, I am certain of it. Now you must go for I have kept you long enough. The others are waiting.'

Merryn got to his feet, crouching low, sensing she had filled as much of the puzzle as she was going to. As he ran the torch across her remains one last time, his eye caught sight of two delicate chains, one around her neck, the other draped across her ribs. On the end of each was a tiny locket, glinting in the torchlight.

'Take them if you like. My body has no use for them now.'

'Are you sure?' Merryn whispered.

'Sir John had them made when first we met. My portrait, it makes me look so pretty though I swear I never was. It's only right that you should have it. You must remember your sister as she was in the flesh, not here in this dark hole. The other is of John.'

Gently, Merryn lifted the chain from around the skull and together with its twin, pushed it into his pocket. 'You shall have your burial.'

'And I shall do whatever is my power to give you the life you deserve.'

Moments later, he emerged from the crypt into the blinding sunlight to find Beatrice, Malika and Miss Kelly sitting on the chancel floor.

'What news?' Beatrice asked, bursting with anticipation. 'Did you find her? Did she speak to you?'

Merryn sat with them. 'Yes, I found her or at least the remains of her body. And these.' He held up the chains with their lockets. 'Shall we open them?'

The others nodded silently, so carefully, he prised open one of the lockets, astonished at how, after so long, the two halves parted so easily. Staring out at him was the tiny face of a pretty young woman, scarcely eighteen he guessed, perhaps younger. 'That's Grace, my sister,' he said matter-of-factly, handing it to Beatrice.

Malika smiled. *Just as I thought.*

The second locket took some gentle persuasion to open but at last Merryn came face to face with the man he had been dreaming of since term began. The painter had, for his own sake, enhanced Wintour's undoubtedly handsome visage while at the same time, smoothing away the heinous lines that betrayed the fountains of evil springing from a corrupted soul, a soul destined to return time and again to the flesh of man.

'And this is Wintour,' he announced, looking up to find a speechless audience staring at him. 'He killed her with a pistol, the one sitting in some private collection in New York.'

'The twin?' Beatrice whispered, struggling to take in what she was hearing. 'How could you possibly know that?'

'She told me. Killed her and her unborn baby but not before she'd used the one we found to kill another man.'

Miss Kelly suddenly stood up and walked wordlessly into the nave, unable to contain the storm of emotion sweeping over her. Malika followed, knowing there was little she could say to soften the impact of what the crypt had revealed.

Beatrice sat staring at the two faces in the lockets. 'Now what?' she asked.

'We arrange for the bodies to be buried in consecrated ground. Without that, their souls can't begin the journey to their ancestors.'

'Mum was right, then.'

'She knows so much more than people here, stuff that really matters; not like all the history crap that sits inside my head. I wish I could wash it all out and start again.'

'There's a lot inside my head I wish I could be rid of,' Beatrice said quietly.

Merryn let the moment pass and then said 'There's more, Bee. Grace won't reach her ancestors unless the pistol saves a life.'

'You told me that before and I still don't get it.' Beatrice frowned. 'To make up for the life it took? That's crazy. It's an inanimate object. It doesn't have a soul.'

'It's the only way Grace can be pardoned, the instrument she used to take a life now saves one.'

'It would make more sense if *she* saved a life.'

'Or used the pistol to save a life,' Merryn suggested.

Before Beatrice could reply, Zac appeared from the nave. 'Well, was she there?'

Merryn glanced at Beatrice and then answered, 'Nope. Only the remains of Wintour's men. Seems like you were right. It was all in my head.'

Zac laughed. 'You're the worst bloody liar on the planet.'

CHAPTER 37

Saturday 26th October
Bristol Royal Infirmary – Critical Care Unit: Room 608

The room was dark when they entered so Miss Grigoryev raised the blinds a little, then pulled a chair up alongside the bed and motioned for Merryn to sit. He stared at a man he barely recognised, lying quite still amid a tangle of cables and tubes. His scalp, largely devoid of hair, wore an ugly mosaic of weals, scabs and hideous yellow bruises.

'George,' his wife whispered, 'look who's here. Just as I promised, your star pupil.'

For a while, Merryn just sat watching the man he had worshipped since his first encounter with the history teacher in Year 8, too shocked, too angry, too upset to say anything. Then, mindful not to disturb the IV drip, he gently gripped Mr Biddle's wrist. 'Mr Biddle, it's me. Merryn.'

The elderly man's eyes suddenly opened, blinking in the unaccustomed light.

'See, I told you!' Miss Grigoryev exclaimed. 'It happened last night. He is coming back.' She leant over her husband until his eyes met hers. 'It's me, darling, Sofiya. You remember? Look who I am bringing to see you.'

Mr Biddle frowned as though struggling to understand the world he'd awoken to. 'Sofiya?' he croaked. 'Do I know you?'

'I'm Sofiya, your wife. We are married two years next week, George. I shall bring you a card. Maybe also something nice to eat if I can smuggle it past the nurses, eh?' She laughed. The music was returning. 'I'll leave you boys a while so you can talk.'

She beckoned Merryn over to the door where she spoke softly. 'It's like I tell you before. He remembers nothing, not even his wife. The doctors, they have warned me this happens but they cannot say when or even *if* his memories return. So we must be patient, always patient. It's hard.' She nodded and squeezed his arm. 'I will leave you a while, eh? Speak to him. Maybe he will remember something from school.'

Merryn returned to his seat. Mr Biddle seemed more alert now and asked for a glass of water. 'Thirsty work, lying here. What's your name again?'

'Merryn. You taught me history at Tidenham Academy before... your accident.' He lifted Mr Biddle's head forward and helped him take a few sips.

'Accident? What accident?'

Merryn needed no second invitation and launched into an account of the events which had befallen both of them, starting with Mr Biddle's first meeting with Mear. It was only when a nurse entered the room thirty minutes later that he paused for breath.

'I think that's enough now,' she announced. 'George needs to rest.'

'According to... Merryn here, I've been resting since the start of term.'

'Then a few more hours won't harm you in the least. Now, say goodbye to your star pupil.' She turned to Merryn and smiled. 'Miss Grigoryev has been telling me all about you.'

He winced. 'I'll come back, maybe tomorrow, Mr Biddle, and we can finish the story. There's so much more about the pistol. I wish you could see it.'

'The pistol. Yes, I should like to hear more about the pistol.'

Left alone, Mr Biddle lay still for a while, Merryn's wild tale swirling around inside his head. Who was the boy, for heaven's sakes, and how on earth had he got himself mixed up with this dreadful Mr Mear? He wrestled with the problem, getting nowhere until finally he drifted off to sleep. Two hours later he awoke from a dream feeling oddly refreshed and immediately sat up. 'Good gracious,' he exclaimed to no one. 'What's Merryn MacIntyre doing with a flintlock pistol?'

CHAPTER 38

Monday 4th November
Tidenham Academy

After two weeks of beating about the bush, Merryn finally plucked up the courage to ask her. 'Bee, are we going out or not?'

Beatrice led him over to a vacant bench where they sat together while she ran over in her head the speech she had rehearsed countless times since her mum had made the decision. In the end, she just told him. 'We're leaving next week.'

'What? Leaving? You mean back to Kenya? You can't! Next week? But what about the appeal?' Merryn stared at the most precious thing in his life, the girl who had gate-crashed his stifled existence, injecting it with a meaning that his obsession with history never could; and now, after less than two months, that meaning was about to be wrenched away.

'Mum's case officer says there's almost no chance the appeal will succeed. Mum's doing part time at the supermarket but she's not earning enough to pay the rent. We can't afford to wait until the Home Office tells us to leave.'

'But the drugs she needs. What's going to happen?'

'The Home Office have told us the reason we're being sent back is that Kenya have made HIV drugs available free of charge so she'll get treatment. But she won't. I know she won't. The politicians in Westminster have no idea what it's like in Kenya, how long it takes to get something done, how many layers of bureaucracy you have to dig through before anything happens. Even if the drugs are free, it'll take so long for the authorities to process her case. And anyway, I told you she needs a special cocktail of drugs that aren't available in Kenya.'

She sat holding Merryn's sleeve. 'Look, I'm sorry. I've treated you badly since that day at the church. I thought I could make it easier just in case this happened.' The tears were running freely now. 'I'm so, so sorry but there's nothing I can do, any of us can do. It's better sooner rather than later, so Mum's booked flights for next Monday. There's a friend we can stay with in Mombasa till Mum finds work.'

Merryn sat numb. The bottom had dropped out of his world. 'Will you text me?' he asked weakly. But what was a text compared to a kiss?

'Skype maybe.' She could tell by the boy's expression he'd never Skyped before. 'I'll show you. Maybe one day I'll come back. You'll be professor of history at Cambridge by then.'

'Don't say that and, in any case, I'm done with history. What's the point in getting excited about stuff you can't change? What matters is the here and now, Bee. You and Malika.' He hesitated, then added, 'And Grace.'

'Grace? But she's from the past.'

'No, she's here, right now, waiting for me to do something.'

'But you have. You've spoken to the Reverend what's-his-name...'

'Chowbury. Actually, I spoke to Isaac and he contacted the Rev.'

'And you told me he's agreed to a proper burial for her bones once the archaeologists have finished with them. If Isaac's involved, then it should happen pretty quick. What more could you have done?'

'She won't be buried for months. I looked online and it takes forever to get a skeleton released for burial. Anyway, it's the pistol I was talking about. It has to save a life, remember.'

'Where is it now? Still at the museum in Bristol?'

'No. According to Isaac, St Pierre has started the restoration in his lab in France somewhere. It will be auctioned when he's finished. Apparently there are only two prospective buyers left – the British Museum and the private museum in New York. The TVC's valuation frightened everyone else off.'

'How much?'

Merryn shook his head. 'He didn't say.'

'You never asked him, did you?'

'What's the point?'

Beatrice let out a deep sigh. 'Idiot. Because you found it. *That's* the point. The greatest single piece of treasure this century. It's been all over the news and you still don't want to know what it's worth.'

'I know already. £400,000. It could have saved my dad's business. And the house. My parents have accepted an offer for it so we're moving in the new year. More important than all that is the money could have…'

'Stop! Don't you dare say it.' Beatrice stood up abruptly. 'How many times do I have to say it? It's not about money. Mum could win the lottery and we'd still have to leave. You've just got to accept it and move on. I'm doing it,' she sobbed, 'and if I can, so can you.' With that, she got up and walked away from the boy she loved.

CHAPTER 39

Thursday 19th December

'Merryn! Zac! Mr Levi's here,' Donna yelled up the stairs. 'Sorry about that, Mr Levi. Please come in, come in.' She glanced over his shoulder into the night. 'Oh my goodness. Looks like the snow's coming down hard now.'

'Not much global warming going on out there tonight,' Isaac remarked, setting down a long, black case while he shed his ample overcoat. 'I see you're moving.'

'Ah, the For Sale sign. Yes, sadly, we are. Contracts aren't signed yet but we should be out of here mid-January.'

'Moving to something bigger?' Isaac asked.

Donna laughed. 'Bigger? I wish. No, the local authority have found us a two-bedroom flat to rent in Chepstow. Temporary until we find something else. Anyway, let's not dwell on our misfortunes,' she said, ushering the elderly gentleman into the living room. 'You have something to show us, I believe.'

Isaac lifted up the case, its lid furnished with four brass latches and a sturdy lock. 'I most certainly do. Something quite beyond your wildest imagination.' His voice was laced with melodrama while his eyes burned bright with mischief. 'I expect the boys are bursting at the seams to see the pistol now that St Pierre has worked his magic.'

'Yes, of course,' Donna answered without much conviction. The truth was her son hadn't mentioned the pistol since the inquest. Once, when she'd brought the subject up, hoping that she might provoke in him some of the fervour she'd witnessed before the inquest, he had quoted some unintelligible gobbledygook at her. 'It's Swahili,' he'd said. 'Something I learned from Bee.' And that was that. No translation, nothing. Since then, events had conspired to worsen his mood still further. Beatrice and her mother had returned to Kenya; Malcolm had filed for bankruptcy and as a result, both house and business had been put on the market; and arrangements were being made for him to move to Chepstow Academy. It couldn't get any worse.

'Ah, here they are, Britain's most celebrated treasure hunters!' Isaac exclaimed as the two boys entered the room. He shook their hands vigorously. 'Getting used to celebrity status yet?' he asked, settling into an armchair.

Before either boy could answer, Donna said, 'Actually, Mr Levi, we've asked the coroner for anonymity. At least for the time being. The last thing they want in their GCSE year is the media hammering at the door day and night.'

Yes, Merryn thought. *Especially when you have to confess that you were breaking the law when you found the treasure.*

'Of course, of course,' Isaac said. 'There's plenty of time for all that.' He laid the black case on a coffee table in front of him. 'Now then, where's the rest of the party? I took the liberty of inviting Sian. I hope you don't mind, Mrs MacIntyre, but she's been involved pretty much from the start.'

'Sian? You mean Miss Kelly, the English teacher? Actually, I've been looking forward to meeting her.' Donna's poker face fooled no one.

'And your husband? Is he going to join us?'

'I've texted him twice now. He went out to walk the dog, so he said. That was a half hour ago. He should have been back by now considering the weather. He knows you were coming but he's got a memory like a sieve. He's got a lot on his mind at the moment. I'll call him.' She left the room to find her mobile. When she returned, she looked troubled. 'His phone is switched off, silly man. But no worries, he'll be here.'

'No rush, Mrs MacIntyre. You've had to wait three months to see the pistol so a few minutes longer won't hurt.'

The doorbell rang and Donna rushed to open it. Moments later, Sasha and Zac's father, Daniel Hunt entered the room, closely followed by Miss Kelly.

Following introductions, Isaac cleared his voice. 'While we're waiting for Mr MacIntyre, why don't I get you up-to-date with a phone call I received from a certain Mrs Winifred Khatri at The British Museum. I think everyone should be seated before I say any more.' The light in his eyes burned brighter than ever, the mischief at boiling point.

He waited until everyone had squeezed onto a seat in the crowded sitting room. 'Winifred was clearly very moved by what she heard at the inquest; by the spirited actions of two boys who set out, determined to solve a mystery that has baffled historians for centuries. Did Wintour actually leap?'

He paused for breath, his audience wondering what was coming next. 'Finding Wintour's pistol was, she said, as miraculous as Howard Carter's discovery of Tutankhamun's tomb. What drove Carter to search in the rubble left behind by the excavation of King Rameses VI tomb? And why did Merryn and Zac choose to ignore the first gap in the railings and instead, gain entry to the cliff top through a second gap? A golden death mask, a golden pistol – both found by luck or was it fate? She's convinced there's a book to be written about the pistol, one that will capture the public's imagination just as the first account of Carter's discovery did.'

Merryn sat in stunned silence. How on earth did the woman know there were two gaps in the railings? It certainly hadn't been disclosed at the inquest. True, he had told his dad that night when he came fishing for details of the pistol but he certainly wouldn't have passed such a trivial detail to anyone, least of all the British Museum. Merryn looked at Zac whose expression said he was equally baffled.

'Now,' Isaac continued, revelling in the drama of the moment, 'Winifred is a force to be reckoned with at the British Museum and while she's not on the Treasure Valuation Committee, she exerts considerable influence over its decisions.'

'Isaac.' Miss Kelly spoke for everyone in the room. 'The suspense is killing us.'

The antiques dealer chuckled. 'Forgive me. An old man's mischief.' He grinned and then said 'Fifty-fifty.'

For a while, no one said anything as Isaac's pronouncement sunk in.

Merryn was the first to respond. 'You mean the finders get fifty percent of the value?' He wanted to hear it spelt out.

'Exactly. The TVC were persuaded that, because you were both clearly unaware of the law regarding access to the cliff top – after all, the warning sign did not include the word PRIVATE – and, what's more, you did not go there with the aim of treasure hunting, so you should not be penalised. Justice has been served, eh?'

Daniel Hunt suddenly got to his feet. 'Mr Levi, I think you've hit the nail on the head. Justice has indeed been served. Zac was right when he said that without Merryn's fall into the crevice, the pistol would never have been found. Fifty-fifty is the right outcome. There's just one point that Zac and I would like to take issue with and that is the word "finders." We believe there was only *one* finder and whatever reward is on offer from the British Museum should go to him.' Mr Hunt looked directly at Merryn. 'Fifty percent, Merryn. You deserve every penny.'

'But it was a joint discovery, was it not, Zac?' Donna heard herself say.

'Actually, it wasn't. When Merryn fell into the crevice, I was some distance away by the railings. I told him to follow my voice but for some reason he moved left instead. He found the pistol because…' – he looked straight at his partner and grinned – '…he ignored me. He's the finder and like Dad said, he should get the reward. In any case, it was his idea to go to the cliffs, not mine.'

Donna, who had been standing up, sank onto the arm of the sofa. 'Twenty-five percent is a lot of money to hand over.' Her voice trembled. 'Surely you can't do that?' She turned to Isaac. 'Mr Levi, just how much are we talking about here? Merryn told us the pistol was worth £400,000. Is that right?'

'Well, yes, that is right inasmuch as a museum in New York paid that sum for an identical pistol some years ago. The TVC has valued this one at £480,000. Inflation and being one of a pair has increased its value. However, at the auction in London yesterday, a bidding war broke out. If you had watched the news this morning, you would already know the answer to your question. The golden flintlock pistol in this case sold for no less than £620,000, a record for a seventeenth century firearm.'

That brought a collective gasp from the room.

'Oh my God!' Donna burst out. 'That's…' She did the maths. 'That's £155,000. Zac, you can't do this. You can't just hand over that much money. Merryn, tell him you won't accept it.'

But Merryn was listening to another voice, one that spoke with even greater urgency. 'Go to the cliffs, Tom. Go there now. You don't have much time. 'Tis your father.'

Merryn leapt out of his seat. 'Where?' he cried, startling everyone in the room. 'Where is he?'

'The leap.'

'Oh my God!' He spun round to Sasha. 'Please, Sasha, I need a lift. As fast as you can. It's Dad.' Without waiting for an answer, he raced into the hall and threw on a coat. 'Please, Sasha, it's urgent,' he called.

'Merryn, for God's sake, have you gone mad?' Donna shouted

after him. 'What are you talking about? What do you mean "it's Dad"?' She followed Zac who was pulling Sasha behind him, into the hall. 'What's happened? Has he had an accident?'

'No time, Mum. I'll explain everything when we get back. Please, just for once, trust me.' With that, he threw open the front door and the three of them disappeared into the snowstorm.

Two inches of snow had already settled on Church Close when Sasha engaged 4-wheel-drive on the Range Rover and hurtled out onto the road leading to the phone box and the junction with Netherhope Lane while Merryn issued directions.

'Top of the cliffs, yes?' she asked, sliding the car round the bend like a rally driver, narrowly missing the phone box.

'Bloody hell, Sash! That was close,' Zac gasped, clutching at a door handle. He turned to Merryn. 'Top of the cliffs? Second gap?'

Merryn nodded. 'That's what Grace said. Dad's at the leap.' His voice cracked as he spoke, for a terrible picture was forming in his mind. 'I told him exactly where it was. The second gap. What's he doing there, for God's sake? He knows Isaac was coming round with the pistol.'

Zac gripped his friend's shoulder. 'Listen, it could all be a mistake. Maybe… I mean, maybe you didn't hear anything or…' He ran out of maybe's because he was starting to believe. In his heart, he wished more than anything that the voice was in Merryn's imagination. But in his head, he knew Malcolm was somewhere on the other side of the railings with only one thought in his mind.

Merryn shrugged Zac's arm off. 'How much more evidence… whoa!'

The car took the next left turn sideways before Sasha regained control and accelerated along the road towards Wintour's Leap. She slid the car to a stop opposite the Keep Out sign.

'You missed your vocation, Sash,' Zac gulped. 'Find somewhere to pull the car off the road and I'll phone you when we're ready.'

'I swear I don't know what you're doing, Merryn, but please take care,' Sasha implored. 'These cliffs, they are not good for you.' The boys tumbled out of the car onto the road and sprinted through the ever-deepening snow, searching for the second gap.

'Look!' exclaimed Zac, pointing his phone torch at the snow in the road ahead of them. 'Footprints. They're not fresh, maybe ten, twenty minutes. And there, the first gap.' The prints led past the gap and on down the road towards the second.

'Dad!' Merryn cried out. 'Oh my God, she was right. What if…?' His voice fell to a whisper. 'What if he's already jumped? That's why he's here, I'm certain of it. I put the idea in his head. He's lost everything, Zac. I should have seen it. But with all this other stuff – Biddle and Mear, Bee, Malika – I didn't see what was in front of my face. My own dad.' He turned away, sobbing uncontrollably. 'I can't do this anymore.'

Zac grabbed him roughly and spun him round. 'You waste another second talking a load of crap and you'll regret it for the rest of your life. You're going through the railings because she told you to and like every time she's spoken to you, it will work out. Tell your dad he's a rich man. £310,000. But for God's sake, *hurry*!'

'He's right, Merryn. There's no time to waste.'

'Did you hear that?' Merryn looked at Zac. 'No, of course not. She called me Merryn. Come on, let's go.'

The two boys careered down the road, slipping and sliding in the snow until the second gap appeared in Zac's torchlight. 'He went through the gap,' he whispered, pointing the beam at the ground. 'Go on!' he urged, 'and take this.' He handed him the phone. 'And whatever you do, don't go near the edge.'

Merryn pushed his way through the gap and stood for a moment, listening to the soft shush of falling snow.

'Dad,' he called quietly. 'Are you there?'

'Merryn?' came the startled reply. 'Is that you?'

Merryn shone the torch beam through the tangle of branches. They had lost their covering of snow so he could just make out the figure of his father, perched on the very edge of the world.

'Grace, help me, please,' he begged, fear paralysing his ability to think.

'Speak to him. Quietly, calmly.'

Merryn took a deep breath. 'Dad, we're all waiting for you. Have you forgotten? Isaac has come with the pistol. And some amazing news.'

For a while, all he could hear in answer was the wretched sound of anguished curses thrown into the night sky.

Then 'It's too late. You shouldn't have come here.' He barely recognised his dad's voice, thin and broken, without a trace of fight. 'I want you to go. Now. Back to your mother. She needs you. I can't do any more.'

Merryn pushed forward through the undergrowth. 'Dad, you've got to listen. We've been awarded fifty per cent of the pistol's value. £310,000. We're rich, do you hear?' A few more steps and he was on the platform, no more than ten feet from his father; ten treacherous, snow-covered feet.

'You're lying! You mean well, Merryn, I know you do, but you're lying. I saw the sign. Keep Out. You were trespassing, just like we are now.' Malcolm sat on the edge watching flakes of snow drifting down into the empty black void beneath him. 'That woman from the British Museum, Winifred somebody, she told me you'd get nothing. The law is the law, she said, so I know you're lying.'

Winifred Khatri. Grace, you spoke to her. You changed her mind.

'I'm not, Dad, I swear it. Dad, please listen. The house, the business, everything you've worked for, it's safe. The TVC gave us fifty per cent. Come away from the edge.'

'Fifty per cent?' There was a long silence before Malcolm spoke again. 'You're not lying?'

'No, about this I am *not* lying. You'll see. Mr Levi, he's at the house right now. He'll tell you. Please, everything's going to be okay.'

'You've done this, Merryn.' Malcolm was crying now, unable to hold back the wave of shame and relief. 'Not me. I was too busy fighting battles I couldn't win.'

'No, Dad. *I've* been so busy looking into the past I couldn't see what was happening in front of me, to my own family. I need you, Dad. We all need you. Please, come away from the edge.'

Malcolm slid back, turned and slowly got to his feet.

'And I need you, Merryn. You and your brother and your mum. You're right. I've been a bloody fool.' He stepped away from the edge and put his arms around his son, hugging him so tightly, Merryn wondered if his ribs would crack. 'I'm sorry. It sounds pathetic but knowing I was letting everyone down just... got to me.' He wiped his face with a wet sleeve. 'I didn't expect it to end up like this.' He loosened his hold on Merryn. 'Come on, we should go. Who brought you here?'

'Zac's mum, Sasha. She's waiting.' For a second, Merryn thought of showing his dad the crack where he'd found the pistol, but then thought better of it.

'I can't believe I've been so stupid,' Malcolm mumbled as he pushed through the gap in the railings.

'Dad, enough. It's been a crazy few months and we've both done stupid things. I haven't helped matters chasing after Mear and ending up in hospital. But it's over now.'

'Your mum is going to go bonkers when she hears about this.'

'She doesn't need to know anything. You went for a walk with the dog. Where is she, by the way?'

'I locked her in the old kennel in the garden. With plenty of food and water, before you ask.'

'So you went for a walk and fell over in the snow and damaged your knee. Where's your phone?'

Malcolm felt in his pocket and produced his phone. 'Why?' he asked.

For an answer, Merryn took the phone and brought it down sharply on his dad's knee. Bruising people's legs was becoming a habit.

'Ow! Merryn, what are you doing? That hurt! And you've cracked the screen.' He felt his knee. 'And probably my kneecap as well.'

'Your mobile fell out of your pocket and the screen cracked. That's why you couldn't answer Mum's call. She's only going to believe you if she can see the evidence with her own eyes. You must know that by now.' Merryn grinned and pulled his limping father along the road to the waiting car. They were almost there when Malcolm stopped.

'You never told me how you found out I was here. And don't tell me you followed my footprints all the way from the house.'

'No, of course not.' Merryn tried to imagine his dad's response if he told him that his once-sister's soul had warned him of his father's intentions. 'I can't explain it, really. It just came over me when Isaac – Mr Levi – was telling us about the fortune that's coming our way. Anyway, we better get back. There's something you've got to see.'

But his father didn't move. 'It just came over you? So what, you're psychic now?'

'Dad! You're talking nonsense.' Merryn took hold of his father's coat and pulled him along the road. 'Come on, I'm freezing.'

*

'Malcolm? Are you okay?' Donna flung both arms around her husband as he limped into the hall. 'I've been sick with worry, for heaven's sake. Why didn't you answer your phone?'

Malcolm held it up.

'Oh, for heaven's sake, not another accident. And Merryn, how on earth did you know your father had fallen over?'

Five minutes passed while Malcolm and Merryn did their best to ward off the interrogation from an increasingly sceptical Donna. It was only when Isaac, who until that point had been suffocating with impatience, tapped loudly on the case in front of him and announced that he was going to open it, that instantly, the room fell silent. He unclipped the latches, fished a key from a pocket in his cardigan and inserted it into the lock.

'Are we ready?' he asked, turning the key. Slowly, he lifted the lid.

'Oh my God!' Donna gasped. 'You found this?'

Zac shook his head. 'That's not it. That's not what we found. It can't be. How's that possible?'

'Monsieur St Pierre, miracle worker,' Isaac declared. 'I assure you, it's the very same pistol that you found at Wintour's Leap.'

'Merryn found,' Zac corrected. 'But the firing mechanism. It all looks like new.'

'That's the art of restoration, Zac. Pascal tells me the pistol is ready to be fired and I believe him.' The old man pulled on a pair of white, silk gloves that he found in another of his cardigan pockets and lifted the pistol from the case. 'Look at the gold smithery,' he whispered, turning it over. 'I've never seen anything finer than this fox. The detail, it's exquisite.'

Malcolm had been standing with his mouth open, unable to speak until finally he asked, 'This came out of a crack at the top of Wintour's Leap after *how* many years?'

'Three hundred and eighty to be precise, isn't that right Merryn?'

Merryn grinned for the old man's point wasn't lost on him.

Isaac continued. 'It was given to Sir John Wintour by King Charles I as payment for cannons. It appears that the king ran out of money during the war and started handing over royal treasures in lieu of money. It's one of a pair; the other, it seems, fell into the hands of Wintour's arch-enemy, Sir Edward Massey. Heaven's knows how he got his hands on it.'

I could tell you, Merryn thought.

'Anyway, at the end of the war, Wintour was taken prisoner and locked up in the Tower for inciting a Catholic rebellion. One record unearthed by the American collector suggests that injuries he sustained during the civil war left him unable to walk. However, that sounds rather improbable because he managed to escape from the Tower – with a little help, presumably – and flee to France where he lived until his death in 1682.'

Zac glanced at Merryn. 'Feeling smug?'

'He was never able to return to retrieve the pistol he'd lost or hidden, a tragedy for him but a blessing for us.' He laid the pistol back into its case and removed his gloves, holding them out to Merryn.

'Put these on, master apprentice, and you can hold it a while. We shouldn't cock and fire it. The flint would dent the frizzen and it's clean as a whistle. Know what that means?'

Merryn slipped on the gloves and picked up the flintlock, as startled by its weight as he had been fifteen feet down the crevice. 'It means the pistol's never been fired. But it has. Just once.'

Isaac stared at him, a look of astonishment on his face. 'Who told you that?'

Merryn's right hand curled around the fox. 'I... I just worked it out. There was a mark on the frizzen when we found it.' He looked at Zac. 'You saw it too, didn't you?'

Cogs whirred in Zac's brain as it got up to speed. *She told you, didn't she? Grace. In the crypt.* 'Er, yes, though it wasn't obvious. At least, not to me.'

Isaac looked at the two boys in turn, sensing that neither was telling the whole truth. 'It took St Pierre the best part of a week working on the frizzen to find the mark, a single, tiny dent made by the flint when the pistol was fired. When he checked the point of the flint under a microscope, sure enough, it had lost its very tip. One shot, he concluded, and one shot only. And you figured that out, a complete novice in the dark at the top of a cliff?'

Merryn stood and lifted the pistol with both arms and for a moment, he held it aloft.

'We're free, Merryn. You set us free. They buried me, just as you promised, and the pistol, it has saved your father's life. It's time now to say goodbye. The journey to our ancestors is longer than you can imagine. I will wait for you there.'

'I think Mr Levi deserves an answer,' he heard Donna say.

'Merryn, are you alright?' Miss Kelly asked softly.

'They're free,' he answered. 'It's finished.' Before she could respond, he turned to Isaac. 'It was just a guess, Mr Levi, which I admit is not very rigorous, discriminating and... something else you told us in your office?'

'Scrupulous,' Zac chipped in, ecstatic that at last he'd remembered something that Merryn hadn't.

'So I suppose that means this apprentice will be getting the sack?' Merryn said, laying the pistol down gently into its case.

Isaac chuckled. 'No, I don't think so. Not when it appears that my apprentice has psychic powers.' Everyone laughed except Malcolm who just stared at his son.

*

It had stopped snowing by the time everyone had said their goodbyes and spilled out into a white world. Closing the front door behind them, Donna turned to Merryn and said,

'Here, Mr Carter, I almost forgot to give you this. It came in the post this afternoon.' She handed him an airmail letter with a Kenyan stamp. 'I'm guessing it's from Beatrice. Have you heard much from her, about how they're getting on in Mombasa?'

Merryn sighed, thinking how quickly life had returned to normal. 'I haven't heard much, to be honest. I guess they've been busy settling in.'

He took the letter upstairs to his room and sat looking at it, wondering if he should bother opening it or simply bin it. If he *had* been honest with his mum, he would have told her he'd heard nothing from Beatrice since their bleak exchange in the school yard six weeks earlier, six weeks that had done nothing to ease the pain he'd felt watching Beatrice walk away.

Then he thought of Malika. Was Beatrice writing to tell him that the drugs weren't working, that her mum was dying?

He had to know.

His heart was racing as he opened the letter and read the contents.

Hi Merryn,

When shall we three meet again? <u>NEXT WEEK</u> *because Mum's appeal was successful!!!! And get a phone because I want to send you a hundred texts.*

Love you so much,

Bee xxxxx

P.S. First thing Mum will do when we get to England is make you a chocolate cake.

THE END

ABOUT THE AUTHOR

Morton Ross, married with two children, spent his whole working life in south-east Wales, a short distance from Wintour's Leap on the River Wye. He has travelled extensively with his wife, exploring many of the world's past civilisations and the extraordinary buildings they left behind. His passion for history, however, began not far from Leicester when, as a student, he was invited to join an archaeological dig at a bronze-age barrow. Set to work in the most unpromising part of the burial mound where he could do least damage, Morton promptly discovered a 3000-year-old cremation urn. Since then, he's been digging the dirt on local legends, searching for clues that separate fact from fiction.

Printed in Great Britain
by Amazon